The Storm Harbour

EST. 2017 | REPORTING COMMUNITY NEWS AND VIEWS | EST. 1901

HARBOUR UPGRADE

The Storm Harbour Chronicle

REPORTING COMMUNITY NEWS AND VIEWS | EST. 1901

TURNED HOME

Harbour Chronicle

TY NEWS AND VIEWS | EST. 1901

WORSENS nicle

m Harbour

EST. 1901

NG COMMUNITY NEWS AND VIEWS

SAILOR FOUND

The Storm Harbour Chronicle

1951 | REPORTING COMMUNITY NEWS AND VIEWS | EST. 1901

OCEAN SHIPPING

# BEFORE *the* STORM

*Also by Di Morrissey*
In order of publication

Heart of the Dreaming
The Last Rose of Summer
Follow the Morning Star
The Last Mile Home
Tears of the Moon
When the Singing Stops
Scatter the Stars
Blaze
The Bay
Kimberley Sun
Barra Creek
The Reef
The Valley
Monsoon
The Islands
The Silent Country
The Plantation
The Opal Desert
The Golden Land
The Winter Sea
The Road Back
Rain Music
A Distant Journey
The Red Coast
Arcadia
The Last Paradise

# Di
# MORRISSEY
# BEFORE *the*
# STORM

MACMILLAN
Pan Macmillan Australia

First published 2020 in Macmillan by Pan Macmillan Australia Pty Ltd
1 Market Street, Sydney, New South Wales, Australia, 2000

Reprinted 2021

A catalogue record for this book is available from the National Library of Australia

Typeset in 12.5/16 pt Sabon by Post Pre-press Group
Printed by IVE
Endpapers designed by Deborah Parry Graphics

Endpapers background image: Titus Group/Shutterstock
Chapter image credits: Prologue, JohnCarnemolla/iStock; Chapter 1, Adrian R. Tan/Flickr, used under CC BY-ND 2.0; Chapter 2, arthurgphotography/Shutterstock; Chapter 3, Annie 888/Shutterstock; Chapter 4, caseyjadew/Shutterstock; Chapter 5, Tero Hakala/Shutterstock; Chapter 6, JCDE/Shutterstock; Chapter 7, FiledIMAGE/Shutterstock; Chapter 8, TassaneeT/Shutterstock; Chapter 9, tsik/Shutterstock; Chapter 10, pisaphotography/Shutterstock; Chapter 11, HadelProductions/iStock.

*To all my friends and colleagues around the world who work in all forms of media, and to those who have lost their lives seeking to tell the truth and shine a light in dark corners.*

*Without free and independent journalism our world is threatened.*

*Honest, independent media is our voice. Please support your local newspaper, TV, radio, public broadcasters and trustworthy online news organisations.*

Di Morrissey, 2020

# Acknowledgements

For my (late) Uncle Jim Revitt, country newspaper reporter, foreign correspondent – radio and TV, ABC TV producer/reporter, the inspiration to all his ABC cadets over the years . . . and who marched a young girl into the heart of a newspaper empire to learn to be a journalist before she became a novelist. How right you were, Jimbo!

My children, Dr Gabrielle Morrissey Hansen and Dr Nicolas Morrissey, who teach and give back to society and the world we share, and for my grandchildren, Sonoma, Everton, Bodhi, Ulani, who are learning about our world through reading a book, seeing in real life, talking, sharing and doing.

Darling Boris, who carries the burden of oiling the wheels, keeping the garden growing, and is there with love and support each and every day.

And welcome to the world beautiful Ellie Janjic! An inspiration and a gorgeous gift to Kathryn and Jeremy.

To editor and friend Bernadette Foley, who has helped me through many books on and off over the many years. Thanks, B!

Brianne Collins, whose sharp eyes and gentle wisdom picks and polishes pages as I go.

The Pan Mac family: Ross Gibb, Katie Crawford, Georgia Douglas, Tracey Cheetham, Milly Ivanovic, Adrik Kemp and my roadie publicity buddy, Clare Keighery.

Those friends you can call and bleat to as well as have a laugh; agent supremo Jane Novak, Jeff Balsmeyer, Joan Frare, Liz Adams. Also Kristy Swift for holding my hand through the world of IT.

To all my compatriots around Australia running independent regional newspapers – good on you. We need you!

With best wishes to my new friend Dan Meehan, in memory of his beloved Sam.

And in memory of a devoted reader, Susan Kelly.

# Prologue

IT WAS THE PLUMES of dust rising into the setting sun that announced that the local Bachelors and Spinsters Ball was underway.

Trucks, utes and cars made their way along the dirt road to the glamorous property where the huge hundred-year-old woolshed waited for the youth of the local farms, towns and cities to descend and party till dawn. Tradition demanded that it be an excessive night of drinking, dancing, throwing up and sex.

Inside the great wooden shed, with its lingering smell of lanolin from the thousands of sheep shorn over generations, a DJ was controlling the music and light show. The bush bands of the revellers' parents' generation had given way to technology.

The bonfire in the yard illuminated the long bar where barrels of beer, an array of good wines, cheap plonk and in-demand spirits were being consumed as fast as the bartenders could pour. Figures settled around the fire, on the trays of trucks or in the woolshed to watch the dancers. The party was just beginning.

For one night it was a blending of the privileged, the locals, visitors and city friends, where letting your hair down took on a whole new meaning. The dress code was fluid – formal, fancy dress or fun.

She was seventeen and this was her entrée into a new world. She'd been invited by a girlfriend from school whose family knew the hosts, and they'd made the trip north in a froth of excitement. The two girls were thrilled to be included and had gone to some trouble with their hair and make-up. Together they giggled at the sight of a burly ringer wearing what might have been his grand-mother's emerald tulle ballerina ball gown over jeans, cowboy boots and a T-shirt. Many of the girls had dressed in expensive formal wear, the boys in good jackets, shiny boots and ties, which would gradually be abandoned through the evening.

A pick-me-up breakfast would be provided in the morning for those conscious and well enough to eat. The shearers' accommodation had been flung open, though many guests came prepared with swags and blankets in the back of their vehicles.

*

It was late. There'd been dancing and then eating and sitting around the fire in various groups as shrieks and laughter came from the darkness and inside the woolshed. She was a little taken aback when a well-known heart-throb,

2

tall and good-looking, started paying attention to her. This was someone you could take home to impress your parents. She found his interest and flirting flattering.

When he handed her a glass, clinking his own against it and waiting for her to drink, she took a cautious sip, swallowing hard at the stinging taste of what he said was a rum cocktail. He made her laugh. She felt clever and funny and . . . attractive. His arm was around her shoulders and her glass never seemed to be empty.

He took her hand and they danced in the shadows outside the woolshed. As they moved together, he pulled her tight against him and kissed her . . . her first real, grown-up kiss.

But in minutes – was it only minutes? – everything was spinning and her knees felt as if they'd buckle. He led her to the dim light of the empty men's quarters – the quiet would be good for her, he said. Her head was foggy and she couldn't see properly. Was she going to vomit? Oh no, that would be too embarrassing. She saw a narrow bed and gratefully fell on it.

But then he was on the bed too, rolling on her, and she felt his naked legs as the room continued to spin. She pushed at him to get off and leave her alone, but then his hand was on her mouth, the other up her skirt, pulling at her underwear. She kicked frantically as he pushed his face into hers, biting her lips.

'Hey, mate, she doesn't want it! Let her be, c'mon . . .' There was the thud of footsteps in the room and suddenly he was off her.

She heard a low laugh outside as she rolled on her side and threw up over the side of the bed.

She ached all over, but the pain in her head was only beginning. She had to get away from here. Stumbling off the bed, out of the room, she somehow found her way outside. Where was her girlfriend? All she knew was that she had to leave.

When she reached the dark dirt road, she began to walk, but knew it was hopeless. She was over a hundred kilometres from home.

Soon a car skidded to a stop ahead of her, and a figure jumped out and hurried towards her as she stood shaking. She had no idea who the couple were who helped her into their car and asked where she wanted to go.

They came to a stop outside her house just as the sky was beginning to lighten. After the woman got out and opened the back passenger door, she rested her hand on the girl's shoulder and spoke firmly.

'Looks like you had a bad night, love. My advice, try to put it out of your head. You're fine. Take care now.'

The girl mumbled her thanks and quietly went inside to her room.

She never told anyone about that night. She buried it deep inside herself, never to think of it again.

Or so she thought.

# I

THE ROUTE TO WORK was etched into her being. Ellie Conlan had walked the same streets for five years now. If it rained too hard, she caught the tram for four blocks, alighting almost in front of the anonymous steel and glass building.

Sometimes she passed familiar faces in the lobby or elevator – familiar only by the fact that they too occupied some small piece of this tower. It seemed an unwritten rule: you might smile or nod, but stepping out onto your floor, you disappeared from everyone else's radar.

Ellie had been swept wholesale into this world, her hours always filled with tasks, meetings, problems and paperwork. It was a consuming life with little else on the fringes – she had lived alone since her divorce.

5

But she loved her job, spent a lot of time with her team, and caught up with friends when she could, which admittedly wasn't often.

She had learned to tune out distractions while inside the glass and bright lights of the open-plan office. It had seemed cutting-edge when she'd first started but now felt outdated. Open-plan offices didn't work, Ellie had decided long ago. Loud music from the week's soundtrack always competed with snappy chatter, and working sessions took place on the scattered lounges and tiny coffee tables that masqueraded as informal creative hubs, people's laptops perched awkwardly on their knees. Like a motel room on a highway, the space was impersonal and there was no privacy; the hot-desking required that nothing denoting the individual, no photos, favourite objects or personal computers, could be left around the place. You finished the day and the next morning another slick empty desk awaited. Ellie had learned to erect a mental wall around her when she needed to think, create, concentrate.

As a project manager she led her team of developers to write and code, designers to create the look and feel of the user experience, analysts to research the market needs, software engineers and architects to deliver the project on time and to gain a competitive advantage. She often felt like an orchestral conductor, guiding her group to be cohesive and in tune with one another.

Ellie and her team had been working on the rollout of a big new program for a major network, and today was D-day; she was going to present the final project to senior management. On her way to work, her colleague Sophia had sent a text telling Ellie to come to a meeting the moment she arrived. Like Ellie, Sophia was also a project manager, but new to the firm and obviously determined to make it to the top, Ellie thought. Ellie hadn't warmed to Sophia. She was five years younger than Ellie but was always patronising, treating Ellie as if she were a junior.

Without a word to her team, Ellie put down her bag, collected her notebook and pen and headed to the boardroom to meet with Sophia and Roger Gladstone, a senior director. The abrupt text had unsettled her, but she didn't want to worry her teammates, whom she had worked with for years and who trusted her judgement. She knew they would have guessed that something wasn't right, as she usually greeted them when she arrived and checked in to see if they had any questions for her before she started her own work.

'Morning, Sophia, Roger,' she said as she walked into the room.

'We need to talk.' Sophia sat down at the long table and nodded for Ellie to do the same. 'Roger has something to tell you.'

Roger tossed a newspaper and an industry magazine on the table. 'Just in case you haven't seen them, there're stories in here about your project. Online as well. Evidently the product is not fit for purpose. There is a flaw in it.'

Ellie's stomach dropped. 'What is this about?' she asked, as calmly as she could.

'We've been sabotaged. It's bad press,' said Roger. 'Got our clients running scared.'

'About what?' demanded Ellie. 'This project has been under wraps. If there's a flaw, and I don't believe there is, my team could have fixed it.' She looked at Sophia, who shrugged.

'Bit late now for a post-mortem,' said Roger. 'There's so much doubt about the efficacy of the project now, you'll never be able to convince the clients to back it.'

7

'But how is that possible? Someone must have deliberately told lies about the project, although I don't understand why. Anyway, whatever has happened, it wasn't done by any member of my team,' snapped Ellie.

'Actually, it could only have been one of your team, as they were the only ones with access to the details,' said Sophia with a tight smile.

'No one on my team would leak this. And they weren't the only staff with access,' said Ellie, her eyes narrowing. 'You're able to access it, Sophia.'

Sophia shrugged. 'Are you suggesting I'm a saboteur?'

Ellie suddenly realised that ambitious Sophia might well be exactly that.

'With big money at stake, the competition is going for us. Which leaves us with no way to catch up. I'm sorry, Ellie,' said Roger, 'but the whole project has to be scrapped and your team dispersed. We need to start again.'

Sophia jumped in. 'It looks bad, but we have to make a stand.'

The injustice rocked Ellie. For a moment her mind was blank with fury. She'd been sabotaged and every fibre of her being knew this smiling assassin of a woman was responsible. With enormous effort, she pushed down her rage.

'You expect me and my team to just walk away? What exactly are you asking me to do? The loss of this project affects the whole company, not just me,' said Ellie evenly.

'Indeed. That's why we need to make a gesture to show that the problem has been rectified,' said Roger. 'We have to show upstairs, the CEO and the clients, that the matter has been resolved.'

'What! What are you implying? Are you going to make *me* the scapegoat for this mess? Or get rid of me altogether?'

'Oh, you're far too valuable for that,' soothed Roger. 'You're always welcome as part of the company, Ellie. But I'm bringing in a new project manager.' He nodded towards Sophia.

'I'll take good care of things,' said Sophia. 'And I'm sure we can find another project for you.'

Ellie couldn't believe what she was hearing. 'If you can't recognise the advantages of our concept and let me and my team see it through, that's your loss,' she snapped. 'Plus, if the project's been leaked and we've not even been given the chance to address the so-called flaw someone has found, then there's no point my being here.'

Roger shrugged. 'I'm sorry you feel that way. Nonetheless, Sophia will be taking over.'

'So, just to clarify, I am to be moved sideways and my team disbanded to fulfil your ambitions, Sophia, is that correct?' said Ellie, finding it hard to get the words out. In spite of her efforts, she could feel herself losing control of her temper. 'You won't replace me easily, you know. Vision, leadership and my skills and expertise are hard to come by.'

She glared at the senior executive, who looked startled.

'I feel sorry for you, Roger. One day you'll find out how you have been manipulated.' Ellie gave Sophia a steely glance and took a deep breath. 'Consider this my formal resignation. I can't stay here under any circumstances now. I feel badly for my team, whose hard work all these months will have been for nothing. I can see how and why you've done this, Sophia. But I can't continue to work in a place that is so dishonest.'

'I think you're being rather rash –' began Roger.

Ellie cut him off. 'I won't work with liars and cheats who sabotage what would have been a fantastic project to further their own careers. I hope it's worth it, Sophia.'

Ellie was churning inside but she held her head high as she walked purposefully from the room.

'It doesn't have to be this way, Ellie –' started Roger, but as Ellie turned at the door and gave him a contemptuous look, he stuttered and stopped.

She returned to her desk, snatched up her bag and jacket and walked to the lift. She was too furious to talk to anyone on her team; she'd call them all later. Right now, she needed some air.

Waves of anger washed over her as she walked outside onto the footpath.

Suddenly the street around her looked foreign. Her routine had lost its usual direction. Checking her watch, she saw that it wasn't even 9 am. Slowly she walked to Degraves Street, a popular gourmet foodie area, and sat at a footpath table in the lull before the coffee and lunchtime crush.

She dropped her head into her hands.

What the hell had she just done?

Where to from here? What to do now?

*

Reaching the warm glow and buzz of the Magic Lantern Café in Fitzroy, Ellie closed her umbrella, shook raindrops from her shoulders and stepped inside.

The smell of coffee, cake and damp coats was welcoming. She pushed her umbrella into the holder by the door and, glancing around, headed to the corner where Mike had commandeered their favourite table.

He rose, towering over her, and gave Ellie a quick hug. 'Hey, you. I ordered coffees.'

'Great, thanks.' She shrugged off her jacket as she sat

down. 'It's so good to see you. It's been ages.' She smiled at her former colleague. 'Too long.'

'It has been. How was your holiday?'

Ellie looked away for a second. 'Actually, I didn't go anywhere.'

'What? Why not?' He stared at her. 'Okay, tell me what's up.'

'Nothing's up. Same old, same old.' She sighed. 'I've travelled plenty, all those IT conferences in exotic places. After what happened, I just went into cave mode.'

He reached over and touched her hand. 'Ellie, it's been a couple of months now. It's not healthy to sit around moping.'

'I know. I just can't work up the energy to move forward.' She realised she sounded a little defensive.

'I get that you're upset about not having a job, but remember, you walked out. They tried to keep you,' Mike said.

'Yeah, well, they didn't try very hard. After they'd undermined me I couldn't stay there. There was no way I was going to be told what to do by Sophia.'

Mike nodded. 'You're right. I'd have done the same thing in your position.' He added gently, 'I just wish I could've helped you more. You should have told me what was going on.'

Ellie shook her head. 'Don't feel like that, Mike. I can fight my own battles. I could see that I wasn't going to win against those guys. I've discovered that you can't fight someone with such hard-nosed ambition that they're prepared to get what they want at any cost, and Sophia's the most devious of all of them.'

A waitress placed coffees in front of them and Ellie wrapped her hands around the warm cup.

11

'You know Sophia wants to jump up to GM?' he said. Although Mike now worked at a different IT company as he had been snapped up by a big firm, they still kept in touch and he kept an ear out for gossip.

'Yeah, well, let's just see if she can get there on her own instead of elbowing everyone else off the ladder on her way to the top.'

'Did you say that to her?'

'Wish I had.' Ellie laughed, but quickly fell silent and took a sip of her coffee.

'I heard that your team appreciated you calling them all. I bet they miss you.'

'I miss them, too. I feel really sorry for the people who are still there and have to work for her,' said Ellie. 'I should have done more for them – I tried to – but it was as if Roger and Sophia built a wall to keep me out as soon as they realised I was serious about leaving.'

'You know corporations are ruthless psychopathic beasts,' Mike said.

Ellie smiled. 'You're right, but this beast was more like a parasite that sucked up all my energy and left me with nothing.'

Mike shook his head sadly. 'Look at how you've been working – multiple projects, high pressure, impossible deadlines, budget constraints, keeping your team on track and, as project manager, the buck always stops with you. I know the toll it takes.'

'Are you saying I should be glad I'm out of it? Glad they've broken me?'

'Not at all. What I'm saying is that it was completely unfair and there was nothing you could have done about it. You're a brilliant project manager and you're completely across your work. Sophia and her circle of

12

acolytes don't understand the developments we're making in this industry at all. And who knows what that Roger thinks about anything.'

'What a creep.' Ellie sighed. 'At least I don't have to deal with him anymore, either.'

'You challenged them, Ellie. And good for you! You should feel proud for taking the high moral ground,' he said, gazing earnestly at her.

'Well, it was either that or a complete breakdown. It's just hard to swallow that they essentially stole my project,' she said, looking away. 'All that work, and for what? I left my job with pretty much nothing to show for it.' She sat up straight. 'Note to self – don't make waves.'

'You know their number one rule: put up, shut up, work longer, harder, faster.' Mike pushed up his tortoiseshell-framed glasses and stretched out his long jean-clad legs.

'Yeah. And the thing about that is, when you emerge from that bubble you realise you have no life. It's taken me years to notice. I don't count office drinks in underground bars talking shop with colleagues I really don't have anything in common with as the highlight of my social life, but I've realised that's all I did outside of work.' She looked at Mike and smiled. 'You were the only person I could talk to. If I'm still sane at all, it's because of you, Mike.'

'Hey, Ellie. You're out of it and free of them. But it's been ages now. You need to find a new focus. You're a hotshot in IT, you're creative. And you're highly organised, good at managing people, a planner and a visionary. Your team adored you. Any big IT company would kill to get you.' He reached over and put his hand on hers. 'Of course, if you'd stayed and eventually been made redundant you would have been paid out.'

'Never! That would have been hell. Imagine sitting there having to watch that woman trying to run things and stuffing up. Then they'd have to ask me to fix it – or just blamed me for it. She thinks she knows more than she does.' Ellie bit her lip. 'I feel steamrolled. I can't work up the confidence – or the motivation, I guess – to do anything. I know I have to pull my finger out, but . . .' She shrugged. 'Am I whingeing?'

Mike pulled his hand back and gave her a lopsided grin. 'Maybe, but you're allowed to. Now, do you want to eat? I'm starving.'

Picking up the menu, Ellie studied it for a moment. 'Let's try the jalapeño mezcal cocktail: "grilled lime, slices of agave, chilli salt. Mexico's sister to tequila".'

'Sure. And what about the blinis, jambon croquettes, mussels . . .'

'Moules marinière, for me, with sourdough on the side.' She smiled at him. 'You always cheer me up. I haven't felt hungry or eaten properly for ages.'

'You're easy to please.' They ordered and Ellie started to relax a little, feeling less like an overwound spring.

Mike and Ellie had met at work and bonded over their interest in new developments in IT and ways to use it to build communities. They had kept in touch and occasionally met for coffee. Sometimes they had dinner or drinks in a favourite wine bar. He was funny, supportive and someone Ellie could talk to easily, though they both avoided talking shop, and Ellie didn't share too much of her personal angst. She looked up to find Mike giving her a quizzical look.

'Sorry, what did you say?'

'Earth to Estelle: I asked, what next?' He sipped his cocktail. 'You said on the phone that you'd had a long talk

14

with your mother. I heard her on the radio the other day, by the way, the "expert psychiatrist". What's her advice?'

Ellie paused, then said, 'I think she's worried about me. She's been giving me space, but she won't let me drag my feet and sit around forever.'

'Neither will I. You'll be boring company if you don't do something soon,' he said briskly, but with a broad smile.

'Mum doesn't push buttons. She's supportive but she doesn't like to prescribe. While everything was falling apart at work, she never once reminded me that she'd said over and over that I was working too hard for too little recognition. You know, she never liked Charlie but she's never said anything against him or muttered I told you so's about our divorce.' Ellie sat back in her chair.

'Maybe, Ellie, but that's in the past. What's done is done.' Mike paused, then asked, 'What's your next move? Have you thought that far ahead? You're only thirty-six. You have to do something and you need to start now.'

'I know.' She fiddled with the stem of her cocktail glass. Ellie had always thought of herself as being confident and self-assured, but after the circumstances that had seen her lose her job, and worse, the unfair accusation that she had mismanaged her project, she felt as if she'd crumbled. She was back to square one and had no clue what she was going to do about it.

She glanced at Mike. 'Why're you looking at me like that?'

'For a slick hipster you look like a ragdoll who's been tossed around by the family dog.' He grinned. 'I like it.'

She ran a hand through her dark brown hair. Normally stylishly scissor-cut by her expensive hairstylist, she'd let it grow out. 'I don't have any clients or anyone important to see.'

15

'So I don't count?' He laughed. 'Well, then, what else did your mother say?'

'Oh yeah. She asked me to drive down south to check on my grandad. Maybe stay with him a while.'

'Is he sick?' Mike asked.

'No, not as far as I know. Mum thinks he's lonely, or in a rut and maybe neglecting his health a bit. He still works, even though he must be pushing eighty. He used to be a foreign correspondent for the ABC and he keeps busy running the local paper. I think he has some good mates, but he lives on his own. It's been eight years since my grandmother died. Mum said he seemed a bit down in the dumps.'

'Has he seen a doctor?'

'Mum told him to see his GP, but Poppy won't take any advice from her. He says there's nothing wrong with him, and perhaps he's right. She asked me to go and visit him and tell him I need a change of scenery – which is the truth, anyway,' said Ellie, smiling when she saw the concern in Mike's dark brown eyes. 'It's no hardship. I adore my grandfather and the town where he lives, Storm Harbour. It's a special place down south on the coast. I spent a lot of time there when I was a kid, even went to high school there for a few terms while my parents were overseas. I know Mum wants to put a bit of a rocket under me, too, so perhaps Poppy is fine and she's come up with this idea to help me.' She looked down at the meal the waiter had just put in front of her, suddenly feeling overwhelmed.

'Maybe,' Mike said. 'But visiting your grandad in a sleepy town doesn't sound like much of a rocket. You're going?'

Ellie straightened up and tried to smile. 'Yes, I've decided I will, and I'm looking forward to it, in a way.

I haven't seen him in a while. He came to Melbourne five or six months ago on business, and he stayed the night. It was great to show him around Fitzroy. Storm Harbour's only four hours away but it's another world, and I haven't been there for ages.'

'Well, perhaps getting out of town will help you,' said Mike quietly.

'Am I in that bad a state?' Ellie asked, trying to keep her voice light.

Mike glanced at her and then looked down at his hands. 'I worry about you. You haven't been my smart, witty friend for months now, and I miss her. I hate to see the bad guys win out. You did the right thing by leaving, but I just wish you knew how clever and capable you are.'

Ellie looked up at him, surprised by the serious tone in his voice.

'They treated you badly,' he added. 'What happened was not your fault.' He took a mouthful of food and held his fork in the air. 'So what's stopping you from applying for jobs at other companies?'

Ellie laughed, but she heard the hard edge to it. 'And get sabotaged again?'

'Listen to yourself, Ellie! My old friend would be giving them the finger and moving on to bigger and better things!' Mike flung his arms wide, almost knocking over his cocktail glass and Ellie's with it.

'Like what?'

'You can do anything you put your mind to. Do your own thing, if you like. C'mon, Ms Estelle Conlan, move on,' said Mike. 'Drink up, let's order another, and some crab croquettes.'

Ellie felt her eyes start to sting with tears. 'You're such a good friend, Mike.'

He lifted his cocktail glass in a toast. 'Here's to you, Ellie. Welcome back to the real world.'

As the waiter put down the plate of crispy warm croquettes and bowls of mussels with their fresh drinks, the two were deep in conversation. Talking about ideas and plans was one of the things they both enjoyed. Ellie liked the way Mike was a futuristic thinker who cared about the environment, about shared information, freedom of the press, and always thought about others. And best of all, he could make her laugh and distract her from thinking about the troubles of the last few months.

*

They paid the bill and left the café, wandering down the bustling street that was filled with the aromatic drift of cooking food and the sounds of music, laughter and a rattling tram stopping nearby. They strolled past couples arm in arm, a man wheeling his bicycle, a woman walking her dog. The rain had stopped, but everything was still glistening wet.

'So when you get back from Storm Harbour, let's do this again,' said Mike.

'I'll look forward to it.' Ellie realised that she actually was looking forward to seeing him again. It was the first time since leaving her job that she'd felt a spark of happiness.

Two blocks from her small apartment building, before Mike cut through to his street via a neighbourhood park, he bent down and gave her a hug and a kiss on the cheek. 'Enjoy spending time with your grandad. Wish I still had mine around.'

Then he waved and she stood and watched as he strode briskly away along the quiet street.

Walking into her lounge room, Ellie opened the laptop on the small dining table and checked her emails. This was a habit that was hard to break. But there was nothing pressing or even faintly interesting. It occurred to her again that her life was pretty damn empty.

Her mother blamed the divorce as much as what had happened at work for Ellie's 'moods'. But Ellie didn't agree; it was coming up to two years since the divorce and it had been amicable. She knew that her lifestyle hadn't helped; she and Charlie had grown in different directions, with different interests and friends. Though perhaps regretful at their impulsiveness in not recognising their incompatibility, neither blamed the other, and both Ellie and Charlie had swiftly moved on. It made life simpler, with no joint commitments and no kids to make arrangements for. He earned good money as a senior officer in a government department – Transport – and while, as Ellie had now learned, she wasn't paid as much as her male colleagues, she had done okay and had put away a decent nest egg.

She knew she'd get snapped up if she put herself out into the IT market. But at what cost? Sophia's deceit had cut deeply. Talking to Mike had made her realise that she'd lost the drive that used to be so much a part of her personality. Instead she'd just been marking time, retreating to her small but smart apartment.

She sat down on the sofa and thought about what she'd left behind – as she did most nights. Even though the thoughts made her feel tense and sad, she couldn't stop them coming, almost as if they were on a loop in her mind. Plus, the emptiness of the last couple of months had shown her with more clarity than ever before that functioning under such intense pressure every working day, as she had done, was insane. But even so, she still missed the adrenalin rush.

Ellie had lost count of the all-nighters she'd pulled at work, the weekends she'd spent there, the 4 am starts to the day. And still, as manager of major IT projects, she'd almost never got through her overcrowded inbox. The pressure to always be ahead of the game, brighter, quicker, smarter than the competition, to problem-solve for clients at a moment's notice as each new obstacle loomed, had been ever-present.

During the day her mind had never stopped whirring, even though she'd sometimes felt burnt-out and exhausted. She'd even thought about work ideas in her sleep, her mind spinning through details and scenarios, and she'd made notes on the pad by her bed through the night.

And then, for all her dedication to the company, Sophia and Roger had pulled the rug out from under her in a single stroke and robbed Ellie of any confidence or trust.

Ellie shook herself. She'd had a nice time with Mike; why did she keep coming back to these thoughts and let them drag her down? She hoped her trip to visit her grandfather in Storm Harbour would be the change of scene she needed to clear her head.

*

The city was a long way behind her as Ellie turned off the Hamilton Highway.

For the moment her life was a blank canvas; no commitments, no pressure, she told herself. Just a visit to Poppy. Then she'd really put her head down and tackle the problem of finding a good job. She gave herself a pep talk: she was capable – more than capable – and had

20

well-honed skills in IT and project management that she could apply to any number of fields.

But her upbeat feeling quickly faded. She couldn't remember when she'd last eaten regularly, or even when she'd last cooked. Her dinner with Mike was already a blur. Had it only been a few days ago? It took just the smallest thing to bowl her over these days. Where had her strength gone? *Stop beating yourself up*, her practical voice whispered, but she felt she could hardly hear it over the cacophony of critical voices that had centre stage.

She lost track of time as these thoughts went through her head. Driving around a bend, along a country road lined with fields and rows of fruit trees, she suddenly had no idea where she was, where she was going, or how she'd got there. She tried to think straight – the scenery around her was beautiful but it was as if she were in a thick fog.

She blinked. God, how long had she been driving in this brain snap? Her lungs and chest felt compressed, her breath started to come in short gasps, she felt nauseous and all she could hear was the throbbing in her head as she clutched the steering wheel like a lifeline.

A truck thundered past, making her veer to the edge of the road where she frantically skidded into a byway and came to a stop.

She slumped forward, her head on the steering wheel, her shoulders shaking, her stomach heaving. Gasping, she fumbled for her phone with one hand while with the other she tried to open the car door, which suddenly seemed as heavy as a tank.

Mounting fear and hysteria started to overwhelm her. Her vision blurry, she stabbed at her phone until she heard her mother's calm voice.

Ellie croaked, 'Mum, Mum, I'm having some sort of attack . . .'

'Where are you?' Sandy's voice was authoritative.

'In the car . . .'

'Driving?'

'No, no, I've stopped. I'm going to be sick –' Ellie gasped hoarsely.

'Turn off the engine,' said her mother firmly. 'Take deep breaths, count with me . . .'

Gently but clearly, her mother talked her through her mounting fear and panic until Ellie was breathing steadily, beads of perspiration running down her face.

'Are you with me, Ellie? Deep breaths . . . one . . . two . . . speak to me.'

'I'm okay. I still feel sick, but I'm okay,' panted Ellie. 'That was so scary . . . What's happening to me?'

'It'll be all right, honey. Just sit there. Do you have some water? Take a sip. Open the window, get some fresh air.'

Ellie gulped down the water in the bottle she'd filled that morning. 'Thanks, Mum. I feel a bit better. Shaky. Tired. I have no idea where that came from.'

'Oh, sweetheart. I think I do. I wouldn't be surprised if you've had a panic attack. You can't get over the stress and pressure you've been under at work without some cost. It takes time. But I know you, and you will be fine.'

Ellie sighed, drawing a deep breath. 'Thanks, Mum. I'm sure you're right. I think I'll be okay now.'

'Drive carefully. Deep, slow breaths. Pull over if you feel wobbly and call me, or if you can't get hold of me, call your father,' her mother said. 'I love you, darling.'

Ellie thanked her again and sighed as she ended the call. She still felt very shocked. Until recently, she'd considered herself mentally and physically strong and stable. This sudden sense of vulnerability, which she hadn't felt for a very long time, was frightening. She pushed the memories of old away.

Back on the road she decided to drive a little slower to try to stay calm. The green paddocks and pretty villages that had escaped the horrendous bushfires of a few summers ago were like glimpses into a world she had forgotten existed, an oasis between cities and towns where villages were linked together, small communities bonded by tragedy and uncertainty that had found strength in their shared experiences. Once or twice she saw scarred hillsides, the blackened remains of a farm or charred fence line, or a brave sign – *We are open for business*. It occurred to her anew how totally immersed she'd been for fifteen years and more in her career. When had she last travelled to places like these? Her world had been bordered by city blocks as she'd paced a well-worn path between her office and her apartment.

The countryside she was driving through now showed many signs of renewal. Lush green had sprouted against a backdrop of blackened bark. There was plenty of rebuilding going on; some locals seemed to have put the past behind them and moved forward as best they could. Ellie guessed that others suffered behind closed doors and endured sleepless nights. While some people grasped opportunities, others struggled. The fires had changed everything that had seemed secure and safe, but life went on, as it always did, Ellie thought, winding down the window and smelling the fresh air.

The beauty and tranquillity around her brought back memories of a golden childhood, and the many idyllic summers she'd spent in this part of the world.

The small town of Storm Harbour, where her grand-parents had settled, where her mother had grown up, was a place of stability, a calm stopover in the mad rush to a future she'd been so anxious to grasp with both hands, before she learned life could be cruel. She longed to feel that optimism about her future, that enthusiasm for life, again. She was in her mid-thirties and, she realised, at a crossroads.

She hadn't been back to Storm Harbour for a couple of years, but no matter where she lived, this township was an anchor in her life. It was the place she knew she could always return to; the sheltered old house on the hill looking out to the Southern Ocean, the familiar landmarks, friendly faces, the gentle pace of local life, and always, beaming a welcome with open arms, her grand-father, Patrick; humorous eyes and wise smile, seemingly as strong as a tree, as warm-hearted as the sun, with his careworn hands that softly stroked her hair.

And next to him, the gentle shadow of her grand-mother who, like all of them, had basked in the strength, laughter and love of a man no longer youthful but with a young spirit, a man with a kind nature, a poetic heart, a steady gaze, and who stood by his principles of honesty, truth and loyalty.

The coast road meandered through the rural landscape with its neat farms bordered by old dry-stone rock walls. Tears of pleasure and joy pricked at Ellie's eyes as the township, spread along the riverfront, came into view. She skimmed past the *Welcome to Storm Harbour* sign, turned left and was soon in the heart of the town. Lining the wide streets were beautifully restored historic cottages and larger homes sheltering behind the magnificent Norfolk Island pines and ancient cypress pines. Some houses were tiny, stone originals with stooping doorways and cosy doll's-house-sized rooms. Others retained their original entrance ways but Ellie knew that beyond the quaint façades stretched spacious extensions and smart, contemporary renovations. Classic pruned gardens were awash with climbing roses or old rosebushes drooping under the weight of glorious heavy-headed blooms. Garden pride and competitiveness was a local obsession, Ellie remembered, thinking about her grandmother's garden.

The lifeline of the town, the Derrin River, flowed into the dark and unpredictable Southern Ocean, which was screened from the township by a protective army of soldier-straight Norfolk Island pines standing shoulder to shoulder. The small harbour was sheltered from the wild storms that sometimes battered this part of the coast.

Ellie parked the car and strolled down the main street, past the beautiful stone library and lecture hall, feeling a tug of sentimental pride as she came to the familiar doorway with its dim windows displaying front pages from previous decades along with that of the current edition. Scrolled across the window in black-and-gold lettering were the words: *The Storm Harbour Chronicle. Est. 1901.*

When she pushed open the door, she heard the bell that tinkled to alert someone to come to the reception desk. Everyone was always out the back in the efficient if messy office next to the editor's small cubicle. An attempt had been made to soundproof the composing room and printer years before, but when the computer age had arrived, it had been demoted to a storage area next to a bathroom and kitchenette.

The smells and surroundings reminded Ellie of her childhood visits. She walked through into the back room and glanced around at the three crammed desks piled high

25

with folders and photo files, a tower of bound newspapers, a couple of ancient desktop computers, an overflowing filing cabinet, a chalkboard, and dozens of framed photos going back decades that crowded the walls.

Jonathan Cubbins, now the sole editorial staffer for the *Chronicle*, as everyone called it, looked up with a big smile and gave her a salute. Pushing his wheelchair back from his desk, he rolled deftly over to her.

'Hey, Ellie. Patrick said you were coming down. Great to see you.'

'Hi, Jon. How're things?' She shook his hand warmly. 'I gather you're "it" now. Shouldering double the reporting duties for the paper as well as taking the photos.'

'Yep. Sally crossed over to the dark side. Got a job with the local radio mob. We still catch up for a coffee now and then. It's not the same, though, 'cause we can't talk story ideas now we're rivals,' he added.

'What about Maggie? Is she still here?' Ellie had always enjoyed spending time with Margaret Berger, who'd been secretary/office manager/researcher/copy-editor and sparring partner to Patrick Addison since he'd taken over the paper in what Ellie's grandmother had described as his late mid-life crisis.

'Oh yeah, Mags wouldn't leave,' Jon chuckled. 'As she says, chuck her out when she loses her marbles.'

'Well, she'd only be in her mid-sixties, wouldn't she?'

'Yep, guess so. But she keeps telling me she's old enough to be my grandmother. She's just popped out of the office but I'm sure you'll catch her at some point.'

Ellie smiled and looked around. 'Is my grandad here?'

'Sure is.' Jon nodded towards the closed door of her grandfather's little office, where a soft rumble of voices could be heard.

'Who's in there?'

'Seamus O'Neill, saying goodbye before he leaves on his his cruise.'

Ellie winced. 'Are the O'Neills still running things? Surely the town has moved on into the twenty-first century!'

Jon shrugged. 'Seamus inherited a well-oiled machine. As will his sons, I s'pose. Do you want a cup of tea? I wouldn't recommend the coffee. It's only instant.'

'Thanks, no. I'll wait till I get home. I should have let Poppy know I was coming here first. A bit impromptu.'

'Well, I know he won't mind; he's hanging out to see you. He's so excited. We're all really glad you've come, Ellie.' Jon paused, then added, 'He gets a bit lonely. I mean, he has a lot of friends, of course. But you know . . . family.'

Ellie smiled. 'I know. I love my parents, but there's a special bond with grandparents, isn't there?'

'Hey! Ellie!' The door of the tiny office opened and the beaming figure of her grandfather emerged. He looked just the way she'd always thought of him – larger than life, radiating love, comfort and protection.

He was followed by a man of about the same age, well groomed and dressed in expensive country casual brand-name clothes.

'Oh, you have a visitor. Good to see you, Patrick.' He gave a polite nod to Ellie and Jon as he headed to the front door.

Ellie hugged her grandfather tightly. He still felt strong, though she noticed his hair had thinned some and was greyer, but the tang of Old Spice was achingly familiar.

'Are you okay, Poss?' he asked softly, using her pet nickname, 'Possum', which made Ellie bury her face in his shoulder. Patrick then held her at arm's length, gazing into her blue eyes. 'It's been too long, Ellie. You look tired. Burning the candle at both ends, eh?'

She sighed. 'Wish I was. Burning the candle, that is – at either end! I sleep too much these days. That's what happens when you have no commitments.'

'Well, that makes a bit of a change,' he said, and looked at her but didn't say anything more about it. 'Now, c'mon, let's go home for a cuppa. Have you been up to the house yet?'

'Not yet. I figured you'd be at work, so I came here first. I'm ready for a cup of tea, though.'

'I'll grab my stuff. You okay to lock up, Jono?' Patrick turned to him.

'Sure. I'll just wrap up this piece on the crab thief. Think there's more to it than petty theft.'

'I'll leave it with you. Talk to old Norm Watson, retired fisheries inspector. He might have a few ideas or leads.'

'Right. Nice to see you again, Ellie.'

'You too, Jon. I'll be around for a bit so let's catch up later.'

He gave a nod. 'Sure thing. Good to have you back in town.'

Ellie waited outside by her car as her grandfather strode out with his ancient briefcase, his shirtsleeves loosely rolled to his elbows and his trademark fedora clamped to his head.

'What time is it?' He glanced at his watch. 'Just on eleven. Too early for a beer. Right, cuppa tea it is. You've had a long drive.' He hopped into his ancient four-wheel drive. 'I'll catch you up at home.'

*

28

Ellie parked under the gnarled trees that sheltered the southern side of the gracious old house and grabbed her bag. Her grandfather was already inside and probably had the kettle on.

She drew a deep breath as she walked up the path she knew so well. The double-storey whitewashed home on the rise above the town was surrounded by bushland. Ellie and her mother had always called it 'the olden days house' because of its spaciousness and its generous, welcoming elegance. It certainly looked the part from the outside, with its wide wrap-around verandah dotted with comfortable cane furniture, but over the years the interiors had been updated and renovated and an open-plan family room had been created off the kitchen. But there remained rooms which were separate little spaces where one could shut the door and sink into a private world; Patrick's study, the formal dining room, a children's playroom with bunks, and a guest bedroom with French doors opening onto a quiet section of the upstairs verandah, which had once been Sandy's room and was now Ellie's when she came to visit. From that verandah one had uninterrupted views straight out to sea. Tucked in a corner of the grounds and curving around the house to the backyard was her grandmother's garden.

The sensations that hit Ellie the minute she stepped inside were as familiar to her as her own reflection; the smell of beeswax and old roses, and a feeling of lived-in love.

In the kitchen her grandfather was setting out the tea things and a plate of biscuits on the table, exactly as her grandmother had done since she'd first set up house as a bride, Patrick always boasted. Ellie realised this ritual was one of her favourite childhood memories.

'Hey, Sam, look who's here!' her grandfather called.

The old dog suddenly appeared and, recognising Ellie, plunged at her, rubbing against her, almost smiling, tail flailing energetically.

'Hiya, old fella.' Ellie squatted and put her arms around the neck of the dog who had been a devoted family member for twelve years. He licked her ear and, as she looked up at her smiling grandfather, she felt her body go limp, as if her bones were melting. The constrictions around her heart seemed to soften and she breathed easily for what felt like the first time in months.

They lingered over the pot of tea, talking of family news, and then moved on to national politics and world events. Ellie was relieved they weren't getting into personal 'deep and meaningfuls'; she felt on safe ground expressing strong opinions about the government, international leaders and her fears for the future of the planet. She'd grown up with her grandfather challenging and questioning her on the world around them, encouraging her to read and listen to the news, as well as think deeply about life in her own little universe. She had given up trying to interest him in IT, even though he always said he was proud that she'd made it so far up her career ladder. They had friendly arguments and sometimes thought-provoking discussions, which made her pause and reflect, or occasionally see things from a different viewpoint.

'I do fear for my generation,' Ellie said. 'The state of the environment, world crises, crooked politicians. It's a relief to escape down here.'

'You're not out of the woods here either,' her grandfather countered. 'This may be a small town but we're a microcosm of the same elements that make up the world at

30

large: families, neighbours, communities, politics, the ties that bind. We have the same issues, if on a smaller scale. That's what makes us who we are. Fracture that, take away our commitment to each other and where we live and how we run the joint, and chaos and corruption rule. We may be just a little place tucked away down here, but we're a link in an invisible chain that holds everyone together.'

'A connection, a community,' said Ellie quietly.

'Yes. We all have our belonging place. Our country, where our roots are.' Patrick paused, and they sat contemplating this for a moment. 'Anyway, it's going to take a lot more than thee and me to solve things,' he said. 'I have a few chores to do. Maybe you could take ole Sam for a walk? See what's changed in the area since you were last here.'

'Nothing, I hope. I like it just the way it is.'

'You can't stop progress, they say. But down here we try to make sure any changes are for the better. So-called progress is sometimes viewed with suspicion and, as I see it, the paper's job is to let people know what's actually going on.'

'Yes. Thank goodness.' She reached out and took her grandfather's hand. 'It's so good to be back here. I missed it. I missed you.'

He squeezed her hand. 'Stay as long as you like, Ellie dear.' He stood up and carried his mug to the sink. 'You settle in your old room. Well, your mum's old room,' he corrected himself, and smiled.

'Lovely. I might go up now and unpack, and then I'll take Sam out.'

As she went down the hall, Ellie felt lighter than she had in a long time. The anxiety attack on the drive down had rattled her, though. She hoped that being here in the place she felt most comfortable would help lift the dark clouds that seemed to obscure her horizon these days.

*

The sun was high in the sky when Ellie set off with Sam for a stroll through town.

As she made her way down the hill, Sam padding along happily at her side, she thought about how things had changed since she'd last seen Patrick. While her grandfather was obviously thrilled to see her and seemed his usual affable self, Ellie had noted a tiredness around his eyes. It was hard to know if it was from work or his health, or just his age. She knew that some of his friends from his time in Vietnam during the war had died recently, and that must have been hard for him. Living on his own for the past eight years, the newspaper had become more than his passion. Ellie's mother had once said to her that perhaps it had become his reason for living.

There it was again. She stopped and blinked as the thought slammed into her. She'd let her job run her life in much the same way Patrick had. Ellie had thought she was doing the right thing – hadn't really questioned it, if she was honest – when in fact the job had come to dictate nearly every aspect of her day-to-day existence.

As she'd been doing a lot recently, she shut down her mind. It was too hard, too stressful, to think about. Ellie broke into a jog and called out to Sam.

Running slowly down the hill and through the streets, she noticed that the town had acquired an affluent veneer over its quaint old seafaring, fishing and whaling heritage. It reflected a comfortable, creative community.

All too good to be true? she wondered. Or was she being a cynical city girl? In Melbourne she loved living close to the city. She had her favourite cafés and shops, and while she knew nothing of their personal lives, she had a casual familiarity with some of the shopkeepers and café staff. No doubt everyone here in this town knew everyone's business and family history.

She stopped jogging and Sam gave her a grateful look, falling into a dignified walk at her heel. Ellie returned a smile from a woman parking her bicycle outside a small gift shop, then glanced at her watch.

'Home time, eh, matey?'

Sam wagged his tail and they headed back out of town, stepping up the pace as the gables of the roof came into view through the trees. There was a red truck parked by the front gate, and Sam seemed to know it as he loped past and up the path, nosing open the front door.

As she stepped inside, Ellie recognised the voice of her grandfather's good friend, Roland 'Roly' Bolton QC. She'd met Roly a couple of times and found him to be forthright, smart and knowledgeable with strong, definite opinions. His bluntness could also make him a little difficult. But her grandfather found his ideas and his sharp, pithy observations highly amusing.

'Ah, Ellie,' her grandfather said as she walked in. 'Roly and I are catching up. Want another cup of tea? Or is it time for a glass of the strong stuff?'

'I'm fine thanks, Poppy. How are you, Roly?'

'As well as can be expected, dwelling as we do in the twilight zone, where very little is as it seems.'

Patrick chuckled. 'Roly sees conspiracy theorists behind trees all over the place,' he said, smiling.

'We must be ever alert to intruders at our gates,' retorted Roly. 'And how about you, my dear? How long are you in town for?'

'Not sure yet. I'm not in any hurry. I want to enjoy time with Poppy, chill out, make a few plans,' said Ellie, trying to sound cheerful.

'Oh, that's right, Patrick told me you've struck out on your own. Wise move. I felt a great sense of freedom when I abandoned my career in the law. It's a world of the pious and the pompous, numbskulls in wigs and frocks, and dubious subterranean evil opportunists swilling at the trough of padded billable hours. Et cetera, et cetera. So what're you going to do now?'

'I haven't abandoned the IT world. Technology is the path to the future, Roly.'

'Give her a break, Roly.' Patrick smiled. 'Like you, Ellie knows when it's time for a change of scenery.'

'Very good then,' said Roly. 'You can help your grand-father control some of the parsimonious wankers in this town who think they own the place.'

'Steady on, Roly,' Patrick said. 'You'll scare the girl!'

'I'll bear that in mind, Roly,' said Ellie, smiling. 'Poppy, I was wondering if you'd like any help with lunch? And would you like me to pick up anything for dinner? I'm happy to pop back into town.'

'Done and dusted,' said her grandfather. 'Roly brought us some grade-A steak fillets from a friend's very much in-demand cattle. He swapped them for some snapper he'd just caught.'

'Thanks, Roly. It's really kind of you, though I have to admit I don't eat much red meat these days.'

'Vegetarian, are you? Or one of those save the planet crusaders?' Roly peered at Ellie.

'Not really,' Ellie replied. 'It's not so much about not eating any meat at all. I just don't want to support those cruel, industrial-sized feedlots where animals are housed in massive indoor sheds and pumped full of hormones and antibiotics. For me it's about encouraging small-scale, healthy and natural farming.'

'Trendy indeed. But you can munch away guilt-free in this case as the beast is a new lowline breed, grass-fed, hormone-free, produces limited methane, and is environmentally friendly as it treads lightly on the land due to its size and appetite.'

'Sounds good. Well, how about I make a salad for lunch and we can have the steaks later?' said Ellie.

'Perfect, thank you,' said Patrick. 'I can see I'm going to be spoiled while you're here, my darling.' He grinned at Ellie. Then, turning to Roly he continued, 'Oh, I meant to tell you, Seamus O'Neill came in for a chat this morning. Poor fellow, I think he's bored to death since his wife died.'

'He's always at the club in Melbourne, I'm informed,' said Roly. 'Maybe it's time the octopi O'Neill clan had a spanner thrown among their nefarious tentacles. Then he'd be too busy to just sit around counting his shares and assets.'

Patrick smiled. 'That's why we put up with you, Roly. You keep us entertained. The O'Neills may be wealthy and have undue influence, but nefarious? Certainly not Seamus or his dear old mother, Kathryn O'Neill.'

'You think this town is upwardly mobile, cherishes its heritage and history, and is full of friendly folk? It may look that way on the surface, but the hierarchy do not like the tables being rearranged from where they've been for decades. Nor do they like anyone nosing into their business. If it wasn't for your paper, Patrick, no one would know anything. You're a brave man with a big heart.'

'What are you up to now, Poppy?' asked Ellie.

'Just doing my job, love. I'm too old and too wily for anyone to go after me and get anywhere.'

'And too stubborn,' added Roly as he reached for his cap. 'Well, I'll leave you to it. Be seeing you, Ellie.' He touched her grandfather's shoulder lightly. 'Stay there, Patrick, I can see myself out.'

'Does Roly still live alone in the caravan park?' Ellie asked curiously after she heard the front door close.

'Yes. But he isn't there due to reduced circumstances, that's for sure. Any time he wants, Roly can go to Melbourne and wine and dine in places I certainly couldn't afford. And once a year he puts on the formal gear and goes to the Silks and Bar Legends Dinners. I think he just likes living here.'

'Do you ever get tired of working?' said Ellie. 'You could swan around too, if you wanted. Not have any pressure. When, or are you, going to retire, Poppy?' she asked fondly.

'I'll get around to it. The town needs the paper. Like Roly said, how else would people find out what's really going on? They've come to trust us and they rely on the *Chronicle* for local news as well as our take on the nation. We might be just a little paper in a little town, but you'd be surprised how word spreads from here.'

*

When they'd finished the washing up after lunch, Patrick suggested they sit out on the cane chairs on the front lawn.

'I take your point about locals liking the physical paper to read,' Ellie said, picking up the conversation about the paper they'd been having on and off over lunch. 'I enjoy browsing through the *Chronicle* with a coffee. But it should be online with a good website as well.'

'This is an older demographic, Ellie. The place is overrun with rich retired Western District graziers and there's also a lot of "ordinary" people retiring here, buying new places out on the coast. These oldies might be computer savvy but the bulk of them still like their news in-depth, with some background analysis and a crossword, and tea and coffee stains all over it.'

'But why not give them a choice between printed and online, Poppy? Don't your advertisers insist on both?' Then, seeing him shrug, she added, 'Well, that's something I can help you with while I'm here, if you like. Who's your IT person? Is Jon across things?'

'Absolutely, he's always talking about stuff to do with computers and technology. He just upgraded his wheelchair to autopilot or something.'

Ellie laughed. 'Sounds good. But I don't imagine Maggie is very high-tech. I noticed she has an ancient computer on her desk. Don't worry, I can be your go-to IT specialist.' She leaned over, touching his hand. 'You've done such an amazing job with the old paper, brought it up to date. We're so proud of you.'

He smiled. 'A town needs a good paper, sweetie. Keeps the bastards honest.'

They sat quietly, enjoying the shade cast by the wide old branches above them.

Ellie shifted in her chair. 'I know the O'Neills are the wheelers and dealers in Storm Harbour and have been since their family were among the first Europeans to settle here. I remember Ben slightly from when I went to high school down here.' She paused. 'I assume the older son is still up on the Queensland property?'

'Actually, no. Ronan and his family live here again,' Patrick replied.

'Oh,' Ellie said, her hair falling over her face as she leaned down to pat Sam. 'I didn't know he was back.'

'It wasn't that long ago that they moved home. As for his and Ben's sister, as far as I know she lives in Melbourne. Ben doesn't live in Storm Harbour anymore, though I gather he's in town at the moment.'

Ellie gave Sam one final pat and then straightened in her seat. 'So what does the family do as a business? Do they still run sheep?'

'Not just "sheep". Stud merinos and new breeds. And they still have the cattle property in Queensland that old man Boyd bought when the wool crisis struck – they have a manager there now Ronan is back. And Craigmore, that historic home of theirs, is getting up into Palace of Versailles territory. Someone sent us some drone shots of the gardens. Unbelievable.'

'Did you print them?'

'Nope. That would have been an invasion of privacy. I wouldn't like sneaky photos of my backyard appearing in the local newspaper.'

'True.' She gently nudged the old dog, who had started to snore, with her foot. 'You know, in your quiet way you wield a lot of influence through the *Chronicle*. I'm sure you're the first person people think of when they want the truth and leadership and the facts. Seems to me if someone has a complaint or a problem, they don't call the council, they call you.'

Patrick gave a wry smile. 'Ain't that the truth. I never set out for the *Chronicle* to be a serious investigative kind of newspaper. Though I can't deny it's been a welcome distraction since your nana passed away.' He was quiet for a moment. 'We know the O'Neills have influence over the council. It's not just that money speaks, it's the built-in

38

power base and control that comes with wealth, position, prestige and privilege. They also do some very good things for the community, of course.'

'Noblesse oblige. It's not hard to do that with authority and money behind you,' retorted Ellie.

'Don't be too cynical. But equally, people in positions of power also take advantage – simply because they can. Over the years that family has built up a sense of right-eousness and entitlement.'

Ellie looked away, frowning, then said, 'Until someone comes along and calls them out. Like the *Chronicle*.'

Patrick smiled and stretched. 'I enjoy the chase for a story. Now, as it's Saturday I reckon it's time for an after-noon nap.'

'Great idea,' she said. 'Sam and I will head out for another walk soon. After hours in the car it felt so good to go for a jog this morning.'

*

Long shadows stretched out over the river, and the water-front was busy with strolling couples and families, people dawdling on the way home.

At the lookout at the top of the headland, Ellie unclipped Sam's lead and he set off at a good romp. Not bad for an old dog, she thought.

Standing against the clifftop fence, she could imagine the cold wind blowing straight in from Antarctica. She shivered, even though it had been a warm day, and walked down to explore the cannon emplacement from the war years that was aimed at the horizon to ward off invaders.

Sam ignored a group of women who were working out on exercise mats and trotted along the path before lurching towards a cluster of trees in pursuit of some intriguing smell. Ellie followed, knowing this was a short cut, if a bit steep, down to the car park.

Sam was sniffing around a tree as she caught up with him, but then he turned, ears pricked, ready to bark. 'C'mon, Sam, let's head towards the river and go home for dinner.'

The dog looked up at her and immediately Ellie sensed something was wrong.

Ahead of them she saw a woman, and barrelling towards them was a solid hunk of dog, fangs bared as it snarled ferociously.

Sam was hunched, growling protectively in front of Ellie. 'It's okay, Sam.' She leaned down, about to clip his lead on his collar, at the instant the powerful dog lunged at him.

As the two dogs rolled and snapped in a snarling, screaming fight, she heard the woman calling her dog, but all Ellie wanted was to rescue Sam. She threw herself at them, kicking the other dog to let go of Sam as the animals tousled on the ground, biting at each other's throats.

There was a stab of pain in her arm as she yanked at the other dog's collar, twisting it. Momentarily the animal must have felt his air waves blocked as it turned to bite Ellie, releasing its grip on Sam, who rolled on his side, gasping. There was blood everywhere. Ellie kicked the other dog in the ribs, screaming, 'Get off!'

'Stop!' the woman yelled at Ellie as she reached down, snapping a leash on the spiked collar of her dog and pulling it to its feet. 'Don't you kick my dog!' she shouted in Ellie's face.

'Your dog is trying to kill my dog! For no reason!' Ellie screamed at her. 'Keep the brute on a leash!'

She fell to her knees over Sam.

'Oh, Sammy, are you okay?' She pulled the scarf from her ponytail and wrapped it around the bleeding wound on Sam's flank. 'Oh my God. It's okay, Sammy, it's okay.'

The woman held her straining, growling dog on its leash.

'He'll be okay, just take him to the vet.'

'It's Saturday and I have no car,' said Ellie coldly. 'Go away and take your vicious monster dog with you.'

Shaking, Ellie picked up her phone. 'It's okay, Sammy, you'll be fine.' She tried to soothe the dog as Patrick answered.

'Sundowners are ready –'

'Poppy, Poppy, Sam has been attacked by another dog. There was this –'

'Where are you?'

'The cliff path near the cannon.'

'Stay there, keep him calm. Try to stop any bleeding.'

The bleeding was staunched, but Sam's gums were pale and his breathing laboured. Ellie lay beside the dear black dog, remembering all the adventures they'd shared over the years. The dog seemed calm, resigned.

'Don't leave me, Sam,' she whispered. 'I need you. You've always been my protector. I came home to see you . . . you look after Poppy, we can't do without you, Sam. Hold on, dearest Sammy . . .' She buried her face in his flank. Flashbacks of shared times together raced through her head as her heart clenched and her breath came in wrenching sobs.

But then she was being eased to one side as Patrick leaned over her and scooped up the heavy dog in his arms with a grunt. Together they got him into the back seat of

41

the car and Ellie sat beside him, his head on her lap, while Patrick turned onto the main road.

'I've called the vet – he's a friend. He'll open the surgery for us,' explained Patrick as he drove.

Later that night, as Ellie lay wrapped in a blanket next to Sam, he stirred and lifted his head. His eyes were untroubled and as loving as always. She hurried into the kitchen and came back with a small bowl of warm milk. Sam lapped slowly, then gingerly shifted his torn flank to a more comfortable position as Ellie moved her pillow.

Curled together, they slept, waiting for the new day.

# 2

ELLIE PARKED BEHIND THE *Chronicle* offices and ducked along the alley to the main street, deciding to grab a coffee before heading inside.

She took in details of the café: the baskets of flowers hanging from the awnings, the colourful artwork and posters on the walls, the little street library of shelves of books tucked into an alcove. The tables outside were being set for the first meals of the day. She ordered her coffee from the footpath takeaway window and, while waiting for it, picked up a book and flipped through it.

'That you, Ellie? You back here too?'

She turned to see a man standing by a table. He was around her age or a bit younger and looked scruffy, with wild curly hair, a five o'clock shadow that was probably the work of a few days, and wearing jeans, a crumpled shirt and loafers.

For a moment her breath caught in her throat at the familiar features. She did a double take, then he gave a lazy smile as it hit her. 'Ben? Ben O'Neill?'

She was rather rattled to see him, feeling almost as if she'd manifested him after the conversation about his family with her grandfather the day before.

He walked over to her. 'Didn't know you were in town. You living down here now?'

'No, I'm in Melbourne these days. I'm just visiting my grandad.'

'He still got the paper?' Ben glanced over at the office across the road.

'You bet. Still stirring the pot. What about you, what are you up to? When we were at school you always said you were going to be a vet.'

'Me? Nah. I'm the oddball of the family.' Ben's smile widened. 'In fact, worse, I'm an artist. I've been bumming around the world. Doing this and that. How're things with you? What do you do now?'

'I've been working in IT.' Ellie quickly changed the subject. 'Are you just visiting too?' she asked.

'Yep. For my grandmother's ninety-fifth birthday.'

'Wow, how is she?'

'I dunno. Haven't been able to see her yet. Family orders.'

Ellie blinked, wondering what he meant. 'That's an amazing milestone.'

'Grandy's pretty special. She still rules the clan.' He smiled at her. 'My mother was ill for a long time and my gran looked out for me after she died.'

'Yes, I was very sorry to hear that. Your grandmother

must be a remarkable woman. How's her health?'

'If you're asking if she still has a grasp on reality, you'd better believe it. I used to love going round her garden at Craigmore with her. She still drives a little motor buggy. Knows every plant like it's her own kid.'

'Oh, I've heard about her garden at Craigmore. It's meant to be amazing. Did she establish it herself?' asked Ellie.

'I think it was my great-grandmother who first put it in, but Grandy has put a huge amount of work into it. She also made the Botanic Gardens near the caravan park her pet project. She loves gardening and played a huge role in making them what they are today. Hey, do you want a coffee?' asked Ben.

Ellie shook her head. 'I just ordered one, thanks. Are you staying out at Craigmore?'

'Nope, much too far out for me. I'm staying closer to town.'

Ellie was trying to recall the gossip that had hung around Ben since he was a kid. She'd only known him during her short time at Storm Harbour High School. But there'd been whispers about him being a bit of a rebel. He was the only one of the O'Neills who'd gone to school locally.

'Will you be here for very long?' she asked.

Ben made a face. 'A little while yet. I'll hang around until Grandy's party. Might see if I can even get a bit more work here in the meantime.'

The fellow doing the takeaways handed Ellie a mug of coffee. 'Careful, it's hot. Return the mug or bring it back for a refill.'

'Thanks.' She stepped away so Ben could put in his order. 'Well, I'm off to see my grandad,' she said to Ben.

'I'm going to sit in the sun and read the paper.'

45

Ben indicated the folded copies of the *Chronicle* on each table. 'How long are you around for?'

'Not sure. No plans as yet,' she said lightly, then stopped and looked at him. Under Ben's bravado she sensed some sort of fragility. 'Well, enjoy yourself, Bennie. I'm sure we'll see each other around.'

He stared past her, his gaze unfocused. 'No one's called me that since school.' He turned his intense blue eyes back to her. 'I don't think "enjoy" is the word. I hope we bump into each other again. See ya, Ellie.'

She smiled at him before walking across the road to the *Chronicle* office.

Maggie looked up as she came in. 'How good to see you, Ellie. I'm so glad you're back. Sorry I missed you when you arrived.'

Maggie was tall and tree-trunk straight, with fair hair faded to grey that framed her face in an exuberant fuzz of curls. Her big smile and friendly expression were welcoming, but Ellie knew she could be as strict as an unamused headmistress if she chose. Maggie was not the hugging type but the warmth of her smile showed how happy she was to see her. Ellie had known her since she was a schoolgirl and couldn't recall a time when Maggie hadn't been part of the team at the paper.

'Good to see you too, Maggie.'

At that moment Jon wheeled himself through the doorway from the editor's cubicle.

'That coffee smells good. Hi, Ellie.'

'Hi, Jon. What's going on?' she asked.

'The usual. Seven stories and leads all at once. Patrick said he'd fill you in when you got here.'

Ellie raised her eyebrows. 'Okay, I'll venture into the lion's den.'

Pat's desk was covered in piles of folders and papers, but Ellie knew he could put his hands on exactly what he wanted in an instant.

'Morning, Ellie dear. How is Sam?'

'He seems all right. When I left he was snuggled up in the old blanket you found for him.' She leaned forward. 'You'll never guess, I just ran into Ben O'Neill. He's here for his grandmother's birthday.' She sat in the chair opposite Patrick.

'How funny, and we were only talking about him yesterday. So what's Benjamin doing with himself these days?'

'Not really sure, though he did say he's an artist.'

Patrick raised his eyebrows. 'That wouldn't go down well in that family of high achievers.'

'He seems to take some pride in being the arty one, if you ask me. He said his grandmother is turning ninety-five.'

'Kathryn is that old?' exclaimed Patrick. 'I saw her a few weeks ago at a function at the library. Smart woman.'

'Mmm, she still rules the clan, Ben said. Do you remember her husband?'

'Boyd O'Neill? Didn't know him well. He died well over ten years ago. Kathryn was always the diplomat, the friendly face of the family. She's behind some good social services the family helped fund.' Patrick started doodling on the notebook on his desk. 'The birthday would be a good time to celebrate her and look back over the family history. I've sometimes wondered where she hails from.'

'Was she a rich debutante or was it a humble love match, do you think?' asked Ellie.

'Damned if I know. While she's still around and

bright-eyed and bushy-tailed, we'll have to ask her. Where did she come from, what were her dreams? It'd be a great little feature to mark the occasion.' Patrick looked at her. 'Do you want to do the story, Ellie?'

'Me? Good grief, no! I'm an IT project manager, not a journalist, Poppy. It's definitely Jon's territory.'

'That's true, but you know, contributors to small-town newspapers aren't just journalists, Ellie. Too few of them around! We get articles from all sorts of people working in all kinds of fields. I recall you were rather good at writing during your school years, and I'm thinking that old Kate O'Neill might respond well to another woman, someone new.'

'School essays turned me off it, Poppy.' Ellie bit her lip. 'But I have written thousands of words for job tenders and helped out the marketing team with their copy writing sometimes. Actually, I submitted a short story about Fitzroy life to a competition a couple of years ago, so I could knock out something for the paper if you need it, I guess.'

'Oh, we don't knock out stories. They have to be well researched, truthful, meaningful, heartfelt, carefully crafted. It's more than just the facts,' said Patrick. 'Ellie, I think you could write something insightful.'

Ellie looked at him, seeing a challenge behind his quizzical smile. To her surprise she found herself saying, 'Okay then. I'll have a go.' After a moment's reflection, she added, 'But only about Kathryn. I don't think any of the O'Neill men need any more airtime.'

Patrick leaned back with his arms behind his head. 'Wonderful! I'm here to help if you need me, but I know you'll be great.'

'Perhaps you'd better tell me a bit more about the

O'Neill history then, give me some background. What was Kathryn marrying into?' Ellie asked.

Patrick nodded. 'The original O'Neills were among the first settlers round here – part of the squatter aristocracy,' he said. 'Boyd O'Neill was a strong personality and businessman, a successful wool breeder and cattle king. His son Seamus inherited the family company when Boyd passed away,' he continued, 'and it's gone from strength to strength since then. Gives them a lot of power.'

'Power? Because they're rich?' Ellie asked. 'And do they think that with power they can do what they want?' She shivered.

'Not blatantly, but I'm sure a bit of quid pro quo goes on.' He sat forward and rested his arms on the cluttered desk. 'In the old days the senior O'Neills put "their" man in as a councillor to oversee their interests. Now they have a middleman and a lawyer who deal with council, so they can keep their distance. But to have the O'Neills on your team is, shall we say, helpful,' explained Patrick.

'So why does Ben seem like an outsider? Did he do something, or just refuse to toe the family line?' asked Ellie. 'Back in our school days he didn't stand out in any way. Come to think of it, he kept to himself, if anything. But he wasn't meek or a wimp. I seem to remember a fight one time when he stood up for himself.'

'Did you keep in touch with any of your friends from when you were at school here?' Patrick asked.

'Not really. I mean, if I run into them any time I'm here, we chat. But I only went to high school here for nine months, remember, when Mum and Dad went to London so Mum could do that course. It was more the case that I kept in touch with my friends in Melbourne while I was going to school here. I hated being away from my friend Julie. Not that I didn't love being here,' she added. 'It was such a special time with you and Nana . . .'

'Yes. And we loved having you.' He smiled gently, then straightened up. 'So you have a bit of time up your sleeve to do a story on our celebrated matriarch, Kathryn O'Neill, who is marking the occasion of her ninety-fifth birthday. If you run into Ben again, maybe suggest going for a coffee. Ask a few more questions about the family in case there're any dark stories they've never told.'

Ellie chuckled. 'You're incorrigible!'

'Hmmm,' said Patrick, flipping over a page in his notepad as Ellie stood up.

She walked back to the outer office as Jonathan was stuffing his phone, notebook, a voice recorder and camera into his bag.

'You still use a big clunky camera? Why don't you just use your phone?' Ellie asked curiously.

'Nothing beats a Leica, no matter how good the phone camera is. The phone's the backup. Sometimes people get intimidated by the camera, but no one thinks twice about a phone. Not that I ever photograph or record anyone without them knowing,' he added hastily.

'I loved those big old flash cameras the news photo boys used to have,' Maggie chimed in. 'Newsrooms were so different then. No one alive knows shorthand anymore – except me. It's all technology this, technology that. Until it crashes.'

Ellie laughed and thought how far she was from the huge IT projects she used to manage. 'Can I please use your computer while you're out, Jon? Save me going home to my laptop.' She gave them a big smile. 'I've just been hired!'

'Hey, that's great!' exclaimed Jon. 'Sure, of course.'

'About time,' said Maggie.

'Here's the password,' Jon added, scribbling on a piece of paper. 'See you. I'll be back after lunch, Maggie.'

'Righto, Jon, see you then.'

Ellie's phone rang and she saw Mike's name flash up on the caller ID. She sat at Jon's desk as she answered. 'Hey, Mike! How're things in Melbourne?'

'Same as always. Just thought I'd check in to see how you're settling in to the quiet life. How's your grandfather?'

'He's well, thanks. In fact, I'm at his office.'

'You helping out at the newspaper?'

'Yep. So much for the quiet life! I'm going to write a story, if you can believe it. Though I have to bring them into the twenty-first century technology-wise. And to think I was starting to wonder how to fill in my days.'

'You went there to hang out, keep him company, wasn't that the plan?'

'Yeah. Sort of. He's certainly not an old man who needs caring for. He makes me feel a bit slack, really.'

Mike laughed. 'So what's the hot story you're chasing?'

'The matriarch of the town is turning ninety-five, so I'm starting to research her and the family history. She's a pretty switched-on lady, by the sound of it. I'm trying to work out the best way to go about it.'

'I guess you could look back through the history of the town if she's been there a long time. Not just what's written down, but stories from locals who know her,' said Mike.

'Yes, that's what I'm thinking. Problem is, it seems the family are very private,' said Ellie.

'Happens where I grew up, too. The old families tend to bury their history if it's a bit colourful. All the more

51

reason to dig and delve, I say. You're almost a local, and you have respected connections. People will talk to you, trust you, I reckon.'

Ellie smiled, guessing that Mike was trying to cheer her up. 'Okay, but don't forget, I'm not a reporter, and I'm not staying. And I don't want to bring down a defamation suit on the *Chronicle* because of anything I dig up.'

'I doubt it'd come to that. I just think you have a lot of skills you could use.'

'Maybe. So what are you up to?'

'Playing squash three nights a week with my mate Bill. I've been too deskbound. But I won't bore you to tears with my very dull life. I just wanted to see if you were okay; check that you weren't sitting on the verandah wrapped in a shawl feeling, well, flat.'

'Thanks, Mike.' She knew he understood her feelings after their conversation the last time they'd met.

'Okay, well, I'll be interested to hear what you uncover about this old lady and her powerful family. I'd better get back to work. Let me know if you need anything sent from the big smoke.'

'Thanks again, Mike. Just a chat occasionally is lovely. I'm not sure when I'll be back, but when I am, lunch is on me.'

'I look forward to it. Take care, Ell.'

After the call, Ellie didn't feel so cut off from her former life. But it had also reminded her of the looming shadow of what she was going to do next, what kind of a job she might find when she returned to Melbourne. She knew she could go back to her little flat in Fitzroy, but then what? To her dismay, a familiar queasy tight feeling began to well up in her.

She stood quickly and looked around. She could hear

Maggie on the phone, as was her grandfather. She hurried to the bathroom, feeling short of breath, and sat on the lid of the toilet, trying to breathe deeply.

Damn it. Much as she loved being in Storm Harbour, the feelings of anxiety had travelled with her from Melbourne and it seemed they were as strong as ever.

*

After a restless night, Ellie decided to burn off some energy and do a massive house tidy-up for her grandfather before launching into more research on Kathryn O'Neill. But she didn't get very far before Patrick came home from his morning walk and stood, arms crossed, surveying the living room.

'I appreciate the effort, Ellie, but I'll never find a damned thing if you tidy it all away!'

'You've got stuff piled on every surface, Poppy! Let's put it into some sort of order.'

'I know what everything is and where it is.' He looked around and went on, 'Maybe you could help with something I've been thinking of doing for a while. Down at the office. If you wouldn't mind.'

'Sure. What's that?'

'You know the storage area where the printing press was in the old days? I've been meaning to clear it out. Figured it would be useful as another little office. Not that I'm thinking of expanding,' he added hurriedly. 'But we could do with an extra workspace that's a bit quieter, or for when Jon needs to interview people in private and he can't use my office.'

'That's a great idea. I can help with that.' Clearing out the back storeroom at the paper was a project that appealed to Ellie. It would be simple and satisfying.

Enthused, she said, 'You know what, I'll also set up a better IT system, as well as a website and a Facebook page, and you could consider moving everything onto the cloud. That would save you money and you won't need physical storage like hard drives.'

'You're the expert, Ellie, and I can tell that you're keen to get us organised and modernised,' Patrick said, laughing. 'Just don't go busting the budget.'

'Of course not.' Ellie smiled. 'I'll start today.'

*

Just before lunch the following day, Ellie stopped, hands on hips, to survey the fruits of her labour. It had felt good to throw herself into clearing out the storeroom. She'd scanned and recycled great swathes of paper, sorted and ordered relevant files and folders, and brought in a table and chairs from the main office. She'd transformed the small space into a useful conference room and started planning ways to upgrade the paper's computer systems, and she'd surprised herself with the sense of achievement she felt as a result. She was back in her element, getting people organised, working with computers, planning new ways to do things. It felt good.

She looked over as Patrick walked in. He stopped short.

'This is marvellous, Ellie, thank you!'

'You're welcome,' Ellie said, smiling. 'Right, Poppy, the next job is to store all the *Chronicle*'s archives on the cloud. Then you, Maggie and Jon will have easy access to any story ever published in the paper via the internet, on any device, any time. If you want, we can provide a link to the archive for the general public on the new website, too.'

'Right, gosh. Not a bad idea, I think. You'll need to take me through all of that again step by step, though, love.'

'Me too,' Maggie called out. 'I know I should know all about the cloud, but I just haven't got around to it. You can be my tutor, Ellie.'

'That would be my pleasure, Maggie,' Ellie replied.

'Now, I'm heading down to see Roly,' said Patrick as they walked back through to the main office. 'I'm going to grab some sandwiches to eat in the Botanic Gardens, want to join us, Ellie?'

'Sure, that'd be lovely.' Gathering her bag and phone from Jon's desk, Ellie noticed Maggie glance at an envelope as she was going through the post and throw it in the wastepaper basket.

'Maggie! You just threw that out without opening it,' Ellie exclaimed.

'I know who it's from. Serial nutter. Rants on at length about conspiracy theories and the like.'

'Trelawney?' said Patrick. 'What's he on about now? Still thinks climate change is a myth?'

'Why doesn't he email?' asked Ellie. 'Writing an actual letter to the editor seems like a lot of trouble.'

'Sometimes he does email. I think he believes a physical letter has more gravitas and he always attaches other documents to supposedly back up his wild theories. He writes well, actually, but he's just too out there in La La Land. Most of our readers are educated and fairly sensible but Mr Trelawney is unique. I only skim every third letter or so of his,' explained Maggie.

Ellie nodded. 'I had a client once, a successful businessman, who had all these theories about his competitors that initially sounded plausible, but then when I questioned even the slightest thing he'd said, he went off the deep end and claimed I was challenging his views; that I was another one "out to get him". Eventually I was told that he was a classic sufferer of PPD. Paranoid Personality Disorder.'

'I'd say that's probably the case with Mr Trelawney, too,' said Maggie. 'You two have a nice lunch.'

Across the road at the café, they ordered their sandwiches and sat down to wait. Patrick spotted someone he knew and hurried over to talk to them, so Ellie pulled out her phone and called Mike. Part of her plan for the paper involved upgrading the office computers to laptops, and Mike had said he could help get her a good deal. As they spoke, Ellie noticed that a woman her own age was sitting at a nearby table. Her long red hair was tied in a ponytail, and the bright scarf draped around her neck stood out boldly against her black T-shirt.

After Ellie had ended her call, the woman leaned over and introduced herself. 'Hi there, Estelle, is it? I'm Cassie. I saw you with Patrick just now. He told us you were coming down.'

'Please, call me Ellie. My grandfather seems to have spread the word that I was visiting,' Ellie said, laughing. 'We're getting some lunch to eat with a friend from the caravan park.'

Cassie smiled. 'Lovely idea. My husband Steve and I manage the caravan park, actually. Been here eighteen months. We often see Patrick visiting Roland.'

They chatted a little longer then Ellie couldn't help commenting, 'I love that scarf you have, is it hand-painted silk?'

'Oh, thanks. No, it's screen-printed, I make them myself. It's a lot of work but I enjoy making my own pieces. I had a store in Melbourne that sold accessories. I might get back to it at some stage but for the moment the park and guests keep us busy. We love it here.'

'Ah. I can just see those scarves in a smart little store. Where in Melbourne were you?' asked Ellie.

'Brunswick. I wanted to be in Fitzroy but I couldn't find the right space. I had a shop with studio space behind, which suited me.'

'I live in Fitzroy!'

'Really? It's such a great area. Do you work there too?'

Ellie hesitated. 'No, in the city. I was – well, I still am – in IT.'

'That can be a high-pressure job, I imagine. No wonder you take time out down here.'

'Time out. Yep, that's where I'm at,' said Ellie. She stood up as the café owner brought out the lunch order.

'Well, we'll probably run into each other again. Bye, Cassie. Good to meet you.'

'Yes. Hey, anytime you want a coffee and a chat, look us up.'

'Thank you.' Ellie was suddenly touched. 'I will.'

*

'Hmmm, it's a nice day to be out,' said Patrick as Ellie linked her arm through his and they walked down to the gates of the caravan park.

'Just wondering, do many people write to the paper about their crazy theories?' asked Ellie, thinking back to the envelope from the eccentric-sounding Trelawney.

'Too often. Maggie goes through the outta-left-field ideas once a fortnight. We miss Sally; that used to be part of her job. But I can't begrudge her wanting to move on with her career. S'pose she'll try for the TV next, although she'll have to give up the black lipstick.' He smiled. 'She's a bright young woman. She and Jon get on well as they're both into that sci-fi stuff.'

'If she wants to get into TV, then it's good to get a foot in the door with radio broadcasting, I suppose,' said Ellie.

'Yes, you're right. She's ambitious. More so than Jon. They're competitive, though – I've heard them go at each other hammer and tongs on occasion. He misses her company at the office but she keeps in touch. Trying to pick his brains, perhaps.'

As they walked together, Ellie asked, 'So tell me again why Roly, an eminent Queen's Counsel who has run some pretty dramatic court cases, is living in a caravan park?'

'Hmmm, I s'pose it does seem unusual. You never really know who's staying in a caravan park when everyone dresses so casually. He hunkered down here after his divorce, which was around the same time as he retired, a year or so ago. He's in his late-seventies now. He told me once he's always loved small towns, and I think he just wanted a real change.'

'Did he lose his home in his divorce?'

'Well, I know that he moved out of the Toorak mansion, leaving his wife to reign over the roses. Says he just took his chess set, his fishing rods, a laptop, his cello and some favourite books. His grand plan is to write a book. Of what genre he's never revealed, other than to say he has no intention of writing his boring memoirs.'

'Is he actually writing, do you think?' asked Ellie.

'So far I haven't seen or heard a reference to any such effort, so I don't mention it,' said Patrick.

'Probably wise,' said Ellie with a smile. 'And look, there's the man himself, sitting in the sun waiting for us.'

'Ahoy there,' called Roly, lifting an arm in salute as he sat in a fold-up chair outside his cabin.

Ellie noticed his fishing gear, his fire pit and a rolled-up hose next to a tub of herbs. It was simple living, but it said home to Ellie, and hinted at permanence. She'd noticed that some of the other cabins had small gardens, clothes-lines, ornamental pots and even statuettes. The cabins had some privacy in that they were separated by lawns and trees. There was a smattering of outdoor tables and, closer to the river, a couple of barbecues, a boat ramp and a fish-cleaning area. A bike path curled along the waterfront, away from the cabins. They were an independent commu-nity removed from the main office, the camping grounds and the rental holiday cabins and caravans, and further still from the wading pool and kids' play area. Behind them stretched the small but lush Botanic Gardens.

'Ready for refreshments?' called Patrick. 'We can go through to the Gardens to eat.'

'Good idea.' Roly stood up and walked over to them. 'This way. The place is a gem, although very few people come here during the week. Perhaps that's a shame, but for us residents, it's a blessing.'

'I've only been to the Gardens a couple of times before,' Ellie said. 'It's unusual for a town this size to have its own Botanic Gardens, don't you think?'

'We are very fortunate, my dear,' said Roly. 'I believe the original plan was for the Botanic Gardens to be devel-oped and extended over stages, but for some reason they never were and the rest of the land became the caravan park.'

'Luckily for you,' Patrick said, laughing. 'You're living in paradise, Roly.'

'I certainly am. So, Ellie, how are you finding your return to your roots?'

'Oh, it's been lovely. I've noticed a few changes, though. It's been a while since I was last here.'

'I believe one sees a place, no matter how well you

think you know it, through the prism of past and present sensibilities, don't you think?' said Roly as they strolled. 'Memories so often dictate emotions.'

Ellie didn't comment, but his words struck home.

'There's a free table under the she-oaks over there,' said Patrick.

Ellie was spreading out the food when a loud sound broke across the tranquil setting and she jumped, realising it was the roar of a chainsaw starting up.

'What the heck?! Who's using a chainsaw?' said Patrick.

'Oh, that's our temporary resident artist. Remarkable talent,' said Roly, reaching for a sandwich. 'Go have a look. Head down towards the water, through those trees, and you'll see.'

Grabbing a sandwich, Ellie and Patrick did as he suggested, and when they reached the riverbank, Ellie burst out laughing. 'That's outrageous! I love it!'

Patrick shook his head as they watched a man in shorts and a hardhat wield a chainsaw like a conductor with a baton. The sawdust and chips flew in every direction from the massive wooden crayfish that was taking shape in front of him, its angry claws looking ready to strike.

'It's half a damned tree,' said Patrick. 'Must be old, look at the girth of the trunk.'

When the wood carver stopped to step back and study his work, taking off his helmet to wipe his forehead, Ellie gasped.

'It's Ben O'Neill! Hey, Ben!' she called.

He turned around and walked over, grinning. 'Well, this is a nice surprise.' Ellie introduced Patrick as Ben asked, 'So, whaddya think?'

'It's amazing. Is it staying in the caravan park?'

'Nah, this is for outside the new fish co-op shop. They thought it'd be a bit of a tourist drawcard.'

'That's for sure. Where did that tree come from?' asked Patrick.

'The family estate. Cassie and Steve suggested I work on it here, out of the way. I'm staying here at the park.'

'You're living here?' asked Ellie in surprise.

'Yeah, till I've finished this job. I was just about to take a break. Are you on a walk?'

'We heard the chainsaw and wondered what was going on,' Ellie said. 'We're having lunch, why don't you come and join us?'

'Ah, Benjamin, nice to see you,' Roly said as they arrived back at the picnic table.

While Ben demolished one sandwich after another, Patrick casually probed him about his return to the area.

'It was a bit of a coincidence,' Ben said to him. 'I got the job doing the cray for the co-op and the next thing I knew there was a family gathering being held while I'm here. It's my grandmother's birthday celebration.' He paused. 'If they hadn't known I'd be here, I might not have got invited. So it kinda all worked out.'

Ellie was about to ask if the whole family was coming to Storm Harbour for the celebration, but her grandad got in first.

'Your grandmother must have some good stories to tell,' said Patrick. 'Some squatters had a lifestyle few people could have imagined.'

Ben nodded. 'Yep. My grandfather was very proper. He talked about when he was growing up and having to wear black tie to dinner, with servants everywhere. All the properties held big balls, polo matches, formal dinners, that sort of thing.'

'I went to university with a few sons from the wool baron families,' Roly said. 'The bright ones. That was when wool was better than gold.'

'They still live pretty well, those who remain,' said Patrick. 'Most who've sold off to corporations and foreign companies have retired to the coast, to towns like this, while their offspring make hay in Toorak and Tenerife.'

'Yeah, maybe. My family is hanging in, I s'pose, while Grandy and my dad are in charge.'

'We're thinking of doing a story about your grandmother for the paper,' Ellie said, reaching for the last sandwich. 'To coincide with her birthday celebrations. What do you think, Ben?'

He shrugged. 'My grandy is very easy to talk to. Unless you're offside and in the bad books, or that secretary of Ronan's is around. Or my brother – then I don't get a look-in,' he added. 'I've always got on great with Grandy. But I haven't been here for some time.'

'So, you're a bit of a drifter?' asked Roly bluntly.

'Roly, you can't say that!' exclaimed Ellie.

But Ben chuckled. 'To tell you the truth, I don't care. I just do my own thing; it's easier that way.' Looking down, Ben brushed the crumbs from his hands. 'I'd better get back to Harry. That's what I call the cray.' He grinned. 'Thanks for lunch. I'll see you round the park then, Roly, eh?'

'What do you make of that?' asked Roly as Ben strolled away.

'There must be some reason young Ben is a loner,' Patrick mused. 'A roving artist, perhaps? Maybe we can ask his grandmother.'

'Nothing wrong with that,' Ellie said. 'C'mon, time

we went back to work too.' She began gathering the sand-wich wrappers.

'Harry will no doubt claw in a new clientele to the fish shop,' said Roly. 'Worthy of the front page, perhaps. Thank you for the invitation to lunch.'

'See you again soon, mate,' said Patrick, taking off his hat and fanning away a fly.

'Indeed.' Roly gave a wave and sauntered back in the direction of his cabin as Ellie and Patrick walked towards the bridge to town.

'I met Cassie today, who runs this place with her husband. She's seems friendly, very warm,' said Ellie.

'Yes, they're a nice couple. I'd say they'd be busy making this a profitable business. It'd take a lot to main-tain, though I s'pose the council does their bit. It does attract lots of tourists and there are the long-term renters like Roly. They're young, they'll make a go of it.'

Ellie was thoughtful. 'I've always loved this town, Poppy. I remember the stories you used to tell me about the fishing families and the history of the whalers and the shipwrecks,' she said. 'Maybe that's something to ask Mrs O'Neill about.'

'You could, yes, but ideally we want personal stuff. The story of the town is in the Historical Society, but people don't know much about Kathryn herself. Do some homework. Put together a bit of a potted family history first, then when you interview Kathryn, get some wise words and advice from the perspective of a long life of achievement. She is a leading light on garden design and the conservation of local flora, among other things. Then get into the personal stuff. And let's set it up quite soon. We don't want Sally to get her on the airwaves first,' said Patrick.

63

'Did Nana ever have much to do with Mrs O'Neill?' said Ellie.

'Well, they knew each other, but not very well. We had different lives and interests.'

'Okay, Poppy, I'll do some research,' she said. 'If Jon's still out and about maybe I'll jump online on his computer.'

'Why don't you start at the library?' suggested Patrick. 'It may seem old school, but not everything makes it onto the internet, you know. If you're going to become a hard-nosed journalist, you've got to cover all sources.'

Ellie laughed. 'All right, Poppy. I'll see if any of the local history books have anything on the enigmatic Kathryn O'Neill.'

*

The library was housed in an impressive heritage building. Inside, Ellie felt enveloped in that special world of books; there was the occasional hum of subdued conversations, the rustling of papers, and an atmosphere of concentration with several people sitting at computers, others browsing shelves of books, and a handful seated comfortably reading a newspaper or magazine.

After talking with the librarian, Ellie settled down to work, but a couple of hours later, with a growing sense of frustration, she decided she'd probably done as much research as she could for the time being. She packed up her laptop and stacked the books and other material she'd been reading on the returns trolley.

The librarian, whose name tag read *Maureen*, looked up and smiled at Ellie as she walked towards the entrance.

'Did you find what you were looking for?'

'Ah, well, I now know a lot more about the many

social events Mrs Kathryn O'Neill attended in Storm Harbour over the years, and I have a bit more information on the causes and charities she's supported, but I can't say I've found everything I need. It's hard to get a sense of the real woman from these public appearances. I'll keep looking – you never know what else might be out there,' said Ellie. 'It would be fascinating to read some diaries by people who grew up here, personal memories or stories about Kathryn, but I suppose that sort of thing often gets thrown away by their families when they die.'

'Oh, don't remind me, I've heard about some tragedies of family memorabilia being tossed on the tip,' said Maureen. 'But you might want to try Tommy's Treasures. It's a second-hand bookshop down behind the railway yards. You know, where they've converted the big old railway goods shed into all those little shops?'

'I know it. My mother talks about playing in there as a little girl, when it was still the goods shed when the railway stopped here. Thanks so much, Maureen, I might pay it a visit now.'

'Good luck,' said Maureen. 'Let me know if you discover anything extraordinary.'

Ellie walked slowly through town, taking in the activity on the streets, the thriving shops, cafés and offices. How many towns were still recovering from the effects of the devastating bushfires and perhaps would never regain their prosperity? she wondered. Storm Harbour had a lot going for it. It had the potential to grow even more, but at what cost? Managing growth and development was a subtle balancing act, she knew. Growth was not always a good thing if the elements that made a place what it was were destroyed in the process. What mattered was the community, families, friends, the little things; like sitting in fresh air to breathe in a sunrise. Home mattered.

It was a beautiful crisp day, and Ellie found herself breathing deeply and feeling calm, steady and purposeful. She felt she was gradually coming out of the fog that had filled her mind since she'd walked out of her job. But it was taking longer than she'd ever have expected.

Turning down a side road towards the old railway yards, the massive wooden structure of the former goods shed stood out. Ellie could see the last stretch of overgrown railway line beside it. A ramp and steps led up to the entrance, above which in new lettering were the words *The Shed*. Once inside its cool, shady interior, Ellie glanced at the tall timber roof. The old shed was still redolent of its first incarnation, where everything from boots to wool bales, sacks of produce and dairy milk cans would be stacked high, waiting to be loaded on the frequent freight trains.

Now it was a bustling marketplace, with stalls and little shops selling craft and art, antiques, gardening and kitchen supplies, homewares, groceries and fresh produce. There was also a flower shop, where buckets of fresh flowers, dried grasses and decorative dried arrangements brightened a dark corner.

Tommy's Treasures was inside at the back of the building. Shelves of books lined the walls and there was a musty rug on the floor, two sagging armchairs, and a desk with a laptop and credit card machine in place along with notes and a pile of books.

The owner, Tommy, presumably, was sitting in one of the armchairs, reading. He appeared to be pushing fifty, his curly hair needed the attention of a barber, and he wore an old sweater over an un-ironed shirt, but it looked to be cashmere.

He looked up as Ellie stepped inside, but waited a few moments before asking, 'Want anything in particular? Mightn't look it but I can put my finger on any title that I have in stock.'

'Wow, that's organised,' Ellie replied. 'I'm actually after anything you have on local history, in particular the early families who settled here. I've already checked the library.'

'You want actual books or information?'

'Ah, either, or both; what makes you say that?'

'You doing a uni course, writing something yourself or digging into genealogy?'

'I'll just cut to the chase, shall I?' said Ellie.

'Go for it.'

'I'm writing a story for the local paper on Mrs Kathryn O'Neill, so I'm looking for some background on her and the family. Do you know anything about them? Are you a local yourself?'

'My parochialism shows, does it?' He smiled, seemingly not offended. 'Depends what you want to know. The O'Neills manage their public profile pretty effectively.'

'Do they? Why? Is there dirty laundry somewhere? Oh, I'm Ellie, by the way. Estelle Conlan. My grandfather, Patrick Addison, runs *The Storm Harbour Chronicle*. You might know him.'

'Yes, of course I do,' he said, smiling. 'I'm Tommy, as you might have gathered.' He stood up and shook her hand.

'I'm just visiting and I'm helping him out while I'm here,' Ellie explained. 'Though I spent a lot of time here as a child.'

'Please, take a seat.' Tommy waved at the other armchair and they both sat down. 'The changes and so-called

67

"progress" in our town sometimes pains me. I tend to lay the blame at the feet of people like the O'Neills.'

'Really? What do you mean? Do you know something about their dealings?'

'I've lived here all my life and I've never really worked out why they have so much power. Is it just because of all their money? Ownership? Because they were the first Europeans to settle here?' He shook his head slowly.

'I'm just interested to know about Kathryn O'Neill. I understand she had a lot to do with the Botanic Gardens. She did an amazing job; they're gorgeous!'

'Too right. Bloody pity they didn't make the whole area the Botanic Gardens. That would have been an even bigger tourist attraction for the town. If one wanted to bring hordes here, that is. Though the caravan park has to be one of the best sites in the country to camp or live, don't you think? I suppose that secret is leaking out. We do seem to have more people coming through. Even in here.'

'I would have thought this place a must-visit.' Ellie smiled.

'You're too young to remember it when it was the goods shed. Thank goodness they kept this place, though.'

'My mother remembers it. And getting the train down here. I love train trips; it's a pity the line doesn't run anymore.'

'So what in particular would you like to know about the O'Neills?' Tommy asked. 'You trying to find out some scandal about them to write up in your story?'

Ellie couldn't help smiling. 'Not quite. The *Chronicle* doesn't run scandals. But I am interested in finding out about their history. You never know. I hear they have long been leaders in the town and are quite philanthropic.'

Tommy screwed up his nose in distaste. 'Well, so

they should be seeing as they've virtually run the place for generations.' He looked thoughtful. 'I'll do some research for you. Might go and talk to my Aunty Mary in St Bridget's Home. She's older than God, but still has her memory.'

'I don't know her; has she always lived here?' asked Ellie.

'Born here, and she's in her eighties now.' He pointed to the newspaper folded on the chair beside him. 'She still gets the crossword out before me every day.'

'Then she would have known Kathryn O'Neill,' said Ellie.

'Known *of* her, certainly. They wouldn't have moved in the same circles.' He smiled. 'Okay, leave it with me. Here's my card; send me your number.'

Ellie pulled out her phone and texted Tommy her details.

'Thank you for your help,' Ellie began, but Tommy waved a casual hand. 'I'd better get going and leave you to your work.'

'The shop's just a hobby, really. I have to pretend to do something with my life.'

'Oh. Why? Did you win the lottery?' Ellie raised an eyebrow.

'Something like that,' he smiled.

*

'I couldn't find out anything much about Mrs O'Neill other than what appeared in the social pages. And there were a few magazine features on her gardens at Craigmore and the Botanic Gardens,' Ellie said to Patrick that night over dinner. 'There was the record of her marriage – I did discover that her maiden name was Kelly – but no details

69

of Kathryn's family or their history. However, I discovered she was a good bit younger than her husband. Surely if Kathryn had come from "good stock" her family would have been mentioned.'

'Mmm, maybe. Although the focus was probably on the bridegroom's family, I s'pose. Considering their standing in this district.'

'Yeah, maybe,' Ellie said, taking a sip of her wine. 'Seamus was born some time after the wedding so it was no rushed event. And within a few years the "*charming hostess and mistress of Craigmore*"' – Ellie made quote marks in the air with her fingers – 'was presiding over social and charitable events, which she then continued to do for decades. She was active in the gardening club and set up a creche for the children of itinerant workers during the shearing and fruit-picking seasons.'

'There you go. I never knew Kathryn set up a creche. She certainly didn't make a song and dance about it, and I admire her for that,' said Patrick. 'Has she agreed to an interview?'

'Her assistant has. She will notify me as to a convenient date and time,' sniffed Ellie. She had found a phone number for the O'Neill family business and been directed to the family's personal assistant, one Susan McLean. 'She sounds a pain. Susan, the PA, that is, not Mrs O'Neill.'

'Better do your homework, then,' advised Patrick.

*

Ellie allowed extra time so she wasn't late, feeling slightly annoyed at herself for being nervous. 'This is just a simple interview about a life well lived,' she admonished herself.

At five minutes to ten she turned through the gates, driving past the mailbox with only a number on it and

70

along the dusty road to the formal entrance to the estate, where wrought-iron gates displayed the word *Craigmore* across the top of the archway. There was a post with a buzzer and speaker, and when she announced herself the gates swung open.

Taking a breath, Ellie stared at the large red-brick mansion, but even more impressive was the rocky red hill rising behind it. The driveway curled around a fountain. Ellie drove past the portico and the ornate front door and pulled up alongside some parked cars.

As she got out, the front door opened and a well-dressed woman in her forties walked out and waited for her.

Ellie stared at her for a moment and then froze in horror.

'You must be Estelle. I'm Susan McLean, the O'Neills' assistant.' The woman walked towards Ellie, extending her hand, then stopped, frowning. 'Oh.'

'Yes, we've met,' said Ellie coolly. 'Your dog attacked mine. It should be kept on a leash.'

'I apologise. There're rarely other dogs there. He's a male breeder so he sees other dogs as a threat.'

'He did more than threaten!' Ellie had to press her lips together to stop herself saying anything else.

'I hope your dog is all right. I am happy to pay any vet bills.'

'That won't be necessary. Our dog sustained a nasty wound but thankfully he's recovering.' With an effort, Ellie changed the subject. 'Shall I leave my car here?'

'Yes. Of course.'

Before Ellie could say anything else, Susan turned inside. 'Mrs O'Neill will see you in the morning room.'

'Lovely, thank you.'

'I hear the photographer is coming later?'

'That's right. Jonathan Cubbins. He'll call to arrange a time.'

'That'll be fine. Most press like to photograph the gardens, too. Mrs O'Neill will take you or the photographer around them, if she's up to it.' Susan strode ahead as Ellie followed.

The hallway was lined with photographs, lavishly framed, mostly of large merino sheep bulked up with their valuable fleece, posing with ribbons and prize cups. Ellie leaned forward, seeing an enlarged photo of a 1950s wool cheque made out for one million pounds.

Susan opened double teak doors. 'In here, please.'

The room was welcoming and cosy despite its grand floor-to-ceiling windows looking onto a formal garden. There was a faint mustiness, possibly from the heavy brocade window drapes.

An elderly woman with pure white hair cut in a stylish bob, who Ellie recognised from the social pages photos as Kathryn O'Neill, was standing, leaning slightly on a walking stick, and smiling. She offered her hand.

'Good morning, Estelle.' Her handshake was firm, although she looked thin, almost frail. 'Please do sit down and be comfortable.' She gestured to the small settee opposite the armchair beside her. A low coffee table was between them.

Susan hovered close as Kathryn O'Neill lowered herself into the chair, resting her walking stick to one side.

'I'll bring the tea.' Susan excused herself.

Ellie pointed to the garden outside. 'Susan tells me you still enjoy your garden.'

'I do. Gives me endless pleasure. And some pride. It's been a great passion for me. Of course, I didn't inherit a blank canvas; my mother-in-law had a tribe of gardeners do a lot of the work. The old photos show a rather modest effort in the early days. A garden was not a priority,' she said and smiled politely.

'I imagine not,' replied Ellie. 'What got you interested in horticulture? Did you grow up with a garden?'

'Not at all. But I loved the wild bush around us . . . ah.' Kathryn paused as Susan returned with a china teapot swaddled in a crocheted tea-cosy. She poured a cup each for Kathryn and Ellie then put down the pot.

'Can I get anything else for you?'

'No, dear, thank you.'

'Well. I'll be just outside if you need me.'

Ellie read the shorthand between them. Susan would be watching the clock, and likely listening to the interview as well. She did not completely close the door behind her as she left.

Ellie held up her phone. 'Do you mind if I record our interview, for later reference, Mrs O'Neill? I don't trust myself to remember everything.'

'Not at all. Memory can be a very fickle thing, as I have good cause to know at my age,' said Kathryn with a chuckle.

Ellie returned her smile and turned on her phone to record. 'I was wondering about your early memories of moving here as a bride. You were very young – and beautiful.' Ellie had found a formal photograph of the couple in a file copy of the *Australian Woman's Weekly* magazine, in the society pages.

'Thank you. It was war time. But I must say, it still felt like a fairytale. Until Boyd had to return to his duties in Sydney, that is. It wasn't till the war was over that we went to Paris for a belated honeymoon. I have spent my married life here at Craigmore. We've made many trips to Ireland over the years, though.'

Ellie leaped in. 'And is your family Irish as well? I noticed your maiden name is Kelly, and there don't seem to have been any Kellys in this district. Where did you grow up?'

For a split second Ellie thought she saw a slight intake of breath as Kathryn sipped her tea, then replaced the cup in its delicate saucer.

'So many questions at once. My father was an accountant so before I married I had quite a different life-style. Very little to do with sheep.' She chuckled quietly. 'You should speak to my grandson if you'd like to find out about our breeding of the magnificent merino sheep and developing the superfine wool that has made them so famous. We supply Chinese, Japanese and British markets these days.' She gave a small smile. 'We also breed high-quality Angus cattle at our property in Queensland.'

This was not the friendly girl talk Ellie had planned. She tried again.

'And where did you and Mr O'Neill meet?'

'Oh, it was all so long ago, I'm sure no one will be interested in those early years. Please, you haven't touched your tea.' She leaned forward. 'And there's some lovely shortbread that the cook made. Do help yourself.'

Ellie could sense a slight resistance in Kathryn to this line of questioning. Was it too personal? she wondered. She thought the questions reasonable enough, but something felt a bit off. Nonetheless, she pressed on.

'So what were your ambitions as a young woman, Mrs O'Neill? What did you dream of being when you were a teenager?'

'Teenagers were not really known then. In my day

young women did not have the opportunities or access to the workforce that they have now,' she replied tightly. 'Therefore one had to cut one's cloth to fit, as it were. Which is why I have been so dedicated to helping women achieve their goals.'

With a sinking feeling, Ellie realised she wasn't going to get anything more than the most general answers to her many questions. Mrs O'Neill wasn't as forthcoming as she'd expected and seemed to feel constrained, but Ellie felt she had no choice but to keep trying.

'You have a son, Seamus, two grandsons, and a granddaughter in Melbourne, I believe. How do you see the generational changes from when you were married?' Ellie said.

'It certainly was a different era. I like to think I grew more progressive as I matured. I certainly had a very supportive husband.'

'I understand you've always been involved in phil-anthropic enterprises. You seem to have been very independent, breaking away from tradition, perhaps? Or because of your family influence?' Ellie smiled.

'You learn that as a woman matures, she finds the strength of character to follow her instincts and, where possible, her interests. Women are standing up for them-selves more and more in these modern times, which is pleasing to see.'

'It's just unfortunate that we still have to battle for it, though; that it's not a given right, be it for equal pay or opportunity,' said Ellie gently.

Kathryn O'Neill shifted in her seat. 'Well, I have to say there are different battles now. I find social media these days dangerous and despicable, I'm sorry to say.'

Ellie decided to steer the interview back to Mrs O'Neill's

own life. 'Do you consider yourself fortunate, privileged, perhaps, looking back on your life compared to when you were a young girl?'

There was a brief pause before Kathryn straightened slightly. 'I have been very fortunate. Equally, I have lived through some perilous times. As, now, has your generation. Our challenges are different, but they are what shape us to be who we are,' she replied.

Sighing inwardly, Ellie wondered what to do. The article would be as dull as dishwater at this rate, beautiful gardens notwithstanding. 'Mrs O'Neill, what do you see as being your lasting contribution to the town and environs? Apart from the wonderful Botanic Gardens, are there any projects you wished you'd been able to accomplish –'

At that moment the door was thrust open and Susan came into the room, saying loudly, 'I do hope you have enjoyed the tea. Are you up to doing a tour of the garden?' Before Kathryn O'Neill could answer, Susan went on, 'Or maybe that would be something to do when the photographer comes . . .'

Ellie put her cup down with a clatter. 'Please, don't trouble yourself.'

The interview was over, Ellie realised, as Susan McLean began to collect their tea things.

'Are you comfortable, Mrs O'Neill? I'll take Ms Conlan to her car,' the PA said firmly.

'Thank you for coming, dear.' Mrs O'Neill reached for her walking stick, which Susan handed to her. Ellie muttered her thanks and a farewell as she followed the briskly walking Susan to the front door.

*

Patrick emerged from his office. 'Hello, Ellie. Sorry, been on the blower. Did you get any gems from the Queen of Craigmore?'

Ellie wrinkled her nose. 'She's a better poker player than I am a reporter, I think.'

Patrick laughed. 'Well, I've been on the phone with the mayor, Meredith Havelock. She's hearing a lot of gossip. Meredith is pretty steamed up about it, mainly because she's got wind that something's going on but still can't get any details.'

'Details about what, exactly?'

'Meredith overheard a conversation at the council chambers. It was something to do with some land Boyd O'Neill gave to his wife decades ago, which could be any of a number of places, Meredith said – Boyd loved Kathryn and apparently gave her quite a few plots and properties over the years for her to use for her charitable endeavours. Anyway, details are very scarce, but Meredith is worried that something underhand may be going on.'

Ellie shook her head. 'I bet Ben doesn't know about any such plan. Besides, he's been away for so long.'

'Well, let's hope not, as he might mention it to Sally. I seem to recall they've always been quite tight. We don't want to be scooped by Sally on the radio station or TV people,' said Patrick.

'We'd better keep in touch with the mayor.'

'Oh, no worries there. Meredith and I go back a long way, ever since she and Jim moved here. Sally goes to all the council meetings to cover them for the radio, and she's a bit of a firecracker. But our Jon keeps his ear to the ground too.'

'Maybe there's something being planned, some announcement for Mrs O'Neill's big birthday?' wondered Ellie. 'I don't know if I'm going to get another "interview" with Kathryn O'Neill. But I'll have a bit of a dig around. I just think there's got to be more to her personal story.'

Patrick reached out and patted her arm. 'Good. It looks like you're still in a job, kiddo. For the time being anyway,' he added with a wink.

*

Ellie sat in the cosy sitting room and started reading a novel, but she couldn't concentrate. Sam lay on his blanket close to her chair, watching her, his head on his paws. Eventually she closed her book and sat sipping her drink. The house was quiet.

Ellie was thoughtful. She went into the formal dining room where she'd left her laptop. Her grandfather liked to eat at the big kitchen table and rarely used the dining room unless he was entertaining. Ellie remembered family meals at the table, when they'd used her grandmother's favourite dinner service and all eaten far too much.

She sat down and opened her laptop, ready to do some more research on the O'Neill family. Maybe, she thought, she could try looking at some more current news about them, rather than just historical detail. But as she keyed in the search terms and started opening articles about Seamus and his children, the now-familiar feelings of anxiety began to bubble to the surface, along with something new, something more urgent. Was this the stirring of another panic attack? She slammed her computer closed and breathed deeply.

She wanted fresh air. Ellie gently nudged Sam, who, though still recovering, had begun to move around again, and they went out into the cool damp garden.

As the dog sniffed around his favourite bushes, Ellie glanced up at the scudding clouds, hearing the distant waves pounding on the reef below. The beautiful old white house and surrounding trees glimmered in the pale light. The upstairs rooms were dark. Only a single yellow beam of light from the lamp in the dining room glowed at the front of the house.

Vibrant, throbbing, late-night Fitzroy seemed very far away. And the memories here were suddenly far too close.

# 3

ELLIE WALKED THROUGH THE leafy park behind the shuttered old *School of the Arts 1883* building. A few people were fishing at the seawall, others were picnicking on the grass, sitting under the broad trees or at wooden tables. She noticed a couple at one of the tables, then she recognised Ben O'Neill.

As she hailed him, the woman he was speaking to turned and Ellie saw that it was Sally, who had previously worked at the *Chronicle*.

Ben waved Ellie over.

'Hey, Ellie, how's it going? Do you know Sally? She used to work with your grandfather.'

'Yes, we've met. Good to see you, Sally. Jon tells me you're at the radio station now,' Ellie said. 'How are you enjoying switching from print?'

'Pretty good, Ellie, thanks. In fact, I'm setting up an interview with Ben, about his wood carving. Have you seen what he does?'

'I sure have,' said Ellie, but privately thought it would be a better story in the *Chronicle* as listeners might find it hard to visualise how spectacular Harry the crayfish looked.

Sally's phone beeped and she glanced at it. Ellie noticed she had a small nose stud and a tattoo creeping along her arm.

'So how're things at the newspaper?' Ben asked.

'Always busy. How're plans for your grandmother's birthday going?'

'I'm not involved with it. Except my grandmother insisted I be there. She always had a soft spot for me; I think it's because I was a bit of a fish out of water in the family.'

'Your family should wake up to themselves and realise how talented you are,' Sally said, looking up.

Ellie recalled Sally as being a rather nerdy, alternative girl who favoured tattoos (which Maggie loathed), was a big *Star Wars* fan, and swung between intense, introverted moods and being outgoing to the point of irritating. In her late twenties now, there seemed a harder edge to her, Ellie thought, or maybe it was simply that Sally had now found her self-confidence.

'Don't let me interrupt your interview – I'll keep moving. Bye, Ben. Nice to see you again, Sally.'

'Yeah. See ya.' Sally turned her attention back to Ben, who smiled at Ellie as she walked away.

'Cheers, Ellie,' he said. 'Come back and visit Harry sometime!'

*

'Where're you off to?' asked Ellie as she walked into the office and saw Patrick struggling to do up his tie.

'I have a lunch date with the mayor every month or so. A friendly off-the-record chat.'

'It requires a tie? Where do you go?'

'Well, there're two places in town that are a bit more formal. But we don't go to either of them. Meredith likes to try restaurants that are doing something different or just starting out. The tie is a gesture of respect. Say, would you like to come along? I'll ring Meredith and check with her first, but I'm sure it would be fine.' Satisfied with his tie, Patrick reached for his jacket. 'Your nana and I and Jim and Meredith used to have outings together on their boat, before Jim died and Meredith became the mayor. I guess that's another reason we like to catch up. We miss our spouses. Like to remember the good times. There, how do I look?' He struck a pose.

Ellie smiled. 'You look fab, Poppy.'

'So, are you lunching with us or not? I'll call Meredith now.' Then, seeing Ellie's hesitation, he added, 'C'mon, love, chin up, things can't be that bad. You know, I've always said you're the smartest chicken in the henhouse. And besides, I need you at lunch to ask innocent questions. Ones that I shouldn't ask.' He winked.

'Like what titbits of news, gossip, happenings are going on in the council?'

He snapped his fingers. 'That's my girl.'

Patrick pulled out his phone and made the call.

\*

Mayor Meredith Havelock had chosen a cottage café at the edge of town.

'This place looks gorgeous,' said Ellie as Patrick

parked outside the quaint old cottage. On its verandah, checked tablecloths fluttered in the breeze, anchored to each table by a small pot of flowers. A painted sign swung gently on two hooks by the gate: *The Garden Cottage Guesthouse and Café.*

Meredith strolled towards them, waving a greeting. 'Hello, Ellie, it's so good to see you again.' She reached out and shook Ellie's hand. 'Shall we go inside? It's more private and it's getting a bit cool.'

They settled at a corner table with a view over fields where a dozen alpacas grazed. Ellie glanced around, taking in the comfortable furnishings: a floor lamp and a small settee in front of the fireplace, paintings on the walls, a bookcase full to bursting with books, as well as five other tables.

'This is like being in someone's home,' she said.

'That's because we are,' Meredith said. 'Lucy and James, the couple who run this place, live here and grow their own produce, poultry and so on, out the back. Lucy's a great cook. I think it's tremendous to see young people get a business up and running. They had some setbacks with the drought and bushfire dramas, like everyone, but if anything it's taught us all to be a bit inventive, to think outside the square.'

The young waiter handed Meredith the wine menu, recommending a Victorian pinot and adding, 'It's from a small but significant vineyard not far from here.'

Meredith closed the menu. 'We like to support our locals. We'll give it a try.'

Waiting for their drinks to arrive, Meredith asked Ellie about her work, and how she'd got interested in working in IT.

Ellie paused, thinking back. 'It started at school.

83

Computers and technology just appealed to me; they made sense. Like when you start to become fluent in a foreign language and it just clicks. At first I kept it to myself as none of my schoolfriends were interested in coding. I don't code now, though. I'm a project manager, so I employ others to do it. But back then I was fascinated by what coding had to offer and wanted to learn everything I could about it. I'm still interested in it, really. But at the time I felt like there was something wrong with me for enjoying it so much!'

'She's being modest, Meredith. She's been managing some high-level projects and a team of specialists that do stuff I can't get my head around,' said Patrick proudly. 'There weren't a lot of women in her field when she started.'

'Maybe that's why you thought there was something wrong, Ellie,' commented Meredith. 'It's hard being a woman in what's perceived as a male profession.'

'It certainly is,' said Ellie. 'Especially when it comes to networking and negotiating and you're one of the only women in the room. I found it hard to promote myself to the blokes. That is, to realise that it was okay to say, "Hey, I'm really good at this. I know what I'm doing. I'm awesome!"' She tailed off, remembering again how she was muscled out of her job and the terrible scene in the boardroom.

'And you *are* awesome!' said Patrick.

The waiter returned with the bottle of wine and handed it to Meredith, who read the label and then nodded. 'This will be fine, thank you.'

She leaned back in her chair and looked at Ellie. 'If you don't believe in yourself, no one else will. Self-promotion is indispensable when you want to achieve a goal, get something happening or close a deal,' Meredith said. 'I know that now, but I learned it the hard way.'

'You should feel proud of yourself too, Meredith, not just for being elected as mayor, but because you are never afraid to stand up to the boys' club if it's in the town's best interests,' said Patrick. 'I know that it hasn't all been smooth sailing for you.'

Ellie studied the older woman, who presented as a powerful and confident person. 'So what did you want to be when you were a young woman, Meredith?' she asked suddenly.

Meredith waved a hand dismissively. 'Oh, when I was in my teens, I didn't have ambitions. Life can take you in directions you never expect. Sometimes I feel I've lived several lives in one.' She changed tack. 'I remember you as a teenager, Ellie. I'd just moved here with Jim.'

Ellie was about to ask more about the mayor's life before she came to Storm Harbour when the chef and owner came to take their orders.

'So lovely to have you back again, Mayor Havelock,' the woman said, then smiled at Patrick and Ellie. 'Hi, I'm Lucy. Chef, gardener and owner along with my husband, James.'

Meredith introduced Ellie and Patrick before they turned their attention to the menu.

After some reminiscing between Patrick and Meredith, their food was served, and Patrick plunged in.

'So, Meredith, have you found out any more about those rumours you heard about the O'Neill land?'

'Not much more than we spoke about the other day, Patrick. Just rumours: something to do with developing some land in town with "sweeping river views",' said Meredith.

'River views,' mused Patrick. 'How much town land is left undeveloped along the river? Not much, I'd say, unless it's way out where the marshes are, past the golf course, before you reach the sea. But I wouldn't want to live there,' he added.

'I agree,' replied Meredith. 'As far as I can tell, there's been no application lodged for a planning permit yet: I'd know a lot more if there had been. That doesn't mean that secret conversations aren't taking place, though, or that deals aren't being struck.' The mayor rolled her eyes. 'Whatever's going on, they're doing a good job of keeping it under wraps at the moment.'

Ellie nodded. 'So what's the best piece of land in town?'

'Well, there's only one piece of land I know of that has "sweeping river views" and that's the land where Boyd suggested Kathryn O'Neill set up her Botanic Gardens.' Meredith looked at Patrick sombrely.

'They wouldn't,' said Patrick. 'It's not for sale!'

'Or open to development,' added Meredith.

'But . . . that's an icon in town!' exclaimed Ellie. 'It can't be touched; surely the council would never allow that?'

'Look, I could be wrong. We don't really know anything – we don't even know if there is a development planned at all,' said Meredith.

Ellie was thoughtful for a moment. 'Ben told me the Gardens were Kathryn's project. I didn't realise she owned the land. How did that come about?'

Patrick turned to her. 'True to form, the first white settlers in this area made a grab for the best land. The stretch along the river has been in the O'Neill family for generations. As far as I know, Boyd O'Neill "gifted" it to Kathryn, for her birthday or a wedding anniversary or something, so that she could develop the Gardens, but legally speaking he retained ownership. I have no idea who he left it to when he died, but I assume it stayed in the family.'

'I think the original idea was to landscape the whole area, but it's far too big. The Botanic Gardens land was sectioned off as it is today. It's such a special oasis,' said Meredith. 'So if this is the land they're talking about, it potentially includes the caravan park as well.'

'So who owns the caravan park?' asked Ellie.

'It's a bit complicated, but as I understand it, the land still belongs to the O'Neills.'

'I'm sure the O'Neills wouldn't sell that land, for practical as well as sentimental reasons,' said Patrick. 'And as you suggested, Meredith, maybe Kathryn doesn't know what's going on. I've heard that the family and the people around her are very protective of her.'

'Yes. I noticed.' At Pat's suggestion, Ellie had tried to schedule a follow-up interview with Kathryn, but Susan had proved to be as responsive and cooperative as a rock.

Meredith picked up her wineglass and turned to Patrick. 'I just hope the *Chronicle* can raise a bit of awareness if this land deal turns out to be really happening, and if it isn't what the community wants. The radio station won't jump up and down, so we need the *Chronicle*. As we always have.'

'Isn't it a community radio station?' asked Ellie.

'It's a small network, a local regional station, and it's privately run. Its owner has money and influence,' said Patrick.

'You look at who pays the bills to find out what their editorial stance is,' added Meredith. 'True community radio and media outlets, like your grandfather's paper, are vital to a small town and the whole community who live in and around it.'

'And they're getting harder and harder to keep going,' said Patrick with a slight frown. 'We can't rely on the advertising income we used to have. So many businesses are struggling. But a town without strong local media is a town without a voice.'

'I agree.' Meredith nodded. 'Over the years I've lived here, I've seen this town change, and generally for the better; younger people are moving here to start up new ventures, creative types, some alternatives, organic life-stylers, couples wanting to get ahead and set up a business. This has all boosted tourism and brought more visitors, which is wonderful. But don't be fooled: this town is still the preserve of the wealthy in many ways.' Meredith looked at them both. 'What I'm saying is, the old brigade doesn't like to let go of the reins of the town. And that's why we need the paper to keep things transparent.'

'Anyway,' Patrick jumped in, 'no matter where a development goes it will most likely divide the town. I'll keep my ears to the ground. Nothing will happen without *The Storm Harbour Chronicle* knowing,' he added with a chuckle.

*

'Meredith is such an interesting person,' said Ellie as they drove back to the *Chronicle* office.

'She is indeed. Strong, focused, unbiased: a very correct and proper mayor. But when she lets her hair down after a few drinks with close friends, she's quite a character. In the old days, before she hit the limelight, she could say what she thought. After Jim died and she became mayor, she quickly realised she had to be more reserved, more circumspect, let's say.'

'Do you see her often socially, apart from your regular lunch?' said Ellie.

'No, not really. I think she's conscious of not being seen to be in my pocket, or too friendly with the media.' He sighed. 'We both feel we have to be a bit careful about what we say in public. Sometimes we can be on opposite sides of the fence. Anything I might publish that's anti-council could be construed as coming from her.'

'You mean it might suggest that she'd leaked information to you?'

'Wouldn't be the first time it's happened. Where would the press be without whistleblowers?' said Patrick with a faint smile.

\*

After spending a couple of hours setting up the *Chronicle*'s new Facebook page, Ellie decided to take a walk through the Botanic Gardens. Along the way, she wondered how the waterfront must have looked when the town was first established. What had it been like when Kathryn O'Neill came to the district as a young bride? How stunning it would have been if the lush and exotic Botanic Gardens had been established all the way along to where the caravan park was, as was originally intended, she thought.

A mournful musical note drifted up from the caravan park, and Ellie stopped to listen. She was drawn to find out where it was coming from and made her way out of the Gardens, across the grass towards the cabins, where she saw Roly, sitting outside his home with the cello between his knees as he played with aching fervour.

Ellie stood at a distance and waited until Roly slowly lifted the bow from the strings, his head down, eyes closed. She walked quietly towards him and he looked up and saw her. He leaned back and lifted his bow in a salute.

'Roly. That was beautiful! But so sad-sounding. May I come over?'

'Of course.' He stood, carefully placing the cello in its case.

'That was a beautiful lament, I must say. And in a beautiful setting.'

'Yes, the tranquillity here is what first attracted me to this place. Social interaction is available when required, but not overbearing. People are here because they truly want to be. They respect the simple and modest attractions of peace, neighbourliness, and a simple lifestyle with fresh air, quietude, and nature's charm and health.'

'Why *did* you move here, Roly?' asked Ellie gently, her curiosity piqued again. 'Just for the fishing?'

Roly gave her an amused glance. 'You are becoming quite the probing journalist! Well, since you ask . . .'

They both sat down and Roly looked thoughtful.

'Many years ago, I called in here overnight and stayed a day or so for a case I was working on. There had been an incident in which a fishing boat had washed onto the rocks with no one onboard; the owner was missing. It was seemingly a tragic accident. But the family refused to believe it, as their relative was too skilled a skipper. Then his body was found, and gradually some forensic evidence came to light that suggested he had not been alone out on the water. Someone had hidden onboard, murdered him, and then removed the body from the boat. So, as it's not uncommon for a barrister to visit a crime scene, I came down here to see for myself. In the course of my early morning stroll I walked through the Botanic Gardens and along here.' Roly leaned back and looked around. 'I met a fisherman who lived here, and I asked him how he liked it. And he told me he'd never been happier. He said none of his kids could understand why he was here, as he'd previously run a big company and never fished in his life.' Roly chuckled. 'I filed it away. Y'know, my kids don't understand why I'm here either.'

'Did you always have a secret plan to one day just sit in a tinny and fish? Never wanted a yacht, or a flashy waterfront apartment?' asked Ellie.

'I made enough money to buy one, I s'pose. My father always expected me to be a barrister and do well. Marry well. It's terrible, the expectations people put on children.'

For the first time since she'd known the ebullient barrister, Ellie sensed a yearning or wistfulness in him. 'What did you *really* want to do, Roly?'

'Be in an orchestra,' said Roly immediately. 'And travel, and play in the world's great concert halls.'

Ellie stared at the man whose presence could be intimidating, who had a fierce and famous reputation in the legal world, and who had probably never told anyone of his private dream.

'I can tell. Your playing comes from your heart.'

'Some of my neighbours might not appreciate it, which is why I enjoy playing with the trees and the river as an audience. Oh, and anyone who happens by.' He straightened up, looking a trifle embarrassed. 'That's why I won't be leaving my pleasant green field here to move into some suburban cement box any time soon.'

'Fair enough too, Roly,' said Ellie. 'I wouldn't want to give up this slice of paradise either.'

*

Ellie was walking back through the caravan park when she noticed a man standing still, looking around. Her attention was caught by the way he was dressed and because he had his back to the river. She edged towards

91

him, and when he glanced at her, she smiled and asked, 'Are you one of the residents here?'

He looked startled and shook his head. 'No. Not at all.' He waved an arm. 'Do I look like I live in a caravan park?'

Ellie glanced at his tailored slacks, the crocodile logo on his shirt, the expensive loafers and smart blazer.

'Nope. You definitely look like a visitor,' she said politely. 'Are you from the media?' she added innocently. 'Or the council?'

'I'm an architect. Down from Melbourne. I'm doing some work for a client.'

'Ah. Would the work have anything to do with this caravan park?' asked Ellie lightly.

He turned to her. 'Why would you ask that?' he said. 'And you are . . .?'

'Estelle Conlan,' she said. 'I'm an IT project manager. From Melbourne.'

'I see. Here on a holiday?'

'Seeing friends here.'

'If you want to build a holiday home, give me a call,' he said, then pulled out a leather business-card holder and handed her a card.

Ellie looked at it. 'This is a very big firm to be doing business in a small town like this one.'

'Money is as good in a small town as the big city,' he shrugged.

'Of course. You must be good,' Ellie said.

'Exactly.'

As she tucked his card away she asked, 'Have you met anyone who lives in the park? There're some very interesting people here.'

'I don't think I need to know them, thanks. I don't do

92

caravans. I'd be renting a nice townhouse with river views if I was staying here,' the man said archly.

'I don't think they "do" townhouses in Storm Harbour,' said Ellie airily. She waited for a reply, but he just looked at her with a raised eyebrow and a somewhat dismissive expression.

'Enjoy your stay, Estelle.' He strolled away towards the car park.

*

Only a couple of days had passed since their lunch with the mayor, so Ellie was surprised to see her car pull up outside the house when she and her grandfather were sitting on the lawn, basking in the afternoon sun.

'Meredith, this is unexpected, but it's lovely to see you. Come and enjoy the last rays,' Patrick called out.

'Thanks, Patrick. Hi, Ellie,' Meredith said as she closed the car door and walked over to them. 'I should have called first, I suppose, but I just wanted to see a couple of friendly faces.'

'Are you all right, Meredith?' Ellie asked, standing up to bring over another cane chair.

'Oh, yes, I'm fine really, but this business with the potential development is getting me down. It's hard to know who's telling the truth. Certainly no one is giving me the full picture,' she said, sitting down next to Ellie.

'You know you can always trust us, Meredith,' Patrick said, sounding serious. 'Anything you say here is off the record,' he added. 'First, though, can I get you a drink? Tea, wine?'

'I'd love a wine, thank you.'

Ellie jumped up. 'I'll get it, Poppy.'

As she walked back out with a tray of glasses, a bottle

of wine and a plate of cheese and biscuits, Ellie asked, 'So what *is* happening?'

'I wish I knew for sure.' Meredith sighed. 'What I *am* fairly certain about is that whoever is involved in this is trying to go around me. Tell me nothing, show me nothing, employ delaying tactics. I sense there's been a few secret meetings in a local bar where a couple of the councillor chaps go for drinks on Friday nights.'

'And you're never invited,' said Ellie. 'You get cliques like that in all organisations, I guess. Do you know much about them?'

'Oh, they're like a bunch of silly schoolboys. They even have a name for themselves – *The Pineapple Club*.'

Ellie snorted. 'What a stupid name,' she said.

'Actually, they've been around a while. One of the secretaries told me about them years ago when I was looking for one of them. They leave early on a Friday afternoon. They consider themselves a "golden circle", so, as that's the name of the famous pineapple cannery in Queensland, they became The Pineapple Club. I wouldn't want to be included anyway, but I am concerned there might be some connivance going on as a couple of the council managers and directors are in the club.'

'So who's on your side?' asked Ellie. 'Other than truth, justice and a fair go?'

'Thanks, Ellie, for that vote of confidence,' Meredith chuckled. 'There are plenty of good people in council, don't get me wrong. But once this group knew I couldn't be bought off, I became rather isolated. If it wasn't for my eagle-eyed assistant, a few shifty things might have slipped past me.'

'Good for you,' said Patrick. He stood up and handed around the cheese and biscuits.

Meredith took a biscuit and sipped her wine, then said, 'Thanks, Patrick. Frankly, I just can't believe these rumours might really be about the Botanic Gardens land. Apart from whether that would even be possible, legally speaking, why *that* land? There are other blocks that are much larger. A bit further out, one near the golf course, like you mentioned the other day, Patrick, and the other oceanfront but set back a little up on a hill. It'd be damned windy, but has spectacular views.'

'Seals, salt and sea erosion might be factors against those,' said Patrick drily. 'In comparison even a small parcel of riverfront in town is prime real estate.'

'There was a smug architect cruising around the caravan park when I was there,' said Ellie, suddenly remembering.

'Are you sure that's who it was?' asked Patrick.

'Yes. We had a bit of an exchange; he came across as such a snob. But he alluded to how nice it would be to have townhouses with a riverfront view in town.'

'Curiouser and curiouser,' said Patrick. 'Well, you'd better do some digging into that Pineapple Club, Meredith.'

'Would Kathryn O'Neill tell either of you anything if you had her on her own?' asked Ellie thoughtfully. 'Surely she wouldn't agree to the Botanic Gardens land being developed, given the Gardens are supposed to be so close to her heart. Would she?'

Meredith frowned. 'Depends if she knows about it. My feeling is she'd stop it in a heartbeat if she thought something might happen to it.'

'The family don't need the money,' added Patrick.

'Rich people, especially the younger generations, always need more money,' said Ellie. 'They're the genera-tion who either spends it, sinks it, or tries to triple it.'

'Well, I think you're probably right then, Meredith. If it is the Gardens land, Kathryn likely doesn't know, and has possibly been kept in the dark on purpose,' said Patrick.

Meredith shook her head frustratedly. 'It's all supposition at this stage, so let's keep quiet until we know more,' she said. 'It's still possible we're jumping at shadows. But I'll start asking hard questions. If I know that the *Chronicle* will give an objective account of whatever happens, Patrick, that would be helpful.'

'Well, of course we will. That's precisely what the *Chronicle* is for!' said Patrick firmly, his eyes flashing.

'Look out, Ellie,' said Meredith, smiling. 'He's got the bit between his teeth.'

Patrick grinned, but got straight back to business. 'These things always leave a paper trail. Can your assistant look into it?' he asked Meredith, who simply shrugged.

'Don't get your hopes up, Patrick: as I said, none of this is official yet. It could just be the boys' club chatting over drinks. And for anything historical about the Gardens, well, when we went paperless, boxes and boxes of files were dumped, if you can believe it. Some were supposedly stored, but I wouldn't trust them on that. I wasn't able to lay hands on anything.'

'Bloody modernisation,' sniffed Patrick.

'C'mon, Poppy, it's not all bad as long as every change and upgrade is well managed,' Ellie said. 'Everything is supposed to be computerised. It's actually much safer that way.'

'Okay. I shall defer to your expertise, Ellie, dear. I must admit, what you've done so far with our computer systems has been excellent.'

Ellie looked from her grandfather to Meredith and asked, 'What's the next move, then?'

'Well, we can't do anything till we have a few facts. If this is what we suspect it is, it won't be long before more rumours and leaks start,' Patrick said, then paused, thinking. 'We have to start at the beginning. We have to speak to Kathryn O'Neill.'

'I'm afraid I might have blown that,' said Ellie. 'And good luck separating her from that watchdog Susan.'

'Why don't you front Seamus O'Neill directly, Patrick?' said Meredith. 'Or Ronan?'

'Hmmm, yes, perhaps.' Patrick turned to Ellie. 'Didn't you know Ronan when you lived here, Ellie? Maybe you could have an informal chat with him.'

'No,' said Ellie quickly. 'I mean, it was Ben I knew, and only a little bit. Ronan went to school in the city, I think. I didn't know him at all. Plus, I think this is too important an issue to trust to an amateur like me. I might accidentally set alarm bells ringing.'

The mayor and her grandfather looking a bit startled at this overreaction and Ellie felt herself blushing. 'Can I pour anyone another drink?' she asked.

'I'm fine, thanks, Ellie,' Meredith said. 'In any case, I agree that Mrs O'Neill is the key. If we can speak to her first, that might be the easiest way to find the answers we're looking for.'

'And if she won't talk to us, then perhaps we can build a story around when she first received the land.' Patrick rubbed his hand across his face. 'Going back to the historical details can sometimes be a good starting point.'

'Maybe, Ellie, you could put some posts on the paper's new Facebook page, asking for information about the Botanic Gardens, that sort of thing?' suggested Meredith.

Ellie took a large gulp of her wine. 'Certainly. But you do the schmoozing, Poppy.' She finished her drink and clutched hold of the glass. 'I'll leave you both to it. I'll just go in and see to Sammy's dinner. Nice to see you, Meredith.'

Ellie went quickly inside, but from the corner of her eye she noticed that Meredith and Patrick exchanged a puzzled look.

*

The *Chronicle* website and Facebook page were up and running, and already getting some attention. For the home page, Ellie had chosen some scenic shots of the town and river, some from the old seafaring days, and a montage of early issues of the *Chronicle* from the turn of the previous century. She also included a welcome message from Patrick as the third and current owner of the paper.

Ellie published brief profiles of the founder and the first editors, and Jon took a photo of Patrick to go with the paragraphs she'd written about him.

'I'm pleased you've showcased Patrick,' Maggie said as she scrolled through the website. 'He saved the paper when the last owner had lost interest and money, and Patrick breathed new life into it.'

'Tommy at The Shed said that people in town think of Poppy as a legend, which is lovely to hear.' Ellie smiled. 'But they probably don't realise just how much time and effort he put into the paper when he first bought it, and still does, of course,' she said.

Maggie nodded, then clicked on another page and started reading.

'Now,' Ellie said, looking from Maggie to Jon. 'We need to post on Facebook a couple of times a day, linking to stories in the upcoming issue, reactions, photos and videos too, if possible. We can write some content in advance and then schedule the updates. We can add things live if they come in as breaking news, and put up a daily post. As the site is public, we need to monitor comments.'

'And take down the bad ones,' said Jon.

'Let's hope there're not many of those!' said Maggie. 'I'll be interested to see what tips and ideas we get that we can follow up on and turn into stories for the paper. Oh, and by the way, we got an invitation to an exhibition opening at the Regional Gallery next week,' she added. 'It's for a local artist who does wonderful portraits, but this show's a bit different; it's an exhibition of her flower paintings, apparently. It's a fundraiser for the gallery.'

'Do you know much about her work?' Ellie asked.

'Heather was hung in the Archibald Prize portrait exhibition some years back, which is a barometer of how highly she's regarded. I know some artists get a one-off in the Archibald and are never heard of again, but Heather has garnered a lot of respect – and commissions, as a result – over the years. This flower stuff she's doing is new,' explained Maggie.

'I seem to recall that the gallery here is very good. My mother is a supporter,' said Ellie.

'What's happening at the gallery?' asked Patrick as he joined them.

'An art show by Heather Lachlan, but what I was getting to is that it's being opened by Kathryn O'Neill,' said Maggie, handing him the invitation and a press release. 'It was Kathryn who Heather painted for the Archibald Prize.'

'Mmm. Botanical works aren't my usual taste in art, but this might be interesting. Ellie, you'll have to come along,' said Patrick. 'This could be a chance to have another try with Kathryn. See what she knows about any family plan for a development. You need more for the profile we're doing, anyway.'

'We have a little time until her birthday,' said Maggie.

'To be brutally frank, Mags, when your subject is about to turn ninety-five, having the story ready to go is sensible,' said Patrick.

'Oh, I've done my share of obits for people who still haven't kicked the bucket,' said Jon.

Ellie shrugged. 'It sounds like a long shot to me. Lots of people will want to chat to her, have their photo taken with her. I hope the family isn't there, or that Susan, her PA.' Ellie pulled a face.

'You called the PA to try to make an appointment for a follow-up interview, didn't you?' Patrick asked.

'Yes, I've rung a few times, and when Susan finally called me back she was polite but a little frosty. Said Mrs O'Neill is too busy. Which is a nice way of saying, "Never. Over my dead body."'

'Susan sounds a charmer,' said Maggie snidely.

'Poor Kathryn, that makes it seem like she's under house arrest,' said Patrick.

'I'm sure Susan would pounce if we said one word off script. Has Meredith found out anything more yet?' Ellie asked Patrick.

'Nothing concrete, though it sounds like this group of councillors may have done the deal before anything formal is lodged and the council meets.'

'It seems as if they're trying to hammer through what-ever it is with as little scrutiny as possible,' said Ellie. 'Makes you wonder what else has gone on in the past!'

Patrick nodded. 'It's a worry,' he said bleakly.

'From what I know, there are ten councillors, some good people among them, plus the mayor, who vote

100

together in a block,' said Maggie. 'But it sometimes seems like a closed club, with other councillors influenced by the O'Neills, the GM and directors, no doubt.'

'I wouldn't mind going to a council meeting with you, Poppy.'

'Of course, and you might be inspired to stand yourself one day. Or be put off local politics completely,' said Patrick dryly. 'I like going, though. Watching all the body language. Seeing who slips out of the room when certain motions come up, which indicates they have a conflict of interest. And now they're using mobile phones to text each other during meetings to influence the voting.'

'Sounds intriguing.'

'It is,' said Patrick. 'And this gallery opening could be, too. Maggie, please accept the invitation on behalf of Ellie and myself.'

*

Ellie's mobile rang as she was finishing off a Facebook post linked to the latest edition. She smiled when she saw who it was.

'Mike, it's great to hear from you. How're you going?'

'I'm fine, but I haven't heard from you for a while so I thought I'd ring.'

'Thank you. I didn't believe this could be possible, but time goes quickly here. Sorry I haven't been in touch.'

'That's okay, Ell. How's the *Chronicle* IT going? I visited the Facebook page this morning. It looks good. A few digs from the locals, though. Didn't expect to find trolls down there.'

'I wasn't expecting them either, but I suppose trolls can be anywhere,' Ellie reminded him. It had only been a few days, and she, Jon and Maggie had only published a handful of articles online, but they'd all received lots of comments, including a handful from trolls. Although they hadn't mentioned the possible development at all, Ellie noticed that whenever Meredith came up in a story, she was often the subject of the more vitriolic posts.

'Listen, I got a great deal on the laptops you wanted. They're available now. You said you might come up. Do you still want to do that? I'm happy to bring them down one weekend, of course.'

'Yes, you must come and visit down here soon. But I need to go back to my flat and pick up a few more things. I have an evening event at the art gallery here soon and I only have casual clothes.'

'Don't they have shops in Storm Harbour?'

'They do! Some cute boutiques. But I need a bunch of other stuff too, so I'll come up to the city. Plus I really want to see my parents.'

'Of course. Can you squeeze in lunch or something?'

'Perfect! Sounds great.'

*

Ellie turned slowly in a circle, arms outstretched as she looked around her Fitzroy flat.

Compact. Cute. Central.

Suffocating.

This had once been a space she treasured because of its location.

But now the walls seemed to lean in on her. Sounds of the street – a car braking, a horn blowing, traffic rumbling, once so familiar she never even heard them – now made her jump. When she opened the window, it was immediately louder and more intrusive. She slammed it closed.

What had she used to *do* in here? Watch TV, read? Sometimes. Work? Yes. All the time.

As she thought about the life she'd been living lately back in Storm Harbour, she wondered how she'd survived so happily here in Fitzroy.

Ellie had seen her parents, gone to dinner in a noisy, crowded new café, called a couple of friends and made plans to catch up in the next day or so. All just as she'd done in her old life.

So why did she feel like this? Why did she feel so . . . unsettled?

It seemed to her that the great moving pendulum of her life had been caught on the downswing and jammed there for what had seemed an interminable time. But standing here now, she felt that something had changed. She didn't feel like the same person anymore, and it rattled her.

The apartment was starting to feel claustrophobic; she had to go out. Ellie wanted to talk to her mother alone, hug her and laugh together. Have her repeat again that this was all fine and she'd be okay.

*What's wrong with me?* Ellie fretted. She jabbed at her phone.

Her mother's voice was calm and cheerful, steadying. 'Oh, honey,' she soothed. 'Maybe coming back to Melbourne has reminded you of everything you went through with your job. Let's meet for dinner tonight, just you and me. Dad's going bowling – can you believe he and his friend Martin have taken it up?'

'What? Lawn bowls?'

'No. Didn't he tell you? He and Martin go tenpin bowling. It's hilarious. Ask him about it when you come over,' Sandy said, laughing. 'So, I'll meet you at Freddie's at six after I close the clinic. Okay?'

'Lovely, thanks, Mum.'

Feeling better, Ellie went out. She found the lanes and streets, shops and cafés of the city village she'd inhabited the same, yet different. She walked slowly, considering whether she should buy food to cook at home, but then she realised she would be out for practically every meal anyway.

Her phone rang and she saw it was Mike.

'Hi, Ell. Welcome back.'

'Hi, Mike. Thank you. How are things?'

'Hectic but productive. I have those laptops for you. How long are you staying?'

'Thanks heaps. I don't know how long I'll be here, but not long. There's that art show I mentioned coming up and a few other things I need to do for the paper, so . . .'

'Seems like you're settling in down there. Which is good, so why do you sound like you're standing in a bucket of cement?'

'Do I? What does that sound like?'

'Mmm, stuck. Down in the dumps. Are you free now, by any chance?'

'Yes, actually. I'm meeting Mum for dinner later, but there's heaps of time. I'm down near Scoop'n'Goop. Want to meet for an ice-cream?'

'Sounds ideal,' he said, laughing.

They sat at an outdoor table, dipping into tubs of raisin-dotted ice-cream.

'It's great to see you, Ellie. Phone calls are fine but seeing you in person is so much better,' said Mike. 'So, tell me all. But first, how are you? *Really*? You sound so happy when I call you down there. Now I'm starting to worry about you again. I thought going to Storm Harbour would help you.'

Ellie heard the concern in his voice.

'Do I need help?' she asked. 'I *was* good down there. I don't know, I just had the sudden feeling that maybe I was settling into a backwater that felt too comfortable – avoiding my problems, rather than dealing with them – and that scared me. I was worried that I was opting out of the real world. So I raced back here with the excuse of getting the laptops and now I'm desperate to leave again! My flat feels like it's closing in on me, the city noises are too loud. I don't know what's happening to me, Mike . . .' She gave him a despairing look.

He reached over and held her hand. 'Hey, hey. There's nothing wrong with feeling comfortable in a place, and Storm Harbour doesn't really sound like a backwater, from what you've told me. Actually, it sounds nice.'

Ellie squeezed his hand and sat up straight. 'Perhaps you're right. I have been wondering where home is for me these days. It's a strange feeling.'

'Tell me more about your life there. Has the paper uncovered any scoops?'

'Well, there is a rumour about a development that the locals might not like. The mayor is trying to find out the details. She seems to attract a lot of public attention: the trolls seem to have it in for her. Anyway, we're still trying to unravel it. The mayor is a friend of my grandfather's and she thinks some councillors might be trying to slide through a potentially controversial deal. Obviously some people don't want the mayor nosing around. But we'll fight for the truth!'

'So are you writing for the paper?'

'I'm trying to get a story on the matriarch of the town, but she's guarded by a dragon. It was her dog that attacked Sam!'

He ate a spoonful of his ice-cream and smiled at her. 'Look at yourself, Ellie.'

'What do you mean, have I got ice-cream on my face?' She wiped her mouth with her napkin.

Mike leaned across the table. 'No, I mean, listen to your enthusiasm, look at the sparkle in your eyes . . . Ellie, there's nothing wrong with you!'

'No, I'm not sick, but –'

'But you're not happy here, in your apartment, in the city. A minute ago you sounded so flat and worried. Now you've come alive with energy and passion. Ellie, you don't want to be here, that's all it is. You haven't got a job, you feel suffocated. Down there you're in a loving, peaceful environment with a role to play. That's why you feel good being there. You're not running away from reality – you've run to a *better* reality.'

She blinked, considering this. 'But I'm not really doing anything there. Certainly not earning anything. I'm worried that if I leave it too long to come back and get a job here, I just won't be able to cope.'

Mike shook his head good-naturedly. 'Ellie, you're super smart. Good at what you do. Interpret it how you want. But you were miserable here, bitter over a job and the arseholes who ripped you off, essentially. While down there you're involved in something where you can make a difference.'

Ellie took a breath. 'And where there's the sound of the ocean at night and I can walk on the beach at sunrise and sunset with the old dog. And I live with my feisty grandad who always has the kettle on or a sundowner at the ready.'

'Sounds bloody good to me,' said Mike.

'So what are you telling me? I need to stay in a back-water, that's my world now?' She frowned.

Mike sighed. 'No. I'm not saying that. What I'm saying is, we should take the lessons of the last few years – all those bushfires and traumas – and change our ways when things aren't working. Sounds to me like you're lucky enough to have the opportunity to do just that.'

Ellie nodded slowly. 'You always seem to put things in perspective, Mike.' She lifted her shoulders. 'Okay. Leaving my job almost made me want to give up and wish I hadn't bothered to stand up to them. I could've swallowed my pride and hung in there as "part of the team". But I did what I felt was right.' She gave a small smile. 'And I'm going to keep doing that: I'm staying in this fight.'

Mike grinned. 'Good for you! You know, I am so proud to be your friend, Ellie. Let me know if I can help. Yell when you need a software developer for anything!'

'You've helped already by getting the laptops for us at a trade price, seeing as I'm out of the industry for the moment. I really appreciate it.'

'I'm just pleased you're enthused again. And helping the town. It's terrific.'

'You really should come down and see it for yourself sometime, Mike.'

'I will. Keep me posted, and I'll "like" the *Chronicle* Facebook page too.'

They stood to leave and Ellie hugged him goodbye. The security of close friends was something no one can take for granted, she thought.

\*

The next morning, Ellie trailed behind her best friend as Julie went through every garment on the sale racks in the sportswear department of a favourite store in the mall.

'Found anything?' asked Ellie.

'Sort of. What about you?' Julie glanced over at her. 'You're not even looking!'

'I've kinda got out of the habit of shopping,' said Ellie. She could hear how lacklustre she sounded and felt bad.

Julie stopped and turned to her. 'Are you okay for money?'

'Yes, thanks. Though I don't like paying rent for my flat when I'm not there.'

'Well, that's easy! Move back so I can see you more,' said Julie with a grin. 'Wish I had room and you could move in with me. Or maybe you could let your place out short-term to some friends of mine?'

'I couldn't risk my landlord finding out.'

'Move back in with your parents?'

'Yes, I could do that. But I'm thirty-six. I really think I need to sort myself out now – and they need their own lives, too.' She sighed.

Julie looked at her, concern in her eyes. 'You really do sound a bit down, Ells. C'mon, let's go grab a coffee and chat.'

'How about we just have a stroll? I'm missing my morning run and dog walk, and I've had enough coffees lately to keep me awake for a week.'

'Sounds to me like you're missing the coast,' said Julie as they left the shop and began wandering down the footpath. 'So tell me, what's Storm Harbour got that Fitzroy doesn't? Don't tell me there's a fella!' She looked piercingly at Ellie. 'Give me the details!'

'Oh, I have a lot of fellas in my life, actually,' Ellie said, laughing. 'Starting with my grandad, and his old mate Roly, plus Sam the dog!'

Julie chuckled. 'Whoa! You're spoiled for choice,'

she joked. 'But seriously, what about people our age, who you can hang out with, you know? Have fun with, spend time with, or more . . . I mean, what are you *doing* down there?'

'I told you. Mainly I'm having a break to decide what I want to do next. But I'm also helping my grandfather with his newspaper. There's an issue brewing and I'm helping him try to figure out who's involved and why.'

Julie stared at her. 'So you're a newspaper reporter, a spy? I mean, what are you doing for *fun*!'

'Actually, I *am* having fun, but I really care about what's happening. I haven't engaged with something so much in ages. You know the feeling you get when you're involved with something, doing something that you feel really strongly about?'

'Yeah, I get it. But for me that always leads to a place where I just want to have it *done* and get on with life!' said Julie with a lopsided grin. 'What's your life down there really, Ellie?'

Ellie had to laugh. 'Never mind, Jules. You have to be there, I guess.'

'Okay, one of these days I'll come down and see it for myself. Just as soon as I get things sorted with Gordon.'

'Who's Gordon?' asked Ellie.

Julie linked her arm through Ellie's as they walked. 'Oh, he's gorgeous. But you know, he's a bit strange, secretive. I'm still trying to figure him out.'

'Is he married?'

'Ell! Stop it!' said Julie crossly. She was silent for a moment. 'Actually, I hadn't thought of that.'

\*

Ellie found she was smiling. The breeze through the open window lifted her hair as she drove back up the hill to her grandad's house. Sam crashed out the front door and loped over to her, clearly much improved after his injury, his tail doing near circles of excitement as she carried in the packages of food and flowers from her mother.

'That you, Ellie? I came home for lunch,' called Patrick. 'Good grief, what masses are we feeding? Does Sandy think we starve down here?'

They walked into the kitchen and Ellie put everything onto the table. 'She's given us goodies for dinner, plus some nice wine and exotic flowers from the markets. And a treat for Sam.'

'We'll have to get some friends in and share this. How is everyone?' Patrick asked as he put the kettle on.

'Mum and Dad are good. Dad's started tenpin bowling, which he's taking very seriously. It's very funny, actually. Mum is busy, as always.'

'I wish she could come down here more often and relax,' said Patrick, 'but I can't see her doing that any time soon.'

'Nope. She's as driven as ever,' agreed Ellie. 'Oh, I picked up the laptops,' she added, smiling. 'You won't know yourself once you start using them.'

'Maggie and I are looking forward to joining the modern world. Though I still don't think you can beat a phone and a notepad and pen,' said Patrick. 'I hope they weren't wildly expensive.'

'No, we got a good deal. My friend Mike bought them for me at a trade price and they're my gift to the *Chronicle*. External storage, Dropbox and other things you pay for as needed.'

'You don't have to do that –' he began.

'I insist. It's my investment in the family firm!'

Patrick beamed at her as he handed her a mug of tea. 'Thank you, love. That means a great deal to me.'

'No worries,' Ellie said, realising that she was starting to feel invested in the *Chronicle* team in more ways than one.

'Did you enjoy being back in the big smoke?' Patrick said as he pulled out a chair and sat opposite her at the table.

'It was nice to see Mum and Dad and catch up with friends,' Ellie answered, but didn't say anything more.

Patrick glanced at her. 'Well, after our tea, we can finish unloading your gear. I'm going to make a toasted sandwich then I'm heading back to work. Want one?'

'Sure. Thanks, Poppy. So, any big news?'

'Not since I last checked. Don't forget we have the exhibition opening at the art gallery tomorrow evening.'

Ellie took a sip of tea. 'That's right. I'm looking forward to it.'

Over toasted sandwiches they talked about Melbourne and family and tenpin bowling, and Ellie realised some of the tension she'd felt in Melbourne had already ebbed away.

'Right,' Patrick said, standing up. 'Thanks for lunch, I'm off. You coming down to the office?'

'Maybe, I'll see how I go unpacking and also working on a few ideas. Might go for a run, I'm a bit stiff after the drive.'

'Good idea. See you at dinner.' He turned at the door. 'Sam and I are really glad you're back, kid.'

She smiled. 'Me too.'

# 4

ELLIE WAS PLEASED SHE'D brought a formal outfit back from Melbourne with her. She felt good in a dress and heels, which she hadn't worn since she couldn't remember when.

Seeing her come down the stairs, Patrick smiled and went and changed his old linen coat, reappearing in a snappy dark blue velvet jacket and a red tie.

'Do I measure up to accompany you, my dear?'

'You certainly do. Add a beret instead of your fedora and you'd look like some famous roué off the streets of Paris.' She laughed.

'Oh, I hope not, I had more the Maurice Chevalier appeal in mind.'

'Is this your strategy to persuade Kathryn O'Neill to chat to us?' asked Ellie with a grin.

'No. That's your job. A woman of her era would never divulge anything personal to a gentleman.'

Walking into the art gallery half an hour later, they were both surprised at the large turnout. The room was decorated with huge urns of flowers and pots of plants amid boughs of greenery, which complemented the delicate colours and brushstrokes of the paintings. An older woman, who Patrick explained was the gallery director, came over to greet them.

'Sonia, this is my granddaughter, Estelle. She's helping me out at the paper for a bit.'

'Nice to meet you, Estelle . . . How lovely for you to be working with your grandfather,' said the woman with a smile.

Ellie jumped in. 'Please, call me Ellie. Yes, the *Chronicle* is such a great paper, we're very proud of my grandfather. Actually, I'm writing a tribute article on Mrs O'Neill for her birthday. I'd love to say hello again. Do you think I could have a few moments with her?'

'Oh, wonderful, yes, she's just arrived. And you must also talk to Heather Lachlan, our artist. She's been painting portraits for years but this is the first exhibition of her flower studies. Such a talent. Mrs O'Neill encouraged her to do this show, partly to raise funds for our gallery extension.' Sonia glanced away as her name was called. 'Oh, I better go, I need to check on some things before the speeches begin.'

After she'd hurried off, Patrick and Ellie turned their attention back to the crowd.

Ellie saw Kathryn O'Neill being escorted into the room by Susan McLean and whispered, 'There she is, Poppy. Don't you go being nice to that PA – I told you, remember, she's the dragon lady whose dog attacked Sam.'

113

'I remember. All the more reason to talk to her,' Patrick said, and made a beeline for the pair. Ellie trailed behind him.

'Hello, Mr Addison,' said Susan coolly.

'I just wanted to thank you for the chat Ellie had with Mrs O'Neill the other day . . .'

Ellie noticed that Patrick edged to one side so that Susan had to turn slightly, putting Kathryn O'Neill out of her line of sight. Ellie hurriedly left Patrick and Susan and approached the elderly lady.

Susan gave a tight smile. 'That was quite all right. Now if you'll excuse me . . .'

Ellie stepped in front of Kathryn O'Neill, ignoring the man standing next to the guest of honour. 'Hello, Mrs O'Neill, thank you for your time the other day.'

'Oh, Estelle, hello.' The elderly woman gave a small smile.

'I was just wondering if you could spare me a few moments to talk about your land at the Botanic Gardens –'

'Excuse me, Ms Conlan, Mrs O'Neill is not here to be interviewed.' Susan stepped between them, taking the older woman's arm. 'Are you ready, Mrs O'Neill? Would you like some water?' she asked, steering her away from Ellie.

'It's just that it would be such a shame if anything happened to the Botanic Gardens,' Ellie said loudly over the background chatter. Kathryn O'Neill's back was turned and she appeared not to have heard.

'Damn,' muttered Ellie, and looked back to see an attractive man smiling rather quizzically at her. She realised it was the man who'd been standing next to Kathryn.

'Oh, excuse me for butting in.' Ellie smiled. 'It's very hard to get any time with Mrs O'Neill.'

The man held out his hand. He had a friendly, open face, and was maybe in his early forties, she thought.

'Hi, I'm Dave Ferguson. So, what did you want to talk to Mrs O'Neill about? Sorry, I don't mean to pry.'

Ellie shook his hand. 'Good to meet you. I'm Ellie Conlan. I'm writing a story about her.'

'Are you from the paper?' Dave asked.

'Er, yes, sort of. My grandfather is Patrick Addison, who runs it.'

'Ah, yes, I've heard of him. Your grandfather is a bit of a legend in this town,' said Dave. 'So you're a reporter?'

'Oh, no, not really. I'm just helping do the occasional story. What do you do?'

Before he could answer, they heard the tinkling of a bell. Ellie looked over to see Kathryn O'Neill standing beside the microphone next to the gallery director.

Ellie studied the elderly woman, who was elegantly dressed and seemed very composed as Sonia fiddled with the microphone. Then Sonia stepped forward, tapped the mic and called for attention.

'Good evening. Thank you all for coming. This truly is a special evening for the gallery as we honour two exceptional women, Mrs Kathryn O'Neill and local artist Heather Lachlan, honoured by the Victorian Art Society. We also want to thank our generous donors, who are all listed in the catalogue, and especially the VicWide Community Bank and branch manager Dave Ferguson, for their support. Thanks also to our hardworking staff and volunteers. Now, without further ado, I want to hand over to patron and friend, Kathryn O'Neill, to do the opening honours.'

The room fell silent as Kathryn O'Neill looked out across the audience.

Ellie found herself genuinely curious as to what the O'Neill family matriarch would be like in a public forum such as this. She knew from her research that Kathryn had often been in the public spotlight over the years due to her contributions to numerous causes and charities, so she found it intriguing that so little was known about the woman herself. This applied to the O'Neills as a family, too. Patrick had mentioned that he put this down to the family's obsessive desire for privacy, or perhaps it was their need to avoid public scrutiny, he'd said. Maybe this was simply what happened when one family held sway over a town – socially, in business, in local government. And all because of money, which bought influence and allowed them to position themselves among the seats of power.

Ellie had assumed such days were long gone, but as Patrick had told her, 'Never underestimate old money. The reins of influence are not relinquished easily. The methods change, and politicians are not always the moral guardians we hope them to be. Technology, money, spin doctors, sycophantic staff, ambition, these have too often put Them and Us on opposite sides of the fence. Good men and women find it an unwinnable war, so they don't participate – unless there's a chance to feather their own nests.'

'That seems a bit harsh, Poppy,' Ellie had said at the time. 'There are good people, young people, out there standing up and fighting for change and recognition of what needs to be done before it's too late.'

As her grandfather's words came back to her, Ellie wondered if this proud and privileged woman in front of them had any inkling of how this different generation thought. Ellie doubted any of the younger members of the O'Neill family felt the need to march in the streets for a cause they believed in.

A hush fell and everyone looked expectant. But this was no quiet old lady propped up to utter platitudes. Her body language was confident as Kathryn handed her walking stick to Sonia and steadied herself, gripping the podium with both hands. Ellie waited for her to lift her glasses on the gold chain around her neck and read from notes, no doubt prepared by Susan. But Kathryn O'Neill did no such thing. She looked above the crowd, speaking to the back of the gallery, where Ellie noticed that Heather Lachlan was standing.

Kathryn gave a slight smile. 'This evening we are fortunate to be among beautiful flowers, which bring us joy in reality and are captured here so exquisitely by a woman who is not only a talented artist but a wise and gentle friend.

'Friendships, like flowers, can fade, be forgotten, or treasured in the everlasting garden of memory. Like flowers, friendships need tending through sun and rain, drought, floods, neglect and absence. Heather has been my true friend for over fifty years.'

This brought a subtle intake of breath; the long association between the two women was clearly news to most people.

'Even if friends walk in separate directions, you carry the seeds of that friendship, knowing they can be replanted wherever you may be. When an occasion comes along which makes you aware of the passing of days, I urge you to reach out, not just to friends of long standing, but to new ones. I encourage you to share life stories and anecdotes, with friends both old and new. I feel nowadays we are living life long-distance, through technology and lack of touch.

'While Heather's flowers here are botanically accurate, she adds an interpretation, if you will, of what

117

each bloom means to her. For, like people, you can make assumptions about what you see on the surface, but you need to go further. Ask yourself, what do your friends mean to you and why? What does someone's story, their history, tell you about them?'

It might have been her imagination, but Ellie thought Kathryn's gaze, which had been sweeping around the room as she spoke, lingered on Heather as she delivered these words.

'I do hope you will treasure one of these unique flowers in your home and know that the funds raised tonight will go towards supporting the gallery. I thank you all.'

There was a burst of applause.

Sonia gave Mrs O'Neill her walking stick and took her place at the microphone. She signalled to the artist and pointed to the mic, but Heather Lachlan shook her head with a shy smile from the back of the room and waved away the opportunity to say a few words.

'Before the formalities of the night come to an end,' Sonia said, 'I'd like to again thank Heather Lachlan for her striking artworks, and Mrs O'Neill for making this event possible and for her beautiful words. Enjoy the exhibition.'

On cue, waiters appeared with glasses of champagne and orange juice, and Dave handed Ellie a champagne.

'Well, that was lovely,' said Ellie. 'I take it you are the local bank manager, Dave?'

'That's right. You're not one of our customers? You should be.' He grinned. 'Even if you're not from here. Where do you call home?'

'I'm based in Melbourne. But my grandfather has mentioned the bank. Community supported by and for the locals. Is that right?'

'That's the essence of it. Let's have a look around. I really like some of these paintings.'

They kept talking as they stopped to look at each of the artworks. Ellie told Dave a bit about herself and asked, 'Where were you before coming to Storm Harbour?'

'I did a stint with a different bank in Melbourne early on, but these days I move around the state, going where the bank sends me.' He pointed to a painting. 'That one's striking. I wouldn't mind buying one of these to hang in the bank.'

Ellie leaned in to look at the details. 'It's great. The artist really has brought out the strength and even the personality of each flower.'

As the crowd started to thin, Ellie noticed Patrick heading towards her. 'My grandad looks ready to sit down in his favourite chair with a whisky. I'd better go. Nice to meet you, Dave.'

'A whisky sounds like a good idea, actually.' He smiled. 'Hey, would you like to have a drink sometime?'

Ellie blinked in surprise. Was he asking her out on a date? She hadn't been on a date for she didn't know how long. Before she could think too hard about it, she said quickly, 'Sure, yes, that'd be nice.' They exchanged phone numbers and then Ellie nodded to Patrick that she was coming. 'It was lovely to meet you, Dave. See you around.'

She gave him a quick wave as she linked her arm through her grandfather's, and glanced back over her shoulder.

Dave was still looking at her with a big smile.

*

The next morning, Ellie put the paper down next to her boiled egg and toast and turned on the radio.

'Let's hear what the local news has to say,' she said to Patrick as he spread fig jam on his toast.

They both paused, lifting their heads to stare at the radio when they recognised Sally's familiar voice.

'*According to an unnamed source in Storm Harbour Council, our council could be considering a plan to redevelop some or all of the land comprising the Botanic Gardens and the Gardens Caravan Park, a haven for visitors, campers and a small community of permanent residents, and also a prime stretch of real estate in the centre of town.*

'*We approached a spokeswoman for the O'Neill family who said only that the family had, quote, "No knowledge of such a plan nor any comment to make", unquote.*

'*When contacted about the issue, Mayor Meredith Havelock stated that she is not aware of any formal application for such a development currently lodged with the council.*

'*Retired horticulturist and landscape designer, Andrew Hayden from Melbourne, whose father was responsible for the design and supervised the planting of the Botanic Gardens in honour of Mrs Kathryn O'Neill, told us he believes the town is privileged to have the Gardens in such a rare setting.*

'*Steven and Cassandra Northcotte, current managers of the Gardens Caravan Park, said they had no knowledge of any such plan.*

'*No doubt if any redevelopment plan is in the works, it will be raised at the next council meeting. This is Sally Gordon for Storm Community Radio.*'

'Holy moly! That'll have everyone choking on their breakfast!' said Patrick.

'It will certainly make the community sit up and take notice. But Sally has scooped us! I wonder who the leak is in council who gave her the story, though? And why they didn't come to us.'

'Well, Sally's in at the council chambers all the time looking for stories. Jon and I decided a while ago that we'd only go to the council meetings if we thought the councillors were going to discuss something really news-worthy. Otherwise it can take up hours of our time for nothing,' said Patrick. 'But if this is on the agenda, I'll be at the next council meeting, that's for sure.'

His phone started to ring. 'Okay, here we go. We say only that we are not commenting, but we are investigating the story, if anyone asks.'

'Got it.'

As Patrick fielded phone calls and rang a few of his council contacts, Ellie went into the sunny room at the back of the house, which she'd taken over as an office. It had been her grandmother's domain where she sewed, read and relaxed.

For a moment Ellie surveyed the little room in the morning sunlight; the softly faded chintz sofa, the antique desk and upright chair with its needlepoint cushion of cheerful flowers and her grandmother's initials in a corner. Patrick had left the framed photos as well as some books and magazines and an unfinished needlepoint where her grandmother must have kept them. He had filled her favourite vase with what he called 'happy flowers'.

The house had more room than Patrick needed, but he refused to downsize, and Sandy and Ellie had given up long ago trying to persuade him to move. Now Ellie found the many private and personal spaces comforting and endearing. And having a space of her own to work in was a joy. It occurred to her again that her compact flat in Fitzroy was going to feel very claustrophobic after living here.

She opened her laptop on the desk and went to the newspaper's Facebook page. She skimmed the comments, pleased to see that all the articles they'd posted had attracted discussion from various viewpoints, but then her hand froze as the words of a standalone post leaped out at her.

*Who does that mayor woman think she is? We're not having some slag with a dirty past tell us what we can and can't do. We know all about what she's been up to, and she'll get what's coming to her if she doesn't shut up and stop asking questions.*

Ellie was familiar with trolling, but she'd never been as close to it as she was since setting up the Facebook page for the paper. At first the comments had been snide but general, and a few had been about the mayor but they hadn't been too personal. That had clearly changed with the comments she'd found now. The fact that they were directed at someone she knew and liked was painful.

She took them down after checking the page of the person who'd posted them. Unsurprisingly, it led to a dead end. She'd need more time to try to work out who was behind the fake name.

People hide behind their social media handles and think they can say anything, she thought as she stood up and glanced out the window. Patrick looked so happy working in his vegetable garden, but Ellie knew she had to talk to him about the comments, even if it might upset him.

'Poppy,' she called out as she walked over to him, 'what do you know about Meredith Havelock? You know, before she moved here? Does she have some sort of, ah, colourful history?'

Patrick straightened up and pushed back his hat. 'What're you talking about? I've no idea, actually. She and Jim settled here when he retired early. Health reasons or something. Why?'

'Where'd they move from?'

'Melbourne, I think.' He went over and turned off the hose. 'What's wrong, Ellie?'

Ellie took a breath. 'There's someone trying to discredit the mayor on the paper's Facebook page. A troll is hinting at some pretty ugly history, saying why does the mayor think she can decide what the town should or shouldn't do . . . that sort of thing. It wasn't nice. I've taken it down.'

Patrick looked outraged. 'She's the mayor, for goodness' sake! She has every right to make decisions for the town! Why would anyone defame her? About what? Who are they?'

'No idea. Probably just a misogynist who can't bear the idea of a woman in charge. Welcome to the wonderful world of social media, Poppy. It's one of the hazards of having a public profile, I suppose.'

'Don't say anything to Meredith. I just hope she didn't see it. Well, we don't want anything to do with this social media stuff then.'

'There're a lot of positive likes, comments and questions,' Ellie said quickly. 'And the website and Facebook page should generate interest in the paper that wasn't there before.'

'How do you know it wasn't there before?' asked Patrick. 'Everyone likes the paper, or else they wouldn't buy it.'

'Poppy, they say that to you, but let's look at the numbers. How many adults live here versus the circulation of the *Chronicle*?'

'Well, that's always hard to quantify. The paper gets handed around and read by more people than just the person who bought it. Let's see, it's in waiting rooms, coffee shops and such,' he said gruffly.

'True. And we need those people to keep paying to read it. Also, there are probably some people who don't like it but they won't say so to your face.'

'People chew my ear about things all the time! But no one would have the cheek to backstab the mayor to my face, I wouldn't think. Must be a nutter with a grudge of some kind,' growled Patrick.

'There're a lot of them out there. Guess we have to expect them to hit on us. There are going to be people for and against the paper, however unbiased you try to be,' said Ellie. 'Does the paper have many readers outside of Storm Harbour?'

'Oh yes, you'd be surprised. As well as the news-agency and the other shops in town, I've now built up a courier army of retired couples who deliver bundles all over the shire.'

'Really?' Ellie said, crossing her arms and leaning against one of the old trees. 'Isn't that expensive?'

'No, not at all.' Patrick grinned. 'They're people like me who want the truth to be reported. And because they're mostly retired they have the time and they do it for free, and the paper pays for their petrol. It started with one couple who came to me with the idea and it grew from there.'

'Poppy, you never cease to amaze me,' Ellie said, laughing.

'It's not me, love. Maggie coordinates them all. I have no idea what we'd do without them,' he said, shaking his head.

124

'Okay,' Ellie said as she patted the trunk of an old tree. 'I'm going into the office to work on the website, and then I'm having lunch with Dave.'

Patrick smiled. 'That's nice. We could do with a bank manager in the family.'

'Poppy! It's just a lunch date! Sheesh.'

*

In Dave's text inviting Ellie to lunch, he had suggested they meet outside a 1930s emporium that had been transformed, with offices on the first floor and an Asian-style marketplace with various food stalls and small restaurants on the ground floor.

'I had no idea this town was so multicultural!' Ellie looked around at the variety of food.

'My office is nearby so I've tried most of the stalls and they're all delicious,' said Dave. 'It was a clever idea from a guy who holidays here a lot and missed Chinatown in Melbourne. He set this up and brought down a bunch of chefs to train the staff, who're mostly locals.'

'Brilliant. I wonder if we can do some articles with them for the paper,' Ellie said, noticing that she was starting to sound like her grandfather. 'I'm not sure I've ever had any Burmese dishes before. Let's go there.'

They walked over to a table and as soon as they sat down a waiter brought them each a menu.

'This all sounds good. Oh, look – it says here they preference local produce,' Ellie said.

'I think most of the stalls do. Some of the people who work here have sidelines growing fruit and vegetables, farming ducks, seafood, lowline beef, goats. I think we're giving Tasmania a run for its money now.'

'We?' said Ellie. 'Do you farm?'

Dave chuckled. 'God, no! The finance for this place was done through our bank so I know a bit about it. We support the town's enterprises, and some of our local investors have been very involved, too.' He nodded over her shoulder as he lifted a hand to acknowledge someone behind her. 'Here's one of the movers and shakers who run this place now.'

Ellie heard someone walk over to join them and half-turned towards them.

'Checking on your investment?' Dave asked cheerfully.

'Hobby, more like it,' came the reply, and Ellie froze. Turning back, she lifted the menu, pretending to study it, keeping her face down.

Dave rose and the two men shook hands. 'Ellie, meet one of the brains behind this establishment,' he said.

She glanced up as Ronan O'Neill held out his hand with a cool smile. 'Nice to meet you.'

His smile didn't reach his eyes and the handshake was brief.

'Do you have time for lunch?' Dave asked him, and Ellie stiffened.

'Excuse me.' She jumped to her feet. 'I have to go to the ladies'.'

She hurried across the large room, realising she had no idea where the toilets were, until a young waitress pointed her in the right direction.

Ellie was walking fast, swallowing hard as her breath came in deep gasps. She prayed no one was in the washroom.

She lurched into a toilet stall and braced herself against the door, not sure if she was going to throw up. Trying to remember what her mother had told her, she started counting while she took deep, slow breaths.

She couldn't have another panic attack here, now. The surging in her chest steadied a bit, and then she found she was crying. Wrenching sobs welled up in her as she leaned her head on her arms against the back of the stall door.

Slowly Ellie gathered her scattered wits, taking a deep breath, then another, as she went to the sinks and washed her face and hands, over and over and over, replaying fragments of a scene in her mind: a narrow bed . . . a spinning room . . . a hand over her mouth . . . another hand clawing at her waist . . .

She looked up and stared at herself in the mirror. The reflection quivered like the surface of still water suddenly disturbed, and in the ripples she saw a teenage girl's tear-streaked face.

A woman came in and Ellie lowered her head, turning away to dry her hands. She walked slowly back out, her knees trembling.

Across the room she saw that Ronan O'Neill was perched in her seat, leaning over the table talking to Dave.

As a waitress came by, Ellie reached out and touched her arm.

'Excuse me, can you do something for me, please?'

'Are you okay?' The girl was holding a tray and she stared at Ellie with concern.

'No. Actually, I'm not. See the two men over there at the Burma stall? Could you please tell the blond man –'

'Mr Ferguson, you mean?'

'Yes, please tell him I've had to leave, I'm having a terrible migraine attack. I just have to go.'

'Sure, but are you okay to drive? I mean, why don't I ask him to get a taxi or something –'

'No, no, really, I'll be fine. I have medication in the car. I have to go and get it.'

127

She just wanted out, to be away. Damn it, Ellie thought. I was sure I was okay.

Why had she stayed down here? It had been a stupid idea; she should have gone straight home to Fitzroy when she'd heard that Ronan had moved back to Storm Harbour. Ellie shook herself. No. She wasn't some little girl here to be spoiled by her grandfather. She was supposed to be looking out for Patrick.

She wrenched open the car door and fell behind the wheel as her phone rang.

'Ellie? Are you okay, where are you?'

'Dave, I'm so sorry. It's a migraine attack, makes me vomit and I feel as sick as a dog. I just need fresh air, I'll be fine. Please, I apologise . . .'

'Don't be sorry. I'm worried about you. Let me take you home.'

'I'm in the car. This has happened before. It's okay, I know what to do. I'm so sorry.'

'Are you sure? . . . She's in the car. Migraine attack . . .' He was explaining to Ronan O'Neill. 'Ellie, call me the minute you're home so I know you're okay. I wish you'd let me drive you.'

'I'm fine, really. I didn't want to throw up all over you. I'll call you tomorrow.' She ended the call and, quickly snapping on her seatbelt, she drove out of the car park behind the old building. But as she drove down the sunny street Ellie felt overwhelmed and desperately sad. Or was she feeling sorry for herself?

She'd thought that quitting her job under a cloud was enough to deal with. It had sent her into a downward spiral, but she'd felt that she was just starting to crawl out of it and find some purpose again. How wrong could she be?

Looking out at the town she loved, Ellie wondered for

the first time exactly why she had come here. Ostensibly, of course, it had been to deal with the immediate problems in her life, and there was truth in that. But a deeper part of her knew there was more to it, and she refused now to let herself shy away from this as she always had done in the past. Trembling a little, she allowed the thought to form. Was it time she actually faced the demons she'd lived with for nearly twenty years?

Ellie had a vague memory of her mother telling her once that the deepest depression was often cloaked by a cheerful demeanour that kept the tortures hidden. Had she been doing this herself, maybe for years?

Ellie had always felt she could talk to her mother about anything, as Sandy often said, 'A psychiatrist has heard it all.' But now, when she perhaps needed her most, she didn't want to disturb or upset her mother. Mothers always wanted to fix things, make things right. And sometimes they just couldn't. Deep down, Ellie knew she needed to help herself. 'Grow up, get on with it, move on,' she'd been trying to tell herself.

But Ellie also knew that helping herself sometimes meant acknowledging that there were things she couldn't do on her own, strong and independent as she'd always tried to be. This was the time to pick up the phone.

Julie came to mind; her best friend, who never kept a secret from her even if Ellie sometimes wished she would. They'd shared a lot, had a lot of history together, and she knew if she were Julie she'd be on the phone to Ellie demanding heart-to-heart time and expecting Ellie to be on the doorstep.

But Ellie couldn't do that. Much as she loved her friend, she knew Julie was a 'me' person at heart – everything was always about her – and Ellie often teased her and told her so. In any situation, inevitably Julie had been there too, done that too, known it too, and would dole out very specific advice on how to overcome the problem. Ellie had always smiled and nodded or shaken her head, but she knew Julie had rarely taken anything seriously, and her advice wouldn't cut it this time. Nope, she wouldn't call Julie.

Charlie was gone from Ellie's life, and they'd never shared caring in-depth conversations, ever, even as husband and wife.

Mike would listen and probably say the right things, but for some reason she was reluctant to let him see she was struggling. She felt she was letting him down. He'd been so proud of her efforts when she was getting on with life, happy to see her using her skills, even at a basic level, to get the paper into the modern world. Mike was a possibility, but not top of her list.

Ellie pulled over and hit the brakes.

She had been driving slowly; there was little traffic in town. In front of her on the corner was the imposing Council Chambers building. Was it meant to be intimidating? she wondered.

Suddenly she knew who she could speak to. She realised she should probably call ahead, but she was afraid she'd be put off to a later time and would then lose her courage.

Ellie got out of the car and went to the reception desk, where she announced herself and requested a meeting, now, if possible.

The receptionist hesitated when she heard Ellie's authoritative tone of voice then excused herself. She returned after a few minutes, Meredith Havelock close on her heels.

'Ellie, this is a surprise. Is everything all right?' She frowned when she saw Ellie's tense expression.

'Meredith, I was wondering if you could spare me some time. Now, if possible? Maybe a coffee . . . somewhere quiet?'

Meredith studied her for a minute. 'Yes, of course. Follow me. Hold any calls, please,' she said to the woman on the desk.

She showed Ellie into her office and shut the door. 'You look upset. Is Patrick okay?'

'Yes, he's fine. I'm sorry, but I need to talk to someone. Not just anyone, but, well, I just . . .' She sank into the chair Meredith pointed to, feeling too drained to sugar-coat her words. 'I'm having a bit of a meltdown. There've been two major issues this morning.'

'Something specific, or is this a long time coming?' Meredith waved at the bench in the corner. 'Bad coffee or cold water?'

'Water is fine. Thank you.'

Meredith studied Ellie, put the water in front of her and sat down opposite her with a mug of coffee. 'Right. Let's deal with this issue by issue. Number one is about . . .?'

'You.' Ellie watched Meredith steadily. The older woman didn't seem surprised and didn't flinch. She raised an eyebrow.

'Yes?'

'I'm sorry to say it, but there's a troll out there who decided to attack you. I don't know what's happening, but someone left some nasty comments on the paper's Facebook page. Whoever decided to target you hinted at secrets and a dark history. A colourful past, that sort of thing. Of course, I took the entry down,' she added hastily.

Meredith nodded. 'Thank you. No doubt there'll be more. An attempt to intimidate me so that I toe the line, I assume.'

'But you wouldn't do that unless you thought it was right, would you?'

'No. I wouldn't.'

'Do you have any idea who could be trying to . . . well, scare you?'

Meredith shrugged. 'I'm the mayor. I've ruffled a few feathers over the years.' She added after a moment, 'Of course, I'd appreciate you removing this sort of thing as soon as possible if it happens again. Which it will. Though even if you block them, trolls are adept at re-inventing themselves online, I've found.'

Ellie nodded. 'Of course.' She felt that there was more to Meredith's story – more than just feather ruffling – but before she could probe any further, Meredith had moved on.

'Now. Item number two. You. How are you feeling?'

'A bit calmer.' Ellie tried to smile but gave up.

'What happened this morning?' Meredith spoke gently, her eyes kind.

Ellie drew a breath. 'I was supposed to have lunch with Dave Ferguson, but suddenly someone came over to say hello to him, and I just fell apart when I saw who it was. We have history, sort of. But I was suddenly swamped. Overcome. I haven't laid eyes on this man in many years and I've never spoken to anyone about what happened between us. I thought I'd put him out of my mind. I've been so much better since being back in Storm Harbour, helping my grandfather with the paper and trying to get my head back together. It's so hard to go back into a world that walked all over you.'

'Is that why you haven't gone back to work in Melbourne?' asked Meredith softly. 'Came to hang out down here with Patrick where you thought you'd find a safe haven?'

'Yes. Safe in one way, but not in another.'

'Perhaps you came back here to face the past without knowing it?' said Meredith quietly.

Ellie looked up sharply when she heard her own thoughts reflected back at her. Meredith was perceptive. She'd been the right person to come to.

'Something like that, I guess,' Ellie replied. 'I thought I was doing the mature thing, putting stuff from the past behind me and trying to move on. And then it all just hit me: I've pushed it away, but I've never dealt with it. It's not something I could talk to my grandfather about, or even my mother and father. I just fell apart. Ran to the bathroom and then out the door. I rang Dave and said I had a migraine.'

'And it was this man walking back into your life that brought this on?'

'Yes. Suddenly I just couldn't handle it.' Ellie's voice cracked as she spoke these last words, and she finally let out a sob in an explosion of breath.

'Oh, Ellie,' said Meredith. 'I'm sorry to see you in so much pain. Life isn't always easy. But you're so much stronger than you think you are.'

Ellie sniffed. 'I know that, in theory. I'm smart and educated and independent. But then I look at my life and it's been two steps forward, one step back. Every time I think I'm getting ahead, I have the rug pulled out from under me.'

Ellie felt Meredith watching her, almost as if in silent sympathy for a moment, then the older woman put her mug of coffee down on the small table and turned to face her, her shoulders set and her face resolute.

'Would it be of any use if I told you something of my own life experience? It might help you to put things in perspective. Or appreciate that you are not alone. Maybe let you see where I stand.'

'It might,' mumbled Ellie. 'I'm not sure. I should say that what happened to me wasn't to do with work. I was only young . . .'

'I sense that. We all live with demons as well as angels, you know. And everyone has a secret history of some kind.'

Ellie gazed at the tall, sturdy woman with whom she'd only recently connected, and realised she knew virtually nothing about Meredith, apart from what Patrick had said about their friendship. It had been enough to know that she was doing a good job as the mayor and that she was honest and principled, strong and defiant too.

Ellie could still feel the pain and anger in her chest, but the frantic sense of injustice had lessened. So she nodded, taking a sip of water.

Meredith leaned back in her chair, her voice calm and low as she matter-of-factly began telling her story . . .

*

The front door slammed behind Meredith as her mother screeched, 'You little bitch! Don't you slam my bloody door!'

'It's my house too,' the girl muttered under her breath as she set off down the lane. Well, who knew whose house it was? They hadn't paid the rent in two weeks. Her mother had been screaming that Meredith was the one who had to deal with the problem with the bloody landlord.

'I can't keep fobbing 'im off! Get down to the pub and find the old goat and get some money off 'im before it all goes on the damned dogs, horses, booze, probably floozies . . . and what a damned waste that'd be.' She'd given a nasty laugh as she shoved her daughter down the hall. 'Go on, go and git 'im, Merry! Just bring back the money!'

'Mum, I don't want to go into the pub. I'm not allowed. I'm fifteen. That's too young.'

'You don't look bloody young. Flash your boobs a bit and you c'n pass for twenty, easy. Tell 'im you need rent money, or we'll be out on our ear.'

'Why don't you go down there and tell him?' Meredith bit her tongue to stop herself from adding that her mother was known for flashing her boobs when it suited her to get what she wanted. Meredith had observed that much, along with too much else she wished she didn't know about.

She kicked a piece of gravel with the tip of her brown school shoe as she dawdled down the back lane that led onto the main street.

Radios and a TV blared through the thin walls of the terrace houses in their inner Sydney suburb. There was little privacy in the semi-detached workers' cottages that stood cheek by jowl in the shadow of the famous bridge.

She could smell the sour pilsner from the beer barrels as she came to the pub on the corner, and heard music drowned out by the broadcast of a horse race and the shouts of the men in the bar who were glued to the snowy images on the TV hanging on the wall.

She pushed the frosted glass door of the public bar open and looked for her father.

'Who're ya after, lovey?' A man in a short-sleeved

135

shirt, partially open to reveal a stained singlet, leered at her from red-rimmed eyes.

'My dad. Fred. It's okay.' Head down, she tried to make herself smaller as she slid across to the men three deep around the bar and tugged at her father's belt.

'What the f– oh, it's you, love. Bloody hell, has your mother sent you down here? Listen, you can't come in here in your school bloody uniform!'

'We need money for the rent, Dad. Mum says she'll be going to jail if we don't pay up. Can I have some, please?'

'Is this yer girly, eh, Fred? How old are you, darlin?'

'Not old enough for a dirty coot like you, Sid. Bugger off,' her dad said.

'Give the kid some dough, Freddie, you bloody had a win or two,' said a man holding two large foaming schooners. 'Hey, girly, put your hand in my pocket, never know what you'll find, eh?' He gave a raucous laugh as he thrust his hips at her.

Her father, swaying slightly, stepped away with his beer. 'Over here, Merry. Listen, keep your mother quiet, will ya. Here.' He pulled out his wallet, which was stuffed with notes, several drifting to the floor as he fumbled. Meredith quickly bent down and scooped them up and held out her other hand.

He thrust a fistful of bills into her palm and she curled her fingers over them. 'Off you go, love. Straight home, I won't be long.'

As she hurried out the door, the man with the schooners was handing one of the beers to a large fellow in a navy singlet. A younger man, smoking a cigarette, was leaning against a large painted glass advertisement for Flag Ale in a wooden frame. He had one foot propped up on the wall.

'Here she is with a pocketful of pounds. Don't spend it on the way home, missy.'

The other man ogled her. 'Where'd she get that? Got any tips for the gee-gees? Bit young to be working, aren't cha?'

'Ah, quit it, leave the kid alone.' The younger man dropped his cigarette and rubbed it into the ground with his boot. 'C'mon, I'll walk you home. You live near here, don't cha? I've seen you round before. Come to get your old man?'

Meredith quickened her steps, shaking her head, looking down as she pushed the notes deep into the pocket of her school uniform.

'S'okay. I'm leaving anyway.' He nodded at the men, who made rude grunting gestures and laughed as they returned to their beers.

Meredith walked faster, ignoring the man who fell into step beside her.

'Listen, slow down. I ain't gonna hurt you or take the money.' He kept pace for a bit and then asked, 'So what's your name?'

When she didn't answer and kept walking fast, still looking down, poised to run if she had to, he said, 'I'm Reg Hunt. I'm working on the building site down near the pub, where they're tearing down the factory. Gonna be flats there. Fancy ones, I reckon.'

Meredith was counting the doorways, just a short block to go.

'Y'know what you should do, miss? Take half that money you got from Freddie and shove it away somewhere. For yourself. You might need that one day.'

Instead of going up the back lane to the gate into their tiny square of backyard, Meredith stayed in the relative safety of her street until she reached her house, when she turned and banged on the front door. Reg waited nearby, pulling off his hat to wipe his brow.

'All right, all right,' her mother's voice came irritably down the hallway. A moment later she opened the door.

'What're you doing here at the front door like the bloody Queen?' She grasped Meredith by the shoulder and shoved her inside, then saw Reg standing on the footpath watching, his hands in his shorts pockets. 'Who the hell are you?'

'Just a mate of Fred's from the pub. Didn't think she should be walking round the pub at this hour. Street'll be full of drunks,' he said.

'Well, bully for you. And don't think you can come here sniffing round my girl. She's only fifteen. What're you? Twenty-five? Ain't you got better things to do?'

'I got a sister like her, back in the country. Don't lose your flaming rag, lady.'

Meredith's mother ignored him and slammed the door, shouting out to Meredith, 'What do ya think you're doing letting some bloke follow you home? And where's the money? Did ya get it from the old bastard?'

'Yeah, yeah,' called Meredith, who had edged into her bedroom, quickly pulling out the high-figure notes and stuffing them into her old teddy bear where a seam had given way.

She came into the kitchen and dropped the handful of crumpled notes that remained in the fruit bowl on the table, letting them fall over a rotting banana.

'Is that all? Bloody hell. Are you sure?' Her mother's eyes narrowed as she glared at Meredith.

'Dunno. He was with some fellas, the races were on. Maybe he'll win some more,' Meredith said hopefully.

Her mother grunted as she scooped up the bills and shoved them in her bra.

*

'Anyway. That's how I met Reg, my first husband,' said Meredith.

Ellie leaned back, trying to hide her surprise. 'You had a bit of a tough upbringing by the sound of it.'

'That's an understatement. More like I dragged myself up.' Meredith shrugged. 'I just wanted to get out of there. Things got really bad. The booze got out of hand, Dad started hitting Mum, then she started hitting me. I suppose she needed someone to take it out on. It was ugly. I left school and got a part-time job in the laundrette down the road. Stashed away my pay and whatever I could lift from Dad's wallet or Mum's cookie jar, so they didn't notice.

'Reg hung around and would come and see me at the laundrette. Took me to the movies and lunch and it started from there. It's a familiar story, I suppose; he was the only one who treated me nicely.

'One day Mum and Dad had a huge bust-up – they were screaming at each other and hitting each other, throwing things, smashing things. It got so out of hand the police came, and I knew it was time to get out. Reg didn't have any work at the time so he decided to go back bush. We got married and I went with him. I didn't love him, but that didn't matter to me: he was an escape, and that was what I needed more than anything.'

*

For a young woman from the inner city where neighbours shared a wall, a backyard fence and knew everybody's business, the isolation of living in a tiny fibro cottage in the country with no neighbours or even a car in sight terrified Meredith.

Reg was working as a rouseabout and handyman on a station three hours' drive away so he only came home at the weekends. And when he did, he'd spend most of his time sitting out the front of the house, drinking.

Once a week Meredith took their old truck and drove into the small township forty-five minutes away. People were friendly but there seemed few young women around her age anywhere. Young wives were at home, others had unseen jobs or were studying and doing courses.

She did become friendly with Lizzie, a woman who worked in a hamburger café and in the front bar of the town pub, the Commercial Hotel, in the evenings and on Saturdays. She was saving up to get out and travel.

Lizzie was cheerful, practical and, in her own way, ambitious. Most Fridays she and Meredith had a late afternoon tea together between Lizzie's shifts. While she wasn't well educated, having left school even earlier than Meredith, Lizzie was street smart in a way that amazed Meredith.

And then Meredith fell pregnant. At first she was thrilled, and Reg was too, but as he pointed out, it'd make little difference to his life as he'd still be away at work most of the time. 'But a baby would give you something to do during the week,' he said.

Meredith found it hard enough to scrape by on the portion of his meagre pay that Reg gave her, and their home was barely basic when it came to amenities. But nonetheless she found herself touching and holding the small bulge growing in her belly with increasing delight. And for brief moments she thought of her own mother and wondered what had become of her, but quickly pushed those thoughts aside. Neither parent had reached out to her and for that she'd been grateful, but a grandchild . . . well, maybe that would change things.

It was not to be. Meredith miscarried alone in the ugly fibro cottage, and by the time she was able to drag herself behind the wheel of the truck to drive to the nearest neighbours for help, she knew she could not stay in this life with an absent husband ten years her senior, whom she knew was drinking heavily.

At the hospital the doctor performed a hysterectomy, and when Meredith was discharged he patted her arm, telling her, 'These things are often for the best. Consider yourself a free young woman in many ways. Maybe one day you might like to adopt a little tot, eh?'

After the loss of the baby, Meredith shut down emotionally. Reg barely seemed to notice – Meredith assumed he was getting his pleasures elsewhere and couldn't bring herself to care. He soon stopped bothering to call her and came back to town less and less often. Eventually he stopped coming home at all.

Lizzie took her in and got her a room near hers, upstairs at the back of the Commercial Hotel. Meredith learned a lot from Lizzie, whose motto was, 'You gotta look after yourself, 'cause no one else will.' Sometimes she'd wink at Meredith and say, 'But, Merry, a little spoiling on the side don't go astray, eh?'

Meredith soon learned, through the thin walls of their rooms, that Lizzie's idea of 'spoiling' was to entertain the occasional chap, and as a result, she might appear in a new dress or pair of shoes. Or she treated herself and Meredith to a night at the pictures and a Chinese dinner.

By that time, Meredith was working at the bakery and hated it. The hours were long, and the fine flour that always clung to her made her cough. Her job was to roll out the dough and do whatever chores Blue, the baker, needed done, as well as serving in the shop. The manager of the shop was a cranky man named Hugo, who'd come to Australia from Yugoslavia with dreams of being a gold and opal prospector and who constantly whined about the fortune he was missing out on in the fossicking fields past Lightning Ridge. He never let Blue have a moment's peace and was always criticising him for one thing or another.

One day Blue 'blew his stack', as he later confessed to Meredith, and dumped a tub of sticky dough ready for the current buns straight onto the boss's head. Blue cowered, waiting to have his block knocked off his shoulders, but instead Hugo stomped out, never to be seen again, they thought.

Blue rang the owner of the bakery down in Sydney and convinced him that he and Merry could run the place. For a raise, of course.

Blue declared that he may be bald and fat but he was as happy as a pig in mud with the new arrangement. 'You gotta grab opportunities by the balls as they come past you, love. You're smart, Meredith, but you can be smarter.'

At Blue's urging she went to night school, where she studied money management, public relations and a subject called 'How to Get the Best from Your Employees'.

'Wotcha doing that for, love? We don't have any staff. You and me are doing just fine,' said Blue.

'I'm learning that we can do better. We need to put a deal to the owner so that we get a share in the profits if we rack up more sales. I've got some ideas,' she told him.

The bakery soon morphed into the Continental Café. Blue embraced the idea of baking 'funny foreign stuff' like croissants and fancy breads, and the shop, now with tables and chairs outside, the first in town to do so, was extended into an unused section of the grocery store next door.

Some Italian men who had moved into town persuaded Meredith to buy a fancy Italian coffee machine and serve 'proper coffee': 'The cappuccino, the latte, the espresso . . .' one man sang in his strong accent, kissing his fingertips. 'You won't regret this one.' And she didn't.

The isolated, nondescript country town was suddenly being featured in magazines and talked about on local radio. Meredith noticed that other people were starting up new small businesses, too, and took some pride in being one of the forerunners of this trend. She had a very comfortable bank account and was starting to feel secure for the first time in her life. But in spite of that, she sometimes felt the itch to do something more, something different.

A few years later, Hugo called in to see them as he was passing through. He shook his head in amazement at the changes they'd wrought and congratulated them.

'And how are you? Did you find any opals? Gold?' asked Meredith with a smile.

He shrugged. 'We never say. I do okay.' Then he winked at her and shoved a hand down into the deep pocket along his trouser leg and drew out a small phial. He tipped it into his hand and showed her.

Meredith gasped at the glowing black opals with fire-red hearts and several chunky gleaming gold nuggets.

'These maybe look small, but best quality.' He gave a wide grin. 'I do okay.'

'Blue will be pleased to know that. He always felt sorry for donking you on the noggin – head,' she clarified as he looked puzzled.

Hugo chuckled. 'You are one clever lady,' he said to Meredith. 'What you are doing next?'

'Good question, Hugo. I'm ready for another challenge. But you know, I've kind of gone off going back to the city. Much as I hated it here when I first arrived, I like this place now. I'm somebody. In business, I mean.'

He carefully put away his little glass phial and looked at her. 'You should go to the diggings. Good money there for someone clever like you.'

'Doing what? I'm not going to mine. And I don't think I have the energy to start a bakery again.' She laughed. 'What do they need out there?'

'Women,' he said bluntly. 'The men, they want ladies. Y'know, for . . .' He pumped his arm suggestively.

'I get the picture, Hugo,' said Meredith coolly. 'That's illegal, for starters.'

Hugo shrugged. 'No rules out there. Coppers, they run it with the owners. The boss – the madams.' He cocked his head. 'Big money.'

'I don't think I would find suitable work there. Wherever it is.'

'Backhill. That's the place to go. Some new mining opening up, men coming in. Bit of a rough little town. Open for business opportunities, if you ask me,' said Hugo. 'Someone like you, good business head. Strong. You go, in couple years you be very rich.' He looked straight at her. 'Finish job. Take your money, make new life.'

'Well, thanks for your advice,' Meredith said. 'I'm pleased to see you've done well. Achieved your dream, Hugo.'

He nodded and smiled, something Meredith had rarely if ever seen him do. 'Yes, I got my dream. Trick is finding what your dream is, eh?'

*

Ellie leaned forward. 'That was a pretty wild suggestion of Hugo's. What did you think?'

Meredith nodded. 'I never considered it for a second. But then after the claustrophobia of my life with Reg, the years of slogging at work, the risks I took trying to build up the café, I thought, what the hell. I need a break. I'll take a little trip . . .'

*

If Meredith thought she'd been living in a backwater, the drive to Backhill was a revelation. The space, the emptiness, the sheer breathtaking monotonous beauty made her feel as if she were shedding the skin of her previous life.

On the outskirts of the town she passed by some camps with tents, sheds and machinery scattered in gullies. She pulled up by the side of the road and stared at the brown creek below and the view out to the plains and distant hills. It was a palette of red dust and ochre against the searing blue of the sky.

Driving down the dusty main street she decided that the town was like a rough dot intersecting the unsealed roads that headed north and south. She cruised along, noticing a couple of pubs, some self-proclaimed clubs of dubious heritage, a few eateries, an aged supermarket, and some stores with windows wired and barred against fights and breakages, she assumed. One heavily barricaded shopfront announced, *All mining needs. We buy and sell gemstones/gold/minerals.* A large petrol station with a tin-roofed motel attached featured vast swathes of peeling paint.

What looked to be a one-man police station had a holding room out the back. A boarding house was on the corner of a lane furthest from the heart of town. Behind

145

it was what looked to be a line of dunnies, till, driving slowly past, she saw that each door had a room attached. A light above illuminated a number on each, and at the end a smaller building was marked *Office*.

Meredith pulled into the petrol station and filled the tank.

'Where you off to, lady? Long haul to the next town.' The attendant slammed the cash register shut and handed her the change.

'Too far to anywhere, I'd say. Which is better to stay at, the motel or the boarding house? Or the pub?' she asked.

'None of 'em would prob'ly suit you, love. But if you don't know the road, wouldn't advise driving through the night.' He rubbed his chin, eyeing her up and down. 'Pub'll be noisy till late, but you should be okay there. Lock ya door. Lot of drunks about and they'll crash anywhere. Big day in town t'day. Few blokes'll be pretty flush, I'd say.'

'Pay day?' asked Meredith.

'Yep. Every couple of months the assayer and buyers come to town. A bloke's digging for months and months and maybe finally got a find; coupla opals, a nugget or two, who knows. Some of that new stuff they're after . . . so they get a sale. It'll be gone by midnight. And tomorrow they'll wake up with a sore head and drag their bums back to a hole in the ground and start over.'

'Sounds like a lot of effort to drink away in one night,' said Meredith dryly.

'Ah, they get their rocks off too, so to speak. 'Scuse the language. Not many women up here. 'Specially since Old Mary kicked the bucket.'

'Oh? Who was Old Mary?'

'Queen of Backhill and Beyond, she used to call

herself. Ran the Ladies' Club. Though "ladies" might be pushing it a bit. It's more like a henhouse at the minute; they need another boss madam in there to straighten them out. Strewth, you should hear the brawling and arguing going on. A lot of the blokes reckon they take their life in their hands the way them girls are fighting for business.'

Meredith was under no illusions as to what the man was talking about. 'That doesn't sound great. Are the women safe, looked after?'

'When Mary ran it, I'd say so. She was a good sort; cared for those girls like they were her own, from what I heard. Shrewd old duck, though. Apparently she left a packet of money to some unknown relative down south. They probably think Mary had a goldmine!' he chortled.

'I'll try the pub. Thanks a lot.'

'Safe drive home, girly,' he called after her.

Meredith almost smiled, thinking she was glad she still qualified as a 'girly'.

She stayed a couple of weeks, living off her savings from the bakery, and soon enough became accepted at the pub, although the locals made it clear to Meredith that they couldn't work out why she was there. A rumour started that she was an amateur jeweller or buyer, though with limited knowledge of anything to do with gemmology, prospecting, mining or fossicking; this just made Meredith laugh. She started to wonder herself what she was doing there. Until she met Dolly.

Dolly seemed ancient, though she was only in her fifties. But years of digging, panning, scratching and noodling in the scorching summers and freezing winters had leathered her skin to the texture of a sun-baked tortoise.

She had bright beady eyes that missed nothing. Her

husband, Ralphie, a slow, quiet fellow, 'did the paper-work' according to Dolly, and occasionally hovered in the bar. Dolly owned the pub. And it was rumoured that she owned half the town as well. She had done well and she wore her wealth.

When Meredith first met her, she was transfixed by the sparkling jewellery adorning Dolly's scrawny arms and fingers. Three or more rings glittered on every one of her fingers, and bracelets jangled. One sharp-eyed observer said to Meredith that Dolly's jewellery regularly changed. She was, as the local said, 'a walking bank'.

Dolly soon took Meredith under her wing, sniffing out that here was a woman with brains who didn't know where to go next in her life.

Meredith, on the other hand, considered herself a woman in control of her emotions, her life, and her future, whatever that might be. In the course of a quiet chat over two glasses of chalky wine that Meredith choked down, Dolly had her number – Meredith's life story, her strengths and weaknesses, and a plan for what would be Meredith's next move in life.

Sitting together in the pub one day, Dolly leaned in close to her and said, 'Listen, Meredith love, you're smarter than you think. Sounds like you made a good business from a nothing bakery. But you can do better. I can tell you got no firm plans. No life; no man hanging on to you, no kids, any of that. First off, you spend a bit of time with my Ralphie – he's the smartest numbers man in the country.'

'I don't gamble, Dolly.'

'Haha. Good one. Nah, he's the number cruncher, smartest accountant and mover around of money and investments you'll ever meet, as I said. Learned it in the clink from the best white-collar fall guys for the rich bastards, who turned them in to save themselves. Now, listen. I need a strong woman who's clever, firm, thinks on her feet and is classy to boot. That's you, right?'

'To do what, exactly, Dolly?'

'Upgrade the Ladies' Club. I'll splash a bit of money to fix it up nicer, and you can do the fixing. Then we get the word out down in Sydney, Brisbane, Melbourne for some city girls. They're keen to get out of the city at the moment, the trade is being hit hard down there. We need a bit of class up here.'

Meredith raised an eyebrow. 'You mean the brothel.'

'Well, if you want to call a spade a fork . . . yeah.' She chortled then got serious again. 'Listen, these fellows here and out of town have got money. Though I accept some hard stuff as payment too if it checks out – opals, gold and such. I know my stones. If the joint gets upgraded, so do the prices. They'll come from bloody everywhere. But I need someone there to run things, keep the customers in line and look after the girls. I took the place over after Old Mary left and I own it outright now, but I have too much on me plate. I need a manager.'

'But it's against the law, isn't it?' Meredith said, shaking her head.

'Ah, you don't have to worry about the local sergeant. You run a good, clean, classy joint with no hassles and the local coppers get a cut: they'll be thrilled. You don't have to do anything you don't want to, and neither do the girls; the girls like it when they have an organised straight-shooting madam to run things smooth and friendly like.'

'That's what you're offering me? A job as a madam?' Meredith didn't know whether to laugh or weep.

'Not *a* madam, *the* madam! Give it a go. Get it up and running and if you don't like it, drive away. With pay.

I know a smart, strong woman when I see one. You're young, and you're a bit lost. Stay here a couple of years. You might never leave. Or else save your money, Ralphie can tell you where to invest it if you want that, and then when you're ready, pack your bags and piss off. How's that sound?' Dolly leaned back and folded her arms, looking as if it was all settled.

Meredith slowly sipped her wine through pursed lips, trying not to gag. Delicately she pulled out her hanky and dabbed her mouth. She thought about the women who'd worked the streets near her home in Sydney when she was growing up. They'd talked to her and Meredith had quickly realised there was nothing glamorous about their lives. The women were beaten physically and their spirits were often just as brutally broken. If she could take care of the women working at Dolly's place, she might be able to do some real good, she decided, and earn a wage.

'The first thing to do is to ask Ralph to order some good wine. This stuff is bilge water,' Meredith said, not daring yet to tell Dolly that she had her own agenda.

Dolly slapped her leg and guffawed. 'Champagne. That's what we'll get. Good customers get a champagne or three to get them in the mood to spend up big. Good thinking.'

*

'So you stayed?'

'I did, after I'd finally made it clear to Dolly that the health and safety of the women would always come first.'

'Was the work hard? I can't imagine it.'

'Well, I was the manager, of course. It was up to the girls to do everything else. But I made sure they were well looked after. We spent time together and I taught them

150

what I'd learned about running a business. I gave some of them advice about managing their money and helped those who were interested to go back to school by correspondence. I even taught a few of the girls how to read and write.'

'What were the women like?' Ellie asked.

'Mostly they were just regular girls who wanted to earn a good living, though there was always a few more desperate waifs and strays who had nowhere else to go. I kept a special eye out for those girls and did the best I could for them. I'd even try to find another job for them in town if I thought our place was too demanding for them. I made a deal with all the women: that I'd look after them if they were honest with me. We were very careful about keeping them safe and healthy. The local doctor, a really intelligent, lovely woman, helped me teach them about health, hygiene and contraception. We also had "specialists" come to teach them, if they were interested, about exotica in the bedroom, even belly dancing. I could've franchised the Ladies' Club everywhere. The girls got the same wage as I did, which I discovered was very different from the way other places operated. We became a kind of family for a while.'

'So it was a success?' Ellie asked.

'It was. Everyone, including all the women, made a lot of money. Ralph was a genius. Dolly was generous. I turned that row of dunnies into a smart private club, where privacy was the key. No one ever saw who came or went with whom. The office became the club room and bar where the punters and the girls mingled like it was the ritziest cocktail party you ever saw.'

She took a sip of coffee and leaned back in her chair.

'But for me the real success was helping the women learn new skills, nothing to do with their work in the brothel, that is. Together we helped each other and some of the women really blossomed and gained confidence. I was very proud when a few of the girls got together and started their own beauty salon in another town. All above board and, as far as I know, it was a great little business.'

Meredith smiled gently.

'I kept my head down for five years and then one day I just knew I wanted my life back. Also, no matter how I looked at it and what good I did for the girls, it wasn't legal. Dolly was upset but she understood. Gave me a beautiful opalised fossil pendant, millions of years old.

'I went to Adelaide, cashed in my investment and then bought a house in Melbourne. I met Jim there. When he proposed to me, I had to try to find Reg to get a divorce, but sadly for him, he'd died in an accident. Eventually Jim and I moved to Storm Harbour.' Meredith lifted her arms. 'Happy ending. Here I am. Except I miss my Jim every single day.'

'What did Jim know about your past?' asked Ellie, utterly absorbed in Meredith's story.

'Nothing. Bless him. He was such a straight and proper guy. I don't think he would have understood.'

'What about your parents?'

Meredith shrugged. 'Collateral damage, I suppose. I found my mother in an aged care home after Jim died. She was very old and frail by then. She patted my hand and said she'd known I'd be okay. Do all right.'

For a moment Meredith's composure wobbled. She looked at Ellie. 'I was probably about your age when I met Dolly. Sometimes in life you turn a corner and end up where you never thought you'd be. To be blunt, as Dolly once told me, "Shove your shit under the bed, hold your head up high, and walk out the door". Whatever happened to you, Ellie, never be ashamed of your past.'

Ellie stared at the confident and poised woman in front of her.

'Thank you. I so admire you. But, Meredith, could someone else know all this? Someone from your past? The threats on the website . . . it would be better to keep them quiet.'

'Ellie, I've never done anything that I'm ashamed about, but certainly if this became public knowledge it would not be a good look. No one here knows anything about my past, including your dear grandfather. But I don't want to be bullied out of standing up for what I believe is right. I can say that I have never been dishonest in my life, and I took good care of those women. Their welfare was always my highest priority – that's why I accepted the job. Many people would assume that no one would want to run a brothel, but they didn't have the good fortune to work with the amazing women I did. Running that business was the first time I really understood the importance of a community.'

'Thank you for telling me this, Meredith, for sharing your story.'

'So, do you feel a little better? I'm here to listen to you, too.'

Ellie gave a small smile and drew in a deep breath. 'I've taken up a lot of your time. I do feel much better. At some time, I'd like to share with you too.'

'Good. I'm glad. You know you can come to me any time.'

'Thank you. The town is very lucky to have you as mayor. And I'm lucky to have you as a friend.'

As Ellie stood up, Meredith also got to her feet and squeezed Ellie's arm. 'Dolly always said to me, "You can only give it your best shot, love. Aim straight".'

# 5

THE NEXT MORNING ELLIE drove a delighted Sam down
to Main Beach, where the white sand and choppy surf
glittered in a stiff easterly wind. There were a couple of
surfers, crouching black figures riding the break, and a
few people walking dogs along the shoreline. The surf
club was closed and the picnic ground deserted and quiet,
save for the whirring of a chainsaw – Ellie could see Ben
from a distance, working away on what must be a new
project.

It was one of those days that reminded Ellie of cut
glass. Everything seemed clear and sharp and bright, both
in the outside world and within her. Perhaps, she thought,
this was because she felt calmer. It was reassuring to
know there was another woman out there who had come

through tough times and kept a secret. And Ellie now knew that, if she needed to, she could share her own story with someone like Meredith. It was comforting.

As Ellie drew closer to Ben, she paused for a moment or two, to marvel at his skill. From the great chunk of fallen bleached cypress tree he had hewn a sleepy-eyed mother seal lounging on a rock. The rough form of two wooden pups was just starting to emerge beside her. He had brought the static piece of wood back to life. Compared to the wild and angular Harry the Cray that Ben had created at the caravan park, this carving had a gentle softness about it.

Ellie walked towards him.

'Hey, Ben!'

As he caught sight of her, he turned off the saw and lifted the visor shielding his face.

'Hi, Ellie. And hello, mate,' Ben said, laughing as Sam bounded up to him.

'Sam, sit down!' Ellie smiled. 'This looks stunning. You got another commission, obviously?'

'Yep,' said Ben. 'It can happen like that: one good project in a local area generates more work, if people like it.'

'I liked the cray, but these seals are even better. I love the tender look in the mother's eyes. What're you doing next? Do you have anything lined up?'

'Nope. But there's a job in Queensland that I *could* maybe do, out in the backblocks.'

Ellie nodded. 'That sounds promising. Is it an art job or on the land?' she asked.

'A bit of both. I like the land. Farming. I miss working at Craigmore. I used to help out in the woolshed,' he said. 'One year I spent time working with Ronan at the family

155

cattle stud in Queensland. That's where he met his wife; I took over while they were away on their honeymoon.'

'You must be looking forward to your grandmother's big party,' Ellie said, wanting to steer the conversation away from Ronan.

'Yes, I might finally get to spend some time with her! She's very "tied up".' He made quote marks in the air with his fingers and rolled his eyes. 'Thankfully I've got plenty to go on with here,' he continued, gesturing towards the seals. 'And I've been hanging out with Sally a bit, catching up.'

'Well, at least you're keeping busy,' Ellie said, patting the seal, then looking sideways at Ben with a smile. 'Sally's a nice person to keep busy with.'

It was a casual remark, but Ben flushed and busied himself with his tools. 'Well, yes. She's smart and warm and quirky, which I like.'

'Are you two serious then?'

'We didn't know each other well at school. She's so different from anyone else I've met, you know,' he said, adding, 'It's nice to have someone on my side.' A hard expression flashed across Ben's face, and Ellie thought she knew what it meant. Ben had always been the kid on the outer. Well, she hoped Sally didn't use him and move on. She couldn't see ambitious Sally putting her career on hold to live in the backblocks of Queensland with a wood carver.

'I'm glad, Ben. Well, I'd better keep going – Sam's busting for a walk. See you later.'

Ellie and Sam headed along the beach, Sam still a little tentative after being confined at home with his injury. In the distance, she saw a figure jogging towards them. After a few moments, the figure grew larger, then lifted an arm to wave to her.

'Hey, Ellie!'

'Dave, hi.'

She stopped as Dave, panting and flushed, reached her.

'This is a nice surprise. Are you okay?' he said, looking concerned. 'Bad migraines can leave you feeling drained for days. My father gets them and he has to go straight to bed in a dark room.'

'I'm okay now, thanks. I'm sorry to mess you around at lunch. Day off?' she asked.

'I try to do this every couple of days. I go to the gym in the mornings, but nothing beats running on the beach. Do you have time for a coffee? Bring the dog, we can sit outside. The café is open.'

He chatted cheerfully as they walked up the beach, telling Ellie about some friends of his who had visited recently and were thinking of investing in the area. As they passed the picnic area and crossed the road to the Beachside Café, she could hear Ben's chainsaw in the distance.

Ellie sat down at an outside table while Dave went in and ordered two coffees, which he brought out a few minutes later. Handing one to Ellie, he sat back, pushing his sunglasses up on his head.

'How come I haven't seen you down here before this?' he asked.

'I generally go along the river and the other side to the beach, down from our house. This end is nice, but more for the serious surfers,' said Ellie.

'It can certainly be more dramatic than the river, when the wind comes up,' he said. 'Hey, I was sorry to hear that your newspaper got scooped by the radio station about the development rumours.'

Ellie smiled. 'We're not worried. As my grandfather

157

said, we'll wait till we have all the facts. Tell the true story. That's what good newspapers do. I suppose you keep on top of money deals, investment opportunities?' Ellie raised an eyebrow, and Dave didn't miss her insinuation.

'Yes, of course, we are always on the lookout for developments, projects to invest in and support, be it a farm or housing, or major infrastructure.'

'Well, yes, I can see that you'd need to be across everything that's going on in the area,' said Ellie. 'I hope the bank looks at the big picture too, and considers what will help the community as well as the investors.'

'Naturally. Don't forget that we're a community bank, after all, Ellie,' Dave said, and changed the subject. 'So what're you doing then? Working on any hot IT projects?'

'I could be.' Ellie grinned.

'Like what, for example?' Dave asked.

'Like, say, a social networking app for the over fifties, alongside a dating app for the same age group,' Ellie replied, saying the first thing that popped into her head. 'Might call it "Boomer". Maybe throw in a slick get fit-style app for those life-experienced individuals with bucks but no bang . . .'

'What?' Dave said, laughing. 'Are you serious? All joking aside, if that's what you're working on, we should talk business!'

'Dave, I'm joking. Sort of. I got the paper into the modern world, and what happened? We got all sorts of comments, some of them not very nice, including one very nasty troll.'

'Really? That's bad. Who or what are they hitting on?'

'The mayor, for starters. The paper. The usual. There was another angry post this morning, actually. I took it down straight away.' Ellie grimaced as she recalled the ugly words, almost identical to the last vicious warning to the mayor that she'd taken down once before.

'Have you reported this to the cops? Though Sergeant Lyons might not be au fait with internet threats,' said Dave.

'They haven't been that specific. Like I said, I pull the posts down as soon as I see them. If no one bites back, they'll eventually lose interest,' Ellie said, adding, 'That's what I'm hoping, anyway.'

'Yeah, you're probably right.' They sipped their coffees in companionable silence for a moment, then Dave said casually, 'Hey, I might go to Melbourne one weekend. Want to come?'

Ellie glanced across at him. 'Oh, thanks, but no. I was there a short time ago. That was enough. Though it's nice to catch up with friends.'

'Sure is, which reminds me, there's a big party coming up at the sailing club with all the movers and shakers in town. Would you like to come? Ronan O'Neill will be there, the guy I introduced you to at lunch –'

Ellie was already shaking her head. 'No. I'm afraid not.' She drew a deep breath. 'I don't mean to sound rude. It's just, you know how these things are in small towns; the newspaper has to be objective, so I don't want to upset my grandfather by appearing to take sides . . .' She leaned down to pat Sam and catch her breath, sure that her excuse didn't really sound convincing.

'Oh, sorry, Ellie, I didn't think of that. I don't want to put you in an awkward position.' Dave shrugged, but looked disappointed. 'Meeting some of the businesspeople from the area has been fascinating – the original families running the big properties outside town, that is. It's an intriguing insight into another world, which I gather has changed a lot over the past couple of decades. The stuffy old squatters' rural lifestyle, posh as it was, has been upgraded by corporate movers and shakers. No farming drudgery for them, they've made their money from start-ups, the tech bubble, or cashed in on the horns of a bull market.'

'The old families, hold-outs like the O'Neills, are still a hangover from the days of the squattocracy, though,' said Ellie. 'Entitled. Like overpaid footballers.'

'Ouch.' Dave winced. 'Seriously, I agree in part. The first settlers operated under the Doctrine of Improvement, and they've been described as small-venture investors with mobs of sheep as their "capital", who "squatted" on Aboriginal land until their claims to its economic use were recognised by officers of the Crown.'

'What's changed then, when rich people use legal loopholes and regulations to manoeuvre their way into taking land they're not entitled to?' said Ellie tightly.

'You're probably right. But as my father says, "If you can't beat 'em, join 'em".'

'Is that what you're doing?' Ellie asked, trying to keep her voice even. 'Why you're in banking?'

Dave looked pained. 'Actually, no. I did choose to work with a community bank for a good reason – to avoid the trap of banking with the big boys, doing as they do or you don't get to climb the ladder. I might be ambitious, but I'm not prepared to walk over the little people.' He chuckled. 'Listen to me! That sounds condescending. I mean, I won't walk over hardworking, everyday people. Like you and me.' He reached over and touched her hand.

Ellie found she was letting out her breath. 'That's good to hear. Sorry for sounding aggressive. Just so you know, I don't want anything to do with the O'Neill hierarchy.'

'Fine. I won't ask why. Except . . . does that include old Mrs O'Neill?'

'I guess not. To be fair, I hardly know her,' said Ellie.

'No one does. Well, have we settled that then? Are we still friends?' he asked disarmingly.

Ellie couldn't help smiling. 'Of course. Thanks for the coffee. My treat next time.'

*

She took Sam home and on the way she waved to the postman, who gave her a thumbs-up as he drove past her.

She filled Sam's dish with fresh water, changed out of her walking shorts and then, acting on a hunch, she took out her phone, looked up the phone number she wanted and hit dial.

'Hello?' said Heather Lachlan.

'Hello, my name is Ellie Conlan. You probably know my grandfather, Patrick, who runs *The Storm Harbour Chronicle*?'

'Yes, dear, of course, I know the paper, though I confess to not reading it often. I suppose I shouldn't say that to you!' Ellie could sense Heather smiling down the phone.

'I'm actually writing an article about Kathryn O'Neill for the *Chronicle*. I was at your exhibition opening and gather that you and Kathryn O'Neill are old friends. I loved the Archibald portrait you did of her, by the way. Even if it was some time back.'

'Thank you, dear. Well, it was a successful painting, that's for sure, rather set me up. I always felt that it was one of the easiest works I've painted, actually, seeing as I know her face so well. We've been friends since we were young women, you know.'

'Yes, and as Mrs O'Neill said in her speech at the gallery, she treasures your friendship. I'd love to talk to you about her as part of my research for the piece.

161

In fact,' Ellie took a punt, 'I was hoping to have another informal chat with Mrs O'Neill herself, and thought that, once we've spoken, you might be able to recommend me to her.'

'Well, dear, your timing couldn't be better,' Heather said. 'As part of Kathryn's birthday celebrations, Ronan has commissioned me to do another portrait of her. She's coming to sit for it in a day or two. Portrait painting can be quite an intimate experience, plenty of time for deep thoughts and discussion: is that the sort of thing you might be interested in?'

Ellie's heart leaped. This was better than she could have hoped for. 'That would be perfect. If you think Mrs O'Neill would be okay with that?'

'I can't see why she wouldn't. I'll ask her and let you know if there's any problem.'

'Wonderful, thank you,' Ellie said. 'If she agrees, may I come a little early to speak with you, for some background before the sitting?'

'Please yourself, dear girl. If you don't mind sitting around while I get paints and materials ready. Of course, we could have a cup of tea.'

'Sounds lovely.' Ellie paused. 'Just one more thing. Mrs O'Neill's minder that her grandson employs, Ms McLean, will she be dropping Mrs O'Neill at your studio?'

'Oh, did you want to speak to Susan? She generally just drops Kathryn at the door when Kathryn visits. She seems to be a very busy woman.'

'Actually, well, frankly, I'd rather not involve Susan. She is very protective . . .' said Ellie cautiously, and waited.

Heather Lachlan sighed. 'Oh, I find her obnoxious. Don't know how Kathryn puts up with her. Don't worry, we'll keep it between ourselves.'

Feeling triumphant after the call, Ellie went to the letterbox to collect Patrick's mail and to her surprise she found an envelope addressed to her. It was a card with a sweet dog who looked a bit like Sam on the front. Inside was a note from Mike.

*How're things going? Let me know when you're coming back to town. I've had a bit of a win, so would be nice to celebrate. How's the paper going? How are you? Best, Mike.*

She phoned him straight away.

'Hey, there. Thanks for the card. It was a nice surprise to get a real letter in the post! So what's your win?'

'Ah, I will explain at length over a long lunch. So how're you?'

'I'm good. There's lots going on with the paper. I'm still monitoring its website and Facebook page, and we still have our troll, unfortunately.' She told Mike about that morning's ugly post. 'Mostly things are going well, though,' she went on. 'I'm doing the research for my feature article, which I'm enjoying.'

Laughing, she told Mike about how the day before she'd showed Patrick some of the work she'd done on her article about Kathryn O'Neill. 'Poppy emailed it back to me covered in comments and questions: *"Expand this"*, or, *"Take this out!"* and *"Why did she say this?"* Jon said they call it Poppy's famous *"blue pencil treatment"*, harking back to the old days of subediting, apparently. Jon says he gets exactly the same sort of comments on his drafts.' Ellie smiled to herself, remembering. Patrick had been proud of her, she could tell.

'Anyway, enough about me,' she said. 'I'm so curious about your "win". Can you give me a clue?'

'Not yet! Actually it's not that major. Just thought I'd

like to share it with you in person, but I can tell you that I do have serious interest and some funding for a project, which is great. Now, what are your moves?'

'Staying put for the moment. Poppy and the paper are all-consuming. But there's always time to have a long lunch. Why don't you come down here instead?' she said suddenly. 'You've never been here.'

'Great idea! It's a long weekend this weekend. Can you recommend somewhere nice to stay?'

'Oh, we have plenty of room . . .' Ellie began.

'No, I don't want to disrupt your grandad's routine. Yours, on the other hand – I suggest you clear your diary!'

'Oh, sure. It's so full of exciting events.' Ellie laughed. 'I'm really looking forward to showing you around. And congrats on whatever your project is!'

'I'm looking forward to seeing you, too. Let me know where I should stay.'

'I know just the place – I'll book it right now and send you the details.'

Ellie immediately called Lucy at the Garden Cottage.

'Sure, thanks, Ellie, Mike will be one of our first guests – the guesthouse has only just opened. I'll throw in a special big breakfast for him,' said Lucy.

'Thanks very much, Lucy. He'll be down on Friday afternoon.'

When Patrick came in, Ellie announced, 'Hey, Poppy, we're going to have a visitor. My friend Mike is coming down this weekend. I booked him into Lucy and James's guesthouse. But what say we have a dinner party while he's here?'

'Well, that'll be nice. A little gathering sounds good, too. You'll have to handle the food side of things; I don't do much more than stews and toasted sandwiches these days.

What did you have in mind? Casual or sit-down? Haven't done that in a while.'

'It's a bit cool for the barbie on the lawn. Let's use Nana's good china in the dining room,' said Ellie. 'And we'd better decide who we're inviting.'

*

Ellie found that she was taking extra care with her hair and make-up to meet Mike down at the River Bar where he'd invited her for lunch, having arrived the night before.

It was hard to miss his tall figure leaning on the railing looking out over the river.

'Hey, you!' called Ellie as she walked along the board-walk towards him.

He turned and spread his arms. 'This is all gorgeous! Why haven't I been here before?' He hugged her. 'Keeping this a secret, eh?' Then he held her at arm's length. 'It agrees with you. You look happy, Ellie.'

She laughed and changed the subject. 'How's the cottage? Lucy and James looking after you?'

'Almost too well – I really overdid breakfast. Let's go for a walk before lunch. I want to see the waterfront here. Look at all these fishing boats! Are those crab traps?'

Ellie chuckled at his enthusiasm. 'You bet. My grand-father has a mate who gets the freshest crayfish for us. They do a great cray bread roll and beer down here.'

'Right. We'll put that on the agenda. Cute houses, I s'pose they're all holiday rentals?' he said as they passed the row of cottages. 'Well looked after. The whole town is, by the look of it.'

'Yes, it's a sweet place and it's great having a river on one side and the sea on another.' They headed towards the park at the end of the seawall and Ellie asked, 'What's new in the big smoke?'

'Oh yes, the gossip. You might be pleased to hear that your "friend" Sophia seems to have bitten off more than she can chew. She's struggling to maintain control and move things along, apparently. The firm lost a big contract.' He grinned.

'No surprises there. And I don't care,' said Ellie.

'Really?' Mike stopped and stared at her. 'Yes, you do.'

'No, I really don't. I could never go back there now.'

'Pleased to hear it. Plenty of other opportunities. When you're ready.'

They turned into the park.

'Over there is the track that leads to a little island,' Ellie said, pointing. 'It's a beautiful walk, lots of birds and wildlife. There's an old lighthouse on it. Are you still surfing? The Main Beach where the surfers go is just on the other side of the dunes.'

'Yeah. I haven't had much time lately, though. Like you say, it must be amazing to have a beach on your doorstep. You could take up fishing.'

They circled the park and then Mike headed towards a row of heritage buildings.

'These're empty? What a waste.'

'They're vacant, but a lot of buildings in town have been restored; the whalers' bluestone cottages, the old pub and boarding houses, oh, and the council chambers. They are listed with the National Trust. The Historical Society's in an old stone heritage house, and a lot of private homes have been renovated in keeping with the original building,' said Ellie. 'Are you interested in heritage places? I didn't know that.'

They turned back towards the path to the restaurant.

'You don't know half my secret passions.' He grinned. 'I'll explain over lunch.'

*

The white wine was crisp and light and local. 'Well, it's from forty kilometres away,' Ellie said. The salad was crunchy and fresh, the crayfish delicate and sweet, complemented by a tangy dressing and crusty, warm, just-baked bread.

'Do you eat like this all the time down here? It's seriously good food,' said Mike.

'We try to eat local as much as possible. Lots of people grow stuff and the markets are wonderful. A friend of Poppy's, Roly – he's such a character, you'll enjoy meeting him – brings us fresh fish from his Italian neighbour and amazing lean beef from a friend's herd of lowline cattle.'

'Ellie, I'm impressed. You're not exactly roughing it away from the city. No wonder you seem so happy here.'

'So tell me about your interest in old buildings. Is this to do with your new success?' asked Ellie.

'Well, yes. Long story short, I've been creating an app. It was just something I was tinkering with, nothing important, but I got swept up in it.'

'Something to do with heritage buildings? How does that work?'

'Yep. It probably hasn't really come up between us before, but I love heritage architecture, have for years. It's long been a hobby of mine to research the construction and details of old buildings all around Victoria, the different periods and styles. So it occurred to me to start a database recording the features of our heritage homes and buildings. That led to developing an app that would be useful for architects, builders, interior designers, history buffs, but especially for people who're renovating old homes. So, for example, if you want to know what colours to paint the interior of a 1920s worker's cottage, you can check out the original colour schemes and swatches on the app.'

'Oh, wow, Mike,' said Ellie. 'I never knew you were keen on old buildings. This is a great idea. I love it.' She grinned at him. 'You'll have to take photos of the details in Poppy's house. I don't think it's been changed since it was built a century ago.'

'That would be great. In fact, from what I've seen of Storm Harbour already, it would be the perfect subject for the app, with the whalers' bluestone cottages and so on.' Ellie could hear the excitement in her friend's voice. 'Another feature is that you can use the information on the app to determine a building's approximate age from the details in its design.'

'Amazing. There're so many possibilities, Mike, and you have the IT know-how to do it at far less cost than having someone else build it,' said Ellie, starting to share his enthusiasm.

'Yes, apps can cost a bomb, but that's because people usually have to pay someone like me to design and develop them.'

'But how will you collect all the data and information?' Ellie asked. 'You'd need images, architect's drawings . . .'

'I know, I know, and it's purely part-time for me so I can't do as much research as I'd like to. I've put the word out on social media and letters in a couple of journals and already people are emailing me with old drawings, and some historical societies have come on board. I'm starting small but I have big plans!'

'So you said you have interest already?'

'Yes. When I'd finished the prototype I tentatively put it out there to see what interest there might be, and I've been really surprised at the support. A few people have come on board as investors and others are considering it. Like I say, the R and D takes time, but it's so satisfying.'

'Wow, Mike, I'm so happy for you, and almost envious. I wish I had something I could lose myself in and get enthused about.'

Mike leaned back. 'Now you know my secret passion, Ellie,' he laughed. 'I'll hang onto my IT job for the time being, though.'

'You never know when an app just appeals and suddenly takes off and becomes a lucrative side hustle,' said Ellie. 'Look at all the apps on our phones! No wonder people are trying to come up with a winning app all the time.'

'Aha, a celebration?' came a voice over Ellie's shoulder.

Ellie turned to see Dave Ferguson standing behind her.

'Hello there!' she said brightly. She introduced the two men. 'Mike is a friend from Melbourne, an IT colleague. Dave is the manager of the community bank here.'

'Please, don't get up,' Dave said as Mike rose. 'You here for the long weekend?'

'You bet. My first time here. Amazing place. A bit of a secret.'

'We try to keep it that way,' said Ellie.

'Whereas I'm not against advancement, done in a sensitive way,' said Dave with a chuckle.

'He's saying that to annoy me,' said Ellie.

'That's the job of a bank manager, isn't it? To support local advancement?' said Mike.

'Only if it's appropriate,' said Dave quickly. 'Well, I'll

let you get back to it – enjoy your lunch, I can recommend the lime meringue pie. Catch you later, Ellie, and enjoy your visit,' he said to Mike and sauntered over to join a table with two other men.

'Seems pleasant. He likes you,' said Mike pointedly.

Ellie wrinkled her nose. 'He's nice. But he moves in a different circle and has friends who come and visit, looking for "investment properties" here.'

'You don't approve? I noticed a lot of land ripe for development on the outskirts of town, and along the coastline. As Dave says, it can be a good thing if it's done sensitively,' said Mike.

'Storm Harbour is wise to treasure its heritage,' Ellie said. 'It has a great setting, high-quality food and a good vibe. It has a lot to lose if new developments aren't in keeping with the rest of the town.'

'You're right, Ell. No wonder it's attracting people like Lucy and James and their business.'

'Yes, and Cassie and Steve, who run the caravan park. It's not just a summer place. I love it here in winter. Always have.'

'Does this feel more like home than the city?' Mike asked gently.

Ellie didn't answer for a minute, then said slowly, 'It's more than that. Might sound silly to the generations who've lived here, but I do feel a sense of my roots being here. That sense of place and belonging people talk about. I hadn't realised it so much until this trip.'

They stopped talking and quickly studied the menu when the waiter came to take their dessert order. Then Mike leaned his elbows on the table and said gently, 'You were very fragile when you left Melbourne. Now you seem stronger. Happier. But you're not just burying your problems, are you? I don't mean to sound like a shrink, but I know enough pop psychology to know that avoiding problems never helps solve them.'

Ellie was thoughtful. 'I don't think I'm doing that. Actually, the other day I was thinking that in a strange sort of way I've come back here to face them properly.' She looked at him and gave a small smile. 'Your branching out with a sideline has me thinking. Maybe I should do some travelling, stay a couple of months overseas, Europe, perhaps. Write something. I don't know. I'd never considered any such thing till this moment.'

'Sounds like a plan,' said Mike cheerfully. 'I'll drink to that.'

'Actually, I've just decided I'm not making any plans. I'll take it as it comes. Who knows where I'll be in, well, who knows when?'

They clinked glasses.

'Send me a postcard now and then,' said Mike.

*

Ellie surveyed the dining table set for Patrick, herself, Mike, Roly, Meredith, Cassie and Steve. She and Cassie had caught up for coffee a few times and had started going for morning walks together, giving them time to build the foundations of a strong friendship. Ellie found she really enjoyed Cassie's company. She'd asked Lucy and James, too, but they were busy with guests and the café.

Mike had come over early to help and now he was sitting on the verandah, yarning to Patrick, while Ellie took care of the final preparations.

She'd kept the meal simple, using fresh ingredients: a leg of lamb with pickled figs, crushed potatoes with herbs baked with butter, broad beans, roasted beetroot and home-baked olive bread that Meredith was bringing. The lamb came from Roly's breeder mate, so it was ethically bred at a small-scale local farm. Dessert was a lemon custard tart Ellie's grandmother had taught her to make, baked with their own lemons.

Mike had brought the wine. He now had a local favourite and was taking a case back to the city, along with a loaf of Meredith's olive bread she'd offered to make especially for him.

'It's seriously delicious. She worked in a bakery once,' Ellie had explained.

The room was cosy, candles burned, and Ellie's grandmother's favourite vase was filled with the last of their roses for the season. As the guests arrived and mingled and chatted over wine and a cheese board, Ellie put the finishing touches on the meal and served up as the guests took their seats around the table.

Roly was in fine form, and Mike kept roaring with laughter or shaking his head in a bemused fashion at the older man's wild stories.

Steve recounted the tale of a huge seal that had hauled its bulk out of the river onto the fishing landing where Roly and his friend Nino were cleaning their catch. It had started barking aggressively, demanding a feed.

'I heard this racket, and there's Roly waving his fist at the seal and demanding that the beast "cease and desist", and Nino screaming at it in Italian. The next thing I know, the old bull puts his head down and charges them!'

'What happened? They can be dangerous,' exclaimed Ellie, who couldn't help laughing.

'Nino was the hero. He flung the bucket of fish at it just as Roly turned around and charged back at the seal, yelling, "Leave me the bloody mulloway!"'

As everyone laughed Roly said, 'Well, mulloway are getting damned rare around here these days.'

Over dessert, Patrick turned to Meredith. 'How're things down at the office?' he asked.

She wrinkled her nose. 'Still very frustrating. I'm making no headway on finding out about this potential development. Like I said before, something's going on, but I'm still not privy to it. You know how a conversation can stop when you walk into a room? Well, that's happened to me more than once lately.' She shrugged. 'By the way, do you know where Seamus O'Neill is at the moment? One of the staff wanted him for something.'

'Oh, it's that time of year,' said Patrick. 'For as long as I can remember, Seamus and his wife took a cruise this time every year. They'd fly somewhere and get on a cruise ship and sail around the Caribbean, South America, you name it. After his wife died, he continued the tradition.'

'Well, he better come back soon, as I imagine he'll want to be here for Kathryn O'Neill's big party,' said Roly.

'Oh yes, good point,' Patrick said.

'When are you going to start taking it easy, Poppy?' teased Ellie.

'Me? Cruises? Never. What would I do with myself? Once a newspaperman, always a newspaperman. I learned on the job how to be a reporter and now a proprietor.' He turned to Mike. 'Speaking of the job, I heard on the grapevine that you're interested in heritage buildings and have built an app? How do you make money from these apps?'

'Poppy!' Ellie laughed.

Mike nodded. 'Hey, this is what everyone is after, an app that a wide range of people are interested in and subscribe to. You can learn a Chinese dialect, become a superior breadmaker, like Meredith –'

173

'I didn't learn from any app, honey!' interjected Meredith.

'– or just play games that go from simple to silly to superior stimulation. Or give you a brain snap.' Everyone chuckled. 'But seriously, I've always had a secret fascination with buildings; I really should have studied architecture. It's not just the way buildings are constructed, it's the world around them that develops as a result. We spend so much time in and around structures, but how often do we really think about how a community is influenced by its surroundings?'

'Which is why walking in a forest is so good for your sense of wellbeing,' said Cassie.

'Exactly,' agreed Ellie.

Roly reached for his wineglass. 'Aspirations can lead us astray until we learn what makes us feel at home in our own skin and surroundings. Unfortunately, we can't all afford to be in the setting we might like. I have a great concern about the way people are often lumped together like sardines. Humans need a bit of space, sun, trees, nature.'

'I agree,' said Mike soberly. 'If governments and developers would work for the people and not their pockets, we could build integrated communities for social housing, people in their retirement, young families all together that allow for, say, a compact back garden, a shady tree, green space, and a shared community garden, or playground, perhaps. Connected by flat paths for bikes and scooters and joggers and walkers. Public transport close by. Planning is the key. These things need to be built into the concept from the start.'

Meredith sighed. 'Good luck selling that to the government,' she said. 'Money rules, and it's wrong, but it's a matter of reworking our lifestyle and work choices within our current circumstances, if we are able to.'

'Hear hear,' said Patrick.

'But it's still the mantra of the majority to maintain mediocrity. And what about people's apathy about climate change?' said Roly. 'We're standing at the gates of hell with the world on fire all around us, and still too many sceptics out there are refusing to take off their blindfolds. Keep pluggin' away with your paper, Patrick.'

'You've got a point, Roly,' said Steve. 'But I have to say, I've observed such a change in people who come through the caravan park here. When they actually stop being busy and doing stuff, and just sit in a chair under a tree, look at the river, maybe with a beer or a mug of tea in their hand, where there's no traffic, no TV or radio, no people in your face, just a few birds, they become a different person. And I hear them say how different they feel, all the time.'

'You could sell a stay at the Gardens Caravan Park as a form of therapy, like those nature clinics and spas,' suggested Roly. 'I will be your spokesperson. On the other hand, please don't let the place get overrun with stressed-out city people!'

'As long as I can prevent it in my little corner of the world, I will,' said Steve quietly, and hearing his words, Ellie thought about the potential development breathing down their necks.

'Let's move to the verandah for coffee and a nightcap,' said Patrick.

'I'll help you clear up, Ellie,' offered Cassie.

'No, that's my job,' said Mike.

It was late by the time Ellie and Mike joined Patrick in the old rattan chairs on the verandah, where a gas streetlamp-style heater hissed above, wrapping them in a soft gush of warm air. Sam had found the direct down-draft and was snoring faintly.

Cassie and Steve had given Roly a lift back to the caravan park with them, and Meredith had left soon after.

Patrick had broken into the whisky Mike had brought him, and had persuaded Mike to share a noggin as Ellie nursed a good shiraz.

'This is a bit hard to take,' said Mike, stretching his legs. 'I didn't know you were such a decent chef, Ellie. I want your grandmother's lemon tart recipe.'

'Ellie learned a lot from her nana. Sandy, her mum, never felt at home in the kitchen, I fear.'

'That's okay. Dad's a dab hand on the barbie,' said Ellie. 'He always made my school lunches too. Some were not as successful as others.'

'I got a bit spoiled working overseas so much, mainly in Asia. The office always gave us a joint with a cook,' said Patrick.

'I think I might have mentioned to you, Mike, that Poppy was a foreign correspondent for the ABC,' Ellie said.

'Yes, but I had to learn the ropes, starting with regional radio. What an eye-opener that was after the big city. At first I thought I was in clover. They paid me fifty quid a week to sit in the sun all day drinking brandy and ice from a long glass, eating home-cooked meals at the Railway Hotel three times a day, roaming the countryside at weekends breathing in smog-free air. Then I'd sit in a cool office punching out little stories to amuse the locals.'

'Sounds pretty cushy,' said Mike.

'Yeah. But the loneliness, the lack of people I could talk to about ideas, theories, thoughts and plans, got to me. The rest of the world didn't seem to exist in that small backwater. And to tell the truth, the work was dull and didn't come with any challenges, so I started to feel I was missing out on everything that was going on in the city. I was in paradise on the edge of hell.'

'Were you there on your own, Poppy? A one-man band?' asked Ellie, who'd never heard much of Patrick's early days as a journo.

'Well, my predecessor had left a list of regular corre-spondents, including one in my town. I spent weeks trying to find this cove and finally rang my predecessor who told me, "He'll make contact when he hunts down a story. He works off the beaten track." So I had this vision of an ABC stringer correspondent with a white pith helmet, Commonwealth of Australia–issue notebook in his hip pocket, pencil clenched between his teeth, poling a bamboo raft up the rivers of the region looking for a story off the beaten track. Never did meet him.'

'When did you first go overseas?' asked Mike.

'Early sixties, to help run the Port Moresby news-room while the senior fellow went to report on how self-government was coming along in Dutch New Guinea and check out the increasing Indonesian threat to its stability.' Patrick chuckled and added, 'I'd heard the ABC offices were basic but I was stunned to find that the studio and record library were in a rusty tin shed built sometime before the Second World War. Accommodation was a post-war prefab with no air conditioning. We had a couple of local cadets, with one doing bulletins in pidgin English and the other in Motu dialect. It was a great experience but the after-work parties and shindigs on the weekends took their toll.' He lifted his glass. 'Cheers.'

'Nana always said that Vietnam was a turning point for you,' prompted Ellie, as she could see her grandfather was enjoying reminiscing and Mike appeared genuinely interested.

'Yeah. For so many. I was sent up on the heels of the Viet Cong's ambush of a small unit of Aussies, mostly kids of nineteen or so, in a rubber plantation at Long Tan. I was only in my twenties myself,' Patrick said, sounding far way for a moment. 'I was in the Caravelle Hotel in Saigon, near the great French-style boulevard, Tu Do, and the famous Continental Hotel. Sipping G & Ts on the terrace where Somerset Maugham and Graham Greene had been. But my favourite place was the roof terrace at the top of the Caravelle, to hang out with people like our cameraman, the legendary Neil Davis. We'd watch the light show on the edge of the city near the Mekong Delta as the war trundled on.'

'Did you work with the Americans at all?' asked Mike.

'Yes. We had a unit seconded to us. Didn't get our sense of humour at all.' Patrick chuckled. 'We were waiting at the Aussie base camp for an aircraft and one of our group had a big feather he'd picked up in the jungle. We were admiring it, and one of the Americans asked what was so special about that feather. Quick as a flash my mate says, "It's a kangaroo feather, mate." The guy looks dubious and says it's the first time he's heard of kangaroos having feathers. So my mate goes on that they're rare because 'roos only had a couple at the end of their tails. The feathers helped them stay on course during very long leaps. And he went on recounting some of those huge daring leaps and pretty soon the chap wants to buy the feather. Our mate says aw, no, his mum gave it to him as a good luck charm.' As Mike and Ellie laughed, Patrick went on, 'Well, he parted with it for twenty bucks, saying, "Jeez, my mum'd kill me if she knew what I was doing!" Yep. We got a lot of entertainment from those guys.'

'Did you get close to any action?' Mike put his glass down and leaned forward.

Patrick looked away, saying quietly, 'Too close. Too often. At one point in ninety days I made sixty-two hazardous flights, hitching around in twenty different types of aircraft. Once I was in a chopper, three foot above ground and about to land, when we discovered it was a minefield. Another time I missed a flight and was cursing myself for losing a story, only to find out the aircraft had gone down and I lost some good mates. I was a wreck on tranquillisers and sleeping pills for weeks after that. I did a few more tours overseas, Japan and India, then I met your nana, Ellie.' He smiled softly. 'Best thing that ever happened to me. We moved here when Sandy was a toddler, and I retired early to take on the *Chronicle*. I couldn't bear to see it fold up. Since Ellie's nan died it's kept me going.'

Patrick drained his glass and put it down. 'Right. Enough of my old ramblings. I'm off to bed. Good to meet you, Mike, come any time.'

Mike stood and warmly shook his hand. 'A real honour to meet you, Patrick. I mean it. You're an inspiration, I have to say.'

Patrick patted his arm. 'You're just trying to get in my good books. G'night, Poss. It was a lovely evening and meal.' He blew her a kiss. 'You coming, Sam . . .? Nope, fickle dog. You'll come slinking back to my bed when our guest has left.' He waved and headed indoors.

'What an amazing man,' said Mike softly. 'You're lucky to have him as a mentor and a buddy.'

'I know,' Ellie replied. 'He's been so special in my life and I respect his advice. Though I don't always take it, I s'pose.'

'Mmm, he's like a wise owl,' said Mike, and yawned. 'Well, I'd better head back to the Cottage.'

'Take it easy driving up there. Thanks for your help tonight. And for listening to Poppy's yarns. He doesn't get a chance to reflect back like that too often.'

'I loved it.' Mike reached over and gave her a hug. 'See you tomorrow, I'll leave a bit after lunch.'

'Mike, I really enjoyed today. See you in the morning.' He gave a salute as he got into his car.

Ellie nudged Sam. 'C'mon, off you go for a quick walk. Then it's bedtime.'

*

Tuesday morning, Patrick was having breakfast when he shouted to Ellie, 'Come quick! Sally's on the radio about the land deal again!'

Ellie raced into the kitchen from the sewing room study and turned up the volume on the radio.

'. . . *and so, a source in the Storm Harbour Council reports that an application for a permit to access and develop the land next to the Botanic Gardens, currently leased by the council as a caravan park, will be formally lodged once certain formalities with the land are dealt with. Our source reveals that a developer wishes to build luxury townhouses along the riverfront. The application will have to go through the proper procedures, including being put to a council meeting, before it can be approved. The council media manager did not return our calls . . .*'

'Who the heck is leaking this to Sally?' said Ellie.

'Not sure, but no wonder Meredith is frustrated. Her suspicions were right, it seems; there are people who have an idea of what's going on and they are keeping it from her,' said Patrick. 'Why don't you ask Sally?'

180

Together they headed into the *Chronicle* office. Maggie was already there, the kettle whistling.

'Morning, Patrick, Ellie. Gosh, did you hear Sally's report? Do you think she's right?' Maggie asked.

'Good morning, Maggie,' said Patrick. 'If I trained her properly she wouldn't be blathering on with unsubstantiated rumours, so she probably is correct.'

Jon was on their heels. 'Morning all. What's going on? Don't tell me Sally scooped us again.'

'No. She didn't. When we have the full story, we'll go to press,' said Patrick firmly, striding into his office. 'So in the meantime, hop to it, Jon. Go back to your sources in council and around the town,' called Patrick.

Jon grinned at Maggie. 'He's cranky.'

'Taught young Sally everything she knows,' Maggie said. 'How was your dinner party, Ellie?'

'Terrific. Poppy enjoyed himself. Did a bit of reminiscing.'

'I love his stories of the old days,' said Jon. 'He should write a memoir. Oh, here are the papers.'

As he spoke a delivery driver backed through the door, pushing a trolley stacked with bundles of papers.

'Howdy, where do you want 'em? The usual?'

'In the storeroom, thanks, Alan, and leave a bundle here, please,' said Maggie as Jon grabbed a pair of scissors to snap the plastic tie binding the fifty papers together. They each took a copy.

'Wow, the layout looks great. The new designer we're trying out really knows what she's doing,' said Jon.

'Is that the paper?' called Patrick, walking into the room to collect one.

Even though the paper came out three times a week, there was always excitement as each edition arrived from the printers in the larger town nearby. They spread open the paper and pored over the pages.

'The two new advertisers should be happy with their pages,' said Maggie.

'Your capture of the crab thief story looks good, Jono,' said Ellie. 'How'd you get a photo of him being arrested?'

Jon winked. 'I have a friendly face in the force. Dropped me a hint and as it happened I was five minutes away. With my camera. So what's Sally's scoop?'

'She had a follow-up on the rumour about the land at the river: apparently an application to develop the caravan park land as luxury townhouses is about to be lodged,' answered Maggie.

Jon looked surprised. 'Wow. None of my sources had anything to tell me before. If a formal application is lodged, though, then it should be easier to get more solid information. I'll get on it.'

'Yes. Great to have something concrete like an application after all the smoke and mirrors. Let's get cracking,' Patrick said, looking at Jon then Ellie.

'So who's going to talk to Sally?' asked Maggie as Patrick went back into his cubicle.

'Ellie, you know her,' said Jon. 'Sally and I have kind of become sparring rivals. In a sort-of-friendly way. You might have more luck.'

'Maybe I'll talk to Ben first,' said Ellie thoughtfully. 'He said he's been hanging out with Sally a bit. He's probably almost finished that carving. It's brilliant.'

Late that afternoon Ellie swung past the house to collect Sam and headed to the Main Beach picnic ground. She found Ben walking around the mother seal and pups, looking thoughtful.

'Oh, wow, Ben! Is it done?'

'I'm not sure. I have to sit and look at it for a bit. Before it gets oiled and polished.'

'It's quite something, Ben. You have such a talent. Do you paint or do other art? Why did you decide on wood carving?'

'I dabble in things. When I settle down someplace with a studio I might get into more into painting. One day I just saw a tree that'd come down in a storm, and I could "see" exactly what was inside it. It's like each tree has a creature at its heart.' He looked at the sculpture a moment longer and then turned to Ellie. 'So, how're you doing?' He bent down and patted Sam.

'Oh, good, thanks. We heard Sally on the radio this morning, she's really going for it. I hope she's on sure ground over this caravan park thing. And I hope it's not true.'

'She says she's on top of it.'

'What do you know about it? The land was in your family, or is it still? I thought council just leased it.'

Ben shrugged. 'I wouldn't have a clue. Not that I wouldn't be interested,' he added. 'But, well, I'm not around much, so I'm not told anything. You could ask my father when he's back. I wouldn't waste your time going to anyone else, if I were you. They won't tell you anything.'

'What about Sally?' How does she find out what's going on?'

'She only knows what some staff person in council is leaking to her. Honestly, Ellie, I don't know who it is,' Ben said.

'Well, when we know details, we might have to see if we can all work together. I'd hate to see the caravan park go under for a few townhouses,' said Ellie.

'Yeah, me too. But people with money would like them.'

'Might have to get people out to protest,' said Ellie.

Ben shook his head. 'Good luck with trying to get people to march in the streets in protest in this town. It's always the nimbys versus the progressives, but mind your manners. This is Storm Harbour, don't you know?' He gave a short laugh.

'Maybe you're right.' Ellie called to Sam, who had wandered into the bushes, sniffing about. 'Well, tell Sally good on her for breaking the news!'

'Okay. Let me know how things go. See ya round.'

Ellie and Sam walked on, Ellie completely lost in her thoughts. Without realising where she was headed, she eventually found herself at the caravan park. Ellie saw Cassie sitting on the step outside their demountable office, her head in her hands.

'Cassie?' she called softly.

The other woman looked up. 'Hi, Ellie. Sorry, I'm a wreck. You've heard the latest?'

'Only what the local radio had to say. Have you heard anything official?'

'Nothing, but all these rumours are so unsettling. We figured we'd be the first to be told if we were about to be turfed out. Or if it was even a possibility.'

'Yes, you'd think so.'

'We were sure we'd found our dream. We've had our struggles. Being here we thought we'd made it through the hard times and out the other side. It felt like a sort of prize after sitting in the proverbial darkness for months and months,' said Cassie.

'Well, my grandfather has the *Chronicle* on the case too,' said Ellie, grateful that she might be able to ease Cassie's mind on this point at least. 'He'll get to the bottom of it.'

Cassie shook her head sadly. 'Hard to fight the big end of town if there's any truth to it. And why?'

'Money,' said Ellie with a sigh.

'Ugh. I know, but I thought we'd all learned that money doesn't buy you health, life, love, luck . . .'

'Which is why we can't let them go back to those old days where money rules. Values have changed.'

'Except for the rich,' said Cassie bitterly.

'Move over.' Ellie sat on the step as Cassie made room. 'How is Steve taking this?'

'He's worried. He contacted council as soon as we heard but hasn't been able to find out anything yet. Our biggest worry is for the residents living here. This is their home and I'm not sure where any of them could go if we have to close.' She rubbed her eyes. 'And we'd have to move back in with my parents, I guess.'

Ellie put her arm around Cassie's shoulders. 'Hey! Don't jump ahead too fast. Like I said, we want to help you. Can you tell me what the deal is that you and Steve have here?'

'Deal? Nothing special. We moved here because we love the area and we had a few ideas for businesses we could run, but then when we saw that the old caravan park manager had retired we went to the council and applied to take over the lease. Steve will know the nitty-gritty of the lease deal.' Cassie was quiet for a moment, then said, 'Coming here, we thought we'd found our own paradise. It's friendly and safe.'

'That's true. Do you lock your door at night?' asked Ellie. 'We don't.'

'Only if we have some out of towners passing through who seem a bit suss. Though we always lock the office, of course,' said Cassie.

'I don't know whether to just enjoy the fact that

we're cushioned from the ugly side of life here, or if it's time to get back into the real, dog-eat-dog world.' Ellie sighed. 'Do you miss the bright lights of the big smoke?' She looked at Cassie. 'Why did you and Steve move away from the city?'

Cassie hesitated, a tear spilling from her eyes. Ellie reached out to touch her hand.

'Cassie, sorry, you don't have to elaborate,' began Ellie, suddenly aware she'd hit a nerve.

'Oh it's not just the thought of being uprooted again after . . . We . . . we had a bit of a hard time, before coming here.'

'Do you want to talk about it?' asked Ellie gently.

Cassie took a deep breath. 'We had a stillborn baby, Ava. She only lived a few hours, but I think of her every day. So Steve wanted to move away, as if we could leave the pain behind.'

Ellie was stunned. 'Oh Cassie, I had no idea . . . I'm so, so sorry. How terrible for you both . . .' She squeezed Cassie's hand. 'How long ago did this happen? Or would you rather not talk about it?'

'It's okay,' Cassie said. 'I don't mind talking about her. Otherwise, it's like she didn't exist. She was so perfect . . .' A tear ran down her cheek.

Ellie leaned forward and said softly, 'Do you want to tell me about her? You called her Ava?'

Cassie nodded. 'After my grandmother, who I adored.'

'Who did she look like?' asked Ellie.

'So much like my grandmother! Though we had the name picked out before we even saw her . . .'

Ellie listened as Cassie talked and talked, her eyes bright with memories. But then she slowly wound down,

186

her words growing quieter, her eyes dimmed and damp with tears. Eventually, after a long moment of silence, she said, 'It was just so unexpected . . . the shock. Steve can't bear me to mention her. He wanted to get away from everything we'd planned. Start over . . .'

'I guess I understand that. But it must be hard to carry this alone, Cassie. Anytime you want to talk, or pick a flower for Ava, please, I'm here.'

'Thanks, Ellie, it's a relief that you know. I get very sad on her birthday each year.'

'If you want to do something special for Ava, any time, just ask me,' said Ellie.

Cassie nodded, unable to speak for a few moments. 'Thanks, Ellie, that's sweet of you.' She straightened up, wiping her cheeks. 'I suppose we should go and find Steve.'

'Where is he now?'

'Talking with some of the locals down at the landing, I think. Some of them get together for a sundowner and a bit of a fish around this time of day.'

'Shall we go talk to them?'

'Sure,' Cassie said. 'I just wish I had some good news for everyone.'

'You can tell them that the paper is going to help. Jon is out poking around – I think he's mad that Sally got the tip before him. Patrick will be on the phone to everyone he knows, too.'

'Oh, bless him,' said Cassie. 'He and Roly are such good mates. Those chess games of theirs are something to watch.' Cassie smiled. 'You know, the residents here are a mixed bunch who get on so well. They've figured out their invisible boundaries, respect their idiosyncrasies, and know when it's appropriate to check up on someone. Of course, people have disagreements. We hear a few sharp words occasionally, but we always manage to resolve them cooperatively.'

'Sounds to me like you guys should be running the council,' said Ellie dryly. 'Show them the importance of community consultation. Hey, I hear music.'

Across the grass they saw half-a-dozen residents seated at tables or on the grass near the landing, and some had brought their own chairs.

Roly was there with his cello, someone else had a guitar, and they were singing a silly whimsical song Ellie didn't recognise, but it made her smile.

Cassie looked at her. 'See what I mean? They come from all walks of life and might never have crossed paths before, but each in their own way treasures what they have here – a home and being part of an oddball family. Some of their real families think they're nuts living in "just a caravan park".'

The song finished and people clapped and laughed. Then Roly spotted them and lifted his cello bow in acknowledgement. Steve was sitting beside him with a beer in his hand.

'Aha, Ellie, are you here as the music reviewer from our favourite newspaper come to critique us?' Roly said as he put away his cello.

'Just a friend dropping by,' she called.

Steve stood, giving Cassie his chair. He squeezed her shoulder, saying quietly, 'You okay?'

She nodded.

'Want a drink, Ellie?'

'Thanks, Steve. A light beer would be great,' she answered.

Roly handed Ellie a director's chair. 'Here you go. Where is our esteemed editor? Hunched over a steaming keyboard with a green eyeshade, chewing a dead cigar? Isn't that what editors do?'

Ellie laughed. 'Maybe in your day, Roly.'

A guy in shorts and a T-shirt wearing a fishing hat leaned over and held out his hand. 'G'day. I'm Nino Baretti. You a local lady or what?'

'I like to think I'm a local. I went to school here for a while and my grandad still lives here. I'm staying with him.'

'That's a good girl. You like fish?'

'I love fishing. And eating them.'

'You want to take fish home to your pop, eh? You cook him, okay?'

'Nino comes from a famous fishing clan,' said Roly. 'He just brought in a good feed.' He pointed to a plastic crate with a wet sack over it. 'He's our weatherman, tells us when we should go out fishing. He's remarkably accurate.'

'Thank you, I'd love a fish.' Ellie smiled at the man and he beamed back.

'And that's Bluey. From the 'Gong up north in New South Wales.' Roly nodded at the man on the other side of him, whose friendly face was crinkled and freckled. He gave a cheerful smile.

'Wollongong?' Ellie said.

'Yep. Got too bloody big for me, 'scuse my French. The missus over there likes it here too.' A woman in casual slacks and a blouse waved to Ellie. 'Once I retired we hit the road and never got past here!' He chuckled.

'Bluey was big in waste management,' said Roly. 'He's got some hair-raising stories you should hear some time!'

'Really?' said Ellie politely.

'Yes, sir,' said Bluey. 'Started as a night carter as a teenager. That's a dunny man, you know. Climbed the ladder and was high up the ranks by the time I was fifty. Then I had to have dealings with the council. I didn't last six months after that.' He shrugged. 'Once they knew I couldn't be bought off, I was out. Bleeding well tried to force money on me. A lot of funny business goes on in some of the big rubbish companies. Lotta money in shi– 'scuse me, trash,' he concluded.

'You should talk to Shirley over there, too. Lot of stories even in this small gathering,' said Roly, leaning back in his chair.

Nino twirled a finger. 'Some of the stories here, you can't believe they're true! Better than anything you read in a book, eh, Roly?'

Roly turned to Ellie. 'Small portraits of a park, perhaps? Vignettes of our small population?' he suggested. 'Articles not for the sympathy vote but to change some perceptions?'

'Yes indeed, Roly. Poppy, Jon and I have already talked about that idea but it seems there are even more people here than we thought who could feature in the paper,' said Ellie. 'Now, if you'll excuse me a tick, I just need to talk to Steve.'

She drew Steve to one side and asked him about the lease arrangement he and Cassie had with the council.

'I don't want to pry into your personal business, but we're trying to help,' said Ellie.

'There's nothing very private or special about it,' said Steve. 'There was what they called the standard lease arrangement where they hired me and Cassie. We live here for free, manage and maintain the place. Any improvements or construction or stuff have to be approved by council. A fancy splash pool area or things like that would have to be approved, but we like it the way it is, really.

So do our guests, so we haven't gone down that route.' He frowned. 'This development business is a nightmare. I've been trying all day to get in touch with the director of the council division that controls caravan parks, but no one wants to tell me anything or speak to me about it. It's like I've been blacklisted. No consultation encouraged,' he said, then sighed. 'There're some people who see our town as an up-market holiday area to come to in summer. But they don't care about the town as a whole the rest of the year.'

Ellie nodded, not knowing what she could say to cheer him up. 'There're lots of us who'll give you all our support,' she said at last. 'Thanks for the beer, Steve. I better head off.'

She called out goodbye and was about to leave when Nino handed her a plump bream wrapped in a tea towel.

'It's all clean for you, love.'

'Oh, how wonderful. I'll return the tea towel.'

'That's okay, you enjoy him for dinner.'

*

When Ellie and Sam arrived home, she saw that Patrick was busy in his study.

Ever since Mike had left, Ellie's mood had shifted. Mike had distracted her, as he always did, made her laugh and look at the big picture, feel energised – and ignore shadows and memories.

But a blanket had fallen over her, not bringing warmth and comfort, but weight and worry.

Night was closing in. Ellie sat on the verandah, wrapping herself in a bulky cardigan as the breeze turned chilly. Her coffee had gone cold. She put down the notepad where she'd been scribbling questions to put to Kathryn O'Neill.

191

The more she thought about this woman, the more the spectre of the O'Neills seemed to haunt her. Shadows of memories shifted like dark clouds on the horizon, heralding a storm.

This house, her grandparents and family, the safety of the town and its people, had always protected and nurtured her, despite the nightmare that hovered at its fringes and never went away. Life did indeed seem to be a process of one step forward and two back.

The darkness was blurring the garden and trees. Sam shifted closer to her chair.

Then the steady step of Patrick came along the verandah.

'It's getting cold, love.'

'Uh-huh.'

He sat in the chair next to her, leaning down to rub Sam's velvety ears. 'Dinner soon, matey.'

They sat together in a silence broken only by the rustling of leaves, the settling of birds.

Whether he saw in the darkness or just sensed that a tear had trickled down Ellie's cheek, Patrick reached out and rested his hand on her shoulder.

'One day at a time, love.'

# 6

ELLIE WAVED AT PATRICK who was standing on the verandah, watching as she and Sam came back along the track from the beach after their breakfast walk.

She knew he used to worry about her setting off down that path when she was young, determined to explore '*on my own, Poppy!*' She'd always come back with treasures for him – a shell, a cuttlefish, driftwood. And he'd helped her when she'd put a message in an old rum bottle and sent it out to sea.

So many memories. But there was one that still haunted Ellie, which she'd never shared with her family. She'd overheard Patrick talking with her mother once, when Sandy had asked him if he knew of anything that had upset Ellie during the time she'd lived in

Storm Harbour while Sandy and Doug were overseas.

Ellie knew they were none the wiser. There was no way they could know what had happened.

Looking up at the house now, she thought that although she was indecisive about her future at the moment, it was clear that she had a deep attachment to this home, this place, this town.

As she and Sam walked back through the garden, Patrick smiled at her.

'Maggie gave me another jar of her famous fig jam. I recommend it on toast with creamed ricotta,' he said as they walked together into the kitchen.

'Thanks, Poppy. I'm starving.' She started cutting thick slices of fruit bread.

'I hope your talk with Kathryn goes well today,' Patrick said, sitting down at the kitchen table. 'You can only do what you can. I'm sure Heather will back you up, since we now know those two have been good buddies for a long time.'

'Yes. I wonder how they first met,' said Ellie.

'Ask her,' said Patrick.

'Hopefully Kathryn will be more forthcoming about her life without Susan the watchdog around.' Ellie paused and looked at Patrick. 'Do you think I should ask her about the development rumours? Warn her, in case she doesn't know?'

Patrick considered, rubbing his cheek with his hand. 'I think you should tread gently for now,' he said eventually. 'We still don't know for sure that an application has been lodged, or anything confirmed really, for all that Sally's mysterious source told her. You could edge around the issue – find out if Kathryn knows anything about plans for the grounds – but until we have something more concrete, I don't think we should upset her with something that might not be accurate or even true at all.'

'Okay, Poppy, good plan,' Ellie said. 'Speaking of Sally, I'm catching up with her before I meet Kathryn. I'll see if she can give me any more information.'

'Good luck, Poss. You know, it's great to have you on the *Chronicle* team.'

*

Sally and Ellie walked through the grounds of the caravan park and sat on a bench facing the river.

'How peaceful is this?' said Sally. 'I can see why Ben likes staying here.'

'Was it by choice? To be near the crayfish sculpture he was working on, or because of the family situation?' asked Ellie.

'A bit of both, probably. He tries not to show it, but I think he feels they don't understand his art.'

'Do you think Mrs O'Neill has any idea about the plans for the caravan park?' asked Ellie.

'I don't think so, or I imagine she'd put her foot down. And Seamus O'Neill is away on his cruise so we can't ask him about any redevelopment.'

'Can't you call him?'

'Tried, but no answer. I asked Ben about it and he says his father turns off his phone and his emails when he goes on holidays.'

'It feels like someone is deliberately keeping things obscure and vague, and until it's brought up at a council meeting we probably can't find out too much.' Ellie looked sideways at Sally and added, 'You seem to have the inside info from someone in council. Can you say who it is?'

Sally smiled but shook her head. 'Now, Ellie, you know

a journalist can't always reveal her sources.' Changing the subject, she asked, 'Have you worked out a way to talk to Mrs O'Neill about the Gardens and all the speculation?'

'I'm seeing her this afternoon, at a sitting for a portrait she's having painted. I'll try to probe a bit, if it feels okay,' said Ellie. 'I also need to get some background material from her for this feature I'm writing, so I have to be careful. I don't want to push her to the point where she just closes down.'

'It would be good to see the plans for these town-houses.' Sally sighed. 'Wait till the locals find out more details . . . I think there'll be a lot of backlash.'

'Yes, but of course there'll also be pressure from some people who see gentrifying a caravan park with expensive townhouses as a good thing. It might be seen as making the town more "up-market",' added Ellie.

'Yep. Lining their own pockets. I bet there'll be a queue to buy them,' said Sally.

'We need to get the facts and let the locals know what's really going on,' said Ellie.

Sally nodded. 'You know, it's always seemed strange to me that anyone would try to do something with this land while Kathryn's still alive,' she said. 'But from what I've been told, I gather it's all very time-sensitive, for some reason, which my source either doesn't know or won't say.'

'Really? That's interesting,' said Ellie thoughtfully. Checking her watch, she stood up. 'Thanks for the chat, Sally. I'd better get ready to see Mrs O'Neill.'

Sally stood too and was silent for a moment, then said, 'Ellie, do you want to team up? We could share info and perhaps even agree what we use and when?'

'Absolutely,' said Ellie, pleased at the offer. 'We can be far more effective if we put up a united front. I'll let you know what I get out of Kathryn O'Neill if it's of any value.'

'It's a deal.'

Smiling, they shook hands.

*

Ellie took her old bicycle, which Patrick had refurbished for her, and rode into town to Heather's quaint bluestone cottage. The artist's studio was attached to one side. She put her bike behind the garage and tapped on the studio door, which faced the street.

'Come in, come in,' said Heather, opening the door.

Ellie smiled at Heather's profusion of grey curls restrained by a colourful scarf that trailed behind her. She wore a paint-spattered smock with large pockets over a maxi dress, and had bright red lipstick and colourful dangling earrings.

'You look just as I expect a working artist to look!' Ellie said, smiling.

It was the smells that entranced Ellie as she walked into the cluttered studio, which constituted one large room with window drapes pulled. There were two easels and a couple of armchairs, stacked paintings in varying stages of completion around the walls, shelves groaning under paint tins, bottles of turps, jars holding brushes, rolled cloths with brushes in them, rags and pots and tubes of paint, books, notebooks, as well as jugs and jars and bowls, candlesticks and strange figurines which, Ellie assumed, could be used as props. The profusion of objects and painting materials was somehow enchanting. The smell of oils, paint, coffee and a fading bunch of lavender filled the room, and at close quarters, Ellie caught the scent of Heather's sweet familiar perfume.

'Orange blossom. Make it myself,' she explained cheerfully when Ellie commented on it. 'Same with the lavender oil. Now. Teabag or over-brewed coffee?' she asked.

She waved Ellie into one of the two armchairs, eschewing the more formal chair on a raised platform to one side of the huge canvas on the nearest easel, which was covered by a cloth.

'Tea would be good, thank you, as long as you have time. I don't want to hold you up,' said Ellie.

'Lovely. It's no bother.' Heather turned on the kettle then started wiping brushes with a cloth and squeezing daubs of paint onto a palette.

'Do you mind if I record our chat?' Ellie asked, taking out her phone as well as a small notepad and pen.

''Course not. You can check with Kathryn too, but I'm sure she'll agree. She hasn't any secrets as far as I know,' Heather said, chuckling.

Ellie pushed the record button. 'Can you tell me about your friendship? You said you'd known Mrs O'Neill a long time. Where did you meet?'

'It was when she came here as a young bride,' Heather said, making their tea and handing Ellie a mug. 'Knocked our socks off. Boyd was quite the catch – had been for years. By then, the matchmaking mothers were coming to the conclusion that he was a confirmed bachelor. So we were surprised when he brought Kathryn home. Not that we saw much of them, mind you. I believe Boyd liked to party, but the wealthy graziers kept to themselves. If you weren't part of their social set you didn't get a look-in. Which is why we always assumed Kathryn came from the same sort of background, not that she ever talked about it.'

'It was also the war years so things were not as they'd been before, I guess,' prompted Ellie.

'It was a crazy time; there was a feeling of "live for today, who knows what tomorrow will bring", that sort of thing. But life had started to settle down somewhat by the time Boyd and Kathryn were married. You know, the locals were very curious about Kathryn because not many people had met her. And there were the inevitable rumours, of course,' said Heather.

'Such as that she might be in the family way, as one older lady described it,' Ellie said.

Heather chuckled. 'There was no way Boyd O'Neill would be trapped into a marriage.' She paused, then said, 'The first time I saw Kathryn I thought she looked like a fairy princess. I was just a teenager and Kathryn was barely twenty. Boyd helped her out of his town car and they went into the old Grand Hotel for a luncheon. I can still remember the dress she wore; a pale lemon silk with sprigs of violets on it. Everyone looked so dowdy during the war, and here was Kathryn, like a breath of spring. Artists remember things like that.' Heather smiled.

'She must have made quite an impression,' said Ellie.

'Oh, she did.' Heather put down her mug and adjusted her easel. 'The O'Neill family lived out at Craigmore, the wool stud. It's not really that far out of town, but it was a world away in those days. Still is, in some ways,' added Heather. 'They owned some land in town, and I think they had an office. I seem to recall my father mentioning it once. They also owned a couple of the heritage homes. Kathryn told me that she and Boyd tended to stay over in town after functions rather than drive all the way back to Craigmore.'

Ellie nodded. 'I know this is a bit off topic,' she ventured, 'but when I went out to Craigmore for an interview with Mrs O'Neill recently, the assistant Susan

McLean was hovering. She cut short our interview when I started asking personal questions.'

'Susan can be a bit of a problem, as I mentioned to you,' said Heather with a sniff.

'How long has she been working for the family?'

'A couple of years. It was Kathryn's grandson's idea to employ Susan when he came back from the cattle station. Poor Seamus was worn out after years of caring for his frail wife Laura and I suppose Ronan thought it was too much for his father to look after Kathryn on his own. Not that she needs much help physically, and Susan's not a nurse,' Heather added. 'She works as Seamus and Ronan's assistant and makes appointments, that sort of thing.'

'And Ben?' asked Ellie. 'He seems a bit of a lone wolf.'

'Dear Ben. We artists don't always fit in,' said Heather. 'I do like what he's doing now with his wood carving. He seems to have found his artistic style. Although I must say I prefer brushes to that dangerous machine of his.' She went on, 'Maybe if they'd let him express himself in his own way when he was younger he wouldn't be such a wanderer. Of course, Kathryn's fond of him. She tries to protect him, as grandmothers do. I don't think the rest of the family understand him. He always used to visit Kathryn and stay with her before Susan came along. I hear he's staying at the caravan park this time, doing a carving.'

Ellie nodded. 'Yes. He was complaining to me about not being able to see her at Craigmore, and I suppose Mrs O'Neill doesn't come into town often.'

'You're right. Kathryn doesn't drive anymore, and she can't get a lift unless it's convenient for Susan,' said Heather.

Ellie checked her notes. 'So tell me, how did you come to know Kathryn?'

Heather grinned. 'Would you believe me if I said we both had golf lessons at the same time? We were partners in a comp and, well, we hit it off, so to speak. We were terrible players then but we had a lot of laughs. I found her such easy company, the two of us with two other ladies in a foursome slicing and slashing our way through eighteen holes. We bonded very quickly.'

'Here? At the local club?' asked Ellie.

'Yes, that's right. It was quite the thing for young ladies to take up. Really, though, we were complete amateurs with no proper idea how to play. But we did improve once we'd had a few lessons, and eventually we played in a comp at Royal Melbourne. Even Boyd O'Neill was impressed at that. He was a member, of course.'

'What else did you get up to? Did you mix socially, or visit Craigmore?'

'Not really. Kathryn and Boyd seemed to have a close bond, which I found unusual for those days. Heaven forbid a man should be affectionate in public! And they kept to a very tight circle of family and their friends. After Kathryn had Seamus she got involved in charity commit-tees and gave away prizes at shows and things. She even set up a creche for the wives of workers on the local farms, which became important for the whole area,' Heather said proudly. 'Her heart was really in gardening, though. She brought in an excellent landscape designer, Hayden, his name was. He did so much at Craigmore. And then came the Botanic Gardens, her passion in life. Anyway, you should ask her about that.'

'I will. The Gardens are a beautiful and precious part of the town,' Ellie said.

'Absolutely, we are so fortunate to have them.' Heather smiled. 'Kathryn and I have always kept in touch, although it's a bit harder these days since the family have taken to treating her with kid gloves. I tell her they must think she's like a fragile piece of glass that's kept in the good china cabinet and only brought out on special occasions.'

The two women laughed, but then Heather continued more seriously, 'I don't think she realises how under the family's thumb she is. I'm just glad she speaks her mind occasionally and comes to visit. It was her idea that the family commission me to do her portrait for her birthday, though Ronan thinks it was his idea. But really we just have a few laughs and reminisce.'

Heather began laying out her brushes as they noticed a car pull up outside.

'I'll go to the door. Maybe you could take the mugs into the kitchen, just inside the house,' Heather said diplomatically.

Ellie took the hint and disappeared into the house as she heard the murmur of voices at the front door. She waited till Susan had left and Heather called her to come and join them.

The contrast between the woman Ellie had met in the sitting room at Craigmore and the one sitting in the chair on the platform could not have been starker. Today Kathryn looked relaxed and happy instead of formal and slightly on edge as she'd been when Ellie had first met her.

'Kathryn, you remember Ellie Conlan? I called you when Ellie asked if she could join us today,' Heather said.

'Yes, of course. It's lovely to see you, Ellie.'

'Thank you, Mrs O'Neill. It's so kind of you and Heather to let me come. I'm afraid we didn't have much time at our last meeting.'

Kathryn waved her hand vaguely. 'Susan keeps me to some silly schedule, although it's not like I'm in a hurry anymore.' She turned her bright, amused eyes towards Heather, who smiled. 'Sometimes I like to escape her clutches, for sheer amusement.'

Kathryn's silver hair was cut neatly and she wore a tailored black jacket over a rose silk blouse with the collar standing up. Diamonds sparkled in her ears and a strand of pearls shone against the blouse, which was tucked into black velvet trousers. She was possibly too thin, but whether it was her bearing, her self-confidence, or just knowing she was Mrs Kathryn O'Neill, something gave her an air one could have considered imperious, Ellie thought, if it wasn't for her warm smile.

'Ellie's hoping you could reminisce a bit about the olden days for her article,' said Heather. 'I suspect she doesn't believe we were great golfers!'

Kathryn chuckled. 'Weren't we just? Remember how horrified the club was the day we turned up in golfing trousers?'

'They wouldn't let us into the dining room, until they saw it was you,' added Heather. 'We broke down a few barriers in our time. Broke a few rules, too,' she added, lifting the cloth from the half-finished painting as she spoke. 'Now, no one is to look, it's bad luck to gaze on an unfinished portrait.'

'She just made that up,' said Kathryn calmly. 'So, tell me, Ellie, are you writing for the *Chronicle* fulltime?'

'Yes, but just for a while. I normally work in IT, computer coding projects and so on.' She wondered how up to speed these ladies were with modern technology. 'But I enjoy writing. And I'm sure you have a wonderful story to share. Did you ever keep a diary?'

Kathryn shook her head. 'No. Only the common garden variety appointment diary, that is; I'm not much of a writer. But Heather did. And she gets on that Facebook place.'

'Just to promote my work,' said Heather. 'Now, get comfortable, Kathryn, and don't jig around too much.'

'My jigging days are over,' said Kathryn, smiling at Ellie. 'You're very pretty. Are you living in town?'

'No, I've been living in Melbourne. My parents are there, too, but Storm Harbour feels like my home now.'

'Are you going to stay here then? You're not married.' She glanced at Ellie's ringless fingers.

'You know what the girls say nowadays about the men here,' broke in Heather. 'They're either taken or terrible!'

Ellie laughed. 'I'm divorced, actually. No kids. I'm just here helping my grandfather, checking up on him. Not that he needs it. The paper keeps him young.'

'I don't read the newspaper regularly anymore,' Kathryn said. 'I find much of the news so depressing I prefer to read a book.'

'You're not alone there,' said Heather with a chuckle.

Ellie decided to steer the conversation away from herself. 'Can you tell me about your special memories as a little girl, Mrs O'Neill? Where did you grow up?'

Kathryn paused a moment, then waved a hand dismissively. 'Oh, you're not going back *that* far, surely?'

Heather leaned in to study the painting, wincing slightly. 'I'm not as strong as I used to be, some brush-strokes are a bit shaky. Kathryn, tell Ellie how you met Boyd.'

Kathryn's face lit up. 'It was the war years. Such a strange time, looking back on it,' she began. 'Tragedy and laughter. Freedom and fear. Many women took on men's work, so there were opportunities to learn new things and prove that women could do the same tasks. Not that we were paid anywhere the same amount, though.'

'That's often still the case, unfortunately,' said Ellie. 'What did you do?'

'I worked as a typist in a solicitor's office in Melbourne. Rather a good one too. There were five of us. So many men and women in uniform. Some women I knew joined the services and the Women's Land Army.'

'Did you live with your family?'

'No. I lived in a house in Camberwell with two other girls. Families took in boarders in their spare rooms for a modest rent in those days. I'd catch the tram to work in the city centre each day.'

'How did you meet your husband, Boyd?'

Kathryn looked away, a soft smile on her face.

'One day, my boss sent me over to the Windsor Hotel to deliver some papers that had to be signed. The hotel was such a landmark; only people with means stayed there. I remember I felt rather overcome when I walked up the steps and into the foyer, because it seemed so quiet and prestigious.

'The concierge offered to deliver the papers for me but I insisted that I had to hand them over in person, as this had been my instruction. So a porter escorted me up to a suite. Boyd opened the door and I delivered the papers, and explained I would come back later that day to collect them if it was convenient. I knew my boss was anxious to have them signed. Well, Boyd asked me to come in and wait. Said he'd look through them on the spot.'

'He always was a considerate man,' commented Heather with a smile.

Kathryn nodded. 'I do remember feeling relieved. So I went in and sat down while he took the papers to his desk in the main room and started to go through them. It was quite a thick pile of documents, so I thought he was going to just skim them and sign, or else I'd be there all day. So I picked up *The Age* newspaper and asked if I could read it. Well, he found some small problems in the documents and scribbled a note and then asked me to have them adjusted by the solicitor and returned the next day.

'The following day I brought a book with me! I gave him the papers and said I'd read in the lobby. So I sat and read, and after an hour he came down and ordered tea for us. He sat opposite me while the waiter poured our tea and he picked up my book and asked me why I was reading about the gardens of Europe. I told him I loved gardens and that I walked through the Botanic Gardens every day. Then to my surprise he leaped up and said he hadn't been out of this hotel for ages, and would I fancy a walk in the Gardens right then?'

'Really? How romantic,' said Ellie, finding herself completely engrossed in the story.

Kathryn smiled. 'I didn't know what to do. He was an important client, though, so I agreed. I decided that as it was daylight, I couldn't come to any harm walking. And I knew the Gardens like the back of my hand.

'Well, we walked and talked. He told me he was a woolgrower so he couldn't join up, as he was in an essential service. Then he asked me all about the plants I liked. I told him I dreamed of having my own gardens one day. We ended up talking for a long time, and it was late in the day when I took the papers back to the office.'

'Kathryn, your memory amazes me,' said Heather, standing back from the canvas and regarding it closely.

'Well, it was an important time in my life. I suppose

that's why I can recall it so well. Anyway, the next day he rang and asked me out to dinner at the Windsor,' Kathryn said, laughing. 'It was a lovely meal and we talked so easily together; it felt like we were friends. Even though he was much older than me, I felt safe with him. At the end of the evening he hailed a taxi for me and paid for it to take me home. He was a gentleman.'

Kathryn gave a small shrug and a smile. 'That was the beginning. Neither of us knew anything about each other. No ties. No issues. I didn't think of him in a romantic way at first, but I enjoyed his company and friendship. In the following weeks whenever he came to Melbourne he took me to dinner and to the theatre and lovely places. We walked in the Gardens regularly, just talking. Sometimes we had afternoon tea. And when he was back at Craigmore he wrote me letters. In retrospect I realised he was visiting Melbourne more often than he needed to for business!'

'Of course he was,' said Heather with a grin. 'I remember you telling me how concerned he was that you were boarding in town, away from your family. I suppose he wasn't to know that you had little other option.'

'Oh?' said Ellie, turning back to Kathryn. 'Why was that?'

Kathryn waved a hand in the air. 'I was an only child and quite independent by then. My mother had died when I was young, and I was estranged from my father.'

This was interesting, but Ellie suspected she should let it lie for now as Kathryn seemed rather reluctant to discuss it further. 'And the rest of your courtship? Engagement?' she asked. 'Being wartime, was it a whirlwind romance?'

'Maybe in a different time, we would never have fallen in love or even been an item. This was an era where many couples were rushing into marriage before the men went overseas. Boyd was different – he was older, very sophisticated and running a large enterprise, and seemed to be in no hurry to settle down. Indeed, he told me he had avoided the persistence of society matrons trying to inveigle their daughters into his orbit. Romance had been the farthest thing from his mind.'

'Well, maybe not entirely,' said Heather with a smile. 'Maybe he just wanted to do things on his own terms, not be dictated to by society.'

Kathryn nodded. 'You might be right about that.' She paused. 'When my boss found out that Boyd was taking me to dinner and spending time with me, he gave me a bit of a fatherly lecture along the lines of not getting my hopes up. I nodded but ignored him. I felt Boyd was lonely and I was too, when I think about it.

'When we got a bit more serious, he gave me some lovely gifts; kid gloves, perfume, chocolates, things you couldn't find in those war years and things I could not afford.

'And then he kissed me. It was under a tree in the Fitzroy Gardens by moonlight as we were strolling back to the hotel to get a taxi to take me home. A few days later he proposed. I was so overwhelmed I didn't give him an answer for a couple of days, which later he teased me about.' Kathryn laughed softly.

'We were married at the church here in Storm Harbour. I wore the most beautiful dress and our photo was printed in the social pages, would you believe?' she said. 'However, as the war was still on, Boyd and I decided to keep it quite small. My boss gave me away and a girlfriend of mine was my bridesmaid. Immediately afterwards, Boyd had some duties in Sydney that he had to attend to, concerning our wool industry here and exports to the UK. So we went there soon after our wedding. We took our honeymoon later, after the war years.'

Kathryn stopped, deep in thought for a few moments. Heather painted on, and a companionable silence enveloped them as Ellie made a few notes. Then, glancing up, Ellie thought she caught a glimpse of what Kathryn would have looked like as a young bride. A smile had brightened the older woman's face.

'We went to Paris,' Kathryn said at last. 'It was an exhilarating time, and so romantic. Then we came home and I settled into married life at Craigmore, which I loved,' she added.

'Did you spend much time with your husband's family, his parents? Did he have brothers and sisters?' asked Ellie.

Kathryn looked at her but answered as if she hadn't heard the question.

'Boyd always made me feel like a princess. He never once made me feel that I was any less than him when it came to social standing when we first married.' She gave a slight smile. 'I suspect there was a lot of gossip, but it didn't bother us. We were truly a love match and we enjoyed spending time with each other, talking about the world as well as plans for Craigmore. And once Seamus came along, we were very wrapped up in our little family life. Sadly, I couldn't have another child. That's one reason why I am so devoted to my beautiful grandchildren.' She looked away for a moment, then, straightening up, she continued, 'For a special surprise one wedding anniversary, Boyd presented me with the "blank canvas" at the river, as he called it.'

Ellie glanced up. 'The land where the Botanic Gardens and caravan park are?' she asked, grateful that the subject had come up without her having to guide the conversation in that direction.

'Yes. We always talked about the beautiful Botanic Gardens where we courted. And Boyd suggested I oversee the Gardens as a contribution to the town, in a way. It was the most rewarding thing I have ever done.'

Ellie saw her opening. 'Actually, I've been wondering about the site, as I heard on the radio that some land near the river may be developed,' she said carefully. 'I knew your family had some land in that area.'

'Well, they wouldn't be talking about our land,' said Kathryn firmly. 'Have you heard this, Heather?' she asked the artist, who was frowning as she concentrated on some detail on the canvas.

'No, can't say I have, though you know me: head in the clouds! People are always threatening developments these days, aren't they? Anyway, stop asking questions, Kathryn, Ellie is supposed to be interviewing *you*!' added Heather.

Ellie didn't want to upset Kathryn, but she didn't want to lose her chance, either. She pushed on.

'Well, while I was looking into the story I found out a lot about the Botanic Gardens. I was wondering, why didn't you plant out the whole strip of land next to the Gardens?' she asked.

Kathryn smiled as if she were looking back in time. 'I had great plans for the whole site, but the Botanic Gardens was a huge undertaking. I planted a lot of trees, which are lovely and tall now, and I so enjoyed working with Mr Hayden, the landscaper and botanist. In fact, so many clever people helped me. Mr Hayden also laid out the gardens at Craigmore.'

'So you planned to do something with the rest of the land but weren't able to?' Ellie hedged.

'Oh, we thought about it – I would have loved to – but by then we had young Seamus and a full life. Boyd was

210

busy diversifying into cattle in Queensland and had also got into polo in a big way, both playing and breeding the ponies and such. Also, I had my charity work and fund-raising for the creche we set up,' she said. 'People started coming to the river to camp and Boyd saw how much they enjoyed it, so he let them do so. In the end, we thought it would be a shame to stop the visitors. As it grew more popular it became too much for Boyd to manage, so he let the council run it and they have done so ever since.'

'It's a very special legacy,' Heather said to her friend, and Kathryn smiled.

'Yes, that's true,' said Ellie. She felt torn. It was clear Kathryn O'Neill was not aware of the development rumours. She wondered if she should say that the park could be in jeopardy, but remembered Patrick's words about treading carefully. Instead she backtracked.

'My, you've had a magical life. Do you feel lucky?'

A shadow momentarily crossed the elderly woman's face. 'I feel very blessed. And very fortunate. My family means everything to me.' Kathryn looked off into the distance, lost in her memories once more.

'When Seamus married Laura I was so happy for him, though she was always a frail girl. Then when Ronan, Linda and Benjamin came along I discovered the joys of being a grandmother. It was such a tragedy when Laura died, though not unforeseen. Of course, the children were grown by then.

'Ronan was working on our cattle station in Queensland; such a clever boy, he managed the station superbly. That's where he met Cynthia, whose parents owned the adjoining property. Ben went up and ran the O'Neill property when Ronan and Cynthia went on their extended honeymoon to Europe.'

211

'I remember that wedding,' broke in Heather. 'Social event of the season!'

'It was,' said Kathryn with a faint smile. 'Then when Ronan and his sister Linda had children of their own, and I became a great-grandmother, I was thrilled. I adore it when they all come to visit and our house is full of laughing, boisterous children.'

'And Ben?' Ellie was about to say more but Kathryn jumped in, smiling.

'Ben is such a gifted and thoughtful young man. He's a talented artist, you know. I think he was rather hoping to take over on the cattle station after Ronan, but Ronan told Seamus he didn't think Ben could manage it . . .' Kathryn trailed off, but then straightened in her chair and continued. 'Their sister Linda married well and lives in Melbourne. Seamus spends a lot of time visiting his grandchildren there. I'm glad he still goes on the cruises he and Laura always liked; it's an escape from real life for a moment, he tells me.'

'Quite a tribe, isn't it?' commented Heather.

'A dynasty,' said Ellie. 'So, how do you see the future for your family?'

'The future? Continuation, dear girl. The sense of continuity, of overlapping circles. We move forward and each of us has a life but we are always joined to those around us. Family is the glue that holds us all together. It creates our world. Family is everything to me,' she repeated firmly.

'For better or worse. Amen,' said Heather.

Kathryn shifted her position. 'Is it time for a break yet, Heather?'

'Of course it is.' Heather grimaced as she straightened up. 'Can't paint for as long as I used to.' She then

212

peered at the canvas. 'Hmm. This is coming along. It's been interesting watching your face as you talked to Ellie, like seeing the years peel away.'

'Oh, good. Ladies like to hear that!' said Kathryn, laughing.

'I'd love to include a photograph of the finished portrait with the article, if that's possible,' Ellie said.

'I can't see why not,' Kathryn responded. 'Especially if, as Heather suggests, she has managed to work miracles.'

Heather smiled as she put down her brush and looked at Ellie. 'When an artist gets a glimpse into the heart and soul of a subject it can be very revealing. I hope I've captured that vulnerability.'

Ellie watched Heather help Kathryn down from the chair, wondering what had caused the sense of vulnerability that Heather had seen in Mrs O'Neill. Most people would not consider this privileged woman to be fragile in any way other than because of her age. But Ellie thought that she, too, had seen something behind Kathryn's eyes as she'd spoken.

'Thank you for your time, Mrs O'Neill. You must feel very proud of your family and the gift of the Botanic Gardens.' Ellie paused, then decided to probe just a little further. 'So there are no plans to change anything at the river?'

'No. Whatever for? It's perfectly lovely. Our gardener looks after the Botanic Gardens. I think it has worked out well, as the caravan park people look after the other section. It's a very happy arrangement and asset for the town.'

Ellie's heart sank. Kathryn knew nothing about the rumours.

'Come on, Kathryn,' said Heather, 'let's sit down for tea before Susan arrives.'

'I'll leave you both alone,' said Ellie. 'Thank you so much again, Heather, Mrs O'Neill. I'm looking forward to seeing that portrait!'

'Me too. Lovely to see you again, dear. Incidentally, would you and your grandfather like to come to my birthday celebration? I'll have Susan put an invitation in the post.'

'Oh, that would be wonderful. Thank you.' Patrick would no doubt go, but Ellie wasn't sure if she'd make an appearance.

She put her things in the little basket on the front of her bike and pedalled home deep in thought.

\*

'So how did it go?' asked Patrick as Ellie came into the office later that afternoon.

'Well, Kathryn obviously knows nothing about any proposed plans. From the way she was talking about the Botanic Gardens and caravan park, I think she'd be shocked if she did. Nor did Heather; the two ladies live in a bit of a bubble.'

'Half their luck!' Patrick sighed.

'She was very friendly and chatty,' Ellie went on. 'Loves her family, sees no flaws in any of them. Obviously adored her husband.' She paused then added, 'Actually, Poppy, the more I think about it, the more I realise that in that whole time, Kathryn only mentioned her background once, and that was in response to something Heather brought up. She deflected questions about her own family and hardly revealed a thing about herself. The only new thing I learned was that she loved playing golf. And Heather told me that!' Ellie shook her head, bemused.

'Clever or cunning?' asked Patrick with a wry smile.

'Why would she have to be either? What's she got to hide?' Ellie wondered. 'In fact, she said her boss gave her away at her wedding, not her father. She was estranged from him, apparently, and her mother had died. They were the only other facts I picked up.'

'Perhaps she feels her real life began when she met Boyd,' said Patrick. 'In a way I'm glad she's being kept in the dark. The loss or development of that land would hurt her deeply, I think.'

'I'm sure you're right,' Ellie said as she picked up her phone. Out in the little back office, she sent a text to Sally: *Interview over. No new info: neither Kathryn nor Heather seemed to have any idea about the development.*

Sally quickly replied: *Okay thanks. Might have a lead. Want to investigate further before I say anything more.*

*Let me know what you find.* Ellie wrote back, but didn't receive a reply.

She decided she needed some time to think, so she headed out to her favourite café and sat at a table in the sun after ordering. She couldn't bear the instant coffee Patrick and Maggie sometimes brewed up in the office.

'Hello.'

Ellie looked up and was taken aback to see Susan McLean standing by the table, smiling.

'How's your dog? I do hope he's all right,' Susan said.

'Yes. Sam is on the mend. The vet put in a few stitches,' Ellie said, not really wanting to get into a long conversation with the woman.

'That's good to hear. May I join you?'

'Of course.' Ellie felt uncomfortable. Why on earth

215

was Susan being so pleasant? Did she feel guilty about what had happened to Sam? Ellie tried to read Susan's expression but was at a loss.

'I thought you'd like to know that we're going to have a little media event prior to Mrs O'Neill's birthday. On the same day, but before the family festivities start in the evening. There'll be a presentation of her portrait. The *Chronicle* might like to come along.'

'Thank you,' said Ellie politely. 'I'll let my grandfather know. He and Jon will definitely be there.'

'Great.' Susan paused. 'Actually, I was hoping to speak to you and your grandfather about the *Chronicle*. We're forming a group – a team – to promote the town. It'll comprise a group of stakeholders; a sort of business hub. Each organisation will do their own thing, but under a team umbrella.'

'What will you be promoting, Susan?' Ellie asked, a little surprised. 'Are you setting up a new business as well as working for the O'Neills?'

'Oh, well, I work for the rest of the family too, in a way. It's in all our interests to promote the area, isn't it?'

'Yes, I suppose it is. What do you have in mind?'

'We'll start by inviting various businesses and organisations in Storm Harbour and the surrounding district to come together to map out ways to promote the area in a positive way. Showcase the opportunities here,' she said, then added, 'There are too many negative stories going around.'

Ellie wondered what Susan was referring to, then thought she might be talking about the riverside land. 'Well, I guess if you've heard negative feedback about local goings-on, it must be for a reason,' she said slowly. 'You really need to talk to my grandfather about your plans.'

'Indeed. But I thought I'd run it past you first. After all, you know about social media, promotion, that sort of thing. I've noticed how the social media for the paper has sprung up since you came to town.'

'I don't have much experience with it; no more than most people, really,' Ellie said. 'I'm just across the technological aspects.'

'Well, we all need to do our bit to stimulate and grow the local economy, Ellie. Bring more people to town to live here permanently or long-term as well as to holiday. To invest by starting a business. There are a lot of assets here that are never showcased or advertised. The town could grow substantially, which would benefit everyone. We need to get advice from good consultants in the city.'

Hearing this, Ellie felt her hackles rise. She felt like asking why they'd need to look for expertise in the city, and how the local business community would cover the cost of these consultants. Why not find bright Gen Y and Z-ers in Storm Harbour who knew how to use social media to 'influence', and check out the savvy old-timers who could offer their advice? she wondered.

Instead she said mildly, 'Sounds interesting, but if you need this, it means there are issues to be addressed. Wouldn't it be better to tackle the systemic problems first?'

Susan had a swift answer. 'The idea is to jump over the negative and not dwell on the problems as so many do, but to go straight to the solutions and future plans.'

Ellie smiled to herself, thinking that there were probably just as many people who didn't want to see the town 'grow substantially'. Plus, she already knew her grandfather wouldn't go for taking a side. It was the paper's role to be objective. He'd write up issues as they progressed, but would not act as a promoter or be involved.

'There is also the potential for decent advertising in your paper,' Susan went on, dangling a carrot.

This sounded like a veiled bribe to Ellie, but she bit back the heated response that was on the tip of her tongue, because it then occurred to her that she might find out more about the O'Neills if she showed some interest in the plan. It was a means of digging around, and innocently probing about the caravan park.

'Sounds interesting. Let me speak to my grandfather.'

'Excellent. We have a one-page flyer outlining the ideas. I'll email it to the *Chronicle* with all the contact details.' She stood up. 'We're all invested in this town, one way or another. So pleased the *Chronicle* can help. I'll be in touch.'

Susan gave a small wave and walked briskly away, leaving a perplexed Ellie sitting there. Shaking her head, Ellie picked up her phone and checked her messages.

The chair opposite scraped as someone sat down.

Ellie looked up, then did a double take when she saw Dave smiling at her.

'Hi, stranger. Are you okay?'

Ellie gave a small smile. 'Yes, fine. How're you?'

'I'm wondering when you're going to come out with me.'

'I doubt that's occupying your every waking moment,' said Ellie lightly. 'Sorry. I've been busy. Lot of things on the go at the moment. Hunting down information for an article for the paper.'

'Yes. In a small town there's not much that escapes scrutiny. Even when there's nothing really going on. Or is there?'

218

'That's what newspapers are for, to find out what's really happening. Not gossip and speculation,' said Ellie firmly. 'However, if you have any rumours to share, I'm happy to listen.'

'My lips are sealed. I can't reveal my customers' secret money-laundering deals, and plots against the establishment.' He smiled. 'Just kidding. Seriously, let's have dinner. Or try to have lunch again. You're not that busy, are you?' he asked, leaning towards her.

Ellie shook her head. 'Of course not. It's just . . .' She paused as she stared at Dave's handsome face and winning smile. He was a decent man, affable, intelligent, comfortably situated, well liked in town and had a sense of humour. What was holding her back?

He reached out and touched her hand. 'Please, I'd like to get to know you better.' He tilted his head as he scrutinised her. 'Or is it me?'

'Oh, no, not at all,' Ellie exclaimed, feeling embarrassed. 'It's maybe just . . . oh, I don't know. I came down here for a lot of reasons. I left my job in some truly horrendous circumstances, and I handled it badly. I'm dealing with a few different things, I suppose. I'm just not sure I'm ready for this.'

'If you only "suppose", then you need to address whatever it is, confront things head-on and deal with them and move forward. Listen, I get it. We all go through stuff. Don't let it beat you.' He pushed back his chair. 'And if you don't want to have a meal, then come surfing with me!'

'Thank you, Dave,' said Ellie. 'I'll think about it.'

'I'll call you before the end of the week. Take care, Ellie.'

'You too, Dave. Thanks again.'

He left the table as Ellie looked into the dregs of her coffee cup. *What the hell is wrong with me?*

Dave's words echoed in her head. *Don't let it beat you.*

*

Ellie watched Sam walking along the empty windswept beach. He was still moving a little gingerly after his injury, but that didn't seem to stop him from having fun.

He came back to her with a found stick, joyously waiting for her to throw it into the waves.

'It's too rough and too cold for swimming, Sammy,' she said ruffling his ears.

The sunset had been smothered by windswept grey clouds scudding low over the tossing waves. To some this may have seemed a desolate, cold setting, she mused. A depressing place to be. But for Ellie this was a place etched into her heart and memory. During the Christmas holidays when she was thirteen she'd had her first kiss in those dunes while her family picnicked below. It was the place she came to in times of joy and sadness. A place to scream at the cliffs, shout at the waves, and sing to the sky. A place where she could be herself.

Suddenly Ellie flung out her arms, and cried to the wind and the sea, '*Who* are you, Ellie Conlan? *Why* are you here? *What* are you running from?'

Sam rushed as quickly as he could to her, cocking his head, looking worried as he dropped the stick at her feet.

She crouched down, hugging the dog. 'It's just me, Sam. I'm running from me.' She stood up, snapped the stick in half and flung it on the sand in front of the bewildered dog.

'Let's go home, Sam. We have stuff to do.'

*

When Sam and Ellie arrived home, Patrick was on the phone in his study and a beef stew was bubbling on the stove. Ellie fed Sam, who fell into his bed in the kitchen as she poured herself a glass of wine and set the table.

Over dinner, Ellie recounted her meeting with Susan. 'So, what do you make of that?' she asked Patrick.

'All sounds like hype. Someone comes up with these ideas every few years. Most of the town likes things the way they are and wants to let the place grow and change organically. If some big-shot developer were to get their way and slap up a monstrosity of a hotel, a high-rise, a hypermarket, a factory or a mall, the little guys would close down. Times have changed. What your Mike said about caring, integrated, clever communities is the way to go. But it does no harm to listen to ideas and assess them. I say worm your way in to hear what that Susan is all about. There's more to this than meets the eye, as someone wise once said.' Patrick leaned back in his chair. 'It's a sure bet: if she's involved, so are the O'Neills.'

# 7

Ellie heard her grandfather walk into her room and her eyes snapped open. It was dawn.

He leaned down, whispering, 'Hey, Poss, wake up, sweetie.'

'What's wrong?' She struggled with the covers as she sat up and Sam stirred on the end of her bed. 'Are you okay, Poppy?'

'Yes, love, I'm all right.'

'What's happened? It's so early.'

'There's a story breaking. We need to go. I'll make a quick cuppa and toast.'

'Do we have time? What's going on?' Ellie leaped out of bed as Sam tried to do a down dog stretch, but opted to sit down again instead.

'Warranghi National Park, a kid is lost. A little boy, four years old.'

Ellie stared at Patrick. 'Oh no, that's a pretty wild place. I remember we went for a picnic there once. And there's a big lake up there.'

'I got a call from one of the men who's going out to join the search. The sergeant told me when I contacted him that they've been looking for about an hour already.'

'Were there other people around?' Ellie asked. 'Oh, this is awful. Are they locals?'

'I don't believe so. Anyway, get dressed now, warm gear and sturdy shoes. We might need to help with the search. I'll get a quick breakfast going.' He hurried from the room.

'No. You can't come, Sam,' said Ellie as the dog looked hopeful at the idea of an early morning walk. 'Oh damn, I only have running shoes. They'll have to do. Raincoat. Wool scarf. No idea what the weather is doing today. Quick shower,' Ellie said aloud, as if checking items on a list.

The local ABC radio news was on and the kitchen was cosy when she walked in, the smell of toast all pervading. It felt safe.

'Poor little kid must be petrified. Anything on the news?' asked Ellie, reaching for the Vegemite.

'Only a brief mention; I suppose they don't know much yet. Hopefully he'll be found quickly. Sergeant Lyons said the family is from out of town, camping up there. One of the parents woke in the night and discovered the boy was missing from his sleeping bag. Crawled out of the tent, they assume, to go for a pee maybe.'

'Wouldn't his parents have heard him moving around?'

'His sleeping bag was close to the tent flap, which

223

wasn't zipped down all the way, so it sounds like he squeezed through without making any noise. That's all I know. C'mon. Bring your phone. The reception is dodgy up there but you never know. Plus you can take some photos for the paper.'

'Have you rung Jon and Maggie?'

'Not yet; could be all over by the time we get up there. Jon won't get his wheelchair off the path anyway as the campsite is in the middle of the bush.'

'That's right, of course. Well, the camera on my phone is pretty good.' Ellie downed her tea. 'Has Sam been out?' When Patrick nodded she handed an inch of her toast crust to the dog, pulled a cap on her head and collected her backpack.

'Right, let's go,' Patrick said. 'We'll take my car. I think it'll be better than yours once we hit the rough roads into the national park.'

'Sam, you stay and guard. Be a good boy.' Ellie closed the door behind them all and patted Sam as he watched them leave.

It was a forty-minute drive into the ruggedly beautiful hills towards the national park, which was popular for hiking, spectacular views, camping and birdwatching. It was raining lightly, the windscreen wipers swishing rhythmically, and Ellie shivered, imagining the little boy out in the cold, wet weather.

'Would've been chilly overnight. Hope he had warm PJs on and found somewhere to shelter,' said Patrick as he drove.

'It'd be pretty easy country to wander off and get lost in, as I recall,' said Ellie.

Patrick was quiet for a moment.

'It's the great Australian fear: "Lost in the Bush",

everyone's horror story since whitefellas lobbed in here. Paintings, stories, books, movies, all based on a child or children lost in the great Australian wilderness outside the back door.'

'And so it goes on,' said Ellie quietly. 'I remember seeing a picture in a book of that Frederick McCubbin painting of the lost child in the bush, a little girl holding wildflowers in her apron, huge eucalypts towering over her. It gave me nightmares.'

'Yes. The lost children. Applies to the stolen generations too. Children separated from family. It's a tragedy no matter what the circumstances. Do you know the story of the Cooper-Duff kids?' asked Patrick. 'I came across a reference to it one time.'

'No. Who were they?'

'It was around the Horsham area in the 1800s. Three kids went missing in the bush. They lived in a shepherd's hut; very remote country. The eldest was a boy of about nine, the younger boy about the same age as this missing kid, four. The sister in the middle was seven. The story goes that they went out to cut reeds for their mother to make a new broom to sweep the mud floor. Somehow they got lost.'

'Oh no. What happened? Were they ever found?'

'They had a mob come and search, following their tracks, but then there was a thunderstorm that washed the footprints away. So they called in Aboriginal trackers. Nine days passed while all this happened.'

'Nine! Oh no!'

'In spite of the rain, the trackers were able to pick up signs of the children. And then they found them. The older children had been carrying their little brother on their backs. The girl had been using her dress to cover them at night when they slept with the youngest between them. They were in bad shape, emaciated.'

'How had they survived?'

'I wondered about that too. The story I read didn't give those details. The girl, Jane, was made something of a heroine for looking after her brothers.'

As they pulled into the camping ground car park, Ellie saw that the rain had stopped and the sky had cleared, and the sun was now shining on the damp leaves and forest floor. There was a small crowd of volunteers gathered around, listening to a police officer while an ambulance team waited nearby and SES crew members were looking at maps or preparing equipment. As Patrick and Ellie walked towards the group, more cars drove into the parking lot.

Patrick went over to shake the hand of one of the police officers he knew, and Ellie glanced at some people who were looking after a distressed couple, clearly the parents. The mother was about her own age, and the father had his arm around her, his face pale and drawn.

'Please, I need to go with you. I've got to find my boy,' the father was saying.

Two searchers nodded, one of them reassuring him.

'Sure thing. We're just getting coordinates so we know where no one has been yet. There's a bunch of people out there already. We'll do everything we possibly can, mate.'

'His name is Peter,' the tearful mother said to those who had just arrived.

'The site where the family was camping is over there,' the coordinator explained, pointing to a map spread out on the ground in front of him, 'and the hiking trails start there: one to the lake, one to the top of the hill overlooking the valley. We'll divide into groups . . .'

As she was listening to him, Ellie felt a tap on her shoulder.

'Hi, Ellie. It's nice to see you, if in unfortunate circumstances.'

Ellie looked up to see a slightly scruffy man dressed in hiking boots and carrying a small backpack. It took her a moment to place him, but then she remembered.

'Tommy, hello, I almost didn't recognise you away from the bookshop. Yes, it's terrible.' She gestured towards his backpack and boots. 'You came prepared.'

'I was a Boy Scout, back in the day. I know this area pretty well, so I drove here as soon as I heard the news from a friend. It's rugged in places. Lot of caves and crevices and gullies.'

'I suppose a little kid could crawl in anywhere if he's scared,' said Ellie. 'Do you hike around here much?' She could only picture Tommy sitting in his armchair at Tommy's Treasures, reading a book, waiting for a customer.

'Yes, I do. Nature is a good antidote to mind-wandering from a seated position.'

'Mind-wandering,' she repeated. 'Reading, I take it? I like it.'

'Do you want to be in my group?' Tommy asked.

'Sure. I'm ready to do as I'm told,' she said as Patrick joined them, nodding a greeting at Tommy.

A dog handler brought one of the sniffer dogs over to the parents and talked quietly to them. As instructed, the father gently eased their son's jacket from his wife's grip, to let the dog smell it.

Ellie's heart twisted. 'What awful thoughts must be going through those poor parents' minds,' she whispered to Patrick.

'Think about their reunion with the boy,' said Patrick. 'Do you want to take some notes, details, names and such, or shall I?'

'It feels so invasive; I don't think I can. You do it, you know more of them than I do.'

Ellie looked around at the swelling group of volunteers, recognising the barista from a café in town, and shopkeepers and locals she knew by sight and casual conversation. Steve and Cassie, Nino the fisherman, and several others from the caravan park were in a group, and she spotted James from the Garden Cottage.

'You up for this, love?' asked Patrick.

'Yes, I'll go with Tommy's group. Don't worry about me,' Ellie said.

'Right. I'll stay back here. If there's any news and you have any reception, call me straight away. Good luck.' Patrick reached out and gave her shoulder a quick squeeze.

Ellie joined Tommy's small group of two women and three men and they quickly introduced themselves. One of them was an SES volunteer who knew the area. Ellie listened quietly as they were given directions to a targeted area and instructions on how far apart to walk and how to communicate; the do's and don'ts. She checked that her water bottle was full and put it back in her pack, and took the whistle Tommy handed her.

They spread out in the undergrowth among the trees, following a pattern, beating the ground, lifting branches and ground cover, the calls and sounds from the other searchers echoing around them. The area was thickly forested and it was easy to lose sight of one another. But some distance away the bright red jacket of Pam, another volunteer in her group, flashed in and out of Ellie's peripheral vision. With every step Ellie strained to hear

228

the sound of a child's call, willing the small boy to reveal himself.

They came out through a stand of trees to a clearing where they could see the still waters of the lake ahead. A couple of boats were out in the middle, and black-clad police divers surfaced next to them. Ellie saw one of the divers shake his head.

By midday the sun was high and hot. They returned to the checkpoint and Ellie was stunned to see how the crowd had swelled. A sense of urgency and concern was palpable. She spotted Sally and a TV news crew, and Ben was standing nearby with his arms folded, listening at the edge of one group.

Ellie went over to Sally, who was recording comments and information from the police.

'Have they found any trace of him?' she asked quietly.

Sally shook her head. 'Nothing. But the police think he has wandered off rather than been taken. They're being cautious; they can't rule out abduction, but they think it unlikely.'

'So hard for the family,' said Ellie. 'Have you spoken to them?'

'The police are keeping them sheltered, no media. I heard that their names are Mia and Luke Jensen but I don't know much more at this stage.'

'I wonder where they're from?' said Ellie.

'They're here on holidays. From Horsham I was told,' said Sally. Her phone started ringing. 'Oops, I have to go.'

Ellie stared after her as Sally hurried off to take the call, and then saw that her own group was getting ready to set out again. Quickly she looked around for her grand-father and saw him talking to an older SES volunteer.

'Poppy, you know the story you told me about the

Cooper-Duff children? Well, this little boy's family is from Horsham. Hope we have a happy ending too.'

Patrick smiled gently. 'Yes, indeed.' He glanced around. 'There's Meredith. I'll go and talk to her. Take care, love.'

As the afternoon wore on, a sense of controlled desperation took hold, and this feeling only intensified when they heard the sound of a helicopter whirring above them.

A coffee truck from Storm Harbour arrived, as well as a group from the local Sikh community, who Ellie remembered reading about in the *Chronicle* after they had given up dozens of volunteer hours to feed the CFA and local community during the bushfires one year. They set up a station providing hot food for the search parties when they came back to the base camp.

After a quick break to rest, Ellie and her group listened to the latest instructions and prepared to resume their search. She did a circuit of the camping ground to take photos and capture the activity at the checkpoint for the paper. Then she hurried back towards her group just as they set off and were disappearing among the trees. She could hear Tommy already calling out, '*Peter.*'

She signalled to Pam that she was back in position as they headed down a gully in a different direction from the track the search parties had taken that morning. In seconds Pam was obscured by the trees.

After a few minutes Ellie emerged into a small clearing, noticing a faint track made by animals ahead of her. A branch cracked nearby and her heart leaped. She was about to call out, but then came the sound of voices. This was not a child; the voices were male and angry.

She stopped and leaned against a boulder, listening. When she crept forward around the rock and looked down into the gully below, she was shocked to see Ronan standing there, his face flushed, his angry tone evident even though she couldn't make out the words. Then someone moved forward, shaking his hand at Ronan, who swatted it away. Ellie inhaled sharply. It was Ben.

Why were the brothers there, arguing, when a child was missing?

If she'd witnessed this anywhere else, Ellie would have walked away. Here she suddenly felt vulnerable and alone.

She shrank down behind the boulder, straining to hear but not be seen. She was too far away to catch what they were saying. Eventually, the men moved away.

As Ellie watched Ronan's retreating back, her pulse quickened and her breath came in short gasps. But before she became overwhelmed by the familiar nightmare of anxiety, she closed her eyes and pressed her palms against the granite. *No, Ellie, no more*, she admonished herself. *No. It's over. You are safe. You have a beloved family and a dear old dog waiting for you, while somewhere close there is a small frightened boy who needs your help. Snap out of it.*

Feeling suddenly determined, Ellie turned, grasping a green branch to heave herself back up the slope and around the boulder, but it bent and sprang back, whipping her shoulder. She stumbled and slipped, hitting her arm. Wincing from the sharp crack to her elbow, she stopped and gingerly pressed her arm with her fingers. A sharp pain spiked through her. She realised she would have to go back to the base camp and have it seen to.

She dragged herself upright and found a sturdy stick to help her up the slope. Back at the top, she spotted Pam in the distance.

'Pam, I'm going back,' she shouted. 'I hurt my arm!'

'Do you need help?' came Pam's voice through the trees.

'No, thanks. I'll be fine. Good luck!'

But after ten minutes of struggling, Ellie was forced to take a rest. She saw another large rock and sat down as the searchers' voices and calls faded into the distance. The soft sounds of the forest, and its silence, were calming. Her fears dissipated, her breathing slowed and she felt oddly comforted. Watched over. The forest was no longer fearful, but benign.

She thought briefly about what she'd seen between the O'Neill brothers in the gully. She resolved to tell Patrick when this was all over, but decided to put it out of her mind for now. There were more important things to focus on today.

She drew a deep breath, wishing that the small boy would feel some sense of the comfort and protection she felt at this moment. Then she pushed on. Her elbow was throbbing; she hoped she hadn't done any serious damage.

Back at the camping ground, a paramedic strapped her elbow for support. 'There you go. It's not serious, just bruised,' the woman said, giving Ellie a smile. 'Just take it easy.'

'Okay, thanks. Can I join the search again?'

'Sure. Go carefully, but you should be fine.'

Ellie thanked the woman and began to walk back towards the main group just as a familiar voice called to her.

'Hey, Ellie, are you okay?'

She turned towards the car park to see Dave climbing out of a battered-looking van with a surfboard on the roof. He hurried over to her, an anxious expression on his face.

'Yeah, I just banged my elbow against a rock. It's fine. You going out searching?'

'Yes. Bloody awful. Poor little kid. I was out on the boat and didn't know about this till after lunch. Then I came straight away,' he said, looking around. 'I'll go and find out about joining in the search. Be careful, Ellie.'

Ellie gave Dave a quick wave then noticed her grandfather sitting on a fold-up chair under some trees, with Roly seated next to him on an upturned plastic crate.

'Ellie, what have you done?' Patrick jumped up when he saw her coming towards him.

'I just fell and hurt my elbow. Nothing serious, Poppy. Hi, Roly. You're not planning to search out there, are you?' said Ellie. 'It's a bit rocky on the tracks.'

Roly shook his head. 'No, I came to see if I can offer any moral support and practical help around the campsite. I got a lift up with Reverend Turner. He came to see the family.'

Ellie glanced at Patrick. 'Oh dear. That sounds ominous. But there are still places we haven't searched.'

'I know, my dear. Let's stay optimistic,' Roly said.

'I might just go and take some more photos before the light goes,' said Ellie. 'I'll be back soon.'

Walking around the camp area, she noticed Sally sitting close to Ben, the pair deep in conversation. Ronan was nowhere to be seen. Ellie decided not to interrupt but kept moving, taking photos as best she could with one strapped arm while breathing in the atmosphere of tension and fear. People were huddled in small groups, volunteers were being briefed, and the number of police and paramedics seemed to have swelled.

The parents of the missing boy, Mia and Luke Jensen, were with Meredith and a man Ellie assumed was the reverend, as well as a woman Ellie could see was with the Red Cross. She noticed how pale and quiet the parents were, and she thought about the feeling she'd had in the bush. The calmness, the serenity. *It's not scary, the forest is wrapping its arms around him, keeping him safe*, she thought. *I just know it*. 'We'll find him and he'll be okay,' Ellie said softly to herself.

She was walking away from the small group when a car door slammed and suddenly an engine roared to life, the vehicle speeding past dangerously close to her. She caught sight of a grim-faced Ronan behind the wheel. Ellie stopped and watched as the car disappeared down the forest track towards the entrance to the park. She instinctively put her hand up to her injured arm for protection, and shuddered.

\*

Voices were subdued. No birds sang, no wind shifted the leaves. Night waited. Small fires were lit around the campsite and emergency lights from a chugging generator illuminated the sad scene. The next group of searchers were ready to go out with battery-powered lights. The sniffer dogs were still there and had apparently picked up a trail in the afternoon, but it had petered out among slimy rocks in a small spring.

Ben had disappeared and Sally told Ellie she was planning to head back to town to do a piece on the evening news. The TV crews had also left to update viewers on the search with images of the anxious crowd, distressed parents, the local volunteers and no doubt stock footage of the rough terrain of the national park, where somewhere a small child was hopefully sheltering during this cold dark night, awaiting rescue.

It was that thought that kept the remaining searchers scouring the bushland in the darkness.

Cassie and Steve, Patrick, Roly and Ellie were sitting together, eating curries and keeping each other company.

'If young Peter isn't found by 10 pm, they'll stop and go out again at dawn,' Patrick said quietly.

'We have to get back, I'm afraid,' said Cassie. 'Steve will come at daybreak unless there's good news. You sure we can't take you home, Roly?'

'I'm with the newspaperman, but thanks.' Roly looked around at the other groups sitting nearby. 'I recognise so many people here. Seems the whole town has come to help,' he said.

'Says a lot about Storm Harbour, doesn't it?' said Patrick. 'We pull together when needed.'

'If you have room, I'll get a lift with you, Cassie,' said Ellie. 'Our old dog Sam's been home alone all day and will need feeding. Plus I drove here with my grandfather and he might need his car. Poppy, are you coming home tonight?'

'I'm staying,' said Patrick firmly. 'Got to be here when they find the lad.'

'You're such a stubborn newsman,' Ellie said fondly, but she wasn't surprised he'd decided to stay.

'It's what we do, love. And it's only by being at the scene that you get the depth and guts of a story. Observation. Listening. Soaking up the atmosphere. A casual comment overheard can be very revealing. But I'm glad you're going home to Sammy. You can take over from me at breakfast, if need be. God forbid we should all still be here then.'

'All right, but take care and try to stay warm. I'll go into the office and see how Jon and Maggie are going on

235

the way home. When I called Jon just before he said they were still there.'

*

'No news, huh?' said Maggie as Ellie came in and shook her head in reply.

'What've you done to your arm?' asked Jon.

She told them about her accident and gave them a rundown of the operation at the base camp and who she'd seen in the search groups.

'It's all really sad and upsetting. Those poor parents. But what's heartening is that so many townsfolk have joined the search. Tommy from the bookshop was leading a group and there were some people from around town who I knew by sight, and a group from the Sikh community up north somewhere turned up and fed everyone a fantastic meal. As well as the volunteers, there were police, rangers, rural fire service and SES teams. As I was leaving, the guy from the hardware store arrived with ropes, tents and sleeping bags. It now looks like it's going to be a night-long vigil,' said Ellie.

'So the parents have no friends or family with them,' said Maggie.

'No, although the local minister and the mayor are supporting them. Peter, the little boy, is an only child apparently,' said Ellie.

'What's happening up there now?' Jon asked.

'Some of the searchers are still out but they're stopping at 10 pm and will start again at daylight. Poppy will stay up there. Roly's with him and Dave has offered for them to rest in his van if they want to. He brought up sleeping bags and pillows, which was thoughtful. Poppy has his old car, so he could sleep in that, but Dave's van looked more comfy. I got a lift back with Cassie.'

236

'Right, well, there's still time for them to find him tonight. Let's keep hoping,' Jon said.

Ellie smiled gently and nodded. 'How's the next edition coming along?' she asked.

'We've got the printers on standby; the layout is all done save the front page. Just hope it's a good news story,' said Maggie.

'Patrick called me late afternoon – the reception up there was pretty bad, but I was able to confirm the plan with him. Good news or not, we'll be ready to go as soon as he calls in with any news,' Jon said to Ellie.

'Hey, the early news bulletin is about to start.' He rolled his wheelchair over to the little TV set in Patrick's office.

'I'll be interested to hear Sally's report on the radio, too. Which reminds me, Ben O'Neill was out there,' said Ellie. Her memory of the argument between Ben and his brother reared up in her mind, but she pushed it firmly away.

'They really seem to be an item,' said Jon.

'You don't mind?' Maggie asked him. 'You and Sally got on so well.'

Jon shrugged. 'Nah. Sally can be a bit of a crazy chick, but we still get on. Friendly rivalry. Hey, did you get any photos, Ellie?'

'Yes, but I doubt they're as good as you'd take. Mainly background stuff, people setting up, the search parties getting ready, the food guys, local people . . .'

'I'd like to be up there. I have such a sensitive zoom, I can get really clear close-ups that capture people's emotions,' said Jon.

Ellie sat down in front of the TV and looked over at the kind and sensitive man next to her. 'We could give it a try, Jon. Would your wheelchair cope with the rocky tracks?' she asked.

'I'd be fine at base camp, where it's flat. But I'm needed here if we have to get something out quickly,' he said. 'You can borrow my camera, if you like. I'll give you a quick lesson.'

'If you're sure, that'd be great, thanks. I'll take good care of it.' She smiled but it quickly faded. Ellie knew she should report what she'd seen, much as she didn't want to talk about it. 'By the way,' she said tentatively, 'I saw Ronan O'Neill up there in the bush. He and Ben were arguing. I couldn't hear what it was about, but it certainly wasn't friendly. Then Ronan sped off in his four-wheel drive, almost knocking me over on the way. Ben stayed on.'

'Really? I wonder what's going on there . . . Look,' said Maggie, 'here's the news.'

The bulletin led with the story of the missing boy.

'Man, that does look rugged,' Jon said, watching the helicopter shots of the gorges and hills, the police divers in the lake and the searchers struggling through the thick undergrowth.

The reporter's voiceover continued: *'There was a moment of hope when a police sniffer dog picked up the boy's early trail near the family's tent, but once into the forest, wet from overnight rain, the dog lost the scent . . .'*

'If he's not found tonight and is alone out there in the wilderness . . . well, the major networks will be crawling over the place tomorrow,' said Maggie.

'There's lots of crews there already, Maggie. Look at that poor couple,' Ellie said as the camera lingered on Peter's parents. 'They're blaming themselves, Meredith told me. As if it was their fault. A curious little kid out in the real bush, perhaps for the first time; maybe he wanted to pee, or heard an animal and went to try to find it . . . to be an explorer.' Ellie stopped; it was too upsetting.

'I'm going home to feed Sam,' she said eventually, scrolling on her phone to find the number of the local taxi. 'If you need me, call anytime during the night. I'm ready to go at a moment's notice. Jon, if you decide to come, maybe give me a call to let me know. I'm planning to head back up there really early tomorrow morning if there's no news before then – I can text you when I'm leaving.'

Jon nodded and then took Ellie through the basics she needed to know about how to use his camera and its different lenses.

'Take care, Ellie,' Maggie said.

*

As Ellie walked into the house, Sam flung himself against her and she hugged him tightly.

'Sorry for leaving you alone, Sammy. There's a poor little boy lost out there somewhere,' she told the dog. 'And our devoted newspaper proprietor is hanging in there too.'

Ellie fed Sam, jumped in a hot shower and carefully pulled on comfortable clothes around her sore elbow. Heading back down to the kitchen, she made a cup of tea. She wasn't hungry after the wonderful meal the volunteers had provided.

Her phone rang and Mike's name flashed up on the screen.

'Hi, Ell, are you okay? I've just seen the news on TV about the lost boy. Awful. Any update? I caught a glimpse of Roly on the telly.'

'Oh, it's terrible, Mike.' Suddenly she wanted to pour out how she felt.

Mike listened, letting her go on, only interrupting when she recounted her fall and injured arm.

'How are you now? Were you scared?'

'For a moment I felt myself going under . . .' She paused. 'I was alone, and I was about to panic. It's very rugged out there. But then, strangely, it was like the forest reached out and embraced me. I felt . . . comforted. Does that sound weird?' Without waiting for a reply she continued, 'All I could think about was that I hoped that the little boy might feel the same way; feel that he was safe, I mean.' Her voice wobbled on the last words.

'Let's hope so, Ell,' said Mike soothingly. 'Where's Patrick?'

'The old bugger is still up there! He's determined to cover this story himself.'

'Ever the journo, good on him. What do you think the odds are of the little kid turning up?'

'Oh, Mike, I can't imagine. The area is hilly, with gullies, rugged crevices and caves all over the place, and a big lake nearby. Dangerous. I just can't help imagining that he must have had an accident . . .' Her breath caught in her throat.

'Ellie, wait. You need to hold on to hope. Be strong. I wish I was there to give you a hug.'

'Thanks, Mike. I'll keep you posted. I'd better ring my parents as they always listen to the national news.'

'Call any time, Ellie, I'm always here for you.'

'I know. Thank you.'

Her mother answered the phone on the second ring. 'Hi, honey. We saw the news. Those poor parents, how dreadful. Is there any update?'

'No. They'll be hunkering down for the night now, I guess. Do you think the little boy will survive out there?

240

It's getting very cold. And Poppy is staying up there too.'

'What! The silly old thing. I get it, though.'

Ellie told her mother about the search and everything that had happened that day. It felt so good to be able to share it all with her mum, she thought.

'Poppy and his team are doing a special front page for the paper,' Ellie said. 'Poppy will write the story from the heart; the way the town has pulled together to try to help. In a way, it's made us realise what's truly important.'

She looked at the bandages on her arm as she explained about her accident. 'I was so strung out, I thought I might have another panic attack, but I didn't. I was okay,' she said.

'That's wonderful to hear, sweetie,' her mother said softly. 'You are more than okay. I can hear it in your voice. You'll go from strength to strength now. You won't know yourself when you come back to Melbourne. The world is your oyster again, Ell.'

'I don't know about that. But somehow I do feel I've reached a kind of turning point. For tonight, though, my only wish is that Peter comes through this safely.'

'Get a good night's sleep, honey. We love you. Give your pop a kiss for me when you see him.'

At some point in the night Ellie stirred and reached for her phone. No messages. Sam continued snoring on the foot of her bed. Her face was cool from the air coming in from the partially open window, and she prayed that somehow some comfort would reach the small boy alone in the bush on this cold night.

It was still dark when Ellie woke to find a text from Jon saying that he was already up and would go in early to the office rather than tackle the rugged national park. After quickly getting ready, she set off; she wanted to be back at the camping ground before daybreak. She'd packed the camera bag, Patrick's Driza-Bone coat, a thermos of tea, some toasted sandwiches, and a bag of fruit.

When she arrived and climbed out of the car, Ellie saw figures moving around a small fire, where a wisp of smoke joined the rising mist of the fading night. She spotted Patrick and Roly sitting in the quiet circle and joined them.

'Hi, Poppy. No news?' she asked her weary-looking grandfather.

'Good to see you, love.' Patrick shook his head and put his arm around her shoulders. 'Sadly, no. As soon as they can see, the teams will start the search again,' he said. 'One or two local fellows who know this area very well told me they're planning to go out soon.'

'Where're the parents?' asked Ellie.

'They're still up there, staying in the tent. The social services mob are looking out for them. They won't leave here, of course.'

Ellie looked around and saw a few photographers and journalists huddled together in a group. Just then a TV outside broadcast van rolled up.

'Are Sally and Ben here?' she asked.

'Ben is, but Sally left last night. She has to do the breakfast show. She'll be on at 8 am with an update, then she said she'll come back here.'

'How did you sleep, Poppy?'

'With some difficulty until someone produced a bit of a nightcap. Roly snores.'

'Don't you believe him, Ellie,' Roly said, smiling at her.

'Well, I brought some tea,' said Ellie, handing over the thermos. 'And some toasted sandwiches for you to share. They're cold, but you could put them near the fire.'

242

'We're told the volunteers from yesterday are bringing more food today. Such generous, good people – those curries were delicious.'

'We even have portaloos,' added Roly. 'Water is a bit scarce, but someone is bringing some more up later.'

'I might just take a walk around and talk to a few people,' Ellie said. 'You been taking notes, Poppy?'

He tapped his top shirt pocket where he kept his notebook. 'Details are jotted down in here and the rest is in my head,' he said, pulling down the brim of his old fedora.

They drank the tea in silence and offered around the sandwiches and fruit.

'Okay, I'm going to have a quiet chat with the commander,' said Patrick. 'Thanks for the breakfast, love.'

Roly stood up too. 'I told Ekam I'd help his mob dish out the food today,' he said, 'and I think that's their truck now.'

Ellie smiled to herself, wondering what his former colleagues at the bar would make of the imperious QC they knew standing at a trestle table with the group of smiling Sikhs dishing up hot food to weary searchers and a community committed to rescuing a small child.

By 10 am, more news and media crews had arrived, along with volunteers from outside the area. Ellie learned that some relatives and friends of the parents had come from Horsham to offer their support and help in the search. She could see that the Jensens were still in a state of shock and deep pain. Mia sat clutching Peter's favourite stuffed toy, which they'd found a few metres from the tent.

The morning wore on and there was still no news by lunchtime, although the camping ground was filled with people – volunteers, service personnel and the media. An ex-court reporter recognised Roly and took him aside for

243

what she probably hoped was an exclusive interview, Ellie thought.

She and Patrick sat together finishing their lunch.

'Roly is at home in the limelight,' observed Patrick. 'Yet he is essentially a loner, I think.'

'I think you're right. He seems content living in Storm Harbour, even though it's not what anyone would expect of a retired QC. He doesn't fit the mould,' said Ellie.

'I agree. It's refreshing, I think,' said Patrick. 'The caravan park is unique; it has a sort of shared privacy. Each has his own little nest where he can step outside the door into a peaceful park.'

'Which someone else looks after for you,' Ellie smiled. 'You can see why people retire and downsize. And here you are still slogging away, Poppy.'

'Yep. And enjoying every day. I miss your nana, but the paper and this town keep me going. I know I've said it before, but that's just because it has never been truer. Look at the cross-section of people who are here. Hard times as well as good bring us together. You hear of people dying in their bed and no one misses them for weeks. That wouldn't happen here.'

They watched as Cassie and Steve came over, his arm around her shoulder. They too had re-joined the search at daybreak.

'Phew, I haven't hiked like this in some time. We're taking a break. Sadly, there's still nothing to report.' Cassie looked distressed.

'It's not over yet,' Steve comforted her.

Ellie exchanged a sympathetic look with Cassie, knowing how she must be feeling; sadness for a woman whose only child was lost, as one who'd lost a child at birth.

'It's getting colder. Do you think the little guy might

244

have found some water?' asked Cassie. 'There was that spring the sniffer dog handlers mentioned. I hope he got a drink there.'

'Sweetheart. Please, try to stop fretting,' said Steve gently. 'Everyone is doing what they can.'

Patrick waved away some flies with his fedora and clamped it back on his head.

'Time to do the rounds and update my notes.'

'He does have a way of getting people to open up,' Steve said to Ellie as Patrick walked away. 'I heard him chatting to some people he didn't know and the next minute they were telling him their life story.'

'He calls it just having a bit of a yarn, but he manages to get people to reveal a lot without them knowing it,' said Ellie. 'Roly says he would have been a good lawyer,' she added.

As the shadows started to lengthen, the campsite fell into a late-afternoon lull and Ellie felt the general mood turn to gloom, tears and fears. This was changeover time for the various groups assembled at the gathering point. Some weary people were packing up to go home, having been there since dawn. Ellie saw Sally kiss Ben and head back to her car, presumably returning to town for her evening news shift. Cassie and Steve were also leaving, and tried to persuade Roly to go with them.

'Thanks. I appreciate your concern, but I am lieutenant to Captain Patrick. He's determined to remain at the front line, so I will too,' said Roly.

'Good on you, Roly. But make sure you guys keep warm. Light rain is forecast for later,' said Steve.

Ellie had struck up a conversation with a journo from a metropolitan newspaper and a presenter from a TV morning show.

245

'Your *Storm Harbour Chronicle* is a bloody good newspaper,' said Phil, the journalist. 'Lots of in-depth coverage, as well as big-picture stuff.'

'Your grandfather is a terrific character. We met him earlier,' said the presenter, who'd introduced herself as Rachel. 'He has some great stories of his own. In fact, I think he's worth a profile on TV. I might suggest that.'

'How long are you staying up here?' asked Ellie.

'As long as it takes,' Phil said. 'Such an awful thing for the parents. I have a kid that age.'

'I find it hard to stay objective doing the bad news stories. It takes real concentration to not get choked up. The news editor hates it when that happens,' said Rachel.

'They can be unsympathetic sods, news editors.' Phil shook his head.

'Well, I'd better get back, but it was nice chatting to you,' said Ellie.

'Might look you up if I come back for a holiday, it looks like a gorgeous town,' said Rachel with a smile.

The commander was speaking quietly to a small group who were preparing to make one last foray into the bush before it would be too dark and risky even with lights.

'One press fellow and a local were injured slightly today. It's rough country out here,' Ellie heard him say. Then her phone rang and she moved away to take the call, seeing Jon's name on the screen.

'Hi, Jon, how are you and Maggie doing? Is everything all right?'

'Well, it's being kept very hush-hush, but Kathryn O'Neill was admitted to hospital yesterday.'

'Oh no! What happened?' Ellie said softly, turning her back and walking further away from the crowd.

Jon replied, 'It's being kept a secret, apparently, but my cousin, who's a nurse there, is finding out what the problem is. The family are not allowing visitors.'

'Thanks, Jon. Keep me posted. I'll tell Patrick if I can get him on his own, which mightn't be easy.' Then she added, 'Maybe that's why Ronan dashed off yesterday. But Ben is still here somewhere. I wonder if he knows. I hope it's not serious.'

'She's in a private room, not the ICU, so that's something. Try to keep in range so I can update you. My cousin is on duty till tomorrow morning.'

'Okay. Thanks again, Jon.'

Ellie kept walking away from the groups and the campfire to the spot at the edge of the forest where she'd found the best phone reception. She looked into the darkening bush as she dialled Heather's number. If the elderly artist hadn't heard about Kathryn, Ellie wasn't going to say anything. It was a long shot, but Heather just might tell her some news if she had any.

'Hi, Heather, this is Ellie Conlan.'

'Ellie, how nice to hear from you. How are you?'

'I'm good, thanks. I was – *Oh my God!* Sorry, Heather, I'll have to call you back!'

Ellie stabbed at the phone to end the call, and started to run.

Holding up Jon's camera, which had been hanging around her neck, she began clicking images of Ben, who was trudging out of the trees, lit by the last glow of the sunset in an almost halo-like way. He walked slowly, bending forward as he balanced a child on his back. Peter's arms were wrapped tightly around Ben's neck, his legs dangling at Ben's hips, and his pale face leaning against Ben's shoulder.

'Ben, Ben, is he okay? Peter . . . Peter . . .' The crowd yelled to him.

Ellie kept shooting as screams and shouts suddenly burst out around them. Everyone in the camping ground seemed to Ellie to have let out a collective breath of relief and now dozens of people were running towards the man and boy. A car horn and a siren went off.

Ben lifted a hand in a halt sign as the boy jerked at the blaring noise and stared at the advancing crowd with some trepidation, then buried his face in Ben's neck again. Ellie rushed to Ben and Peter, stopped and framed a shot, then clicked.

'He's okay,' called Ben. 'Where're his parents?'

'They're coming,' called the first person to reach Ben, and stopped respectfully so as not to scare the child.

The Jensens raced forward. Luke lifted Peter from Ben's back and the child held him tightly as the sobbing mother, almost fainting, fell against her husband and son, embracing them in a tightknit knot.

The cameras and TV lights began illuminating the trio clinging together, a family again.

'He looks so tiny,' said one woman who was tearfully watching the little figure in his dirty camouflage combat pyjamas.

Paramedics hurried over and wrapped him in a blanket, then they escorted Mia and Peter quickly to the ambulance. Around them, laughter, cheers and applause broke out. People were congratulating and thanking Ben and slapping him on the back as he walked slowly behind the paramedics.

The senior ambulance officer lifted Peter from his mother's arms. 'Let us check how he is, Mia, but he seems pretty good to me,' the woman said gently.

Mia turned and, too tearful to speak, took Ben's hand and squeezed it tightly.

Ellie snapped a photo of Ben with Mia Jensen holding his hand in both of her own, tears streaming down her face, managing a grateful smile. Looking on, Luke was smiling. Straight away Ellie knew it was the hero shot for the front page.

Patrick, slightly out of breath, followed by Roly, arrived at her side.

'Bloody magnificent. Did you get shots? Quick, let me see them.'

'Ben, Ben, tell us how you found him?' Ellie and everyone else in the media was calling out, cameras, microphones and lights trained on him.

Ben was encircled. Ellie noticed his arms were badly scratched and one leg of his jeans was torn. She turned her phone recorder on, held it up and then asked, 'What made you go back down there, Ben? Alone, and with darkness falling?'

Someone handed him a bottle of water and Ben sipped it before speaking slowly.

'It was suddenly so quiet. I just thought that it would be good to go down alone, and then I might just hear him. So I set off. I walked for at least half an hour, I reckon. Then I slipped and rolled down a narrow ravine behind some boulders. It ends in a bit of a small creek, only a few inches of water, but there's a tiny overhang you wouldn't notice unless you were on the ground, or very small. It's a shelter of sorts but hidden by bracken. I wouldn't have seen it, but then I heard whimpering. I called out Peter's name and he suddenly just peeped out at me. Gave me a shock, I can tell you.'

'What did Peter do when he saw you?' Patrick said.

'He just stared at me for a minute. I didn't want to scare him, so I said quietly, "G'day, Peter, how'd you find this special spot?" And he said, "Bobbly". Took a bit of interpreting, but it seems he followed a young wallaby and fell down the ravine, just as I did.'

Ellie looked at the circle of faces standing around Ben. Glancing beyond them, she saw the tall figure of a man a metre or so away. Ronan.

His expression was impossible to read.

He caught Ellie looking at him and turned his head back to Ben, ignoring her. And, Ellie realised with a shock, there had been no recognition in his eyes. He had no idea who she was. Who she really was.

Ben was the hero, and would remain so, but she knew he'd never milk it or trade on it.

'It was just luck,' he was saying modestly. 'I'm used to being in the bush, but with the light fading and not looking where I was stepping . . . well, it was a lucky fall, I guess.'

'Why do you think he didn't hear us calling him?' one of the volunteers asked.

'I don't think he could've heard the calls from the top of the ravine, and if I hadn't fallen, it's not likely he would have heard me either,' said Ben.

After a few more questions, everyone started to disperse, pack up and head home. Ben was escorted by a couple of paramedics to the ambulance to be checked out. Ellie stopped when she heard a car engine she recognised starting up behind her in the car park. Then she watched as Ronan sped away.

The medical team had given Peter back to his parents for the moment. The little boy seemed to be taking the attention in his stride now that he was reunited with his stuffed toy, which he clutched as he was held in his mother's arms.

'He's dehydrated, has a few cuts and bruises, but nothing's broken. He's incredibly lucky. A tough little fellow,' said his father proudly. 'But he's still going to the local hospital now to be checked out.'

'Ben too,' said one of the paramedics.

'Nah, I'm okay,' started Ben.

'Grab the lift, Ben, save Sally coming back to get you,' said Ellie, smiling. 'Let her interview you from your hospital bed!'

For the first time Ben smiled and gave her a thumbs-up.

'Ben, just before you go,' she said quietly. 'Do you know about your grandmother?'

'Yes. I found out after she was admitted. Sounds like she'll be okay, it's not serious. The doctor said they were just taking precautions, apparently. Ronan wouldn't let me go and see her yesterday, claimed the hospital had said no visitors, but I don't believe him. I'll go in and see her now as I'm going to be there anyway.'

'You're the hero of the hour, I reckon they'll let you do whatever you want,' said Ellie.

Patrick appeared beside her and shook Ben's hand. 'Good work, lad. When you're ready, we'll do a longer interview with you for the paper, if that's all right. Maybe in the morning?'

'Sure, but I don't have much to add. I'll be in touch.'

'Right, thanks, mate. You better go over to the ambulance, and Ellie, we have to get back and put the paper together,' Patrick said.

'Guess who's on the front page, Ben!' Ellie grinned.

'Don't overdo it. I won't hear the end of it from the mob at the park!' said Ben.

'Too late, old son.' Roly pushed forward to pump Ben's hand. 'When the fans have all left, come round to my spot for a noggin.'

'Sounds like a plan,' said Ben, and with a wave, he left with the paramedics.

'C'mon, get your stuff, Ell, I have a front page to write. Let's get those photos to Jon and tell them we're on our way,' said Patrick, firing on all pistons. 'Want a lift, Roly?'

Much later, after watching the TV news at home with Sam, Ellie rang Heather to apologise for hanging up on her. Heather had no idea of the drama that had unfolded, so Ellie suggested she make sure she bought the next edition of the *Chronicle*. Nor did she seem to know that Kathryn was in the hospital, so Ellie didn't mention it.

After she'd ended the call, her phone immediately rang again. It was Sally.

'Thanks for sending that recording of Ben for the news bulletin. He's here now, out of the hospital, and we've done a long piece for the backgrounder program. Do you want to meet for a drink at the pub? Ben's being shouted drinks on the house!'

'That'd be great, thanks, I'll head down. How's Kathryn, do you know any more?'

'Ben snuck in to see her. Seems she just had bad heart-burn; ate something that disagreed with her and had some pain. Ronan's wife rang the ambulance in case it was a heart issue. Susan was off duty at the time.'

On her way to the pub, Ellie called in to the office where Patrick had a bottle of whisky open and was banging the keys of his computer like a maestro at a grand piano.

Jon was busy editing and proofing the copy that Patrick was forwarding to him, while Maggie was on the phone, talking to the printer.

'Patrick said they came from Horsham,' said Jon. 'I've been on Trove looking for background stuff. We have a copy of the photo that Patrick wanted, that old story about the siblings lost in the bush.'

'The Cooper-Duff kids? Fabulous.'

'Your photos are great, Ellie,' Jon said as she put his camera bag down on the desk next to his computer. 'Where're you off to?'

'The pub. They're shouting Ben free drinks and we're going to celebrate. Want to come along?'

Jon looked over to Maggie, eyebrows raised. 'Do you need me for anything here, Mags?'

'You go ahead, Jon. We're just about finished, I think. I'll hang in here and send the old boy home to bed,' Maggie said, smiling.

'Great. I've got a couple more things to do, then I'll meet you there, Ellie,' Jon said.

'Perfect,' said Ellie. ''Night, Maggie.'

News had spread and the pub was jammed. Sally waved to Ellie.

'We've nabbed the big table here. The whole place cheered when Ben came in, he didn't know what to do,' Sally laughed.

'Jon's coming along, he'll be here in a tick.'

'Oh, terrific. And Patrick?'

'He and Maggie are still doing the paper.'

Ellie squeezed in across from Ben and clinked glasses with him.

'You deserve all this,' she said.

At that moment, a group came over to salute Ben.

'Hey, we saw you on the news tonight! Well done, mate!'

The group swelled and before they knew it a small party was in progress.

Ellie didn't stay long. The two eventful days had caught up with her and her elbow was aching. She said her goodbyes, blew a kiss and gave a thumbs-up to Ben, and went outside to her car. Then she stopped.

A piece of paper was tucked under her windscreen wiper. Carefully she pulled it free, and found a message scrawled on it: *I have information concerning council that may be of interest to you.*

Below the message was a phone number.

Deep in thought, Ellie folded the note and put it in her phone cover. Under her tiredness and the huge relief after Peter's recovery, she felt the stirring of excitement. They were getting somewhere with the development story, slowly but surely. And then there was Kathryn O'Neill. Why would Ronan have wanted to prevent his brother from seeing their grandmother? There was something strange going on, she just knew it. But right now, she'd had enough news for one day. She would think about it all tomorrow. Wearily, she climbed into her car and drove home.

Pausing outside her grandfather's bedroom door, she heard the sound of light snoring. Peeking in, she saw a rather contented expression on Patrick's face, and couldn't help smiling.

Quietly, she and Sam headed for bed.

# 8

THE NEXT MORNING ELLIE and Patrick, with Sam in tow, went downtown for a celebration latte and were stopped every few metres by enthusiastic locals. The overflow of delight, curiosity for even the smallest details and the congratulations to anyone who'd been involved in the search and rescue consumed Storm Harbour.

Patrick had taken a punt and upped the print run of the *Chronicle*, and the printer had worked through the night to have copies ready by mid-morning. Locals and now, it seemed, a growing stream of visitors, all wanted a souvenir copy. The photos on the front page, of Ben trudging out of the forest with little Peter clinging to him like a baby koala, the tearful, grateful mother clutching Ben's hand, the generous Sikh volunteers and their food feast, and a drone shot of the weary searchers and rescue teams combined to tell an emotional story. Also, running over to page three was the parallel story of the other 'lucky' Horsham rescue and the tale of the Cooper-Duff children, with the historical photos Jon had found on Trove alongside the article.

Once they'd settled at the Riverside Café and given their coffee orders, Sam settling comfortably in the sun at their feet, Patrick smiled at Ellie.

'So, did you celebrate with Ben at the pub till the wee hours? I didn't hear you come in.'

'Actually, I only stayed for a while. I was exhausted. It was a huge day, but it turned out to be a happy one, didn't it? Now, look at this, Poppy.' Ellie took the piece of paper she'd found on her windscreen from her phone cover and handed it to Patrick.

He peered at it then looked up. 'Where'd you find this?'

'It was under my windscreen wiper when I came out of the pub last night. It might be from Sally's contact, her source in council. I'm not sure about that, of course.'

'Are you and Sally still collaborating?' asked Patrick.

'We're trying to. Although I have a feeling Sally's not being completely forthcoming, and I haven't had much to give her,' said Ellie. 'I'm keen to make contact with this person. See what they have to say.'

'Well, yes, we should definitely find out what they have to offer. Then we'll need to work out if their information is legit, whether it can be backed up. And we'd have to ask how they obtained it and so on,' advised Patrick. 'It might be useful but we'd need to check it out carefully.'

'Noted,' said Ellie lightly, though Patrick's advice made her nervous.

As if he were reading her thoughts, Patrick said, 'We are insured against defamation, but even so, we have to be cautious. It only takes one rat to make a spurious claim and then you have to defend it, and imputations are a nightmare to prove. And it all costs. A claim against the paper would send our insurance sky-high. That's why I won't let us publish anything until we've done our research and can verify all the details.'

'That's wise,' Ellie said, taking a sip of her coffee, which the waiter had just brought over.

'Now, I had a call first thing this morning from David Ward, an old mate who owns *The Horsham Times*,' Patrick said, leaning back in his chair. 'It was good to make contact again. David's son and daughter are now running the revamped paper. So encouraging to see independent papers doing well.'

Ellie smiled at her grandfather. 'Yes, it's terrific. Look how people value the *Chronicle*'s coverage of Peter's rescue.'

'Thanks, love.' Patrick laughed but looked a little embarrassed by the compliment. 'Anyway, David told me a bit of background on young Peter's family. Seems the Jensens are doing it tough; they're hard workers but struggle to make ends meet. The camping trip was their big holiday for the year, and, well . . . David has hatched a plan to do a fundraiser for young Peter's future education.'

Ellie nodded enthusiastically. 'Great idea.'

'Certainly is. He's thinking of a community fun run and fundraising day. They want Storm Harbour's hero Ben to be there, to give out prizes.'

'Fantastic,' said Ellie. 'Does Ben know yet?'

'David said he'd ring him later today to ask him.'

257

'Ben will be modest and downplay his role, but perhaps Sally will make sure he goes,' said Ellie. 'In fact, why don't you do a profile on Ben?'

'Good idea, but why don't *you*?' countered Patrick with a grin. 'You went to school with him, if only briefly. The piece you're writing on Kathryn O'Neill seems to be coming together well. So I know you can do it.'

Ellie was thoughtful. 'A piece on Ben would be a good way to follow up on all that's happened. Everyone is asking about him. I'll give it a go, if he's willing.'

Patrick looked up as a man came and slapped him on the shoulder. 'Great paper today, Patrick! Bloody wonderful outcome.' He nodded at Ellie and moved on.

'You know, Ellie,' said Patrick thoughtfully, 'when you interview Ben, you might find out why seems so different to the rest of the O'Neill family.'

'Mmm, you're right. I will certainly ask him.' Ellie finished her coffee. 'You should relax today and enjoy the sunshine here for a while, Poppy. I might take Sam for a walk.' She blew him a kiss and went to the counter to pay for their coffees.

As she headed down the street with Sam, Ellie rang Sally, who thought the story on Ben was a great idea.

'If he gets funny about it, I'll give him a push,' said Sally. 'He's very modest and doesn't think he's done anything special.'

Ellie also mentioned the invitation for Ben to go to Horsham for the fundraiser, explaining, 'Mr Ward is going to ring him later today.'

'Terrific, I'll encourage him to go.'

'Have you heard anything more from your source at the council?' Ellie asked.

There was no reply and Ellie started to think the line

had dropped out. Finally, Sally said, 'I can't say anything, Ell, so please don't ask.'

'Oh, Sally, are you okay?'

'Yeah, I'm fine, but my boss has got involved and all I can say is that if I report anything more about the development rumours, it could cost me my job.'

'That's terrible –'

'Listen, I have to go,' Sally said, cutting her off. 'I'll talk to Ben about the interview and the fundraiser. Bye.'

Ellie stood staring at her phone, amazed at this latest development. Reading between the lines, it seemed clear that Sally was being silenced. What happened to freedom of the press? she wondered. And what did Sally mean about her boss getting 'involved'? She'd talk to Patrick, but there was nothing more she could do about it now, so she decided to tackle Ben about the interview while everyone was on a high over the rescue. She wandered into the caravan park, looking for him, but he wasn't at his campsite. Instead she went to ask Roly if he'd seen Ben, and found the two of them sitting outside Roly's caravan. They waved her over.

'We have muffins, courtesy of the bakery. A token of their esteem for the hero here,' Roly said, smiling and patting Sam when the dog ran over to him.

'I wouldn't say that,' said Ben. 'I'm not used to all this attention. It feels weird.'

'You'll be forever known as "the fellow who found the lost kid in the forest". So get used to it, my friend,' said Roly.

'That's true, Ben,' said Ellie. 'People are curious to know more about you.'

Ben stared at her in surprise. 'Yeah? Really? Why?'

'Because you were the one who found Peter when the

259

search parties all missed him. In fact, I'd like to interview you for the paper. At first my grandfather had planned to talk to you about the rescue, but we've decided it would be great to go further. Explain to everyone who Benjamin O'Neill is . . . talk about your art, growing up here, your very special grandmother . . . whatever you want to share,' said Ellie.

'Damned good idea, Benjamin,' Roly said. 'Ellie knows you; you can count on her to write it sensitively. Not many people I'd bare my soul to, but I reckon Ellie and Patrick would be the ones to trust.'

'Wasn't thinking of baring my soul to anyone, actually,' said Ben. 'Why would I?'

Ellie smiled. 'I wouldn't ask you to do that. But you're a local boy, people are proud of you. You're one of them. I'll do it in a way that satisfies their curiosity,' she said.

Ben looked at her and gave a slow smile. 'Funny, we only knew each other briefly at school and we went off to do our own things. Never really thought we'd see each other again.'

'And here we are,' Ellie said. 'Please think about it.'

'Think I'll have another muffin, for starters,' said Ben, breaking off a morsel for Sam.

'We'll walk it off on the long way home, Sam,' said Ellie as the dog swallowed the bit of muffin and looked hopeful for more. 'Thanks, Ben, see you two later.'

As she walked away, Ellie hoped he'd agree.

She took a short cut along a back street of recently renovated older cottages with freshly painted picket fences and new landscaping. She was deep in thought, mulling over how she'd approach Ben's story if he agreed to be interviewed, when Sam started barking and growling. A dog in a front garden suddenly lunged at its gate.

Ellie jumped back, dragging Sam away from the snarling, snapping dog as it threw itself at the fence.

'Take no notice, Sam. Let's cross over to the other side of the road.'

After she'd stepped up onto the opposite footpath, Ellie glanced back at the angry dog, its hackles raised and teeth bared, and she shuddered. It was the same dog that had attacked Sam before . . . Susan's dog.

She looked at the pretty cottage with its drawn curtains and manicured garden, thinking that Susan should at least have a *Beware of the dog* sign on the gate.

'C'mon, Sam,' she said, gently tugging on his lead. 'We know where we're not wanted.'

*

Early that evening Ben called and agreed to sit down for a bit of a chat the following afternoon. Ellie didn't know if Sally had persuaded him to do the interview or he'd decided on his own, but whatever the case, she was thrilled he was willing to go ahead with it. She began work on the questions straight away.

The next day they met at the caravan park and sat at a wooden table at the edge of the river in the quiet afternoon. The wind had died down and the river was lazy and glassy before the turn of the tide.

'What are your first memories of growing up in Storm Harbour?' asked Ellie once she'd started the record app on her phone.

'Good ones. Working in the garden at Craigmore with my grandmother, swimming in the river, fishing. I had my own canoe which I preferred to Dad's big boat. Feeding a bottle to a baby lamb. Sitting close to my mother as she read to me. Occasionally going to town for treats

261

with Grandy, especially when she took me to visit Aunt Heather. She wasn't my real aunt, of course; she's an artist friend of Grandy's. I loved watching her paint. She always let me mess around with paints and brushes and gave me objects to draw like jugs and flower arrangements and things. I learned a lot from her without knowing it.

'I thought Grandy was so special. She was very devoted to her Botanic Gardens. My father worked in the family business with my grandfather, Boyd, but I loved it when my grandparents looked after us while our parents went on their annual cruise.'

'How come you stayed here to go to school?' asked Ellie, knowing that Ben's brother and sister had been sent to the best schools in Melbourne as boarders.

'Well, I tried boarding school, but I hated being away from home, so they eventually agreed I could go to high school here in Storm Harbour. After that, Dad wanted me to do an Ag course at uni to help out at Craigmore in the family business. I was keen to work on the family property in Queensland but my brother talked Dad out of that. Ronan, being the oldest son, was expected to take over the business,' Ben said, then added, 'Maybe don't print that bit. Anyway, if I couldn't learn how to run the Queensland property, I didn't see any point in studying Ag.'

Sensing that Ben wouldn't be drawn much further about this, Ellie stopped herself from asking him for details about his relationship with Ronan. After all, this was meant to be an article to celebrate the local hero, not an investigation into the workings of the O'Neill family, she thought.

'What were you interested in? What was your passion?' Ellie asked, wondering for a minute how she would answer that question herself if someone asked her.

'I really wanted to do art. That surprised Mum and Dad, my father in particular, and we had a bit of a battle over it. But he finally agreed to let me do what I wanted, and paid for me to go to art school in Melbourne.'

'And your sister, what did she do?'

'She was never keen on farming so when she left school she studied Accounting and got a job with a friend of our father's in Melbourne.'

Ellie nodded. 'So what did you do after art school?'

'I travelled, did odd jobs, painted when I could. Then after a few years I went up to Queensland after all. Straight after they got married, Ronan and Cynthia were going on a flash honeymoon to Europe, so my father asked me to manage the place while they were away. Perhaps he thought it was a way to make up for not letting me be more involved in the property before then.' Ben smiled. 'I discovered that I'm not as fond of cattle as I am of sheep, but I love being in the open spaces.'

'And what about your art? Did you keep up with it while you were there?'

'One of the old fencers used to sit around and whittle wood every night. When he saw that I was interested in what he was doing, he taught me how to use a chainsaw to carve and showed me which wood to use. There was also an Indigenous stockman who taught me about trees and what was special about them. How to "read" them, as he explained it. Did you know some trees are sacred?' he asked Ellie, then went on. 'He showed me the way his ancestors made bark canoes and carved tools and even containers to carry food. I was totally hooked and that led me into the wood carving.'

'And you mentioned that you paint, too, when you can?' asked Ellie.

Ben gave a shrug. 'I've experimented a bit; I like doing charcoal sketches. I always keep a little art book and charcoal and pencils with me to sketch outdoors. Sometimes I set up an easel and paint with oils or do a watercolour. But the wood carving was what caught people's attention, and I've been able to make a living from it. Not exactly steady, reliable work, though.' He grinned. 'But enough to survive on, and I get to work outside.'

'So you feel at home in the bush. Did that help you when you were looking for Peter?' said Ellie.

'Yes. I feel confident in the bush. I felt like a bit of a goose slipping down the gully, but it turned out to be a lucky fall as that's when I heard Peter crying.'

'I had a funny experience when I fell while we were all searching for him,' Ellie said. 'Like the trees were protecting me. All of a sudden I wasn't scared, I felt safe.'

Ben gave a small smile. 'Yep. Trees communicate, they breathe, we need them. Do you know, I can tell from their wood if they've been stressed or had a good life? Mind you, I don't cut them down. I only use a tree after it's fallen,' he added.

'Is that what you're going to do now?' asked Ellie. 'Continue with the wood carvings?'

'I'll always do it when the right wood turns up. The other thing I'm interested in is creative natural buildings. I might try to do a course or some sort of training in building eco-friendly structures. I suppose it depends where I end up. Sometimes I still wish Dad had made me manager of the cattle station but, as I said, Ronan didn't think I was up to it . . .' His voice trailed off.

Ellie looked closely at Ben, and decided to have a go. 'I know this is personal, but can I ask you, how do you get on with your brother? I saw you arguing with each other in the forest,' she said carefully.

Ben glanced at her and then away. 'Well, off the record, and only between us, I'm a bit pissed off at Ronan.'

Ellie paused the recording on her phone and nodded for Ben to keep talking.

'He said I couldn't go to see my gran in the hospital. Such bullshit.'

'That's what you and Ronan were talking about up in the national park?' Ellie said.

'Yeah, among other things. I wanted to let Dad know that Grandy was in hospital, but Ronan said that he didn't want to interrupt Dad's cruise.'

'That was probably reasonable, in hindsight, as it turns out it wasn't too serious. And it would be hard for him to get back home from a cruise ship,' Ellie said.

Ben shrugged. 'You might be right, but Ronan just doesn't like me getting involved in anything. He's always resented how well I get on with Grandy and done whatever he can to get in the way of that. Now that Susan's on the scene, it's the worst it's ever been. She makes it so difficult to see Grandy and I can't work out why. I've spoken to Dad about it but he said he didn't want to make waves.'

Ellie nodded and was about to say something about Susan, but when she noticed that he was patting Sam, she kept quiet. She didn't want to upset Ben even more by telling him about Susan's dog's vicious attack.

'As I'm asking personal questions, can I ask about you and Sally?' she said, changing the subject.

Ben grinned and shrugged. 'It's okay. I'm not sure what'll happen there. It kind of depends on what Sally wants. She's got her eye on a stellar career in the city, so who knows where we'll end up? Besides, I still have an offer of a big carving job in Queensland, the one I was telling you about the other day.'

Ellie leaned forward. 'My grandfather's mate who runs a newspaper in Horsham wants to do a community fundraising day for the Jensens to help Peter with his education,' she said. 'Has he rung you yet?'

'Yes, yesterday. Mr Ward, wasn't it? It sounds like a great idea,' said Ben. 'They want me to be guest of honour.' He laughed. 'And Sally's talked me into it.'

'You'll be treated like royalty,' Ellie said, laughing with him.

'Gee, I hope not!' He smiled. 'Is there anything else?'

'Oh, for my story! I was forgetting, it was just nice talking,' said Ellie with a chuckle, pressing 'record' again on her phone. 'Okay, last question, where would you like to settle down one day?'

Ben looked away, and Ellie noticed that he was staring at the river. 'It's funny, I never thought I was the settling down type. I came to do the carving for the fish co-op, then I got together with Sally, so maybe I'll stick around for a bit after Grandy's birthday. Both of them are pretty special women.' Ben gave a small smile. 'Anyway, we'll see.'

*

When Ellie got back to the *Chronicle* office Maggie was just finishing a call and Ellie could hear raised voices in Patrick's office.

'Visitors?' She nodded towards the cubicle door.

Maggie said quietly, 'Susan McLean and friend.'

'Friend?'

'Some stooge councillor,' said Maggie in a whisper. 'Not my sort.'

266

Ellie leaned against Maggie's desk and asked in a low voice, 'What do you mean? Oh – don't tell me they're trying to get Patrick in on their talk-up-Storm-Harbour good news business scheme? He won't like that.'

'What's it all about?'

Ellie shook her head. 'Susan tried to talk me into getting involved when I was at the café the other day. I think it's their way of, let's say, encouraging the paper to lay off criticising the council. They want Poppy to only run "positive" stories. Which of course he will, but only when they turn up and are worth telling. I reckon what they really want are targeted stories that are just fluff pieces to promote some of the town's businesses, especially the top-end ones.'

Maggie sighed. 'I can't see Patrick going along with that. And how would that help the whole town, anyway? People would see through stories like those.'

The voices in the little office rose, and Ellie and Maggie could tell Patrick was getting cranky.

'I think I'll intervene,' Ellie said to Maggie.

She tapped at the door and went straight in. 'Hi . . . Oh, hello, Susan, may I join you, Poppy?'

Ellie extended her hand to a sallow-faced man standing beside Susan.

'This is Councillor Lowe,' said Susan.

Grasping his limp hand, Ellie immediately disliked him. His disdainful look, small, mean eyes and the arrogant expression on his pinched face set her teeth on edge.

'I'm Ellie Conlan. Patrick's granddaughter.'

'I'm aware of that,' he replied.

'They're here to ask us about doing stories that make the council look good,' said Patrick bluntly.

'Now, Patrick, that's not quite true. Surely we're all on the same team here,' said Susan with a tight smile. 'We all want to promote the town, and make sure everyone knows this is a feel-good place with great opportunities.'

'We have an impressive online presentation to attract families and businesspeople here to make this a place to visit, to retire to, to invest in. We want people to see that this is the perfect town to move to, somewhere they can raise a young family and start a business,' said the councillor briskly.

Patrick continued to look unimpressed. 'Before I'd encourage people to move here, Councillor, there are a few pieces of infrastructure that need fixing. The coast road is the pits – literally – and the internet's dodgy. Maybe council should cool it with some of their more expensive projects that direct money away from what the community wants and needs,' he said impatiently.

'What do you see as a priority for the town?' Ellie asked the councillor, trying to be conciliatory.

Lowe straightened slightly and launched in, as if reciting a rehearsed spiel. 'Every community has to grow and flourish, be viable, and in order to expand we need to promote the good news about our town . . .' But then, seeing Patrick roll his eyes, Lowe changed tack, saying briskly, 'We want to attract people here, yes. But the right kind of people.'

Patrick snorted. 'And who might the "right kind of people" be, Councillor? Cut to the chase. What's this really about? Why should the paper do a tap dance about people and businesses, many of whom are already doing rather nicely, thank you very much? And how much money are you asking people to put up to be featured in this campaign?'

'Mr Addison, Patrick, the council has great respect for the *Chronicle*, but you do have a tendency to point out negative issues and that is not always helpful –' began Councillor Lowe.

'Rubbish! Look at the front page; a little lost boy is rescued, how good is that?' snapped Patrick.

Ellie could tell he was fast losing patience now. 'Just what would you like the *Chronicle* to do?' she asked as Patrick shot a frown her way.

'Support the council,' said Councillor Lowe, sounding annoyed. 'It's bad enough that our mayor finds it difficult to support her own team –'

Susan quickly interjected. 'It's your decision what goes in the *Chronicle*, of course, but it is a newspaper *for* the community. The council would like to be able to count on your support for its new ideas and projects,' she said.

'Excuse me, Susan, I'm a little confused,' said Ellie. 'I thought you worked for the O'Neills. Why are you lobbying for the council?'

Susan frowned. 'That's not what I'm doing at all. The O'Neill family are stalwarts of this town!'

Ellie thought this an odd answer to her question, but she let it go.

'So what's it going to cost these businesses to support your idea?' asked Patrick. 'Is everyone paying the same? Are the small businesspeople being asked to throw in the same amount as the big guys? And what do they get for it?'

'It's promotion for everyone!' cried Lowe. 'The town. And council will match this campaign, dollar for dollar. That includes your newspaper. So we hope you will commit to selling the good news too. Forget attacking the council, as it could work against you and the paper.'

Patrick's voice rose as he glared at Lowe. 'Are you

threatening me? This feels very much like a case of bullying, obfuscating, shuffling cards. You'd get a lot more from the town if you were upfront about things.'

Lowe's face reddened. 'I've had it. You're stubborn and no help to this town –'

'Enough!' bellowed Patrick. 'I run this paper. Council runs the town. Let's stick to what we do, whether or not we agree on the ways in which we do it. I don't try to run the council, so don't you try to tell me how to run my newspaper,' he thundered.

Susan scrambled to her feet. 'Well, thank you for meeting us, even if we don't always see eye to eye.' She glared at Councillor Lowe. 'I think it's time to go. We're wasting everyone's time.'

She turned on her heel and walked to the door, followed by the scowling councillor.

Ellie signalled to her grandfather to calm down and stay put, then followed them out to the main office.

Susan was yanking at the *Chronicle*'s front door as Ellie caught up with them.

'While you're here, Councillor Lowe, I wonder if you know anything about a proposed development on the site of the caravan park?' Ellie asked.

'We came here to discuss a potential campaign, not to indulge your idle questions,' said Susan. She looked furious. 'And what business is it of yours, anyway? You don't even live in Storm Harbour.'

'I work for the *Chronicle*, and what happens in this town is certainly the *Chronicle*'s business,' Ellie replied coldly, before turning back to Councillor Lowe. 'So if you do have any comment to make, Councillor, we'll be sure to include it in the paper's published investigation into the situation.'

Councillor Lowe was stony-faced. 'As Susan said, we came here to discuss what could have been a mutually beneficial collaboration. That conversation is evidently over.'

This time it was Ellie who lost her temper. 'Well next time, tell us what you're really after,' she said, unable to mask the angry tone in her voice.

'Won't be a next time. You've had your chance.' Lowe shepherded a glaring Susan out the door, slamming it behind him.

'What was all that about?' asked a bemused Maggie.

'A whole lot of hot air and none of it good,' said Patrick, walking out of his office. 'The way Lowe was threatening makes me think we might lose some council advertising. Not good for our bottom line.'

'It was as we thought, Maggie. They're trying to persuade us to write only good news stories about the council and the town,' explained Ellie. 'They don't want us criticising them.'

'The mayor supports us so we must be doing something bloody right,' muttered Patrick, grabbing his fedora. 'I'm going over to see Roly. I promised I'd join him for a game of chess.'

Ellie sat at her desk in the back office and played the recording of her interview with Ben. She had enough to make an outline of the story, she decided. She'd call him with any follow-up questions that came to mind as she fleshed out the article. You're still learning this business, she reminded herself. And, she had to admit, she was enjoying the process.

Two hours later, she had a draft outline, and several more questions for Ben. She also made a note to ask him if it was all right if Jon took some photos of his wood carvings to go with the story, as well as including those of him at the rescue of Peter Jensen.

Ellie knew there was another story to be told – about Ben's difficult relationship with Ronan – but he obviously didn't want to talk about it. The little he had said, he'd asked her to keep off the record. She'd respect this request, of course, although it didn't stop her from wondering what Ben's life must have been like, growing up in the shadow of his confident and perhaps bullying older brother.

Reading over the draft again, Ellie thought Ben came across as a modest, quiet local boy hiding his light under a bushel. Storm Harbour was lucky to have someone with his talents. The fact that he was part of the most influential family in town was of passing interest.

Feeling quite pleased with her draft, she emailed it to Patrick for his 'blue pencil treatment'. Then with a wave to Maggie, Ellie made her way outside to head home. She was getting into her car when her phone rang. She smiled when she saw who the caller was.

'Hi, Mike. How're you?'

'I'm okay. I have interesting news.'

'Oh, do tell, I can hear the excitement in your voice.'

'Your nemesis, Sophia, has been fired!'

'No way!' Ellie sat in the car and pulled the door closed. 'Well, I can't say I'm not smiling! Please spill the beans!'

'I'm an outsider so I don't know all the details. But it was hot gossip at the bar last night. Evidently the whole thing totally unravelled. Sophia put up a good front, but she also put her team off, your old team, that is. The company let her drive the bus and it crashed.'

'Sounds like it fell apart at a bad time. They should be ready to launch by now,' said Ellie.

'I have the feeling she was in over her head. See, you made it all look too easy!'

'Oh, Mike. Well, I'm not surprised. She was so full of herself. Thought she knew it all. Doesn't make me feel any better about losing my job, though.'

'I think you have every right to feel smug.'

Ellie laughed. 'Maybe. But I am sorry for the team that had to work with her.'

'From what I heard, they didn't race to her rescue,' Mike said.

'Knowing Sophia, she wouldn't have listened to them even if they'd tried.'

'You're probably right,' said Mike, suddenly sounding distracted. 'Listen, gotta go. Couldn't wait to let you know, though. I'll pass on anything else I hear.'

'Thanks, Mike.' Ellie hung up feeling like she was a million miles away from inner-city Melbourne. As she went to put her phone in her bag, she saw the note tucked inside the cover. No time like the present, she thought. She pulled it out and dialled the number written on it.

'Hello?' It was a man's voice.

'Hi. This is Ellie Conlan. You left a note on my windscreen.'

'Ah, yes. When your car was outside the hotel. Can we meet?' The man had a pleasant voice.

'Can you tell me what you want, what this is about exactly?'

'Not over the phone. I'm no conspiracy theorist but I don't trust my phone completely. I'm close to town. You know the rocky path that goes out to the lighthouse island? There's a seat and a bench at the seawall. Can you meet me there, early tomorrow morning? Say six o'clock?'

'I guess so.' Ellie knew the little park from her walks with Sam.

'I don't want to sound paranoid, but it's best we're not seen together so I don't want to meet in town. Your paper should know what's going on in council. See you there.' He hung up.

The man seemed reasonable and Ellie was sure she'd be safe, but she thought it would be sensible to ask someone to keep an eye on her from a distance when she met him. The caravan park wasn't far away, so she decided she'd ask Steve or Cassie.

As Ellie was about to turn on the ignition, a van pulled into the carspot next her. She realised it was Jon behind the wheel. She took the key out again and climbed out of the car to speak to him.

'Hey, how's your investigation going? Finding anything of any interest?' asked Ellie as Jon transferred to his wheelchair and came towards her.

'Could be,' he said. 'Are you just arriving or leaving?'

'I was just going out, but I'll come in and hear your news.'

Inside, Jon wheeled his chair to his desk and Ellie sat opposite him.

'I've just been poking around, talking to people. I went down to see the gang at the caravan park,' he began.

'Has anyone heard anything?'

'No one that I spoke to. But I saw a guy there. He seemed to be working, making some notes, which seemed like an odd thing to do by the river, especially as he was wearing a suit. Well, no tie, but it was an expensive suit.'

'So probably not a local,' said Ellie. 'Did you talk to him?'

'I did. He wasn't very friendly. Or forthcoming.

274

Definitely an out-of-towner. Said he was "making some notes about the place". Just getting some ideas. He slammed his notebook shut but not before I noticed he'd drawn some diagrams and plans.'

'So he's no artist,' said Ellie.

'He said he might be coming up here for a couple of weeks, so he asked where he should stay. He gave me his card. He's from Melbourne. Seems he's a surveyor.'

'Did he say what he was doing or who he was working for?' asked Ellie.

'The more I asked, the more tight-lipped he was. Oh, and I forgot to mention that before meeting this bloke, I went to the pub for a counter lunch and started talking to a couple of tradies. They were saying there should be a lot of work coming up soon. When I asked them about it, they clammed up,' Jon said. 'Anyway, I took a few photos at the caravan park because the light was so good and I noticed that when the guy was leaving, he put something in his car boot. I thought it was a tripod, and that he'd been taking photos too, but now when I think about it, it could have been a theodolite, you know, that surveyors use.'

Ellie nodded. 'I don't know what, but there's something happening,' she said.

'If anyone knows anything, then they're not saying. It doesn't make a lot of sense. I tried to ask council if a permit to develop any land along the river had been lodged but they wouldn't give me that sort of information. Just said to keep checking the council website.'

'We'll definitely do that, and more,' said Ellie. She thought about asking Jon to keep an eye on the meeting but knew that he usually went swimming at dawn with a few mates and she didn't want to upset his routine.

Instead, she said goodbye to him, got back into her car, and pulled out her phone to call Cassie.

After talking to Cassie for a minute or so, Ellie told her about the meeting.

'Six am at the lighthouse. This guy has some information for the paper. I think it might be a leak from council. I just wondered if you or Steve would be able to hang about and keep an eye on me, in case I'm grabbed and thrown in a car and driven away . . .?'

'Oh, Ellie, stop. That's not funny!' exclaimed Cassie. 'Of course. I'll ask Steve to go and watch out for you. He'll love pretending he's James Bond,' she said, and Ellie could hear the smile in her voice.

'It's not a trenchcoat job! Perhaps he could take his rod and pretend he's going fishing on the other side of the island.'

'Absolutely. He'll be there. Might catch something for breakfast. Do you want him to snap a photo or something?'

'Definitely not. Now, it's at the end of the little park, just after you cross over to the island,' said Ellie.

'Where that table and bench is, I know the place. He'll be there, Ellie. It all sounds very cloak and dagger.'

'Not really. Just council stuff!'

They both laughed.

'Well, I hope whoever it is has something useful,' said Cassie. 'We're still on tenterhooks about the rumours that council or developers are planning something for the caravan park.'

'I'll let you know any news, if I can,' said Ellie.

No sooner had she hung up than her phone rang again.

'Hi, Meredith, how are you?'

'Hello, Ellie,' said Meredith. 'I'm glad I caught you.

Do you have a few minutes to talk?'

'Of course,' said Ellie, concerned at hearing the stressed tone in the mayor's voice. 'What's up?'

'I think things might be coming to a head. Councillor Lowe is being very cocky, pushy, arrogant . . .'

'More so than usual?' commented Ellie. 'I only met him today but he was all of those things.'

'Yes, if that's possible. Smug is more his usual demeanour, so I know he's up to something. He pushes things through for mates and he's devious enough about it that I haven't been able to catch him out.' She paused then asked, 'How did you come to meet him today?'

'My grandfather had a visit from Councillor Lowe and Susan McLean,' said Ellie and she proceeded to fill in the mayor on all the details.

'I'm not sure if they're stupid enough to believe such a spurious effort at heavying the *Chronicle* would work,' Meredith said. 'To think they can control what goes in the paper! "Good news only." What crap. 'Scuse me. There's no good news coming out of council at the moment. It's disappointing that the decent people in there are so easily intimidated by the likes of Lowe.'

'But why would they pressure us to lay off criticising them in the paper?' asked Ellie. 'Surely that would be enough to make us want to find out what's going on.'

'As I see it, their method is to dilute the scrutiny. Divert attention from something they want to slip through unnoticed. Try to make you investigate one thing while they work on another.'

'Surely that can't happen?' said Ellie, then quickly added, 'I suppose that's naive of me, given there've been so many instances all over the country of corruption in some councils in the past.'

'Sadly, that's true,' Meredith said, then went on, 'Ellie, I'm ringing because I'm under attack again. Trolling on the council social media now and nasty notes in my letterbox. It's unnerving. I was wondering if you've deleted any more posts like the one you told me about before?'

'Just one or two,' Ellie said. 'Almost exactly the same as the first one I told you about. They seem to have stopped, though. Maybe whoever wrote them realised that I'll just delete them immediately, so they've started contacting you directly instead. What do the notes say? Is someone trying to frighten you off something? Shut you up?'

'Yes, someone is definitely trying to intimidate me, but I'm confused about their motives. Whatever they want, it's obviously in their interests to unsettle me and make me think that they can get to me. As the mayor I have to expect criticism and there's very little I can do about it,' said Meredith.

'This sounds like more than criticism,' said Ellie.

'Exactly, and I feel it's starting to escalate,' Meredith said.

'Listen, Meredith, tomorrow I'm meeting someone.' She paused, not sure she should say too much, even to Meredith. After all, the man was cautious about being seen talking to Ellie. 'Um, it might be the person who gave Sally her info for the radio broadcast. Did you know that Sally has been heavied by her boss? My guess is he didn't like her saying anything against the council,' Ellie said. 'She more or less said she's been told not to pursue the development story anymore.'

'I didn't know, but I'm not surprised. The station is privately owned, so you know what that can mean – the integrity of its objectivity and reportage depends entirely on the mindset of the owners. So it's all too easy for freedom of the press to go out the window. It's particularly murky in this case as that station gets council funding as a "community" resource,' Meredith said.

'Which the *Chronicle* doesn't get,' said Ellie. 'Our funding comes from advertising, and Poppy told me once that even if businesses have the money, he won't always let them advertise in the paper. If he thinks the business is doing the wrong thing by their workers or for the environment, for instance.'

Meredith laughed. 'We need more people with your grandfather's commitment and integrity.' There was a moment's silence. 'So are you going to share what this person tells you?'

'Meredith, you know a journalist can't always disclose their source,' Ellie said lightly, trying to sound more relaxed than she felt.

'Of course, I just want to help. The pressure is starting to get to me.'

'I'm sorry about that, Meredith.'

'Keep doing what you're doing. The town so needs Patrick and that paper. And you. You've revved the old boy up no end.' She paused. 'And how are you doing, Ellie?'

Ellie knew the gentle enquiry referred to her meltdown and panic attack when Ronan joined her lunch with Dave.

'I'm doing well, thank you. Really well. I'm feeling stronger about things. It's been good being here.'

'You're not leaving, are you?'

'No, no plans just yet.'

'Ellie, you've become part of the town, a local.'

'I feel that way too. So I'm here for the moment.'

'Good on you, Ellie. That's the spirit,' Meredith said warmly. 'Well, I just hope this information proves useful for you and the paper. Keep me updated if you can.'

'Thank you, Meredith. You hang in there too.'

Over dinner, Ellie told Patrick she was meeting the mysterious source at six the next morning.

'That's early. I guess there'll be a few early morning bods about,' he said.

'I called Cassie. Steve is going to go fishing around near where we're meeting so he will be close enough to shout to if needed,' said Ellie.

'Well, if you're sure. Plus it's close enough to people if you shout bloody blue murder,' said Patrick.

'I think this is someone who wants to see us, me, rather than the other way around,' said Ellie. 'Why do whistleblowers and people leak information, Poppy?'

'Mostly it's not to be mischievous but to set off alarm bells,' said Patrick. 'They wouldn't take the risk otherwise.'

\*

Early the next morning, Ellie drove to town along the quiet back street where Susan lived with her angry dog. As she cruised past Susan's cottage and drove on further, Ellie glanced at a car parked beneath the overhang of one of the magnificent old Norfolk Island pines lining the street and saw a woman sitting in the driver's seat, motionless, clutching the steering wheel and staring at Susan's front door. It seemed odd to Ellie, especially so early in the day. She hoped the woman was okay. She looked at her from her rear-view mirror and she seemed fine, so Ellie kept going.

Thankfully the wind had died down by the time Ellie parked her car. She walked over the causeway to the island and the lighthouse at its southern rim, facing the ocean. The lighthouse was unstaffed now, but there was a picnic table near some trees and it was a popular place for walkers and daytrippers. Steve was already there, setting out his fishing rods, preparing to wander off and fish.

Ellie sat down and put her phone on the table alongside a notebook and pen. Her contact probably wouldn't want to be recorded so she might need to make notes. She looked at Steve, who happened to glance around at the same time, and they exchanged a quick smile. She was so grateful he was there. This all felt very odd.

Ellie opened her phone to check her messages and suddenly there was movement as a figure sat opposite her. She jumped and looked up.

The man was a pleasant-looking fellow in his late forties, maybe early fifties.

'Sorry, didn't mean to startle you.' He held out his hand. 'I'm Russ.'

She shook his hand; he had a firm grip. 'I'm Ellie.'

'Thanks for meeting me.'

'Thank you for wanting to help the community . . . if that is why you're here,' Ellie said, smiling.

'Yes. I work at the council. I'm staff, a backroom boy, really. But I often deal with sensitive information.'

'I think you're being modest. First off, do you mind if I record our conversation?'

'I guessed you'd ask that so I've given it some thought,' Russ said. 'Perhaps at this stage you can just take some notes.' He reached over and tapped her notebook. 'This information is particularly sensitive, you understand.'

'Of course,' said Ellie, picking up her pen. 'Okay, let's get started. Why are you doing this?'

'Same reason you're here meeting me. There's

something happening at council that doesn't smell right. More so than usual, I mean. Normally when things don't run smoothly, or there's a hiccup, or a bit of fudging over documents and figures and such, it gets tidied away, covered up or buried, without any drama in the community.'

'Because no one knows?'

'Correct. But this is more than fudging the budget figures or pushing through a mate's development.'

'Why, what's happening?'

He hesitated. 'It's more a matter of what's *not* happening, and the results could be extremely serious for the majority of the town.'

'Is this to do with the caravan park?'

'Yes.'

'So there *is* a plan to develop the park?' asked Ellie. 'For what? I heard there were rumours of townhouses.'

'Possibly. There's no doubt certain people will be ready to jump in with plans and a proposal should the lease not be renewed.'

Ellie looked puzzled. 'I don't understand. Are you able to fill me in? There're some conflicting assumptions. The current managers of the caravan park have a lease with council, which leases the land from the O'Neills, is that right?' asked Ellie slowly.

When Russ nodded she went on, 'As I understand it, the land always belonged to Boyd O'Neill so presumably his wife owns it now. He allowed her to use a section of it, which she turned into the Botanic Gardens for the use of the town. She told me they had originally planned to develop the whole parcel as public gardens but didn't get around to doing the other section.'

Ellie stopped talking and looked at Russ, who

282

nodded. 'That's right,' he said and paused, so Ellie kept talking.

'As people were discovering the area back in the fifties and sixties and camping there, Boyd was okay with that. Until council stepped in and wanted him to care for it, put in a few amenities. But Boyd didn't want to be bothered with all that according to Kathryn, so he leased the caravan park site back to the council.'

'Correct. You're well informed. But that parcel on which the caravan park sits is only on a fifty-year lease. The Botanic Gardens are on a ninety-nine-year lease.'

'Ah,' said Ellie. 'Mrs O'Neill didn't mention that. I wonder if she even knows. Though she came across as being very sharp, still fully across these matters.'

'Well, that's possible. I deal with leases and documents and development permits. I notify owners when leases are coming up for renewal and such,' said Russ.

'So how could this land be targeted for development unless the O'Neills take back ownership and undertake the development themselves, or put it up for sale? Which, from my understanding, it's unlikely Seamus and Kathryn would allow. Ultimately, they control what happens to it, don't they?' said Ellie.

'For the moment. But the fifty-year lease runs out very soon. If a new lease is not negotiated in time, the council will own the land. And that means the council will be able to do whatever they want with it. For the past few months I've been waiting to hear about the lease from Seamus O'Neill and haven't received an answer.'

'I guess you didn't know that Mr O'Neill is away on a cruise,' said Ellie. 'Can't it wait till he comes back?'

'I just have a hunch that something's not quite right. Seamus O'Neill is usually very prompt in all his dealings

283

and correspondence with the council. It's strange that we haven't heard from him at all.'

'Hang on, did you say you sent the first letter months ago?' Ellie asked, thinking back.

'That's right. How long has Mr O'Neill been away?'

'I don't know, maybe a few weeks, but I don't think it's been any longer than that.'

Russ shook his head. 'Well, someone must have received them.'

'And when does the lease expire, exactly?' Ellie asked.

'I don't want to provide too many details,' Russ said, looking alarmed. 'I can't have anything traced back to me. I don't want to lose my job!'

'Of course,' Ellie said soothingly, worried for a moment that she'd lost him. 'The *Chronicle* always protects its sources.'

Russ took a few deep breaths. When Ellie thought he seemed calmer, she asked, 'So, why have you contacted me?'

'I was hoping the paper might do some investigating.'

'I'll try to help,' said Ellie. 'Russ, I'm not sure if you want to answer this, but have you given any information to the local radio station?'

'Me? No, that wasn't me. The reason I thought I'd talk to you people is I had similar information and I reckon it's my duty to share it.' He paused for a moment, then added, 'I can't answer too many questions. There's a limit to what I can say – you understand?'

'Of course,' Ellie said, then quickly moved on. 'We know there has been a Melbourne surveyor looking around the caravan park.'

Russ frowned. 'They must be feeling confident.' He stared up at the lighthouse and finally said, 'I would hate to see the riverside and the caravan park disappear under buildings. It's such a pretty setting. If the community knew for certain of any such plans there'd be an uproar. Which is why I'm hoping you can help.'

Ellie nodded. 'Thank you for alerting us,' she said.

'Please keep me out of this. As you can imagine, I'd be fired immediately if anyone discovered I'd alerted you to these details.'

Russ stood, thanked her and walked quickly away, passing the first of the early morning walkers and Steve, reeling in his catch.

*

Patrick was munching on a piece of toast as Ellie came into the kitchen.

'How'd it go? Useful?'

Ellie nodded. 'Very interesting. The contact seemed genuine. But it's raised more questions than answers, though.' Quickly she filled Patrick in, and he scratched his head.

'Hmm, all very perplexing. Surely the O'Neills wouldn't be willing to let that land go. But if that is the case, then it's no wonder the developer vultures are hovering. Something very odd is definitely going on in council. I can't imagine that Seamus or Kathryn would let the lease on that land expire and the land go into council hands permanently.'

'When I asked Kathryn about the rumours she dismissed them out of hand,' said Ellie. 'And Seamus seems to be uncontactable. What do you think, Poppy? Should we do a story on this now?'

'I know it's frustrating, Ellie, but we still don't have anything concrete to publish. It's all very interesting, but neither we nor the O'Neills want to have bands of lawyers coming down on us like a ton of bricks because of what could end up being just some confusion over paperwork in council.'

'So we say nothing?'

'That's right. At least for the time being. Let's keep digging and listening first.'

Ellie nodded. 'I promised Russ I would keep our meeting confidential.'

'We'll keep this just between ourselves and do our own investigations as well,' Patrick said. 'Until we come up with something definite, we can't print a word, unfortunately.'

It was frustrating, but Ellie could see the sense in Patrick's words. She made herself a coffee and went into the old sewing room, now her study and workplace.

Ellie checked the paper's website even though she knew Maggie would too, as the lovely responses to the rescue of Peter Jensen were still coming in. But then she froze. She blinked, leaning forward as the harsh and cruel words emphasised in capitals leaped out at her. She was being attacked.

*BITCH, LIAR, CHEAT. THAT CONLAN WOMAN CAN'T BE TRUSTED. NO ONE KNOWS THE TRUTH ABOUT HER. DON'T BE CONNED. SHE THINKS SHE'S CLEVER BUT SHE'S A BITCH TRYING TO TAKE OVER.*

With tears springing to her eyes and anger almost choking her, Ellie slammed the cover of her laptop shut.

The cruel and vile attack stunned her. Who would write such a thing, and why? And so viciously? She felt vulnerable and exposed, as if her skin had been peeled back. It was so unfair. Untrue.

Swiftly she re-opened her laptop and deleted the

painful words. How many people had seen the post? Ellie wanted to throw something. This was horrible. She wanted to run and hide. How could she walk through town? Who would even think such things about her?

Suddenly she thought of Meredith. No wonder the tough and strong mayor had been so upset at being trolled. The trolls were such cowards. Why didn't they call her out in person instead of hiding behind an anonymous post on social media?

*Because none of it is true*, a voice answered her.

The only person Ellie could think of who would do such a thing was Sophia, to get back at Ellie for losing her job. Thank goodness Ellie's Melbourne friends probably wouldn't see this. Mike, and perhaps her parents, were the only ones who checked the website regularly, and the post hadn't been up for long.

Ellie headed into the *Chronicle* office and the minute Maggie saw her she leaped up and wrapped her arms around her.

'I've seen them, it's awful. Take no notice,' said Maggie comfortingly.

Ellie stopped short. 'What do you mean by "them"? I deleted the post. Oh no, don't tell me . . .'

'I took them down, don't worry.'

Jon looked over his shoulder from his desk. 'Sorry, Ellie . . . there's another one.'

The belittling and nasty comments kept rolling in all day. She, Jon and Maggie took turns monitoring and deleting them.

By the afternoon Ellie was convinced the only person who would do this was Sophia, but she had no proof and didn't know what to do about it. Eventually, Maggie gently pushed her out the door. 'Go home. We'll monitor the page from now on and get rid of them. Whoever is doing this will get tired of it eventually.'

*

The sky was darkening as Ellie drove up to the house. She felt completely rattled; it was as if she'd been punctured by a barrage of arrows. And because they'd been monitoring the posts all day, she'd got hardly anything else done.

She opened the front door and called Sam, who came bouncing down the hall, though there was no sign of her grandfather. She let Sam out and watched as he began sniffing, then raced across the garden, his nose to the ground. Ellie stepped onto the verandah and saw him snuffling and pawing at something near the fence.

'Sam! Leave it!' Ellie shouted, surprising herself at the tone of her bellow. A warning instinct had kicked in. Sam had his head down and looked as if he were trying to eat something.

'*Leave it*,' screamed Ellie.

She stumbled down the steps, shoving Sam to one side as she looked at the bloody lump of meat. '*Inside*, inside now,' she shouted, chasing the bewildered dog up the steps. As she fumbled to unlatch the door, Sam turned back down the steps and Ellie screamed at him to stop.

Sam froze, looking back at her, confused at the loud and firm command. There was a note in her voice that he obeyed instantly. Taking him gently by the collar, she put him in the house and closed the door behind them. She ran to the kitchen and grabbed a plastic bag and the little shovel from beside the fireplace, then raced outside again and scooped the smelly lump of meat out of the grass and into the bag.

She washed her hands and went back to Sam, who was lying with his nose on his paws, watching her warily. She crouched down, opening his mouth to look at his gums, and sniffed his breath. His gums were pink and there were no traces of the smell of the putrid meat.

Shaking, Ellie sat back on her heels, stroking the dog. Then she rang the vet.

# 9

THE DRIVE TO THE vet with a subdued Sam in the back felt to Ellie like a mercy dash, though she drove steadily. Tears streamed down her face. She couldn't be sure the meat had been poisoned, but after the horrendous trolling and the unlikelihood of a strange hunk of odd-smelling meat just turning up in the garden, it seemed likely Patrick, and maybe even Ellie herself, were being targeted. How could anyone do such a thing to an animal? she wondered.

At the doorway Sam hung back, perhaps smelling the familiar scent of the clinic, and Ellie had to urge him inside. The vet, Richard, wearing a colourful smock printed with dancing bears, listened to Ellie's explanation and then took Sam straight into the surgery and examined him.

'He seems fine, which would suggest he hasn't ingested anything harmful,' Richard said to Ellie when he'd finished. 'He might have licked the meat, but if he did, it doesn't appear to have done any damage. However, you'll need to watch him closely tonight, just in case.' Richard turned to the meat in the plastic bag. 'I'll run some tests on this sample. From the odour, I'd say it's deliberately poisoned bait.' He patted Sam. 'You're lucky, old fella. Just as well you obey orders.' He looked at Ellie. 'If there's poison present, I'll have to report it to the police. Would anyone have a reason to do this?' He raised his eyebrows.

Ellie shook her head slowly. 'Of course, we all have our ups and downs with people, but I can't think of any reason why someone would throw a poisoned lump of meat into our yard to intentionally harm an innocent pet. Thank goodness I was with Sam and stopped him from eating it,' she said.

'What about the *Chronicle*? Would someone want to get back at the paper for any reason?'

'I just don't understand how anyone could be that horrible. They don't like something they read in the paper and so they try to poison our dog?'

Richard shrugged. 'Who knows? Maybe somebody is trying to stop something going in the paper in the first place. Though I can't recall anything like this happening in town before, not a deliberate bait. What did Patrick say?'

'I haven't told him yet. He was out walking when Sam found the meat. As soon as I realised what he was trying to eat, I drove Sam straight here. We'll both need to be careful now.'

Darkness had fallen when Ellie arrived back at the house. She still felt rattled as she led Sam inside and closed the door after him. She could hear Patrick in his study,

291

but before going in to talk to him, Ellie went out and used the light on her phone to search the garden in case there were more baits. Looking around the spot where the meat had been, she concluded that someone had most likely driven or walked past and hurled it over the fence. They were surrounded by trees on a large block so their neighbours weren't close enough to have witnessed anything.

Ellie wished she didn't have to tell her grandfather this news as she could guess how upset he'd be. And his reaction proved her right.

'What the hell!' he said, quickly standing up from his desk. 'Are you sure it was poison? Who in this community would do such a vile thing?'

'Sam's okay, Poppy. We've just come back from the vet. I wanted to get Sam to Richard as quickly as possible so I just got in the car and raced there. Richard's testing the meat to find out what it is.'

Patrick sat back down slowly, suddenly looking old and a little frail, Ellie thought. She sat on the small sofa by the bookcase and took a deep breath.

'I got such a fright, Poppy,' she said softly.

'You did very well, Poss. Probably saved Sam's life . . .' His voice trailed off. 'We'll get to the bottom of this,' he said at last. 'We just have to watch the old boy. Labs will eat anything, as you know.'

'Why would someone do this? It's so cruel.'

'I don't know, love. Perhaps it's about the land development rumours. We haven't published anything yet, but someone might not like us even sniffing around. But if that someone is so desperate to make a point, my bet is that they'll inevitably show their hand. Let's get on with things discreetly until we get more facts and can run with a story.'

Ellie went to bed but slept badly, reaching out in the night to pat Sam, who was curled up by her side. He was in a deep sleep, twitching and making small noises, chasing rabbits or seagulls in his dreams, Ellie thought, and smiled.

She got up early and checked around the garden again before calling Sam for a morning run along the beach. As soon as she opened the car door, he jumped into the back seat and they headed off. Ellie was very relieved to see that her old mate seemed as healthy as ever.

The wind was up, the surf churning, and the sand flew in stinging little gusts. Sam looked like he was enjoying the challenge of the biting breeze. He bounded along the water's edge, stopping to sniff at some seaweed and a dead fish.

Ellie thought back to her old life, as she had begun to refer to it, even though it was such a short time ago. Mentally she ran through her days at work; the pressure of deadlines and meetings, the long hours as she lost track of time, night or day, keeping on top of what her team was doing as well as her own jobs, managing the constraints of budgets and timeframes. The socialising where they only talked shop and rarely seemed to venture below the surface to discuss anything really important or interesting. A meal in a nearby café or restaurant on her own or with Mike. Going to parties at Julie's insistence, where she usually left alone at the end of the night. Returning home to her quiet, compact apartment where she hardly ever cooked and never entertained. And where, inevitably, she'd find herself sitting at her laptop, answering emails while drinking a glass of wine, the unwatched television murmuring in the background for company. Pretending to friends she had a lover.

Though she liked her small rented apartment, Ellie had long been considering buying a flat in Fitzroy. But deep down, if she was honest with herself, she knew she was hoping for something else, and that had always stayed her hand. In a moment of clarity, as she stopped still on the beach, she realised she'd been like this for many years. She'd been waiting for something as time had gone by . . . but what was it?

Sam nudged her, holding a stick, his tail wagging.

'Clever boy. Okay, go fetch!' Ellie flung it as a happy Sam raced after it. And she started to jog after him along the sand.

She was picking up a good pace when her phone rang. Pulling it out of her pocket, she saw that the call was from an unfamiliar number. As she slowed down, she caught her breath and then answered.

'Hello?'

'Ellie?'

She froze. This was a voice from another life. Another planet.

'Ellie, it's Roger.'

'Yes. Hello, Roger.' She paused, wondering if she should tell her former boss that she knew Sophia had been fired. But he saved her the trouble.

'I suppose you may have heard that we had to let Sophia go.'

'I'm down in the country, Roger.' She settled on a deliberately obtuse comment so she didn't have to give away what news she'd heard from her old work.

'Oh, I see. A holiday?' He hesitated for a few seconds, then went on, 'I'll cut to the chase. We'd like you to come back, Ellie. I apologise for the hasty way in which we acted, and it appears we were rather misinformed.

Could you meet me for a chat? Lunch, perhaps? Just to talk; no need to commit to anything yet.'

Ellie felt her head starting to spin as a range of emotions swirled through her: satisfaction, surprise, excitement, reluctance, sadness, indecision. She had no idea how she really felt about this so she took a moment before replying.

'Roger, thank you for the call. Do you mind if I digest this and ring you back? I'm in the middle of a project with my grandfather's newspaper –'

'Of course, I understand this comes slightly out of the blue, but we would value having your expertise back in the company, Ellie. I can offer a very generous remuneration. Call me when it's convenient, say in a day or so? Take care, goodbye.'

He hung up and Ellie gritted her teeth. Typical of the man and the way in which he ran the company to demand that she jump up and down, work to his timeframe and do it *right now*. He hadn't even let her finish her sentence! Well, she'd let him wait a while.

Ellie took a deep breath. She felt as though her life was starting to tip upside down again, and the trolling and the attempt to poison beloved Sam had her more rattled than she cared to admit. And now this: what was she going to do about Roger's offer? She was torn between elation at Roger having to eat humble pie and invite her back into the company, and the niggling thought that she wasn't actually as excited about the prospect as she once might have been. The events in Storm Harbour seemed more real to her, more important, than she had realised.

As Sam dashed back over to her and licked her hand, she thought again about the poisoned meat. The dog would have been the victim of an act that was presumably meant to unnerve and threaten Ellie or her grandfather, or both of them. But why?

It suddenly occurred to her that someone might have seen her talking to Russ, the council source. Maybe she'd better tell him what had happened, just in case.

She rang his number.

'Hello?'

'Do you know who this is?' asked Ellie.

'Yes. I do.'

'Is it convenient to speak at the moment? Or just listen to me? I won't be long.'

'Yes. Go ahead.'

'Someone attempted to poison my grandfather's dog after I met with you. I don't know if it's connected but I thought I should let you know. It's possible someone saw us together.'

'I appreciate that. Thanks for letting me know. I do hope all is well with you,' he said politely, and Ellie realised he was not alone.

'The dog is okay, but I feel I'm being frightened off. And it's working.'

'That's unfortunate. Do keep me updated.'

'And could you keep me updated too?' said Ellie.

'Thank you for calling.' Russ hung up, but Ellie knew he'd got the message.

She put a damp, sandy Sam in the car and drove through the awakening town, cruising down Susan's street on her way home. Ellie noticed that the same car – a small, white sedan – was parked near Susan's house. As she drove towards it, she saw the same woman she'd seen the other day sitting behind the wheel, watching the house intently. As Ellie drove by, she was sure the woman glanced at her then turned away.

At home, Ellie made a cup of coffee while going back over Roger's phone call in her mind. Her first instinct was to ring Mike, but she already knew what he'd say: that it was her decision. She needed to think through her options, the pluses and the minuses.

She paused. What made her think there'd be a minus? she asked herself. The offer was flattering and she felt vindicated. Her team, if they were still all there, would be thrilled if she returned, she knew. She could move back and settle into her life in Melbourne again.

So why did she feel so confused and conflicted?

Ellie wanted to talk to her grandfather. She knew that, like Mike, her parents would say it was her choice and they'd support whatever decision she made. But Patrick would speak his mind.

She tried to be objective about it. Had she become so wrapped up in the minutiae of life in a small town that a move back to the city might do her good? But then, when she thought about it, the city was a series of small communities too; the interplay of personalities in the office, the people in her apartment building and neighbourhood, her circle of city friends. Yes, there was the opportunity to meet new people all the time in the city but, equally, fostering deep and true friendships there was not so easy. Everyone was scattered around the city, always in a hurry, and social occasions were generally conducted in crowded places. She knew most of her acquaintances there only superficially through other friends or her work; she had little idea of their family life, their backgrounds, what they did away from each other, nor they her. Most people seemed too busy to form close friendships in the workplace.

The cohesiveness of the community in Storm Harbour felt very different. Look how the people of the town had come together, bonding over the search for the missing boy. But then, of course, someone had tried to hurt Sam . . .

Ellie finished her coffee, rinsed her mug and headed down to the *Chronicle* office, deep in thought.

She walked into the back office and paused as she looked at Maggie peering over her glasses rather than through them while she studied her computer screen. Jon waved at her and leaned back in his chair, schmoozing someone on the phone. Patrick's voice, strong and determined, came from his small office.

As if experiencing the office anew since her conversation with Roger, Ellie noticed that there was no longer the smell of lead and ink from a printing press, nor the chemical smell from the darkroom where they'd once printed photographs from film before the space was repurposed as a kitchenette. But the piles of files, the old framed photographs and front-page posters going back decades all testified that this was still a place that produced a newspaper. A newspaper that had served and supported, fought for and celebrated its community for decades. And would continue to do so.

Patrick had breathed new life into a fading institution all those years ago and, now in a new era, local independent newspapers were coming to the fore as a reliable source of information. Communities were starting to realise that it was up to them to fight for, support and promote their papers. As Patrick kept saying, 'If we don't look after ourselves and fight for our community, no one else will, because no one will know what's going on!'

As he bade farewell to an irksome caller and jabbed the button on his phone, Patrick looked up. 'Hey there, Poss,' he said to Ellie as she walked in. 'How was the beach?' She could tell he was studying her. 'What's up? Is Sam okay?'

'Yes, he's fine. Sleeping off a big run. I locked him inside the house when I left so he'll be safe.'

'What's bothering you, then?'

'Well, a few things, actually. One especially.'

His eyes narrowed as she sat down opposite. 'Spill the beans.'

'My old boss rang while I was down at the beach. He offered me my old job back.'

Patrick didn't react, but he leaned forward, elbows on his desk. 'And?'

'I don't know what to do.' Ellie sighed. 'I mean, I'm feeling vindicated, of course. He admitted they'd been misinformed.'

'Did they offer more money?'

'We didn't get that far but he hinted at it. He wants me to go and meet him for lunch.'

'Why not a meeting in his office? Sounds more professional to me.'

'I assume he doesn't want anyone to hear anything about it yet. Especially if he's going to offer me a higher wage.'

'Puts you in a strong bargaining position, doesn't it? So . . .?' Patrick stretched back and folded his arms behind his head. 'Now you have this offer in your back pocket, could you look for work with another company? Go out and sell yourself?'

'I suppose so, if that's what I want to do,' Ellie said.

'How long do you have to shop around before giving him an answer?'

'In his usual pushy, aggressive way, Roger will be expecting my answer within a day or so.'

'Well, tell him to cool his heels. If he wants you, the whole city does too. Write your own ticket, Ellie.'

'Maybe. It's just . . . I'm not sure what I want. All I know for certain right now is that I'd hate to leave you and Sam, especially after finding the bait in the garden. Sam'd have to be locked up all day when no one's home. It wouldn't be fair on him.'

'You're right, we'll have to keep Sam out of the garden as best we can for now. I know – I'll put up outdoor lights and a camera,' said Patrick firmly.

'Even that wouldn't be foolproof, Poppy. Someone could still fling a bait into the garden or drive past and toss a lump of poisoned meat out the car window without being seen. It's just terrible.'

'Then I'll bring Sam to work with me. He'd be happy as a clam in here with so much company. Put a bed under the desk for him. At least until we find out who's behind this despicable act.'

Ellie felt a rush of relief. 'Yes. Good idea. So do you think it was a one-off, Poppy? A warning? Or do you think they might try again?'

'I just don't know, love. I reported it to the police this morning, though.'

'What did they say?' Ellie asked.

'Not much, really. They were sorry it happened, but there isn't much they can do about it,' Patrick said. 'Now then, back to your dilemma, love.'

'Well, I have to do something, my holiday funds are running out.' Ellie tried to smile.

'Is that what this has been? A holiday jaunt?' asked Patrick quietly.

'No, not at all,' Ellie was quick to exclaim. 'I guess I was just trying to make light of it. You have no idea what being here has done for me, Poppy. I love living with you and Sam, and I feel like I'm part of the town now. I've made friends here and I enjoy writing for the paper.'

Patrick leaned back. 'That's good. It'll be yours one day. And the old house. You can sell that, of course. I won't be around to break my heart over it. But I wouldn't like to see the *Chronicle* disappear.'

'Poppy! Don't say that,' she burst out, her eyes filling with tears. 'You're going to be around for ages and ages. And I promise you, the *Chronicle* will never stop coming out on my watch! I promise you, no matter what. Besides, you're *not* going anywhere.' The events of the past few days suddenly overwhelming her, Ellie started to cry.

Patrick got up, came around his desk and wrapped his arms around his granddaughter.

'Hey, Miss Media Mogul, settle down. We have plenty of time to plan things. I've been meaning to tell you, I joined the gym. The old folks' weights program. I fling dumbbells around. I'm going to live forever. Now I can throw out the dumbbells who come into my office!'

Ellie managed a smile. 'You're joking. About the gym. Aren't you?'

'You should join too. Bruno, the instructor, is quite a hunk.'

'Poppy, you're incorrigible. I love you so much.'

Patrick perched on the edge of his desk and took her hand. 'Listen, my love. Maybe go to Melbourne, see the big boss, let him do some crawling. And say no. Or yes, if that's what you decide. Because you are the one with the power here. If it's no, you'll be on a high and can walk into any big IT firm. They'll fall over themselves to have you – your friend Mike told me that.' Patrick cocked his head. 'And what does Mike say about this offer?'

'I haven't told him yet. Last time we talked, he said that the woman who undermined me got the sack. Big news in the small IT world in Melbourne.'

'What about your friend Julie? And your mum and dad?' asked Patrick.

'They'll all say it's my decision.'

'Yes, we're not much help, are we? The ball's in your court, Poss. Don't let this Roger rush you. Think about it some more, and see how you feel in a few days.' Then he grinned.

Walking around his desk, he typed some words into his computer and pulled up Ellie's early draft of the article about Ben, beckoning her to come and look at the screen. She saw that the document was covered in his trademark blue notes in the margins.

'In the meantime,' he said with a grin, 'this should keep you occupied. It's a fantastic effort so far. Go get 'em, Poss!'

*

After a quick check through the website comments – nothing further from the troll, she noticed with relief – Ellie spent a few hours at her desk working on her story on Ben, which was going to run in Wednesday's paper. It felt good to focus on what was on the screen in front of her. Patrick was right: she shouldn't let Roger bully her into making a quick decision.

Maggie and Patrick had gone out and she could hear Jon talking in the front office. When he started laughing, her curiosity got the better of her and she went out to the reception desk to see what was happening.

Jon was talking to two good-looking men, probably in their early forties. He gave her a big smile.

'Hey, Ellie, this is Grant and Howard. They've just moved here to start a business.'

'Hello. Nice to meet you.' Ellie shook hands with each of the men. 'That's great. What kind of business?' Ellie was guessing they were foodies.

'A garden cinema,' said Grant.

'The cinema is indoors. In our house,' Howard explained. 'Grant is a projectionist and a collector of movie memorabilia.'

'They bought the old Robertson house at the edge of town. The heritage one with the ballroom,' said Jon.

'Sounds fabulous,' said Ellie. 'What sort of movies will you show? Will you get the new releases?'

'We will, after they've done Melbourne. As well as some of the classics and foreign films. Grant has a lot of useful contacts in the business,' said Howard.

'They've transformed the ballroom into a theatre with movie memorabilia, seats, stage curtains, the whole thing. Sounds amazing. I'm going over now to take photos,' said Jon.

'We came in to ask about advertising. Didn't expect a write-up,' said Grant, smiling.

'Well, it's a brilliant story. When are you opening?' asked Ellie.

'In three weeks. We'll serve twilight cocktails in the gardens before the movie and nibbles at intermission,' said Howard. 'We'll do special events, too. Kids' birthday party sessions, stuff like that.'

'What a great idea,' Ellie said. 'The town will love it.'

'I hope so,' said Grant. 'We're living upstairs and eventually we'll do something with the other rooms downstairs, like the drawing room and library. The place was pretty rundown when we bought it, and it's taken the builders months to renovate; we've only just been able to move in. We got a small government grant to do it up, which helped.'

'Grant and Howard have saved that place. It was going to be demolished but I remember now that there was an outcry about that. The paper covered it,' Jon said to Ellie. 'Can you look after things here while I'm out?'

'Of course. Congratulations, that's so enterprising of you both. The *Chronicle* will give you as much support as we can. Let me know when I can buy a ticket to the opening night,' said Ellie.

'Count me in too,' said Jon. 'I'll get a group together.'

Ellie went back to her desk as Jon left, following Grant and Howard out to drive to the old mansion. When she sat down her phone pinged and she found a text message from Richard the vet.

*Hi. Results from the meat sample are in and as we suspected a poisonous substance was detected. It's a now discontinued product, a sheep-dip chemical used for the control of external parasites. Across the state there have been plenty of incidents of deliberate poisoning with this product, sadly, including against birds of prey like wedge-tailed eagles as well as wild dogs. Probably there are left-over stashes on many sheep properties. I'll inform the police. Cheers, Richard.*

'Oh no!' Even though she'd been fairly sure the meat had been poisoned, having it confirmed brought the reality of the situation home to Ellie. This really had been a deliberate act against them, and as the poison was a fairly common substance, it could happen again.

When she'd been trolled on the newspaper website, Ellie had had the niggling feeling that spiteful Sophia, after losing her job, might have been behind it. Ellie couldn't be sure if this were the case, but in a way it had made her less anxious, knowing that Sophia was physically so far away in the city. The baiting, though, had most likely been done by someone local and someone aggressive. It made her shiver.

Her ringing phone broke into her thoughts.

'Hey, you, wotcha doing?'

'Hi, Mike. I'm at the paper polishing a story, how're you?'

'Cold. Wet. Tired. A bit over it all. Apart from that, I'm terrific.'

'That doesn't sound like you, what's up?' asked Ellie. In her experience, Mike never sounded downbeat. If he was, he hid it.

'Oh, the usual; difficult client, someone made a miscalculation with the budget, my washing machine broke down and flooded the laundry. Anyway, I thought I could do with hearing a friendly voice. So, what's happening? IT is a small world, Ell, and there are rumours doing the rounds about you.'

'Like what?' Ellie said.

'About going back to work for Roger.'

'Well, he did ring me, but that's very different from agreeing to work for him again,' Ellie said, laughing.

'When did he call?'

'When I was walking on the beach this morning, deciding what to do with the rest of my life.'

Mike paused for a moment, then said, 'I hope you didn't jump at the offer. If you want the job, make him beg you. Play hard to get.'

'I told him I needed time to think about it.' Then she burst out in a rush, 'Mike, I don't know what to do, and that makes me feel crazy. Why wouldn't I jump at the chance to go back there and sell myself for a fat salary? A piece of the action? I feel so . . . torn,' she finished lamely. 'Besides, someone tried to kill Sam.'

'What? Are you sure? What the hell happened?'

She quickly filled him in. 'I'd just worry the whole time if I left Poppy and Sam at the moment.'

'Are the police investigating it?'

'Poppy and the vet reported it, but they said there's not much they can do. Oh, Mike, I just don't want to leave Poppy and Sam right now. It's too hard a decision!' she cried.

'It's not as simple as here or there, is it Ellie?' And when she didn't answer, he went on, 'Storm Harbour is a place of shelter for you, always has been. You adore your grandfather, who treasures this time with you. You have a gentle, fulfilling lifestyle in a stunning place. You cook, walk on the beach with Sam, you're involved with, and passionate about, the community. You have friends, you're contributing to the newspaper, which is the life-blood of the town. So why don't you start your own IT business and work from home out of Storm Harbour? You'd have clients falling over themselves to use your expertise. They don't care where you are so long as you have reliable internet. Come to Melbourne as and when you need.'

'Why don't you work from home?' countered Ellie.

'Don't think I haven't considered it, but there are reasons. My apartment is smaller than yours. I need company, and I can't have a dog. Imagine working out of that sun-filled study you have there,' Mike said.

'I'd be competing with my old boss and his well-established company,' said Ellie slowly.

'Look at all the start-ups that are being run fully

306

online now. You can do anything online from home these days for fun or money. Teach yoga, join a choir, pickle yams or whatever . . . you know it, Ellie. What's holding you back?' said Mike, and she could hear the growing excitement in his voice. 'You have the expertise and your overheads are minimal.'

'Okay, okay.' Ellie laughed. 'I'll give it some thought.'

'Don't fob me off. Promise you'll call me back with six ideas.'

'Okay. All right. I'll think about it. Thanks, Mike,' she said. 'I suppose I could work on some concepts. Maybe I could develop some apps. I could build them myself, although my skills are a bit rusty. Might be better if I call on you and my other development friends to work with me to bring my vision to reality,' Ellie said laughing, but starting to share Mike's excitement.

'Ellie, you have the perfect skill set to start up on your own. You're a senior IT project manager, so consultancy work would be second nature to you.'

'*Was*, Mike! I *was* a project manager,' Ellie explained, then changed the subject, not wanting to think about her old job just as her mood was lifting. 'Here's some good news! Next time you come to Storm Harbour we can go to the movies. Two guys have transformed an old mansion into a cinema that's opening soon. The nearest one has always been a half-hour drive away before now.'

'Really? A whole thirty minutes away. You forget the time you spend travelling just to get across town in Melbourne, Ellie.'

'True. We're spoiled, there's no traffic here.'

'I like the idea of the house cinema, and visiting Storm Harbour again,' said Mike.

'You're welcome anytime,' Ellie said. 'All right, I'll give Roger's offer some thought and send you some IT business ideas just to prove I still can.'

'Looking forward to it. Talk soon.'

Ellie put her phone down and stretched. She'd been sitting at her desk for too long.

The front office doorbell jangled, and she jumped up and walked into the reception to see Meredith standing there.

'Hi, Meredith, how are you? Did you want to see Patrick? He's out at the moment.'

'Actually, I wanted to talk to you. I was wondering if you were free for a coffee. Somewhere quiet.'

Ellie noticed the stress and tiredness in the mayor's face. 'Everyone else is out so we can talk here. I'll make some coffee,' said Ellie as Meredith followed her into the main office.

'So how're things going with you?' asked Meredith.

'Okay, apart from someone trying to poison Sam. They threw a bait into our front garden!'

'No! Is he all right?'

'He didn't get to it, fortunately. But only because I was with him. His roaming has now been curtailed and it's rattled us a bit.'

'It's hard to imagine this isn't connected to everything that's going on at the moment,' said Meredith darkly. 'Like I told you on the phone when we last talked, Ellie, it's getting out of hand.' Meredith sat in the spare chair as Ellie made the coffee. 'Toto, I've a feeling we're not in Kansas anymore,' she quoted.

'Life does seem to be moving into *Wizard of Oz* territory,' agreed Ellie. 'Spooky. I just never thought anything like this would happen in Storm Harbour.'

'Me either. That's why I wanted to talk to you privately.'

Ellie looked at the mayor, who was obviously concerned. 'Are you still being harassed? Have you found out anything more about what might be going on in council?' Ellie didn't want to say anything about what she'd learned in her meeting with Russ. He had asked for anonymity, as any connection between them would put both him and the mayor in a compromised position. She just hoped Meredith wouldn't raise it.

'No,' Meredith replied. 'But it feels like the calm before the storm. I have no evidence that anything will happen, of course, apart from the nasty posts.'

Ellie passed her a mug and sat down. 'How can I help you, Meredith?'

'You know I told you about letters in my mailbox? Well, the notes have become even more aggressive. Threatening.' Meredith took a sip of her coffee.

'Oh no. Have you spoken to the police?'

'I reported it, but without more evidence there's not much they can do. I've taken their advice on security and being cautious, but we don't know who's behind it. Hearing what happened to Sam makes it even more frightening. There's the chance the incidents are connected; perhaps it's even the same person.'

From her handbag she produced a sheet of paper and handed it to Ellie, who quickly read the typed text.

*We know everything about you and we plan to tell it all on social media unless you resign from council immediately.*

Ellie gasped. 'Are you okay living alone? You're welcome to come and stay with us until this stops,' she said.

'That's sweet of you. I'll see how I go.'

'Why would they want you to resign?' asked Ellie.

'I assume it's because they're worried I'm going to make waves or interfere with something they're trying to do with the council.'

'But it's your job to oversee what goes on in council. How could they stop you?' asked Ellie.

'Perhaps they're convinced that if my life story is made public, I'll be forced to stand down. I've never done anything I'm ashamed of, but it mightn't look good if they revealed what they call "*my colourful history as a madam*" in their own way. I mean, I can't be sure who in the town would believe me over them.'

'Whoever is doing this is getting out of control,' Ellie said, concerned for her friend.

'Well, you know my story, Ellie. I've been here twenty-something years, and no one has a clue about my past. They never cared; at least, that is what I assumed.'

Meredith sat back and sighed.

'I can't dispute the facts,' she said. 'I'm sure if it goes public I will be made to sound sleazy, dishonest even. After all, it *was* illegal to run a brothel back in those days. To be clear, I *never* lied or covered anything up when I took office as mayor: you have to declare any criminal convictions, and I didn't have any. But it's possible that damage to my reputation and to that of the position I hold would be untenable,' she added. 'I'd love to know who cares enough to go to so much effort to trace my background.'

'My grandfather thinks that the person who tried to poison Sam will eventually reveal themselves. The same could be true for whoever is threatening you. Like you said, it might even be the same person,' said Ellie.

'I didn't think anyone in council was that devious,' said Meredith, shaking her head.

'So how can we help?' said Ellie.

'Well, sometimes the best defence is a good offence, as they say. I want the *Chronicle* to tell my story. Get it over and done with. Better it comes from me rather than from someone who wasn't there, doesn't know how it was, and may well wish me ill,' Meredith said calmly.

Ellie stared at her. 'You're asking us to print your life story, truthfully, unabridged and straight from the heart?' she said slowly.

Meredith nodded. 'In for a penny, in for a pound. Better that my version, the truth, is out there before any other. And it takes away the ammunition for their threats.'

Ellie smiled broadly. 'Genius. That's so brave of you! But are you sure?' she asked. 'We'll need Patrick in on this.'

Meredith gave a slight smile. 'This'll rock him. He thinks he knows me backwards.'

Ellie was moved once again that Meredith had shared her story to help her at a time of crisis. The trust and friendship the older woman had shown her touched her deeply.

'Before we go any further, do you have any clues at all as to who might want to shut you up?' Ellie asked.

Meredith shook her head. 'I did do some checking. Remember the women who started a beauty salon near Backhill? One of them – Amelia – is still there, so I contacted her. Amelia said someone emailed the salon's business address asking for details about me. She couldn't tell from the address who the sender was, and they didn't give a name in their message, so she ignored the email. Who knows who else this person has contacted, though, and what they've found out.'

'Those days must seem almost like another lifetime, Meredith,' said Ellie quietly. 'Listen, just be absolutely sure you're not being shanghaied or tricked into this. Deciding to go public with your story is pretty brave.'

Meredith flung up an arm dismissively. 'Whatever. Water under the bridge. As I said, I've never done anything I'm ashamed of or regret. Why is it women are so often put in a position where surviving as best they can, for themselves, their family, or whatever reason, means they sometimes have to make a hard choice, or have no choice at all? It seems to me that women nearly always have to carry the load, especially when there are children involved and family to provide for. And that fight for survival, the battle to stay afloat, costs them dearly. That was the story of many of the women I tried to help. That's the story I want to tell.'

Ellie shook her head in admiration. 'Meredith, I'm so proud to know you. Of course we'll help. If you're free, come round for dinner tonight and break the news to Patrick.' She gave a small chuckle. 'I'll make sure his good whisky is on hand.'

'I hope he isn't too shocked and disillusioned when he hears what I have to say,' said Meredith.

'I doubt he will be.' Ellie smiled.

*

As soon as she arrived home, Ellie lit the wood-fired oven and, once it had heated up, cooked a chicken she'd marinated in brine that morning. She knew that it would crisp up in the old stove. Then she made her grandfather's favourite dessert, baked egg custard, using her nana's recipe and cooking it in her brown pottery baking dish.

Meredith, Ellie and Patrick enjoyed a quiet meal sitting

312

around the big kitchen table. After they'd finished eating, Patrick rose and thanked Ellie for the amazing food.

'Now,' he said, turning to Meredith. 'Tell me what all this is about.'

Meredith gave Ellie a wink as she and Patrick headed for Patrick's study with the whisky and two glasses.

Ellie stacked the dishwasher and took Sam for a walk to the top of the hill behind their house, where she looked down from the cliff at the roiling sea foaming around the dark rocks. Outwardly, Meredith was such a strong and sensible woman, Ellie thought. It simply couldn't be allowed to happen that she could be blackmailed and lost to the community.

Walking back home, she had the uncomfortable sense that her idea of Storm Harbour being a safe haven was slipping away. Was someone out there, watching, wanting to harm them? She clipped the leash on Sam, who looked rather puzzled at being fettered instead of snuffling ahead at his own pace as he usually did.

Returning to the warmth of the kitchen, Sam stretched, ready for bed, and looked at Ellie. A burst of laughter erupted from Patrick's study, followed by the sound of Meredith's steady voice.

Ellie smiled and took a glass of wine and a book into the old sitting room and settled by the fire. Sam spread out at her feet and started to snore.

It wasn't till Patrick rested his hand on top of her head that Ellie realised she'd dozed off.

'Hey, Possum, bedtime. Thanks for a beaut dinner.'

'My pleasure. So, what did you think of Meredith's story?' asked Ellie.

'I always knew she was a strong woman, and your nana greatly admired her. We'll help her, Ellie. Whoever's out there won't beat us.' He reached out his foot and gently nudged Sam with his boot. 'Bedtime, mate.' Patrick blew a kiss to Ellie. 'I've locked up, sleep tight.'

*

The days had flown by. Ellie had texted Roger and told him firmly that she would need at least a week to consider their conversation, and been pleased when Roger meekly acquiesced to this request. This gave her time to think about things and see how she felt about it all. She had fun doing her 'homework' for Mike, dreaming up a few IT ideas. And she put the finishing touches on her article about Ben, asking him a some final follow-up questions before he and Sally headed to Horsham for Peter Jensen's fundraising day. They promised to take photos for the paper so Jon could write it up, and Sally was taking her recording gear to cover it for her radio program.

When the article came out – her first published article for *The Storm Harbour Chronicle* – Ellie was surprised by how overwhelmed she felt, seeing it in print. She had worked hard on it, and was proud of what she'd done. She knew that Patrick felt the same: the day it was published, he tied a big red bow around Sam's collar and took a bottle of champagne into the office, leading Jon and Maggie in a toast to 'my granddaughter, journalist extraordinaire'. Ellie wasn't the only one who wiped away a tear or two.

For the rest of the week, though, Patrick had secluded himself in his office with Sam, banging out Meredith's amazing story, telling Ellie, 'It's a fine line to tread between exposé and being objective and balanced. I hope people read it with an open mind and heart. She's such a trouper, and she's been so disarmingly frank. It was a different time and place back then. Context is everything in stories like these.'

'Yes. I think it's so much better that we're telling this story rather than allowing it to appear as a sensational tale on social media. When is the printer set to roll? I'd hate the story to leak before the paper comes out,' said Ellie.

Patrick chuckled. 'You sound just like a newspaper editor!'

Finally, towards the end of the week, Patrick strolled out of his office with Sam at his heels. His glasses were pushed up on his head, his hair was mussed from running his hands through it, and he looked faintly pleased with himself.

'I've just emailed you the piece. See what you think,' he said gruffly. 'I'm going to take a stroll, get some air.' He clipped on Sam's lead and the two of them disappeared out the *Chronicle*'s front door.

Ellie read the story and forwarded it to Maggie.

'A sneak preview for you, Maggie,' she called out across the office. 'Poppy's captured Meredith's story so well. It's balanced and has a real sense of compassion for her and the women she worked with.'

She went and put the kettle on as Maggie read the article.

'Astonishing! I had no idea the mayor had done any of this,' Maggie said, looking up from her computer when Ellie handed her a cup of tea. 'How brave of her to open up like that. And you say Patrick didn't know anything about this before this week?'

'That's right. Meredith had told me, but I don't think anyone else in Storm Harbour knew. Well, that's not right, of course. Somebody does know and they're threatening to expose her.'

'So you knew?' said Maggie, sounding surprised.

Ellie sat down opposite Maggie's desk and nodded. 'I was in a bad way one day. Meredith shared her story with me, to help me, which it did,' she said gently, and Maggie looked at her with concern. 'How do you think the article will go down in town?'

'Tricky. It will depend on where people stand regarding council and community, morals and values. You can't tell me there aren't a lot of people around here with more than a secret or two lurking in their past. So you say she's doing this because she's being threatened?' Maggie asked.

'You got it. Vicious letters dropped in her mailbox and the trolling on social media,' said Ellie. 'I bet there are a lot of women who have been put in a similar position; that is, who've been threatened, overtly or more subtly, by someone who thinks they're more powerful. Which they generally are, because they're a man, or have money and position, or who use standover tactics to get what they want.'

'Even so, this will rock a lot of people,' Maggie said. 'But I think Meredith is smart. Publishing her story with us doesn't leave her enemy anywhere to go. Patrick has written such a fair and even-handed yet heartwarming piece. I didn't think the tough old boy had it in him. Why didn't he ask you to write it?'

'Because it needs wisdom, astuteness as to how far he can go legally, objectivity, fairness and heart – as you said. Everything that makes him a great newspaperman,' said Ellie fondly.

'We'd better ask the printer to increase the print run,' said Maggie. 'Wait till Jon reads this!'

The front door opened and Patrick walked back in, taking off his fedora as he did so.

'Hi, Poppy, the article is great,' Ellie said to him.

'Patrick, well done!' Maggie stood up and gave him a hug.

'What's that for?' He looked sheepish.

'For writing something so sensitive with such grace and heart and truth,' Maggie said.

'Oh, is that all.' He couldn't help a pleased smile. 'Ellie showed it to you?'

'It's going to be the talk of the town. Have you alerted Meredith that it's finished?' asked Maggie.

'Yes. I just went down to her office to give her a heads-up. In case she wanted to leave town! Just kidding. Meredith said she won't vary her routine tomorrow. We are, however, going to meet for a drink at the end of the day . . . just in case.' Patrick put his hat back on and pushed it to the back of his head, then rubbed his hand across his eyes. 'Now I'm going to take Sam home and have a nap. The paper goes to the printer tonight. I want to be there for the morning delivery.'

'Why, Poppy?' asked Ellie.

'I just like to see people's reactions,' said Patrick with a smile. 'Can't help myself. There are always people who get up early, wanting to be the first with the news,' he added. 'Maggie, what say we all meet for breakfast in town, around eight o'clock? Market morning, everyone will be about. Can you let Jon know, if he's available? The more the merrier.'

'To man the barricades, you mean?' Maggie smiled. 'You bet, I'll be there.'

'What's Meredith doing tomorrow morning?' asked Ellie.

'Says she's going for a walk, then to the markets, and after that she's doing some work and then meeting a friend for lunch, as she always does.'

317

'Poppy, what about Sally? Does she know about this? We are supposed to be collaborating. I feel badly not giving her some notice.'

'Radio is live and instantaneous. I'm not saying Sally would do this, but if they knew they could winkle a copy out of the printer and beat us to it, I'm sure her boss would do just that. Besides, she's in Horsham right now and probably having a grand time.'

'Sally is a pretty ambitious journo, as I recall,' said Maggie. 'This is better kept in the tent.'

'Just tell her in the morning that we're doing a story on the mayor. If she wants to follow up after the paper comes out, that's up to her,' said Patrick.

Ellie worked in the office for the rest of the day, not wanting to disturb Patrick, who was resting at home. She set up an alert on her computer to notify her any time the mayor's name came up so she could monitor the troll and take down any nasty attacks. She also worked on a few business concepts to prove to Mike that her brain was still churning out ideas.

In the late afternoon she rang Cassie.

'Hi, Cass. I'm heading home, just thought I might come over for a sundowner. Are you busy with guests or anything?'

'We've just booked in two couples in their motorhomes but I'm free now, so a sundowner would be terrific. Actually, I was going to call you. I have some news, but it can wait till you're here.'

'Okay, great. I'm on my way.' Ellie smiled at the cheerful note in Cassie's voice. She and Steve had been so worried about the rumours going around about the caravan park; it was nice to hear her sounding upbeat.

Cassie waved as Ellie drove in the main entrance.

She was seated at a little table outside their cottage. She'd made a small garden bed for flowers, herbs and vegetables by the side of the house and Ellie noticed that the flowers were blooming.

'Hi, Ellie. How're you going? Would you like a glass of wine? Or do you want to try my fruit cocktail? There's no booze in it, but it tastes fantastic. Lucy and James gave us a bucket of fruit from their orchard.'

'Yum, sure, thanks. It sounds delicious,' Ellie said, sitting down.

Cassie went inside and came back with a tall glass filled with the orange-coloured drink.

'Cheers,' she said, handing it to Ellie.

'So, you said on the phone you had some news?' Ellie said.

Cassie glanced down, then looked over at Ellie with a broad smile on her face.

'I'm pregnant, Ellie. It's early days, but I just feel so happy.'

'Cassie! I'm thrilled for you. Oh, congratulations.' She reached out and squeezed Cassie's hand.

A shadow briefly crossed Cassie's face. 'It will be all right this time, I just have a feeling. Steve does too,' she said. 'But we're not telling many people yet.'

'Your news is safe with me,' said Ellie.

'Don't put anything in the paper!' Cassie winked, and Ellie chuckled.

'Front page, obviously!'

'Introducing her or him to Storm Harbour will be enough to start with.' Cassie laughed. Then her expression changed, and she said, 'We just hope we're not going to be evicted and have to start over somewhere. That would be harder with a baby in tow.'

'We can't let that happen, Cass. The town will fight any development here, believe me.'

'Mmm, let's hope so.'

'I'm so happy for you both,' said Ellie brightly. Then, steering the subject away from the development, she added, 'I wonder how Ben and Sally are going in Horsham.'

'Well, it sounds like they're having a ball. Ben's being feted around town as the hero, which he is. He rang this morning to tell us he's moving out.'

'Of the park?' said Ellie in surprise. 'Is he moving up to Queensland to work on that new job he mentioned?'

'No.' Cassie smiled. 'He doesn't want to make a big noise about it, but he thought he should let us know in case someone wanted his spot. Ben and Sally are moving in together! Looks like it's getting serious. I'm so pleased for Ben. He seemed a bit of a loner when he turned up here.'

'Oh, wow, what fabulous news! I'm so happy for them,' exclaimed Ellie.

They chatted for a while, then Ellie finished her drink. 'That was delicious. I'd better go and see if Patrick has thought about dinner.' She smiled at Cassie as she stood up. 'Don't let all the rumours, innuendo and stuff get you and Steve down. And please thank him again for shadowing me at the lighthouse.'

'I won't pry and ask who you were meeting,' said Cassie. She put down her glass, stood up and reached out to her friend. 'Thank you for sharing our secret.'

'Cassie, it's the very best news.' Ellie hugged her. 'I'm really excited for you both.'

She walked towards her car, then turned back and looked at Cassie, who was taking the glasses inside. Ellie thought about the friendships she had made since moving to Storm Harbour and smiled with delight at the good news about Cassie and Steve's baby.

*

Sam stirred and raised his head. Sleepily Ellie glanced at the window, where a glow of backlit clouds glimmered in the still-dark sky.

'Too early, Sammy. Go back to sleep.'

She listened as Patrick's car headed into the predawn. Off to the printer, she remembered, as she slipped again into sleep.

By the time Ellie and Sam arrived in town, shops were opening, early morning walkers and exercisers were out and about and people were strolling along the main street, looking for coffees.

As Ellie walked up the street with Sam on his leash, she started to notice people carrying or reading the paper. A youthful photo of pretty Meredith was displayed under the banner headline on the front page – *A Mayor for the People*.

Patrick, Jon, Maggie and Roly were sitting at a few small tables they had joined together outside Patrick's favourite café, and some copies of the *Chronicle* lay around on them.

They made room for Ellie, and Sam settled at their feet with a water bowl.

Roly raised his coffee mug and saluted Patrick. 'Award-winning journalism, old chap. And bravo to Mayor Meredith!'

As they all raised their coffee mugs with cries of, 'Here's to our mayor!' and 'Go, Meredith!' several passers-by nodded and lifted a hand in greeting and support, while others frowned and looked disapproving.

It seemed as though every second person walking by wanted to stop and chat and give their opinion on the piece.

'Have you spoken to Meredith today?' asked Ellie.

Everyone looked at Patrick.

'I haven't heard from her this morning,' he said. 'She spoke. I wrote. That's a lot of trust. I hope she approves. She's a very decent person.'

The waitress took Ellie's order while she quietly texted Meredith. *R U OK? Reactions??*

Meredith answered almost immediately. *Mixed reviews so far.*

*Want to join us?*

*Maybe later.*

As if on cue, alerts started to come in on Ellie's phone that Meredith was being mentioned on the newspaper's website. Ellie quickly checked, and deleted any aggressively negative comments.

She looked up and saw Patrick watching her. She raised an eyebrow and said, 'Mixed reviews – that's all Meredith said in her text.'

'Well, I think we've achieved the aim of getting Meredith's story out first, as she told it. People can give us their views about it, and there's no doubt they'll be mixed, but at least they won't be based on potentially untruthful anonymous posts on a computer screen,' he said.

'You're right, but nonetheless this could divide the town,' said Roly.

'Perhaps, but does that matter?' said Maggie. 'People love to gossip and take sides. But when it comes down to who is going to look after their interests, I think people will still side with the mayor. She has only ever done her best for this town. Dedicated her life to it, since becoming mayor. You can't fault her there, no matter what you might think of her history. And who hasn't looked back on their youth and thought, "Oh I shouldn't have done or said that"?' she said firmly.

'Well said, Maggie,' agreed Patrick.

Ellie's phone rang. She stood and walked away to answer it.

'Hey, I just read the paper online!' said Mike. 'What a brilliant piece on Meredith. Please congratulate Patrick for me. It's very balanced, especially knowing what good friends they are.'

'Thanks, Mike. You've read it already; that was good of you.'

'Well, I don't read every issue, but I had to see today's after you hinted that there might be something special in it. How're you?'

'Fine, thanks. Yes, it's a terrific piece. Of course, reaction so far has been a bit split.'

'Yes. I saw some of the comments. How is Meredith taking it?'

'It was her idea to do it, but I'm not sure how she is finding the reaction. It's only early. We'll know more as the day progresses, I guess.'

'You know, what impressed me the most was how she turned an average bakery into a continental café in some dead-end town way back then. She was quite an entrepreneur. She must have some good ideas about spruiking tourism in Storm Harbour.'

'Yes . . . actually you've just reminded me that Poppy told me about her ideas about town development when she was first elected, but which got voted down,' mused Ellie.

'So, what are you doing this morning?' Mike asked.

'We're all having a coffee in town. I sent Meredith a text to check she's all right and we might meet later.'

'Well, let me know what the official reaction to the story is from the council. And by the way, I enjoyed your story on Ben.'

'Pleased to hear it.' Ellie laughed. 'Sounds like you're becoming one of our regular readers, Mike.'

'Ha, maybe. Now, what about you, Ellie? How are you going with the brilliant ideas challenge?' he asked. 'Have any more to send me?'

'I knew you'd ask! Okay then. What about a video-conferencing app that allows, for example, a TV talk show host to have an interactive video audience? Say, two hundred people with lowered volume to allow viewers to hear collective reactions? It must also have good admin or a moderator who can dim or spotlight certain members of the audience and the host. The rules are that the audience must dress appropriately to the theme or mood or setting and have no distracting backgrounds, and also have good internet speed. Then away the show goes. How's that for starters?'

'Boom to Zoom!' Mike laughed.

'Well, I had fun thinking about it,' she said, laughing with him. 'Do you think I'm going to share my real app ideas?' she joked.

'No. Of course not. But I see you're still firing, despite being a newspaper journo on the side. So. Have you called Roger?'

'Not yet. I texted him to say I'd need at least a week to think it over.'

'Good. He won't like that,' said Mike. 'Do you want to meet up with him to find out more about his offer?'

'I'm still not sure. I want to think about it all a bit more,' she replied.

Ellie looked up to see Dave waving at her with a woman she didn't recognise walking beside him.

'Mike, I have to go. I'll call you tomorrow.'

'Sure, Ell. Speak then.'

As she hung up, Dave came over to her. 'Hi, Ellie. Congratulations to you all. Great paper this morning.'

'Thanks, Dave.'

'This is a friend of mine, Lauren.'

'Hi, Lauren,' said Ellie.

'Lauren is visiting from Melbourne. We're on our way to the markets.'

'If you see the mayor you might want to tell her you think the article's terrific,' said Ellie.

'Well, I do think that. I had no idea Mayor Havelock had such an interesting background. It's refreshing, frankly. Okay, see you round.'

'Enjoy Storm Harbour,' said Ellie to Lauren.

'I will, thanks,' said Lauren with a smile.

Ellie walked back and joined the group at the table just as Jon pushed his wheelchair out.

'Thanks for the coffee, boss. I have to take my cousin to a Little Athletics sports meet in half an hour, so I'd better get going.'

'See you, Jon,' said Patrick. 'Check the newsagent on the way, see how the paper is doing, would you please?' he called.

'I'd say it would be running out the proverbial door,' said Roly.

'I think I might do a patrol around town, see what feedback there is,' said Ellie, tugging on Sam's leash. 'In fact, we might check out the markets too.'

There was a stream of people coming in and out of The Shed shopping centre. Immediately Ellie saw a knot of shoppers near one of the stalls. She and Sam walked over to find Meredith surrounded by what seemed to be mostly wellwishers. However, as Ellie stood nearby, listening in to the conversations, one older man with a dour expression said loudly, 'Maybe some people should keep their dirty washing to themselves.'

'Yeah. It's just a stunt,' said the woman with him. 'Elected officials are supposed to be upright citizens –'

'Oh, and what grubby little secrets are you keeping?' snapped another woman, turning on them. 'I could tell a few stories about you, Naomi Rawlings,' she added.

'Hey, hey, ladies. This is our mayor, we elected her, we respect her and the office she holds,' someone else said.

'Yeah, but for how long?' came another voice.

Meredith merely smiled and handed her money to an embarrassed stallholder in exchange for a bag of lemons.

'Listen, folks, Meredith has done a damn good job for us for years. There's a reason for this morning's paper. And that's to tell the truth. I for one think we have the best mayor in Victoria.'

Ellie turned and saw that the person standing up for the mayor was Tommy from the bookshop. She went over and stood with the mayor as Tommy joined them.

'Hey, Ellie,' he said. 'Good on you, Mayor Havelock.' He shook the older woman's hand.

'Thank you for speaking up back there,' Meredith said to Tommy as the three walked away from the stall, Sam following along behind.

'I think you'll find the majority of the town is with you, Mayor. It's the few naysayers who shout the loudest, unfortunately,' said Tommy.

'Well, we'll see,' said Meredith. 'I think I'll head off home now. I need a cup of tea.'

'Where's your car?' said Tommy. 'I'll walk with you, if you like.'

Meredith smiled at him. 'Thank you, Tommy. That's very considerate of you.'

'Not at all,' he said. 'I admire the courage it must have taken for you to tell your story.' He looked around. 'Let's go now, otherwise you might be here a while.'

Ellie noticed that a few people had stopped nearby and were staring at the mayor.

'Good idea, Tommy. See you later, Meredith,' she said as she watched Tommy march beside the mayor. They passed a couple who smiled at them, the man tipping his hat in a salute to Meredith.

Ellie and Sam started a circuit of the stalls. So far so good, she thought. But somewhere there was someone who would not like the fact that Meredith had got in first to tell her story. What would their next move be?

As Ellie and Sam walked back up the street, she received a text from Patrick.

*Going for lunch with Roly and Nino down at the river. See you later, sweet potata!*

Ellie smiled. Patrick sounded a bit pleased with himself. And so he should, she thought.

Putting her phone away and setting off again, Ellie spotted the tall figure of Heather chatting to someone up ahead. Heather saw Ellie coming and lifted an arm to wave.

'Hello, hello, Ellie. You been to the markets?'

'Yes I have. How are you? How is Kathryn?' asked Ellie.

'All good, thank you, dear. Did you hear about Seamus O'Neill? His travel agent has just let the O'Neills know that there's a hurricane in the Caribbean, and his

327

small cruise ship has been forced to take shelter. Evidently there's no communication in the Caribbean at present. Seamus might not get back in time for Kathryn's birthday party. Isn't that right?' She turned to the woman beside her, who nodded.

'Have you two met?' Heather continued. 'Cynthia, this is Ellie, Patrick Addison's granddaughter from the newspaper. Ellie, this is Cynthia O'Neill. Ronan's wife,' she added.

Ellie turned and smiled at Heather's companion, then froze as she suddenly realised where she'd seen this woman before. Heather was talking about the hurricane again as Ellie, careful to keep her expression neutral, politely excused herself and pulled Sam away.

She hurried up the street, trying to work out what was going on. Why would Cynthia O'Neill sit in her car watching Susan McLean's house in Pine Street at odd times of the day?

# 10

THE RELEASE OF THE controversial issue of the *Chronicle* was generating great interest.

An impromptu gathering arranged by Patrick on Saturday afternoon turned into an early evening barbecue, with Meredith the centre of attention among good friends. While no one asked her any personal questions, she did regale them with some very funny stories of the 'old' days. Patrick also had great yarns to tell, and when Roly suggested Patrick should write his memoirs, everyone agreed.

The only shadow over the occasion, which nobody mentioned but which was felt by all, was the spike in nasty posts on social media. Twitter had been running hot with a lot of aggressive and unpleasant tweets about

Meredith being 'unsuitable' as a mayor. Ellie checked the paper's website constantly and took down the worst of the comments there as quickly as they appeared.

Before the guests started to leave, James and Lucy brought out a big basket of fruit and other produce from their farm to share around.

'Lucy is bottling preserves and pickles like a fiend while everything is in season,' said James. 'The guests always ask to take some away with them, so we might have to set up a small shop in the café next.'

'I'm still trying to get Meredith's secret bread recipe for the café, too,' said Lucy. 'We could sell some loaves. Also, we have two friends who want to buy our alpaca wool to have it made into knitwear. Their plan is to commission people in the local area to knit it up. Here, I brought you a sample,' she added, handing Ellie a soft ruby-red jumper. But when Ellie unfolded it, she did a double take.

'It's for Sam!' James laughed. 'For the winter. He's getting on a bit, isn't he?'

'Oh, it's gorgeous! Hey, Sammy, come and try on your new jumper!' When the old dog trotted up to her, Ellie slid the garment over his head and did up the buttons on the side. 'It's a perfect fit. Thank you so much, Lucy.'

Sam wagged his tail, looking pleased and probably hoping all the attention meant he'd get a treat of some kind.

'Our neighbour knitted it. She's in her eighties but she has amazing energy. She's now running knitting, crochet and needlepoint classes for the young people in the area who never learned how from their grannies,' said Lucy.

'Something else to put in your shop,' said Ellie. She looked at Cassie. 'Do you knit?'

'I did once,' Cassie replied. 'I might go and join in, I'd love to get into it again.' The two women exchanged a smile, both thinking of baby clothes.

*

On Monday morning at breakfast, Patrick looked weary.

'Can't party like I used to, I reckon.'

'Take the morning off and relax. You've earned it, Poppy. Sit in the sun on the verandah where it's sheltered from the wind.'

'Not a bad idea. What are your plans for the day?'

Ellie groaned. 'Well, first I have to ring Roger.'

Patrick put down his mug of tea and looked at his granddaughter. 'What have you decided?'

'It's a "no" from me.'

'All right,' said Patrick neutrally. 'And what next?'

'I'm not sure. I know what I *don't* want. I haven't thought past that. If it's all right with you, Poppy, I'd like to stay here till I figure things out. Also, I want to give up my flat. It's sitting there empty but still costing me money. The lease runs out soon and I don't think I'll renew it.'

Patrick took a sip of tea. 'Of course, love. You're welcome to stay forever if you like,' he said casually, but Ellie could see he was pleased.

'I'll go into the office this morning and see what's going on,' said Ellie. 'What were you thinking for the front page on Wednesday?'

'Not sure. Let's have one more crack at trying to get corroboration from council about details for any proposal for the caravan park site. Then, of course, the next paper will be all about Kathryn O'Neill and her big birthday bash.'

At the mention of Kathryn O'Neill, Ellie's thoughts

jumped unbidden to Cynthia O'Neill, hunched in the seat of her car outside Susan's house, and then, inevitably, to Ronan. Ellie shuddered: did every O'Neill have some sort of hidden story? Resolutely, she pushed the thoughts away, turning instead to Patrick with a bright smile.

'I don't think "bash" is the appropriate word! Every minute of the evening will be stage-managed by Susan, no doubt. And don't forget, we're invited,' Ellie said.

'Oh, gawd. Do I want to go?' mused Patrick.

'Yes, you do. You've known Kathryn for years and years. Plus, you're my date.' Ellie paused and cocked her head. 'Who's that on the radio?'

She stood and turned up the volume to hear the now familiar whine of Councillor Lowe.

'Sourpuss himself, what's he on about now?' muttered Patrick.

Ellie started buttering her toast, then banged the knife on the table.

'Listen to that horrible rant! How dare he say such things about the mayor. So snide!'

'. . . *it is more than embarrassing. Her disgraceful revelations will make us a laughing-stock. Anything the mayor says or does from here on will be dismissed as being of no value, coming from such a person . . .*'

'He'd better be careful. He's sliding a bit close to maligning her publicly. He can't go about accusing her of deceiving council about her history,' exclaimed Patrick. 'I bet he doesn't have a lilywhite background himself. You know what they say, people who live in glass houses . . .'

'Listen, the radio announcer is agreeing with him! Sally would never do that,' said Ellie.

Ellie's phone rang.

'Are you listening to that scumbag on the radio?' stormed Tommy.

'Yes. Hang on, I want to hear the rest – I'll call you back, Tommy.'

Hanging up the phone, Ellie listened in growing horror as the interview went on.

'Bloody outrageous jerk,' muttered Patrick when the segment ended and the news came on.

Ellie phoned Tommy back.

'Hi, Ellie. Can you believe it? That slimy Lowe fellow is an idiot. He came very close to slandering Meredith,' said Tommy.

'Poppy was just saying the same thing; he's fuming.'

'We have to stop the rot. The social media comments are bad enough, but that interview was the pits.' Tommy stopped, as if taking in a deep breath, then said, 'I have a plan that will shake up council. This is not the type of town where people protest and march angrily in the streets, but I really feel we need to do something.'

'Er, just what did you have in mind, Tommy?' asked Ellie cautiously.

'A friendly, supportive "Rally for the Mayor". To show her that many people here think she's doing a great job. And that we think she's a tremendously strong and honest woman.'

'Well, that sounds good, I think. I've never heard of a rally in support of a politician before,' Ellie said, laughing. 'Let me talk to my grandfather.'

'Of course, of course. But we have to get moving. Strike while Twitter is hot and the interest high. Come over to the bookshop for a chat. It'll be action HQ.'

When Ellie told Patrick about the plan, he shrugged.

'Tommy's heart is in the right place. He's a bit of an

odd bod in some ways, though. He's been through some terrible sadness. Lost the love of his life, actually. Then he came into a big inheritance from a long-lost relative who turned out to have made millions digging holes in the ranges in remote Western Australia.'

Patrick shook his head and went on.

'Tommy's very embarrassed by the way the money was made, so he tries to put it to good use and supports good causes when he can. He prefers to keep a low profile most of the time, which is a loss to the town as he's a very bright bloke. I'm pleased that he sees you as a friend.'

'Ah, that explains a few things,' said Ellie, nodding slowly. 'I like the way he's passionate about causes, although this idea about a rally for the mayor seems a bit strange. I hope it doesn't just make Meredith feel embarrassed.'

'Actually, this sort of thing isn't so unusual around here,' said Patrick. 'There was a get-together a few months ago to raise awareness of mental health issues among rural communities. We're not into noisy, flashy protests so much, but we have always rallied together when the need arises. I'm sure Meredith will see that Tommy has the best intentions,' Patrick continued. 'Plus, Tommy has always been a big supporter of the paper. In fact, he supports a lot of things in town that no one knows about. And I'm sure that's the way he wants to keep it.'

'Really? When I first met him, I flippantly asked him if he'd won the lottery and he said, "something like that". I guessed then that he wouldn't say anything more about it.' Ellie stood up and took their breakfast plates to the sink. 'Even if he's embarrassed about the way his money was made, why does he bury himself away in the book-shop and do good deeds in secret?' she asked.

Patrick shook his head. 'It's his choice and I've never asked. So his offer to come out publicly like this for Meredith is a big deal. We have to support him.'

'You never know about people really, do you?' said Ellie thoughtfully. 'I bet everyone in this town has a story of one kind or another.'

'Probably. But the *Chronicle* isn't going to tell 'em all,' Patrick said, smiling.

Ellie picked her phone up from the table. 'Okay. I'm going to call Roger.'

'Be strong but polite, sweetie. I'll be honest: I'm pleased you're not going back there. Now, I'm going to sit in the sun for a bit and do the crossword. C'mon, Sam, you can help me.'

Ellie smiled as she watched Patrick and Sam head outside. Then she found Roger's number in her phone and listened to it ring, feeling a little nervous.

'Hello, Roger. This is Ellie Conlan.'

'Hi, Ellie, I've been waiting to hear from you. I realise you must be busy down there on the coast.'

Ellie gritted her teeth at the slight hint of sarcasm in his tone. 'Depends how you define "busy". I'm certainly treasuring this special time with my grandfather.'

'Very good of you to spend time with the oldies. Is he being cared for in a home, or managing himself?' Without waiting for an answer – because, as Ellie knew, he wasn't interested in her grandfather or her personal issues – he continued, 'Of course, one has to move on in life. So, what are your plans?'

Ellie had framed a few phrases to lead into her decision, but Roger was being so blunt she figured she wouldn't waste time, either. As he was fond of remarking, unoriginally, 'Time is money', so she got to the point.

'Well, Roger, I have decided to say thanks, but no thanks, to your kind offer.'

There was a pause on the other end of the line. 'I'm not being kind. I respect your talent. You can make a huge contribution to the company.'

'Thank you. It's nothing to do with any personal grudges or animosity either,' she added quickly. 'But I'm saying no to life in Melbourne for now. No to the pressure and hassles of a city. I'm using this chance to explore some creative ideas I've never had the time to focus on before. But thank you for contacting me and making me the offer.'

'Well, I must say I'm surprised you'd opt out of the fast lane. Would an incentive package of more money and a piece of the action help persuade you? A seat on the board?'

Ellie blinked. This was quite a concession, a major offer. Shares, no less. In the moment she paused to take this in, Roger pushed further.

'You can understand I'd need your answer without any protracted negotiations. You know how this industry works.'

'I do, indeed, Roger.' She took a breath. She found that the answer was clear in her mind. 'Thank you again, but I think I'll stick with my decision.'

'I see.' She could tell he was surprised. It was a generous offer, and one that many would proverbially kill for. 'Well, there's probably nothing more to say, then. Best of luck down there, Ellie.'

'Thank you, Roger. Goodbye.'

Ellie hung up and looked at her phone with a wry smile. 'And good luck to you too, Roger,' she said aloud.

Ellie went out onto the verandah to find Patrick, who glanced up at her with a questioning look.

She shrugged. 'It went just as I expected. And I feel great.'

She leaned down and patted Sam, who looked up at her lovingly, tilting his head, tongue lolling.

'You know what, Sam? That was really easy. Now it's onwards and upwards.'

'No regrets?' asked Patrick.

'Nope. Actually, I feel like a weight has lifted off my shoulders.' She grinned, and Patrick chuckled.

'So, do any new opportunities beckon?'

'You know what, Poppy? I feel in control of my life and destiny for the first time in ages and ages,' said Ellie. 'For better or worse.'

'Excellent.' Patrick smiled. 'I'm so glad, Ellie.'

'Okay, I'm off to work,' she said. 'Enjoy your morning off, Poppy.'

'Go get 'em,' said Patrick, and turned back to his crossword as Ellie went inside to gather her things and head down to the *Chronicle* office.

'Patrick won't be in till later,' she said to Maggie and Jon as she walked into the main room. 'A weekend of celebrating took it out of him.'

'I can imagine, but it was lots of fun,' said Maggie. 'Did you hear that ratbag Councillor Lowe on the radio this morning?'

'I thought he was making it all too personal, the way he was bagging Meredith,' said Jon.

'She might say something privately in council about it,' said Maggie. 'Have you heard from her today?' she asked Ellie.

'Not yet. There weren't so many bad posts on the website when I checked this morning. I suspect now that people have actually sat down and read the article they might see her worth.'

'I think the majority of people in town would admit that she's been a darn good mayor,' said Maggie.

'Tommy from the bookshop says he's organising a "Rally for the Mayor". He was pretty outraged at Lowe's comments,' said Ellie.

Jon laughed. 'Great idea!' he said. 'Crazy, but good.'

'What do you know about Tommy?' Ellie asked them both.

'I believe he never got over losing his young wife. She was killed by a hit-and-run driver,' said Maggie. 'You know the lookout at the top of the hill coming into town? Well, Tommy had the lookout built, with support from the roads people and council. He paid for it and worked with the project manager. It's a scenic spot with a seat that overlooks the town. I sometimes see him sitting up there, just gazing out to sea.'

'I never knew that about the lookout. It's really sad in a way,' said Jon. 'But you know, Tommy's done lots of really wonderful things for this town. The paper's covered a few of them – the ones we hear about, anyway. He never asks for any recognition and I reckon he tries to fly under the radar, even from us.'

'What sort of things?' asked Ellie.

'He donated money for a residential home for disadvantaged children,' Maggie chimed in. 'It's attached to a school but it's not a traditional boarding school. He helped find some amazing woman to run it and set up a board to oversee it. Although he doesn't go there often, I've heard he keeps tabs on it. He told me all about it once when I was in his shop. I'm sure he'll talk about it if you ask privately. Not for the paper or anything.'

'I understand,' said Ellie.

'You know, Ellie,' Jon said quietly, 'Tommy insisted on

338

paying for my adaptive car, with the hand controls, swivel seat and hoist and so on. It's given me so much freedom.'

Ellie shook her head in admiration. 'I knew there was a reason I liked Tommy. And now I understand why he seems like such a loner. He still has a broken heart,' she said. 'In some ways I'm surprised he still lives in Storm Harbour. You might think it holds too many sad memories for him.'

'Maybe,' said Maggie. 'Remember, though, Storm Harbour's a place where people look out for each other. We want the place we live, where we have our roots, to be that sort of community.'

'We're a tribe,' said Jon with a grin.

Ellie was thoughtful for a moment. 'And like all families, we have our tiffs and arguments, but hopefully we can resolve them, too. So let's get on with sorting out the ruckus over the mayor then.'

*

Tommy and his friends had hit the phones. That afternoon a small group gathered outside The Shed with hastily painted signs on boards and cardboard. Another group was in the bookstore, listening to Tommy who was organising everyone. He spotted Ellie and Jon and waved.

'Aha, the first of the media to arrive!'

'Who else is coming?' asked Ellie as Jon took out his camera.

'Whoever feels moved to do so, to show support for a very fine mayor. Ah, here comes esteemed Queen's Counsel Bolton.'

Ellie turned to see Roly rocking up in a jacket and tie, looking formal and professional.

'So, what is the order of the day?' asked Roly.

Tommy pointed to a propped-up chalkboard. 'The route is marked here, through town, with a final assembly point outside the council chambers, where,' he pointed to a huge bouquet of flowers, 'they will be presented to the mayor. She has been notified to appear to accept them, which she agreed to – after some persuasion,' said Tommy. Then added, 'This is a rally of support *for* our mayor. It is *not* a protest march.'

'Who's going to present the flowers?' asked Ellie. 'You should, Tommy.'

'Yes, hear, hear,' came shouts from the people gathered.

Tommy grinned and nodded.

They set off in a ragtag group, chattering and laughing. The march along the footpath swelled as passers-by joined them. Talking to people along the way, Ellie discovered that some had come along especially, while others had simply joined in when they'd read the signs.

As they headed down the main street, people came out of shops and cafés to applaud and call out, 'Good on Meredith!' Many snapped photos on phones.

They stopped outside the council chambers, and a spontaneous cheer went up as well as a chorus of 'Good on Meredith'.

Ellie was surprised to see Dave in the crowd with his friend Lauren beside him. In fact, Ellie noticed there were a lot of businesspeople on the footpath as well as Tommy's friends who had set off from his bookshop. There was a jolly feeling in the group, as if it were a picnic outing for some club.

Finally, a faintly embarrassed but smiling Meredith appeared on the front steps.

Tommy handed her the flowers, shouting to the crowd, 'A small token of the town's esteem for you, Mayor.

We appreciate all you have done, are doing, and will do for Storm Harbour.' Tommy smiled at Meredith then looked back at the crowd, which burst into cheers and applause.

'Sometimes we take our elected officials and all who work for this town for granted, or we only seek them out when we have a problem. This is an opportunity to say thank you to everyone in council who works in the back rooms, out in the paddocks and streets and on the river – you name it. We know you're there for us when we need you, led by our able mayor. So on behalf of the town, thank you.'

Meredith stepped forward. 'And I want to share this tribute with all our hardworking council staff and workers, community volunteers, and every person who loves Storm Harbour,' she said in a loud, firm voice. 'Thank you!'

As the cheers died down and the crowd began to chat among themselves, the mayor turned to Tommy and said, 'Thank you, that was a lovely gesture. Would you mind if I sent the flowers over to St Bridget's to share with the old folk?'

'Wonderful idea.'

Cradling the flowers, Meredith gave a wave and called 'Thank you' once more, then headed back inside.

Tommy looked over at Jon and raised his eyebrows. Jon gave him a thumbs-up. Ellie knew he had a stack of terrific photos.

The crowd began to break into small groups, pausing to talk and mill about before wandering back down the street.

'That went well,' said Patrick, coming over to join them.

'Where are the naysayers?' Roly said.

'Vanquished,' replied Tommy. 'It was a modest event, a nice stroll in the sunshine. But I feel it made its point.'

'I think Meredith was hugely touched. It wasn't aggressive and didn't ruffle feathers,' agreed Ellie.

Tommy said his goodbyes and the others headed back to the *Chronicle* office.

'So where to now?' asked Jon. 'Are we writing up the "Rally for the Mayor"? I have some great shots.'

'Yes, but it has to be in the context of *why* there was a rally,' said Patrick. 'Perhaps we can include some quotes from Councillor Lowe's radio interview, and maybe extracts from the story we published on Meredith.'

'And we still have to print a story about the threat to the caravan park,' said Ellie.

'Alleged threat,' said Patrick. 'The problem is that we're still low on facts, which always rings alarm bells with me. We have no corroboration of any plans or details. It's risky to allude to things without corroboration.'

'I could try ringing that architect I met, and the surveyor Jon talked to who was nosing around the site, making notes,' said Ellie.

'I did that already,' said Jon. 'Got completely stone-walled. May as well have questioned my back fence.'

'Let's start with what we already know, then,' said Patrick.

'Right,' agreed Jon. 'Ellie, didn't your source say it all has something to do with the lease arrangement with the owners, the O'Neills?'

'That's right,' Ellie said, and looked up at her grand-father, who was pacing the room.

'Which is Seamus O'Neill, whom they can't reach as he's stuck in the aftermath of a hurricane somewhere in the Caribbean,' said Patrick. 'I've been trying to contact him as well but it's terrible over there, apparently. Fallen trees on the runways have meant the airports are closed and no one can get in or out by air.'

'I wonder if he'll make it back for Kathryn's party,' said Ellie. 'It's only four days away. His homecoming might change things. For starters he can deal with the letter from the council, which might make all the difference.'

'Why don't you give your contact from the council a call and see if he has anything more?' suggested Jon. 'Sometimes these people know stuff without knowing it or are just too cautious to follow up.'

'Okay. I'll try him again,' said Ellie, but she didn't hold out much hope, and said so. 'He was very jumpy. He's worried about losing his job if he's outed as a whistle-blower, which is fair enough.'

'Speaking of the O'Neills, Ellie's feature on Kathryn will run before her birthday, won't it?' said Maggie. 'It's such a good profile, Ellie,' she added. 'As was the one on Ben.'

'Of course it is,' said Patrick. 'The timing is perfect. We need photos of the finished portrait to go with it. Unless Susan the guard dog puts the kibosh on it,' he added.

'The portrait's supposed to be unveiled at the birthday party,' said Maggie. 'Apparently it's being kept under lock and key, metaphorically speaking at least, until then. I think no one is allowed to see it, let alone photograph it.'

'Well, we'll promise to keep the pictures confidential until the paper is printed and delivered on Friday,' said Patrick. 'We can only ask.'

'I wouldn't hold your breath,' said Ellie. 'Heather said the unveiling of the portrait was to be a highlight of the birthday party, and I can't imagine Susan letting anything jeopardise her precious plans. But it's up to Kathryn and Heather.'

'Let's see what we can do. Now, I'm off to the gym,' Patrick said, flexing his biceps and laughing.

Ellie sat down at her desk, resting her feet against Sam who had made himself comfortable at the *Chronicle* with a bed in Patrick's office and another under Ellie's desk. He had quickly learned that Maggie was a soft touch for a small treat from the kitchenette.

Before plunging back into work, Ellie took her phone out of her bag, dialled the familiar number and leaned back in her chair, phone to her ear.

'Hi,' she said.

'Hi, Ell, how are you?' Mike's voice was full of warmth.

'Better than I've felt in ages. I've done the deed. I told Roger no thanks.'

'Well done! Did he dangle bait in front of you?'

'He certainly did. A piece of the action, too.' She filled Mike in on the details.

'Wow, I bet he was pissed off. Not many people in your position would knock him back. I'm proud of you.' Mike paused. 'And you feel good about it?' he asked tentatively.

'Yes, surprisingly. Or maybe not so surprisingly, given how my life has changed since coming to Storm Harbour. I know Julie and others will think I'm mad, but my parents will be supportive. I've decided to give up my flat while I work out what to do. I'll stay here for now. I want to help Poppy through this mysterious drama with the caravan park.'

'Oh yes, what's the latest?'

'Wish we knew. It could be something or nothing. If it's something, it's the best-kept secret in town.'

'And what are your long-term plans? Well, after you sort out Storm Harbour's problems?'

She laughed. 'I honestly don't know, Mike. But for the first time in a long, long time, I'm feeling okay about my future. Roger did me a favour. It felt pretty sweet knocking him back, I have to say.'

'I bet,' Mike said with a laugh.

'Anyhow, that's enough about me – what are you up to?'

'Well, actually, I'm coming down your way again, to do some research. I've made enquiries about that row of warehouse buildings along the river there.'

'The ones we looked at, the old hall and School of Arts building? Do you want to put them in your app?'

'Sort of. I have a few ideas. I rang Lucy and I've booked to stay with her and James again. I can't come till Saturday, but let's get together then, if you're free? I'd love to see Patrick and that gang of his again too.'

'That's wonderful! Of course. Poppy and I are going to Kathryn O'Neill's ninety-fifth birthday event out at Craigmore on Friday night, but I'm free over the weekend.'

'Great. Maybe we could go fishing. I'd kind of like to play tourist,' said Mike. 'I'm a bit over the city at the moment; too many meetings.'

'I can understand that,' said Ellie. 'I'll see you on Saturday, then.'

After she'd hung up, Ellie pulled out the scrap of paper with Russ's phone number on it. Deciding to stretch her legs while she talked to him, she nodded a goodbye to the others and stepped out the front door, hitting 'call' as she did so.

'This is Ellie Conlan, Russ. Can you talk for a moment?'

'Well, yes, for once.' He gave a nervous laugh. 'I'm outside on my own.'

'Good to hear,' Ellie said, wondering how best to start. 'I assume you still haven't heard from Seamus O'Neill?'

'Not yet,' replied Russ. 'Though there's still time. Just.'

'You mean time to renew the lease?' Ellie confirmed.

'That's right. Remember I told you that if Seamus doesn't respond to the renewal letter and renew the lease before it expires, the land becomes the property of the council?'

'I remember,' Ellie said. 'You said if that happens, council can do what they want with it.'

'Quite. And, given the rumours swirling around, one might take a pretty good guess at what they'd like to do.'

'So you think someone has plans in the wings, ready to submit an application to develop the caravan park?'

'Seems a logical move to me. The timing couldn't be worse for Mr O'Neill to still be away. But, like I said, there's still just enough time.'

Ellie saw her chance. 'So you haven't heard the news?'

'What news?' asked Russ.

'Apparently Seamus O'Neill's cruise has been affected by a severe storm – a hurricane, actually. So no one knows how or when he'll get back. He'll probably miss his mother's birthday party this weekend.'

'Oh! I hadn't heard. Well, that is a shame.' Russ sounded genuinely surprised. 'So . . . Seamus could be away for quite a while yet?'

'That's right, which from the sounds of things might make the timing of the lease renewal very tricky. When *does* the lease expire, exactly?' she asked.

There was a long silence. Ellie began to think Russ wasn't going to answer, then he cleared his throat.

'This is confidential information, of course. The lease expires on Tuesday next week.'

'What?' Ellie gasped, unable to keep the surprise out of her voice. 'So soon!'

'I truly thought Seamus would make it back in time,' Russ said apologetically. 'As I said, I've sent out several renewal letters for the lease over the past few months. He should have received at least one of them before he left. But if it's not signed by next Tuesday's deadline, the land becomes the property of the council.'

'Are you sure there's no way of reaching him?'

'I have tried all the avenues that were available to me. Also, there's a limit on how far the council staff can and will go to track him down,' Russ said.

'I understand,' Ellie said, although she wished Russ had told her about this before now. 'Is there anything else you can tell me? Or any documentation you could show me?' She knew how much she was asking of Russ but she figured it was worth a shot.

'I wish there was more I could do for you,' Russ said. 'But I can't risk losing my job.'

'Of course,' Ellie said. 'We're so grateful for your help so far.'

Thanking Russ, Ellie finished the call. Wanting a moment to think, and finding herself outside Patrick's favourite café, she decided she'd have a coffee before heading back to the office and telling them Russ's news. She was about to order when she heard someone call her name.

'Hey, Ellie!'

It was Dave.

'Hi, Dave.' She turned towards him as he hurried over.

'Just the person I want to see. Got a minute?'

'Sure, I was just about to order a coffee.'

'Mind if I join you?'

They sat at an outdoor table and Dave ordered two slices of cheesecake. 'You have to have a piece, it's delicious.'

They chatted amiably and then Dave leaned back.

'Now, the reason I wanted to see you is about the paper,' said Dave.

'What about it?' asked Ellie.

'Don't go on the defensive, I think everything the *Chronicle* does is terrific. Especially that story about the mayor. Go Meredith,' he said.

'Yes. I saw you earlier at the rally. Good on Tommy for getting it organised so quickly. It might really turn things around,' said Ellie.

'Common sense will hopefully prevail. People should actually read the article before jumping to conclusions.' Dave sipped his coffee. 'Now, I have a client, a small group actually, who have an idea that I think is smart and important. It's more than an idea. It's to do with a development –'

'No! Not the caravan park!' Ellie dropped her cup in its saucer with a clatter.

Dave held up his hand. 'No. Not at all. What's going on at the caravan park? I thought that talk was just gossip?'

'So you don't know of a development at the river where the caravan park is?' asked Ellie.

'Only what I've heard from a few tradies at the pub.' He frowned. 'Some talk about townhouses. But I swear this new project is nothing like that.'

'Okay, what can you tell me?' Ellie asked.

'I can show you all the plans and details if you want. The group want to know if the *Chronicle* will help them advance this idea, if you believe in it in the way they do, and I do,' he said, smiling. 'They'll pay for advertising, too, but I know you'll want to get across the ethics and concept first.'

'And that is?'

'I call it "Ageing in the 'Hood",' said Dave. 'It's a new model to replace the outmoded retirement villages. It's where families, singles, retirees – anyone, really – all live in a specifically designed mini-suburb or community that is created for integrated living for all ages. Young parents with kids would live next door to a couple of retirees, near single working people, next to active stay-at-homes . . . you know, all ages, all combinations of specifically designed homes and low-rise two- or four-unit blocks set amid gardens and a park. They'll all be within walking distance of a convenience store, a café, a chemist, a hairdresser and a play centre, with ample accessible parking and a local bus service that runs into the main town or to sports complexes and the like. A neighbour-hood where everybody looks out for each other. As it should be.'

'It sounds like a great idea in theory . . . but where would such a place be built? There's no room for some-thing like that in Storm Harbour, is there?' said Ellie.

'There's a chunk of land designated to be opened up for development between Storm Harbour and Malonby – have you been there? – fifty minutes' drive away. Not on the coast but inland a bit. They want to develop a satellite community from the ground up; not by completely clearing the land, but by designing homes and streets among the trees and around a small tributary that runs from the hills down to the river. Natural shade, well-maintained gardens and level paths in a clean, environmentally friendly and safe community with public green spaces. I could go on; they've thought of everything. I'd live there,' he said, then took a bite of cheesecake.

'Is it stuck in the middle of nowhere, though?' asked Ellie.

'Whenever you want, we can drive out there, Patrick too if he likes. It's just off the main highway, going around hills so you hear nothing of the traffic and see nothing but greenery and birds. Listen, if development is coming to the regional areas, then let's get in first and make it the kind of space we'd all like.'

'Hmm, well, it sounds interesting. Better than townhouses blocking everyone's view and taking away our caravan park. But we'll have to see the detail. I'll talk to Patrick about it. The mayor would like to see it too, I'm sure.'

'She's already seen it, and she loves the idea. She told me council needs to get in and plan the future of the whole area, not just piecemeal pop-up developments that look plonked down and not sensitively integrated like this plan is,' Dave said. 'I'll send you everything. They haven't spent a fortune on fancy presentations and stuff. But look at the plans and walk around out there, as that'll give you a feel for the place.'

Ellie nodded slowly. 'I can't speak for my grandfather, but if we think it's a smart strategic plan, the paper will get behind it. Not just for the advertising dollar but because it's a good idea. That's how the *Chronicle* works. Ethics first,' said Ellie. 'We'd have to be open to all sides of the debate about it as well, of course.'

'Okay, boss,' said Dave. 'I wouldn't expect less. Another coffee?'

'Thanks, but no, I have a bit to do. That cheesecake was amazing, though!'

Dave relaxed back in his seat, hands behind his head. 'So when are you heading back to the city?'

'Not for a bit. I'm helping Patrick and sorting through a few things. Suddenly the big city doesn't appeal so much,' Ellie sighed. 'Used to be you'd go where the job is. Instead I intend to create my own work if I can. Be my own boss.' She looked at him, and thought how their relationship had found its rightful place, as a strong friendship. 'What are your plans?' she added. 'Do they give you much notice about where you'll be moving on to?'

'Well, actually, I've asked for an extension here. Thought I might buy a place. That's always a good investment.'

Ellie looked surprised. 'Just an investment? Will you stay here?'

'I've lived and worked in a lot of different places. This place has a really strong community spirit and I like the lifestyle. Maybe I'll stay here for a while.' He smiled. 'You met Lauren, she's an old friend from uni, a single mum with a little girl. She's interested in moving here too. We might even buy a boat of our own.'

'That's really good news, Dave,' Ellie smiled back at him. 'I'd better head back. I'll talk to my grandfather and call you. See ya.'

\*

Back at the *Chronicle* Ellie found Jon getting ready to go out on a story.

'Patrick is still at the gym and Maggie's gone to meet

351

with the printer,' said Jon. 'Patrick asked if you could check with Heather about taking a photo of the portrait, to go with your article. Reckons she's more likely to say yes to you than to me, and he's probably right.'

'Mmm, wish me luck with that! Susan said no one could see it before the unveiling event just before the party,' said Ellie.

Jon rolled his eyes. If the painting is already out at Craigmore, forget it. But if it's still in the artist's studio, it's worth asking. It'll make it so much easier for us if we can lay out the space for the story with the photo.'

'Okay, I'll ask,' said Ellie. Then she had a thought. 'If I see Kathryn when I view the portrait, do you think I should tell her about the lease?' Quickly, she filled Jon in on her conversation with Russ. 'Is there someone else in the family who might know what's going on or who could sign the lease, do you think?' she asked.

'Ronan, maybe?' Jon suggested, then frowned. 'But Seamus is head of the family and I don't think he would ever allow someone to make decisions without his input. I can't believe he's let all this go till the last minute. It's not like him.'

'He was expecting to be home a week or so ago, I suppose,' said Ellie. 'But Kathryn didn't seem to know anything about all this last time I saw her. Should I tell her now?'

Jon considered. 'I'm not sure that's our place, and it could get your source in hot water. Look, I'll fill Patrick in while you speak with Heather. But he didn't think we should say anything to Kathryn that we couldn't corroborate, and nothing has really changed, unfortunately.'

'All right,' Ellie said. 'I'll give Heather a ring.'

*

'Well, hello, Ellie,' said Heather, opening her door on Thursday afternoon. 'You've arrived just in time to photograph Kathryn and me staring at a sheet covering the painting. I don't think either of us is brave enough to pull it off.' She laughed.

'Oh really? Have you just finished it?'

'It took a week to dry. Kathryn came into town to have her hair done for the party, and now we're having afternoon tea. Susan isn't coming back to pick her up for an hour or so, so we have time for a cuppa together. Please join us.'

'Wonderful, thank you, Heather,' said Ellie, handing her a white cake box she'd picked up at the bakery in town on her way over. Jon's camera, which she'd borrowed, was hanging from her shoulder.

When Heather ushered her through the open studio door, Ellie saw Kathryn sitting in a vintage armchair with her feet up on a pouf.

'Hello, dear. Oh, how kind, you've brought us a little something,' she said, spotting the box Heather was holding.

'It's a sponge cake with strawberries and cream,' said Ellie.

'It looks delicious,' Heather said, carefully lifting the cake onto a plate and cutting them each a slice. 'Pour yourself some tea, Ellie, I just made it.'

Settled with their tea and cake, Ellie asked Kathryn, 'Are you excited about your birthday party, Mrs O'Neill?'

'Dear girl, please call me Kathryn. I've had an awful lot of birthdays, and the family are making such a fuss. But it's lovely to have everybody together for a change. They all lead such busy lives. Of course, we're so worried about Seamus making it back in time.' She sighed.

'Tell her about Ben,' Heather prompted her friend.

Kathryn smiled broadly. 'Oh, such lovely news! Yes. Ben rang me in the middle of some event he was at to say he and Sally are moving in together! Different from when I was young, but still, I'm so looking forward to meeting her tomorrow night.'

'Oh, you spoke to Ben?' Ellie said in surprise.

'Yes, Susan put his call through,' said Kathryn.

'And hovered to listen to the whole conversation, no doubt,' said Heather.

'Well, Ben *did* mention he'd tried calling several times.' Kathryn frowned. 'Anyway, it was such wonderful news, I suppose not even Susan could begrudge anyone wanting to share it.'

'It is wonderful news, isn't it?' said Ellie.

'So, he hasn't proposed?' asked Heather.

'No, but I'm happy for him, anyway. I thought it very lovely of him to let his grandmother know. Kind of him,' said Kathryn. 'I've hardly seen him these last few years, except briefly at the hospital the other day.'

She was silent for a moment and Ellie wondered why Ronan and Susan didn't let Ben spend time with his grandmother. She'd probably never be able to understand the way this family worked, she thought.

'I suppose lately he's been preoccupied courting Sally,' Kathryn said at last. 'He's always been so sweet to me. He's a gentle and kind soul who has always walked his own path in life. And I'm proud of him for doing that, though I do miss our special times together. But he had to find his own feet, out in the world. You young people have to do that before you come back to the nest, isn't that so?' She smiled.

'I suppose so,' said Ellie quietly.

Kathryn sat up straight and sipped her tea. 'Tell me, how are you, dear?'

Ellie smiled brightly, trying to lighten the mood. 'I'm doing really well, thank you. I love living in Storm Harbour – I'm actually thinking about staying here a while longer.'

'Oh, how lovely. Your grandfather must be pleased about that,' said Kathryn.

'Yes. I think he's happy, but he didn't want to let on at first because he didn't want to influence my decision. He's very considerate. Now, is that *the* portrait?' Ellie asked, glancing at the easel draped with a cloth. 'What do you think of it, Kathryn?'

'Well, actually, I haven't seen it yet. It's supposed to be my big surprise gift. Susan has the whole unveiling arranged, but I'd love to take a peek.'

'Are you pleased with it, Heather?' asked Ellie.

The artist shook her head. 'It's always difficult painting those you know well and feel for. We go back a long way. When I look at Kathryn I see her as I remember her in our younger days. You were such a beautiful bride.'

'Boyd called me his bride till the day he died,' Kathryn said softly. 'Heather, do you realise we've been friends for more than half a century?'

'I can do the maths,' said Heather with a chuckle. 'You were very shy and private at first, though. Then before you knew it, we were golfing partners!'

Kathryn gazed past Heather, looking reflective. 'Yes. I know. I remember the year we met almost to the day.'

The tone of her voice caused Ellie and Heather to exchange a quick look.

Ellie sensed Heather was about to make a flippant remark but there was something in Kathryn's expression that made Ellie ask gently, 'Why is that?'

'I felt free for the first time in a long time. Sad. But free.' She paused. 'It was when my father died.'

Heather looked at her and said quietly, 'You told me your mother died when you were a child, and gave me the impression you were also quite young when you became estranged from your father. It seemed painful so I never asked or mentioned anything.'

Kathryn looked at Ellie. 'Cynthia showed me the story in your paper about our mayor. Remarkable woman. Her honesty embarrassed me. Not because of what she said, but that she was brave enough to tell the truth.' Kathryn was still looking at Ellie. 'Secrets steal your soul. Even those you keep from yourself. I've kept a secret for most of my life and now I've finally come to understand how it eats away at your heart, even if you don't admit it.'

'What are you talking about, Kathryn?' asked Heather quietly.

'I want you to know what I've ignored for decades, Heather. And what I should have told you, Ellie, when I did the interview here with you when Heather was still working on the portrait.'

'I don't understand,' started Ellie. There was something in Kathryn's eyes, in the tone of her voice, that was slicing through Ellie's tightly wrapped inner self. The part of her that hurt.

'Keeping some things to yourself is not brave. It eats you up,' Kathryn said. 'I see that now. Let me share this now with you, young woman. And Heather, I've kept this from you, from everyone, for decades, and suddenly I see there was no reason to do so.'

Ellie sat clutching her teacup. This elderly woman couldn't know how she felt and what she suffered in her dark hours. Or could she? Did she want to hear what

Kathryn had to say? Ellie didn't move, she simply stared at Kathryn, who had turned her head and was looking at the sheet covering the painting.

'Then go ahead, Kathryn. Get it off your chest.' Heather folded her arms and rested her head on the backrest.

'I adored my father. I suppose little girls always do. Especially after my mother died. I was nine years old when she passed away. I know it must have been a struggle for him on his own. It didn't occur to me that, unlike most of my school friends, we seemed to have no relatives, or none that we ever saw or talked about. I remember only once a visit from a woman whom my father spoke to in a whisper and with sideways glances at me before he shook his head vehemently. He almost pushed her out the door, slamming it, then called me to him. He held me so tightly it frightened me as I could barely breathe. I had no idea then who she was and she never appeared again. Now I think she may have been a relative – maybe an aunt – who wanted me to live with her.'

Kathryn was looking ahead but seeing the past. She was there, as if it were yesterday.

'I realised much later that our reduced circumstances had come about because my father no longer had any money. I couldn't understand why; after all, he was a successful accountant. Dad used to be very smartly dressed but eventually he started to look unkempt. He was going to the local hotel more and more and I began to resent being left alone at home,' she said. 'I was upset when he announced he was taking me out of the school I loved to go to the local state school, away from all my friends.'

Ellie leaned forward and smiled at the elderly woman, urging her to keep talking.

'The bottom fell out of my world one morning when I was fifteen and the police knocked at the door of our flat to arrest my father. It appeared that my father had been embezzling funds from the firm where he worked on a very large scale over many years. He had been using the money to cover his gambling debts for years. The police took him away.

'I lived with a kind neighbour, Mrs Olsen, who took me in for a few months while I finished school. While I was with her, my father's trial for embezzlement came to court. Mrs Olsen took me to the courthouse in my school uniform and she dressed up with a hat and gloves like she was going to church. I was so fearful, so embarrassed, so scared, so ashamed. My photograph was in the newspaper and then everyone knew. Mrs Olsen was also photographed and mistaken for my mother, which shocked her and her friends so much that she decided to move away.

'I was saved by an old friend of my father, who offered me a job as a filing clerk in his firm and arranged for me to move to a boarding house in Camberwell. At night I studied shorthand and typing. I worked hard and became very proficient and reliable at my job. My boss let my father know where I was and that I was doing well. But I couldn't bring myself to answer my father's letters from jail as I was so angry and ashamed.

'Eventually I was promoted. I grew to like city life. I found my independence and made many friends. But the stigma of what my father had done still haunted me. I was sure that one day my family history would be revealed.'

'And then you met Boyd,' Heather said softly.

'Yes. I never believed someone like Boyd O'Neill would ever cross my path, let alone take an interest in me. Fall in love with me. And I with him.'

'Did you ever tell him about your past?' asked Ellie.

'I was torn, at first, about whether to tell him or not. It was wartime still; people did rash things they might not have done in peacetime. I began to think, who would ever reveal my secret? I dared to dream. But I needed to know that I was safe. That my secret would never be found out.'

'What did you do?' prompted Heather.

'One weekend I went to the jail to see my father. I didn't recognise him, he looked so ill. His first words to me were, "It took you long enough." He said he'd written to me but the letters were never answered. He was bitter. Angry. Hurt. I couldn't blame him. I should have answered his letters. He said he hoped I was making a decent life away from him. I wanted to cry and shout that I had to, I had no choice. But I had managed, and without his help.

'He gradually simmered down. Maybe he thought this was an opportunity to make contact again, when in fact for me it was the opposite. I told him I was planning to marry a respectable, well-to-do man who knew nothing about my past.'

Kathryn paused. Both Ellie and Heather were watching her closely, but said nothing, waiting for her to continue.

'He didn't react, didn't show that he was happy for me. There was just a stillness as he looked at me, as if it would be the last time. Which it was.

'Then he said, "Tell him. Tell this man about me. Or you will live with a lie and a shadow all your life. Never keep a secret, Kathy. It will be either the biggest gesture of trust and love you can show him, or he will turn his back and reject you. Either way, doubt is removed. I kept my gambling obsession a secret and look where it got me."'

There was a weighty silence in the room. Ellie noticed

that the elderly woman had gripped her hands tightly together.

Kathryn drew a breath. 'And so I told Boyd. I told him that my father was a notorious embezzler who'd used the funds to support his gambling habit, and that I had been abandoned when he went to jail. This was not a play for sympathy, but a simple fact. I never wanted to deceive Boyd.

'Boyd looked at me and simply said, "You didn't deceive me. Now I know everything about you." He said he was proud of me for making a successful life for myself after all that had happened to me, but mostly he was proud of me for being honest with him. And he opened his arms, and said, "It doesn't make me love you less, it makes me love you even more!"'

Ellie let out her breath, closing her eyes a moment. When she opened them, Kathryn was staring steadily at her. 'Never keep a secret, Ellie,' she said softly. 'You not only deceive others, but you deceive yourself.'

Heather gave a low whistle. 'No wonder you kept to yourself when Boyd first brought you to Craigmore. All that curiosity and scrutiny from the locals must have been hell for you.'

Kathryn gave a small smile. 'Yes. It was. I kept to myself but I found beauty and a haven in my garden. I still felt I was living a lie and someone would find out about my father; the stigma of such things was very strong in those days, you know. I worried more for Boyd's reputation than my own, as I loved him so very much. And then we had Seamus. It was a difficult birth and the doctors told us I couldn't have any more children. I told you that, I know, but now you know the reason I was so afraid to mingle with people.'

'And your father?' asked Ellie.

'After Seamus was born Boyd suggested I write to my father and send him a photo of his grandson. Which I did.'

'What did you write to him?' asked Ellie.

'I put the photograph in a card and thought and thought. In the end I just wrote, "*This is your grandson Seamus . . . No secrets.*"

'My father died in jail but I still worried about his sordid past coming to light one day. As I told you before, I didn't make friends until I started to play golf; nor was I able to be myself. But when I found some courage, I started to change the way I thought, and to my surprise I began to like myself. And I met you, Heather dear. You didn't ask questions or pry. You made me laugh. You have been the best of best friends anyone could have.'

Ellie felt tears spring to her eyes. These were not two elderly women, wrinkled and worn, living with ailments and afflictions. These were vibrant, beautiful souls who shared a bond that was perhaps even stronger than family, stronger than anything they'd planned; the unity of friendship.

Kathryn looked at Ellie. 'No secrets. That's *the* secret.'

There was silence in the room for a heartbeat or two. Then Heather broke the spell, rubbing her knees and saying, 'Well. The driver will be here to collect the painting soon.'

Kathryn straightened up and held out her hand to Ellie, who reached over, helping her to her feet.

'Heather, dear. I'm going to rip the sheet off that damned painting. And if I don't like it, I'm going to get Ellie to burn it in the back garden,' she said, laughing.

'Excellent idea.' Heather grinned, pushing herself to her feet.

'Wait, wait, I have to take a photo of this,' said Ellie. 'Of you two crazy ladies!'

She turned the camera on, adjusting the focus as the two women, arm in arm, moved to the tall easel.

'After you, m'dear,' said Heather with a slight bow and a wide smile.

Kathryn dropped her arm from Heather's and reached forward, and then with an elegant sweep, she pulled off the covering sheet.

Ellie had the camera glued to her eye, taking shot after shot, moving to catch their expressions. She stood beside the easel, focusing on their faces as the portrait was revealed, zooming in on Kathryn's face as the older woman saw the work for the first time.

The painting showed the gentle face of an elderly woman, at peace with herself, the lines of her life etched deep. And in the shadow behind her shone the same face but that of a shy young woman, her eyes full of love and sadness, shadowed by a secret. But in the clear eyes of her older self, her steady warm gaze reached out to touch those who stood before the painting.

'It's honest, Heather. I like that. You know me,' said Kathryn softly.

'No, I didn't really know you, till now. Now I understand what it is I've done.'

'It's . . . unbelievable. It's stunning. It's captured . . . everything,' said Ellie, unable to see though the camera's eyepiece for tears.

'It's so, so special. Thank you, Heather,' said Kathryn simply.

'I didn't know what I was painting,' said Heather softly. 'But it's there, isn't it? The truth.'

Ellie looked at the two women. 'Kathyrn, as you know,

I've written your story for the front page of the next issue of the paper, which will be coming out tomorrow before your party and the grand unveiling,' she said. 'Unless you tell me otherwise, we'll be including a photo of your finished portrait.'

Ellie watched Kathryn and Heather share a conspiratorial smile, then Kathryn just had time for a tiny wink and a nod to Ellie before there was a rap at the door.

'Oh, Ellie, for goodness' sake throw the sheet over the darn thing and say nothing,' said Kathryn as Heather went to the door.

'All right all right, I'm coming,' she called out as the knocking came again. 'I'm an old woman, keep your hair on.'

While Heather was answering the door, Ellie gently spoke to the elderly woman.

'Kathryn, the story I've written shows the important place you hold in Storm Harbour today, as you have for decades. Things like setting up the creche for the children of the area and the Botanic Gardens,' she said. 'Would you like me to write about your personal story too?'

Kathryn turned to her and smiled.

'Thank you for asking, dear girl. Many journalists would not be that courteous and would print what they wanted.' She paused, shook her head and said at last, 'I should talk to my grandchildren about it first. I'd like them to hear it all from me and I can answer their questions. Do you mind?'

'Of course not,' Ellie said. She wanted to talk more about Kathryn's past, but she knew the man would be in any minute to collect the painting.

Ellie gently hugged the women goodbye as the driver fussed over the wrapping of the painting in a doona to be transported in a small truck to Craigmore. Then she drove back to the office.

'How'd you go with the portrait picture?' asked Patrick as she came through the door.

'Success. It's stunning. Kathryn decided she wanted to see it before the unveiling and whipped the sheet off. It was an act of defiance – as if to say, to hell with Susan. It was a sight to see; those two women are amazing.'

'Good. I'm keen to see it. Heather wasn't an Archibald finalist for nothing, you know. Can you please give the camera to Jon now? He'll work on the images.'

Ellie nodded. 'Poppy, there's more to Kathryn's story. It was a revelation. She just told Heather and me about a secret she's been sitting on.'

Patrick's eyes narrowed. 'What do you mean exactly?'

'You know how we were wondering about her background when we first spoke about writing Kathryn's story? Her family history?'

Patrick nodded. 'Yes indeed. I'm listening. You have my attention.'

Ellie quickly sketched for him the painful story Kathryn had shared.

Patrick leaned back in his chair. 'The poor girl. Boyd was a good man. And a lucky one. They were so in love. What a brave woman, to risk her marriage for the sake of the truth. It explains a lot.'

'I feel sorry that she felt she had to hide her history,' said Ellie.

'Times have changed. Or have they?' Patrick said, and looked at Ellie. 'Secrets. They always come out in the end. And it's for the best that they do.'

Ellie blinked, feeling the weight of words unsaid in Patrick's gaze. She glanced quickly away. 'Poppy, I asked

Kathryn about adding this into the article. She felt better having shared it, but she wants to be the one to tell her family about it. So we can't print it. Is that okay?'

'I'm pleased you asked her. After all, it's up to Kathryn to choose to tell the world or not. It's her business. We are not a scandal sheet. Meredith wanted her story out there. Kathryn trusts us to respect her request. I knew there was a shadow in her life. It seems she's let it go now, and good for her. We shall celebrate her birthday for the milestone it is. For her and for this town.'

Ellie nodded. 'It's a special feeling to have someone put their trust in you, as Kathryn did today,' she said softly.

'Certainly is, kiddo,' Patrick said. 'Right, I'll sign off on the layout once Jon and the designer are ready.'

As Ellie rose and left Patrick's little office, she heard him say to Sam, who was sitting under his desk, 'We're getting on, old boy. And still the world is full of surprises.'

A little while later, after Ellie had settled herself at her desk with a mug of tea, Patrick walked out into the main office, Sam at his heels.

'I just checked the forecast for Kathryn's party tomorrow night,' he said, pushing back his hat and staring out the window. 'It looks like we're in for a storm.'

# 11

FRIDAY MORNING WAS ALWAYS busy around town, but today there was heightened activity, a tension, thought Ellie, as warnings about the approaching storm circulated. It was threatening to be a severe one; even though it wasn't due to hit until that evening, the sky was already overcast and the wind was picking up.

Patrick stayed home to 'batten down the hatches', and as Ellie bought her morning coffee, she saw shopkeepers along the street moving signs and furniture indoors.

'It can be bad if it comes in from the south. We're damned lucky those early settlers planted the cypress and Norfolk Island pines to protect the town,' Maggie told her when Ellie came into the office and described the scene.

'I hope it will be okay driving out to Craigmore

this evening. It would be a pity if the storm washes out Kathryn's birthday,' said Ellie.

'The forecast says it's due to hit around 10 pm, so you should be okay,' said Maggie. 'Perhaps try to get away early, though. Patrick doesn't usually stay at these things very long, anyway.'

'Yes, once the formalities are over we'll head home. My friend Mike is driving here tomorrow. Hope the storm's cleared by then.'

'I've been re-reading your story on Kathryn,' said Maggie. 'It's really lovely and I'm sure she'll like it. The headline says it all, really – *"Town doyenne Kathryn O'Neill celebrates 95 years of generosity"*.'

'Thanks, Maggie, that means so much to me.' Ellie smiled. 'The town needs to know a little more about her so they can get to know the real Kathryn O'Neill. After all, her Botanic Gardens are a big attraction here.'

Ellie's feature article on Kathryn was on the front page alongside a beautiful photo of Kathryn's portrait. The article ran over to page two, which also, as Jon had suggested, had an old photo of Kathryn and Boyd on their wedding day.

As the day wound to a close, Ellie decided to go home early with Sam to get ready for the party. When they got there, Sam paused on the verandah, sniffing the air with his ears back, not liking what he knew was coming.

'You'd better hunker down somewhere safe while we're out tonight, Sammy,' Ellie said, giving the old dog a quick pat. 'We won't be gone long but I'll have to lock you inside.'

As she slipped into a soft apple-green dress, Ellie realised she hadn't dressed up for weeks. She'd had her long hair trimmed and she swept it up onto her head with one of her grandmother's tortoiseshell combs, which she'd found in a drawer in the her grandmother's sewing room.

Ellie and Patrick had wondered what to give Kathryn on this special occasion, because, as Patrick said, 'She doesn't need a thing.' Finally, he'd come up with an idea they'd agreed was perfect. He'd had a specially printed and retouched blow-up made of the page in *The Storm Harbour Chronicle* that had featured a photo of the newlywed couple with the caption, *Mr and Mrs Boyd O'Neill welcomed home*, which he'd had mounted in a simple silver frame.

Once she was dressed and had done her make-up, Ellie wrapped the present in tissue and crimson paper with a silver ribbon.

Patrick came home muttering about going out on a night like this, but nonetheless when he 'turned out for inspection', as he put it, Ellie had to applaud his choice of a midnight-blue velvet jacket and polka-dot tie with a crisp new white fine linen shirt. His best boots were polished and he, too, had had a haircut. He took pride in showing her that he was wearing the woven leather belt with his initials on it that Ellie and her parents had given him years ago.

Ellie settled Sam in the warm kitchen in his basket, with the blinds down around the house as she knew he hated lightning and thunder. She left some lights on and locked up while Patrick did a quick final circuit of the verandah and lawn, making sure nothing was left out that could smash into doors or windows, or blow away.

As Ellie waited for him in the gathering dusk, the stiff breeze pulling at her hair and clothes, a low, far-off rumble made her look up. The sky to the south was the colour of a bad bruise. The storm was definitely on its way. She and Mike would not be fishing tomorrow. She pulled out her phone and looked at the Bureau of Meteorology website. The rain radar looked so bad, the storm cell moving inexorably towards them, that she double-checked she was looking at her locality and not the Caribbean.

'You okay driving out to Craigmore, Poss? We could get the taxi fellow to take us,' said Patrick as he opened the car door.

'I'm fine, thanks, Poppy. We'll be okay in your four-wheel drive, and I'll only have one glass of champagne,' she said, smiling, 'but I think I'll be pleased to get back home to the fire and a glass of wine later.'

'You're not the only one,' said Patrick with a chuckle. Then, as they climbed into the car, he added, 'You know, there's still no sign of Seamus. I tried calling him again this afternoon. He'll be upset at missing this.' After a pause he went on, 'It's just so odd that he neglected to deal with those letters from council. Not like him at all. He must be getting a bit past it. You'd better boot me out when I start losing the plot.'

'That's a long way off. Hey, speaking of parties, what do you want to do for your eightieth birthday, Poppy? We should mark that occasion next year.'

Patrick waved a dismissive hand. 'I'll be quite happy to go down to the pub with my mates. Maybe a barbie at the river with the caravan park mob.'

They were silent for a moment, both thinking the same thing – *Let's hope it's still there!*

As Ellie headed out on the coast road, the car was buffeted by a strong wind. The first spats of rain started just as they reached the ornate gates of Craigmore. As they wound their way up the drive, they saw that an elaborate marquee had been well anchored on the front lawn, sheltered by the solid stone walls of the large house. Oil lamps and flame torches were spluttering as guests milled about inside the marquee.

The caterers had a team of staff on hand to look after parking the cars and to take coats and gifts, as hors d'oeuvres and drinks were offered to the guests on silver trays.

'Fancy. No expense spared,' said Patrick as they hurried across the lawn and into the relative comfort of the marquee.

'What did you expect?' said Ellie, smoothing her hair and adjusting the strap of Jon's camera on her shoulder. 'Oh, there's Heather.'

'I hope the unveiling isn't going to be drawn out. Ronan will be running things as poor Seamus has missed it,' said Heather after they greeted her.

'Where's the portrait?' asked Ellie.

'In the main room in the house; we'll go in there for the speeches, apparently. Susan's calling it a preview before the actual party begins.' Heather laughed. 'Although everyone in town has already seen it,' she added, winking at Ellie, who grinned.

'Is Kathryn here yet?' Patrick asked.

'She's inside. Too risky for her to be out here in this weather.'

'It's cosy here in the tent. But if a big wind gets up, I'll be hightailing it inside too,' said Patrick.

'Hey, look who's here,' said Ellie as a smiling Sally and Ben came towards them. 'Congratulations, we're so happy at your news.'

Ben grinned. 'I'm just moving out of the caravan park over to Sally's place. But we plan to look for a place of our own when I come back from Queensland.'

'So you're doing another carving job up there?' asked

370

Heather. 'Are you going too, Sally, or can't you get time off work?'

'I could go, I guess. I quit my job.'

'What!' Ellie said. 'Why?'

'The guy who owns the radio station is such a jerk. I didn't like my stories being censored because he didn't want to upset advertisers and the council.'

'Yeah, that'd be right,' said Patrick. 'He has fingers in pies all over the place. In my opinion, he's only in the media to use it for himself. He thinks it's a way to get rich. We know better, eh, Ellie?'

Ellie smiled at her grandfather. 'You do okay, Poppy. And you make more friends than enemies,' she said, and turned to Sally. 'Good on you for taking a stand, Sally. So what are you planning to do next?'

Before she could answer, Patrick handed Sally a glass of champagne from a passing waiter and said, 'Well, if you're sticking around, Sally, you'd better come back to work at the *Chronicle*. Unless you're going on to TV or have some other ambitious plan? That's if you'd like to, of course,' he added.

Ben looked at Sally, who was grinning broadly. 'See, Sal, I told you. That's where you should be,' he said.

Ellie reached over and took Sally's hand. 'It's a great idea.'

Sally smiled at her and then turned to Patrick. 'You've already got Jon and Maggie and now Ellie. I didn't think you'd need another journo, Patrick, much as I'd like to come back.'

Ellie jumped in and said quickly, 'I'm keen to keep writing, Sal, I'm starting to love it. But I have some other plans too, back in the IT world. Ben's right – you belong at the *Chronicle* and the paper needs your skills.'

'Well, if you're sure the paper needs me,' said Sally almost shyly, looking at Patrick.

'Definitely,' he said. Then he grinned. 'I trained you well – think of it as me cashing in on my investment.'

'You're on,' said Sally with a laugh. She looked at Ellie. 'You're not thinking of leaving Storm Harbour, are you?'

'No. Well, not at the moment. I'm still giving it all some thought.' Ellie looked around. 'C'mon, let's go inside. Seems like everyone else is heading in.'

'Good idea. I want to get a front-row seat to see this painting in the flesh,' Patrick said.

\*

The tall folding timber doors had been slid aside to open the room up to its maximum capacity. Rows of chairs were set out in front of a small dais on which the covered painting on its easel took pride of place. A small table with a bowl of roses, a glass of water and a hand microphone sat to one side. Several chairs were set up on the platform facing the guests.

Tall tables were scattered through the room for people to rest their glasses and small food plates on, and the catering staff circulated as the guests began to file inside. Ellie moved through the room, taking a few photos for the paper.

She had never seen the whole O'Neill clan – with the exception of Seamus – together before. Ronan and Cynthia and their children were with a group Ellie didn't recognise. When she asked, Patrick whispered that it was Seamus's daughter Linda and her family. Ellie turned away from Ronan and relaxed her hands, which she realised she'd been holding in a tight grip.

She nudged Patrick as Susan appeared carrying a sheet

of paper. She wore a black silk dress sashed with a wide red belt and a dramatic brooch of a glittering spider with ruby-red eyes pinned to her shoulder. She was talking to the head caterer.

'Bossy Boots is here,' muttered Patrick.

'Of course she is. Running everything,' said Ellie.

Heather excused herself to talk to someone she knew, and Patrick went to move away as well, but suddenly Ellie clutched his arm in alarm.

Walking towards them was Ronan.

She felt hot and cold, then faint, and unable to move. He seemed to come towards her in slow motion and, to Ellie, his smile looked predatory and evil. He was looking at Patrick. Ellie grasped Patrick's hand beside her and leaned against him slightly, her knees trembling. She dropped her gaze as she heard from some far-off place the sound of Patrick's voice introducing her . . . *'Do you know my granddaughter . . .?'*

How to avoid him? She wanted to run but was frozen to the spot. Her mind felt as though it was not connected to her body. *Don't touch me!* she silently screamed in her head. Her worst nightmare was coming true . . . No, oh no, her hand was lifted and she felt his flesh on hers. She swayed . . .

'Ellie! Are you all right?' Patrick was gripping her other arm.

She felt herself go limp, as if her body was melting and she'd just be a puddle on the floor in a second. But then a rush of something surged through her, and Ellie blinked and shook her head, jerking her hand away from Ronan's to brush her hair out of her eyes. *No. No.* She did not have to let him touch her. 'I'm sorry. I just felt faint for a moment.'

Obviously noticing her white face, Patrick said kindly,

'Go and get some water. I'd like to have a quiet word with Ronan, please, Ellie.'

'Of course,' she said, grateful to escape.

As Patrick stepped between them, taking Ronan's arm, she heard him say, 'I feel there's something going on at council. Have you heard anything at all about a proposed development?'

'What on earth makes you say that?' said Ronan.

Ellie was shaking as she moved away. She sat down, hoping no one would notice her, and took a glass of mineral water from a tray. After a few sips, she felt calmer. She glanced at Ronan talking to her grandfather. Ronan's hair was thinning and he looked unfit. This was not the handsome, arrogant youth who had appeared to think he owned the world. Who haunted her nightmares and had scarred her soul.

Slowly she let out her breath, her body relaxing as it released the tension and tightness of their latest encounter. What had brought her back from that precipice, though? She had somehow managed to stave off the panic attack she'd felt coming. What was different?

For a moment Ellie felt she was alone in the room but, like the volume of a radio turning up, the sounds around her filtered back into her consciousness. The chatter and laughter, scraping of chairs, clatter of glasses and bottles, all returned, as if she had stepped outside her body for a few seconds and was now back, somehow renewed.

Ellie turned to look for Patrick, but he and Ronan had both disappeared. Instead she saw Susan making a beeline for her, her lips pursed and her eyes cold.

Ellie gave a tight smile and decided to stand her ground. 'Hello, Susan,' she said calmly, rising from her chair.

Susan didn't bother with niceties.

'I am very disappointed in the *Chronicle*,' she hissed under her breath. 'So is Mrs O'Neill. Deeply disappointed.'

'Really? Why might that be?' said Ellie.

'For goodness' sake. Why do you think? You have ruined the highlight of the evening. You took photos of the portrait while it was still in the artist's studio. No one was meant to have seen it until now.'

'I don't understand how that could be a problem,' said Ellie.

'You have ruined the unveiling of the painting for everyone. Look: it's covered. To be unveiled *this evening* as a *surprise*. Fortunately, Mrs O'Neill doesn't read your grandfather's wretched newspaper. You haven't spoiled the surprise for her, but you have for everyone else.'

Ellie was going to remark how nice it was to know that *everyone* else read the *Chronicle*, but bit her tongue. Should she say Kathryn had encouraged her to take the photos of the painting? she wondered. No. Susan was mad enough. Ellie was rather pleased at getting under Susan's skin.

'I believe Mrs O'Neill was aware the article would be out ahead of her big day, so I'm sorry if it doesn't suit you,' said Ellie calmly.

'What you think is not the point. I have arranged this viewing now, before the party gets properly under way, so everyone can see it at the same time.' Her face was turning red. 'You saw it before Ronan did, and he commissioned it! And you put it on the front page! It was to be a surprise!'

'I'm sorry you feel this way, Susan. Heather invited me for afternoon tea with herself and Mrs O'Neill. They were both happy to let me see the painting and photograph it.' Ellie didn't add that she had the perfect photo of Kathryn's reaction to first seeing the painting herself.

'It seems you continue to deliberately go behind my back to make trouble,' snapped Susan, her voice rising. A few people nearby glanced her way. Ellie noticed that Susan had balled her hands into fists and her face was flushed a deep crimson now.

'Well, I'm sure everyone will be thrilled to see the actual portrait now,' said Ellie. 'Excuse me, Susan.'

She headed across the room to join Patrick, who was speaking again with Heather.

'Ellie, I'm sorry about Susan. She saw the *Chronicle* and she's as wild as a skinned cat.' Heather gave a mischievous smile. 'I'm so pleased.'

'As long as they all liked it, that's the important thing,' said Ellie with a grin.

'Now, if you'll excuse me, we have to toe the line. Let's hope the storm holds off!' Heather said and, as if on cue, there came the distant rumble of thunder and the sound of heavy raindrops against the window. She sailed over to where Susan was beckoning her to a seat on the dais by the painting.

The room had now filled with party guests, who were greeting friends, eating, drinking and standing around chatting. A few sat down near the front, but Patrick selected a seat towards the back of the room and gestured to Ellie to sit beside him. Perhaps he guessed that she wouldn't want to sit too close to Susan and Ronan, Ellie thought.

Ronan, Kathryn and Heather were seated by the painting facing the guests. Susan stood to one side. Cynthia and the children sat in the front row, next to Linda and her family. Ellie looked for Ben and was pleased to see him sitting in the front row too, with Sally.

Susan picked up the microphone and waited for the

chatter to die away before saying, 'Welcome and thank you all for coming. To begin the proceedings, Mrs O'Neill would like to say a few words.'

Ronan stood, leaned down and helped Kathryn to her feet. She took the microphone and said warmly, 'My dear friends and family.' She paused, looking down at the front row, and smiled. 'Thank you so much for being here to mark this occasion. We are disappointed Seamus isn't with us, but I know he would be if he could. However, we shall celebrate with champagne at the conclusion of this little ceremony, and please stay on for the party. Many thanks to my family for commissioning this portrait, and to my dear friend Heathler Lachlan. I am always deeply touched by her insight and talent. It is a wonderful, wonderful gift. Thank you, Heather.' Kathryn reached towards the tasselled cord that would release the velvet covering from the painting. 'And so without further ado, I will –'

Before she could unveil the painting, there was an almighty thunderclap at the same time as a massive flash and crack of lightning, and all the lights went out.

There were immediate squeals, gasps and raised voices.

Ronan called out loudly, 'Please remain seated. Don't move, we'll have the generator on in a minute. Please stay where you are.'

Guests took out their phones and small beams of light waved around the room. Ronan was standing next to Kathryn, having helped her back into her chair.

Looking outside, Ellie saw that the rain had become torrential and was pounding against the French doors and windows, so loud that people had to raise their voices to be heard, adding to the pandemonium in the room.

Ellie reached for Patrick's hand. 'Hope this doesn't last long!' she shouted.

Suddenly, in spite of the noise, they noticed a commotion coming from the front hallway: voices raised and clattering footsteps. At that moment the lights flickered and came on again as the generator started. Everyone turned towards the voices and movement at the back of the room.

A shout went up and there was an explosion of talk, laughter, cheers and applause. Standing in the doorway, soaked to the skin, was a dishevelled but smiling Seamus O'Neill.

'Did you swim back, Seamus?' called one voice cheerfully.

Ellie noticed Ronan, Linda and Ben hurrying through the gathering to reach their father as people clustered around the new arrival. Their voices were drowned out as the rain beat down even more heavily. The windows rattled and shook in the wind. Ellie heard a distant crash, and wondered if the marquee was secure.

'Oh, my goodness, how wonderful! You made it!' cried Kathryn, clapping her hands.

Heather leaned over and picked up the microphone from Ronan's chair. Her voice boomed into the room. 'Seamus, your mother says to go and put on dry clothes. Ronan will tell us what's going on. I suggest the caterers bring around drinks.'

There was a loud round of applause and laughter at this suggestion.

Seamus raised his hand in acknowledgement and headed back out into the hall while Ronan strode over to take the microphone, his expression serious.

'Everyone, please stay where you are. Some of the

378

lights are not working. We'll continue when my father gets back.'

As Ben made his way out the door, Patrick called out, 'How'd Seamus manage to get here, Ben?'

'He flew into Melbourne and hired a car and a driver,' he called over his shoulder. 'Just in time. Decided to surprise us.'

Patrick turned to Ellie. 'Well, the driver of that car is going to get a fat fee. He'll have to stay the night, I reckon.'

'Really? What about the rest of us? I don't want to stay here,' Ellie said vehemently, her eyes flicking to Ronan on the dais. 'Besides, Mike's arriving tomorrow.'

'We're not driving anywhere in this madness. Check the BoM website on your phone. Sometimes the fiercer the storm, the quicker it passes.' He paused, giving her a look. 'You okay?'

Ellie nodded.

Patrick hesitated, as if searching for words, but seemed to change his mind. 'Look, Seamus being back changes things,' he said quietly. 'I want to talk to him on his own about the caravan park lease before he joins the party. I know the timing isn't great, but it's urgent now and we might not get a chance later. I'll go and find him. Will you be okay here?'

'Yes, I'll go and see Heather, she's talking to Sally.'

Ellie made her way to the front and sat down beside the two women. 'This is unreal. No one will forget this party! Where's Kathryn?'

'Susan took her out to see Seamus once he's in dry clothes. What a miracle he made it back in time!' said Heather.

There was another thunder crack and bolt of lightning, making everyone jump nervously.

Guests who'd gone outside to help make sure the marquee and everything in it was safe in the gale returned, looking somewhat damp and windblown and brushing water from their jackets as food and drinks were passed around.

Soon Seamus, accompanied by his daughter and sons, came back into the room, and Susan helped Kathryn back to her chair. Ellie couldn't see her grandfather and wondered if Patrick had managed to talk to Seamus.

Seamus picked up the microphone. 'Sorry for my late arrival, everyone, but I wouldn't have missed this occasion for anything, whether it be a storm in the Caribbean or one in our own backyard – or in this case, both!' There was laughter from the crowd, then he turned to Kathryn. 'Mother, you are an inspiration to us all. A very happy birthday to you.'

Ronan leaned across, retrieved the mic from his father and said, 'Let's go on with our little ceremony. Grandy, please unveil the portrait.'

Susan helped Kathryn to the easel, where she pulled the cord and the velvet covering slipped to the floor.

There was an intake of breath and a loud burst of applause. Ellie snapped some photos of the moment and the crowd's reaction. A minute or two later, a waiter walked up to the platform pushing a trolley table holding a magnificent three-tiered birthday cake, the candles alight.

Patrick appeared beside Ellie and sat down, shaking his head. 'No luck talking to Seamus. I'll try to catch him when this is over,' he whispered, and put his arm around her shoulders.

Voices were almost drowned out by the pounding rain and rolling thunder as the guests sang 'Happy Birthday', and Kathryn blew out the candles arranged in the shape of the numbers nine and five. Then, beaming with happiness, Kathryn cut her cake with Seamus's help as everyone applauded.

The waiter wheeled the cake away again to be cut up and served on dainty plates, while other waiters moved the chairs aside so guests could mingle. Ellie could hear a few people discussing whether they should leave before the storm worsened, while others thought it safest to stay till it subsided. The rain was still torrential and the wind continued howling, although the lightning and thunder appeared to be moving away.

Ellie watched as, across the room, Patrick managed to take Seamus to one side and talk to him. As Patrick spoke, she saw a look of shock and alarm spread across the other man's face.

Then Seamus marched over to Ronan and took his arm, indicating that he wanted his son to come with him out of the room. Ronan began shaking his head but Seamus snapped something back at him, his voice raised, and then both men strode towards the hallway. A few heads turned curiously. Seamus looked over his shoulder and gestured to Patrick. 'Come and tell them what you told me,' he said.

Patrick hurried over and grabbed Ellie's hand. 'Come with me. You're the one with the information from Russ.'

She was about to say no, but seeing Patrick's face she quietly followed the group, which now included Susan, and they walked down the hallway towards the library.

It was quieter in there, but the constant thrumming of the rain and wind against the window panes was loud in their ears. Standing just inside the door, Ellie tried to be as unobtrusive as she could.

'What's this about, Dad?' asked Ronan.

Seamus gestured at Patrick. 'I have just been informed, not by any member of my family but by Patrick here, that our lease to council for the caravan park is about to expire. It has not been renewed despite several reminder letters being sent, apparently – letters I have not seen. Which means the council will be able to acquire our land and sell it on, or do whatever they want with it, if we don't renegotiate the lease. I don't know what has been going on, but that land is not to leave this family. My father was definite about that, and so am I.'

'Then why weren't the documents signed?' Patrick asked reasonably.

'Well, Dad was away,' Ronan said.

'Ellie, can you please explain what you found out?' said Patrick. Everyone looked at her.

'What do you mean, "found out",' demanded Susan. 'What is this – an inquisition?'

Ellie took a breath. 'I was told that three letters were sent to you, Mr O'Neill, in the past several months, reminding you that the lease on the caravan park was due to be renegotiated or the land would become council property,' she said. 'That was part of the conditions in the original lease signed by your father, apparently. But there was no response to any of the council's letters.'

'Where did you get such information?' snapped Susan.

'Is this true, Ellie?' asked Seamus, ignoring Susan. 'Are you sure about this information?'

'I am not able to reveal a confidential source, but yes, I'm sure it's accurate. If you contact the council, they'll confirm what I've told you,' she answered calmly. 'One or perhaps even two of the letters were sent before you went away.'

Though it was subtle, Ellie was certain she saw Ronan and Susan exchange an uneasy glance.

'Patrick, since when was it your business to poke your nose into our family affairs?' said Ronan.

Patrick shrugged. 'Ever since a concerned friend reported hearing a rumour about that land. And the town is naturally worried about the possibility of development on that site.'

'What would they know?' said Susan.

'Well, if letters were sent to me, even before I went away, why didn't I see them? Who opens the correspondence? Isn't that your job, Susan?' Seamus said, glancing at her, but without waiting for an answer, turning to Ronan. 'Did you see those letters from the council, Ronan? You must have seen the one or two that arrived while I was away. You had power of attorney to run things in my absence. Why didn't you re-sign the lease? You have always known your grandfather's and my wishes for that land. It should have been a simple matter.' Seamus glared at his son, whose face suddenly reddened, and then Ronan pointed to Susan.

'Susan is in charge of the mail,' he said quickly. 'She should have dealt with it.'

Susan took a step back, clearly surprised. 'What? Don't you dare try to lay the blame on me!' she shouted at Ronan. 'I brought that letter straight to you, and it was all your idea! You said it was an opportunity for us, that it was prime real estate going to waste! And it was you who brought in your mate the developer.' She sounded panicky and Ronan had turned pale.

'That's enough,' he said, pressing his lips tightly together and glancing at Seamus, but it was too late. Seamus looked horrified.

'You opened my mail and didn't notify me? Even before I left on my cruise?' he said. 'Am I to understand that my own son is trying to deprive me of our family land? And what's this about a development?'

Ronan lifted his hands as if to placate his father. 'Look, Dad, you're being too sentimental. I knew you would be. It's just an old caravan park,' he said. 'You've no idea of the potential there. You haven't seemed interested in the business much at all lately. I made a business decision.'

Seamus was speechless with anger and hurt.

Taking advantage of the silence, Ronan turned his attention to Susan. 'I was trying to do a great thing for the town, you know. Not just make a buck, like some people.'

Susan gasped. 'I can't believe what I'm hearing,' she yelled. 'You couldn't care less about this town! You thought the whole idea was brilliant and would make us a fortune. You were in it for the money all along.' She gave a bitter shrug. Ronan looked like he wanted to step over and make her stop talking, but it seemed Susan was on a roll. 'You're the one who decided to let the lease lapse and then buy the land cheaply from the council so your contacts could develop it and make us all big bucks. That was our agreement. And it would have been fine, too, if the media hadn't started poking its nose in,' she added, shooting a cold look at Patrick and Ellie.

'They never had any facts,' Ronan shot back at her icily. 'It would have been all right except that you lost your head and went overboard with your crazy threats.'

'I'm not the only one! It wasn't me who "persuaded" certain councillors that they should sell us the land for a song and approve our development plans. Obviously we knew that goody-two-shoes mayor wouldn't help once she found out what we wanted to do,' added Susan.

'Wait a minute,' said Ellie slowly, as certain pieces of the puzzle fell into place in her mind. 'Crazy threats . . . So it was you who decided to get rid of the mayor? You did the trolling? Spread the nasty rumours?' she continued, staring at Susan and shaking her head. 'I don't know how you dug up Meredith's history. Fortunately, that backfired on you.'

Susan seemed to have realised she'd said too much and fell silent, but her face was still mutinous. A loud boom of thunder made them all jump, and the lights flickered again.

'The councillors you "persuaded" to support your future plans,' said Patrick, 'was Councillor Lowe one of them?'

'Lowe was keen,' said Ronan. 'It was a great opportunity for the town. Still is.' He put his hands on his hips defiantly, but Ellie noticed the tension in his clenched jaw.

'But you thought you had to steal your own family's land to do it,' said Seamus in an appalled voice.

'And did your methods of "persuasion" include poisoning my dog?' asked Patrick quietly. 'Sam, my dog, is okay. Luckily. Ellie got to the bait first,' he added.

'What?' Ronan turned to him. 'I was never part of any plan to poison your dog.'

'Poison!' exclaimed Seamus. 'That's beyond the pale. Patrick, I'm so, so sorry.'

Ellie broke in. 'The vet said it was a chemical that's now banned. He said there's probably plenty still lying around in woolsheds as it was used to treat sheep.'

Seamus looked at Ronan. 'I thought we got rid of that stuff,' he said tightly.

Ronan was pale. 'I thought so too. I asked Susan to take care of it.'

There was a brief, shocked silence in the room as all eyes turned to the O'Neills' assistant.

'You were in this as a partner, all the way,' hissed Susan. 'Now that you've been caught out, you're dumping me in it. What kind of a man are you?'

'But why hurt our dog, Susan?' Ellie said, her voice filled with anger and disbelief. 'It was cruel and senseless.' A thought occurred to her. 'And I suppose it was you who put those posts against me up on social media. What have I ever done to you?'

Susan glared at Ellie and snapped, 'You came to Storm Harbour and acted as if you owned the place! What would you know about what's good for this town?'

Ellie found herself leaning back, trying to distance herself from this woman and her hurtful words.

'I spoke to Keith, who owns the radio station,' Susan continued. 'He was happy to help me and put a stop to that smart-arse Sally's investigation. I tried the same with the *Chronicle*, by offering a lot of advertising, but you were a loose cannon.' Susan shook her fist at Ellie. 'I had to stop you and your grandfather putting something in the paper that would have killed off our deal –'

'Enough!' Seamus raised his voice. 'This is my mother's birthday!' He paused, shaking his head. 'I just can't believe any of this. Mother would never agree to parting with any of Boyd's land. The very idea would kill her! Surely you both knew that?'

'Susan made sure she never found out,' Ronan started in a rush. 'She was protecting Grandy. But I felt that when we showed her what we planned to do, and how good the new development would be for Storm Harbour, well, that she'd love it.'

Everyone simply stared at him as the unlikelihood of

this statement sank in.

'Thank goodness I got home in time,' said Seamus coldly.

'They told us you have till Tuesday to re-sign the lease,' said Patrick to Seamus.

'That's a relief. I'll get my lawyer onto it over the weekend.'

The library door opened and Cynthia stuck her head in. 'Everyone is wondering where you all are.' Her eyes wandered over the group and her expression hardened. 'Am I interrupting something important?'

'Come in, Cynthia dear, we're attempting to resolve a family issue. Of course you're welcome,' said Seamus.

'What about Linda and Ben? And Kathryn, for that matter? Why weren't we included in this family discussion?' she asked tightly.

'It would appear that your husband and Susan have been trying to swindle me out of some valuable O'Neill land,' said Seamus evenly.

The well-bred Cynthia then stunned everyone by marching in and pointing a shaking finger at Susan.

'I *knew* something was going on between you both, and it's still going on.' Then her face crumpled and she began to cry.

As Seamus moved to calm his daughter-in-law, she turned to point at Ronan, tears running down her face. 'I don't know how long your affair with this woman has been going on, but you can have her. I can't stand any more. It's not fair on me or the children. I'm leaving you, Ronan.'

'What are you talking about?' said Seamus, looking confused.

Ronan reached out his hand. 'Please, Cynthia, you've

got it all wrong. For goodness' sake, settle down. We can talk about this –'

'Wrong? Am I? Am I? I've watched you spend hours in that woman's house when you told me you were staying in Melbourne or working. And now I find out that she seems to have taken over the family business. She has her nose in everything, and you've let her.'

Ellie exchanged a quick glance with Patrick. That explained why she'd seen Cynthia parked outside Susan's house.

Susan's eyes had narrowed. 'How would you know any of that, Cynthia? Have you been spying on us?'

'I watched your place because I needed evidence of Ronan being there,' said Cynthia in a cold but calmer voice. Turning back to Ronan, she continued, 'So I have decided I'm leaving you and taking the children with me and moving back to my family in Queensland. The deceit and humiliation are too much to bear.' She turned and made to leave the room.

'Cynthia, please, wait,' began Ronan, reaching towards his wife. 'We need to talk. It wasn't like that at all, it was business –'

'Oh sure. As if!' she spat.

'No, you've got it all wrong,' said Ronan.

Susan snorted and snapped, 'That's not what you led me to believe, Ronan! So you never had any intention of keeping your promises to me? Were you just leading me on so I would help you get that land?'

Ronan looked away, not answering as Cynthia turned on her heel, a disgusted look on her face, and hurried from the room, slamming the door behind her.

Ronan turned quickly to Seamus. 'Dad, let me explain and make it up to you. It was all Susan's idea.

It sounded good and she did everything –' Ronan began, with growing panic in his voice.

'Not quite everything, it would seem, Ronan,' interrupted Seamus, barely controlling his anger. 'I really don't know what to think. We will talk in private later. Don't discuss these matters with anyone outside this room. Right now, I wish to go and celebrate my mother's birthday. Patrick? Ellie, shall we?'

Seamus strode out, Patrick behind him, but something made Ellie hesitate. Her mind had been racing as the revelations of the last few minutes had tumbled out. There was something she needed to do, she realised.

Ignoring Ellie, Susan moved towards Ronan, who took an involuntary step backwards when he saw her furious face.

Giving him a hard look, Susan said, 'Did you really mean everything you just said? This is your last chance. Are you in or out?'

Ronan and Susan seemed oblivious to Ellie as they glared at each other.

'Out. I want out,' said Ronan finally. 'The whole thing is stuffed now anyway.'

Ellie froze as Susan reached out and whipped her hand across Ronan's face, snarling, 'You used me and misled me. You're a weak, pathetic arsehole, Ronan.'

Ronan recoiled but said nothing, his hand on his cheek. Susan pushed past him to wrench open the door, pulling it shut so hard behind her it felt as if the house shuddered. But in the raging storm, it was not heard.

Ellie and Ronan were left alone in the library.

Ronan looked at her. 'I'm sorry about the dog. I didn't know.'

Ellie stared back at him. What had been dawning on

her, what she realised she should have seen long ago, was that the young man who'd had the world at his feet – good looks, wealth, position, fawning friends – someone who could surely have had any girl he fancied, was nothing more than a shallow, weak, cringing husk of a man, full of self-pity.

He had briefly paid her attention. And she'd felt her dreams of love and romance were coming true as any love-struck seventeen-year-old would. That was until he'd plied her with strong drinks and tried to force himself on her, leaving her not only with a torn dress but physically hurt and emotionally damaged.

Ellie now realised that Ronan's attack had crippled her for so many years, and in so many ways. Because of him, she had locked herself in a fragile body, afraid to let go of her heart and emotions. She'd only allowed herself to go through the superficial motions of love, never believing she could truly engage emotionally or physically with a man again, not even Charlie, her husband. She could see it clearly now: what had happened with Ronan had contributed to the disintegration of her marriage. She'd kept Charlie at arm's length, never fully giving him her heart or indeed, her body, emotionally rejecting him until he'd finally given up on ever breaking the barrier around Ellie's heart. Trust had gone, and Ellie had felt foolish and at fault. For years she'd suffered because of this pathetic man standing across from her.

'You don't even remember me, do you?' she said in a calm voice.

Ronan blinked. 'Why? Should I?'

'You should, but I know you don't. There would be no reason for you to think of me. But I've thought about you, too much – far too much. I've tortured myself and others in my life because of those memories, for years. Ever since the night you tried to rape me.'

Ronan reared back as if stung. 'Bullshit! I've never done any such thing.' He lifted a shaking finger. 'Listen, don't you start blackmailing me or whatever you think you're doing. You've caused enough trouble.'

His voice was angry and hard, but frightened. There had been other girls, Ellie guessed. He stepped back again and Ellie had the sudden feeling that if they'd been outside he would have run away. She was sure he wanted to escape, but she was closer to the door. And she wasn't finished.

How many other women had felt like this? she wondered. Slowly, anger mingled with an ache for the young girl who'd dreamed of love and tenderness, a handsome boy who would open doors to a magical life. She was angry at herself as much as with this shell of a man; a ghost who for years had haunted her, frozen her heart in fear and shame, and over whom she'd wasted tears, anger and stress. But no more.

'I've heard of women who try this. Don't think you'll get anything from me. Because I won't give you a cent,' Ronan began, then stopped as he saw the disdainful look on Ellie's face. His babbling threats hung in the air, leaving only the sound of the steady rain outside.

Ellie stared unflinchingly at him. 'I wouldn't take anything from you, ever. I just want you to know that I see you for what you are now. You have a daughter, don't you, Ronan? I hope she never knows a man like you.'

Calmly she walked from the room, closing the door gently behind her.

'Hey, there you are, I was looking for you. C'mon, have some birthday cake,' said Patrick, coming towards

391

her down the hallway. 'The storm is finally blowing away.'

'I know,' said Ellie, linking her arm through his.

*

The mains power had come back on, and they could hear the aftermath of the storm rumbling in the distance. The atmosphere in the large room was happy and friendly, and Kathryn looked delighted at the attention. Susan and Ronan were nowhere to be seen. Heather told Ellie that Cynthia had taken the children to eat and go to bed.

Ellie was hungry. She took a small plate of hors d'oeuvres and sat down next to Ben. Sally was talking to friends.

'What a night. Your grandmother looks so happy,' said Ellie.

'Yes, she really does, doesn't she? It was such good luck that Dad made it back in time. That was the icing on the cake,' he said with a smile. 'And I had a good chat with Grandy. It's the first time I've seen her properly since the hospital. She said she didn't realise I'd been trying to ring her. She's invited Sally and me here for dinner tomorrow.'

'That's so good, Ben.' Ellie suddenly realised that she now had a fair idea why Ben had been kept at arm's length from his family. Given his good relationship with Kathryn and Sally, plus his easygoing manner, he might have been far too likely to mention the rumours about the caravan park development to Kathryn – especially as he was living at the park while he was in Storm Harbour. Ellie bit her lip. It wasn't her place to tell Ben what had just happened in the library – she was sure he'd hear soon enough.

Ben glanced around the room. 'We had a high school formal dance in here one year. Did you come to that?'

'No. I must have been back in Melbourne.'

'It was fun, but I preferred the woolshed dances. This is a great old property, though. Lot of history here.' He paused, looking thoughtful. 'Actually I think my father mentioned that Craigmore is coming up for its 150th birthday soon.'

'That'd be a great story for Sally to do for the *Chronicle*,' said Ellie.

'Yeah, it would,' Ben said, grinning. 'She's so keen to go back and work with you all. She loves that paper. It turns out radio wasn't her thing. Well, not that particular station, anyway.'

'She'll be welcomed back with open arms,' said Ellie.

Ben nodded, then stood up. 'Well, I have to go help Grandy decide where to hang her portrait while Heather's here,' he said, and Ellie returned his broad smile as he turned and walked away.

*

The storm had dwindled to a light rain buffeted by a slanting southerly when guests began to say their good-byes and head for home. Looking around as she walked to the car with Patrick, Ellie noticed debris from trees and gardens, and that some of the caterers' boxes and food covers were scattered about the grounds, but there didn't seem to be any major damage.

'Ready for take-off?' she asked as Patrick buckled his seatbelt.

'You bet. I feel rather weary. But it was an interesting evening,' he said, yawning.

Ellie smiled. 'Yes, it was, in more ways than one.'

'The main thing is that Kathryn enjoyed it, and all the drama happened out of her hearing. I don't think Seamus

393

or anyone in the family wants her to know anything about this. Even an abridged version,' said Patrick.

As they headed onto the coast road, the big swell of ocean was lit by a pewter gleam when the pale moon broke through scudding clouds.

'Bet there'll be a few stars out by the time we get home,' Patrick said. 'Sam will be happy to see us.'

And he was, giving them a bit of a chastising bark as they came inside.

Ellie yawned, suddenly feeling exhausted. 'Right, Poppy, I'm going to bed. Good night.'

''Night, love,' he said. 'We'll have to write an article for the paper about tonight.' He chuckled. 'I'll write the polite, censored version, but it will be great to publish the story of saving the caravan park.'

'That's what we've been waiting for!' Ellie said, smiling and heading up the stairs. As she passed Patrick's open bedroom door, she noticed Sam sleeping on his favourite blanket on the floor beside his master's bed, snoring gently.

*

The unusual sound of a chainsaw woke her, and Ellie dressed quickly and hurried into the kitchen.

'You're up early after a big night, Poppy. What's going on with the chainsaw? I hope the tree-loppers from the electricity company you told me about aren't back?' Ellie asked, sitting down at the table.

'Don't worry, it's just Mal clearing the fallen branches. I've got those electricity fellows under control now. Their company brought in a decent arborist to talk to them about koalas and the best way to prune trees near the powerlines instead of just hacking at them indiscriminately,' Patrick said, putting the kettle on to boil. 'Mal runs a mowing and pruning business. A big branch came down in the storm, so I rang him first thing this morning and now he's cutting it into firewood. Sorry to wake you, kiddo.' He turned to her and smiled.

'You're very chirpy.'

'Yes.' Patrick chuckled. 'There's a certain satisfaction in knowing you're starting the day with a win. In fact, I'm heading out now to meet Seamus in town.'

'Let's wait until Seamus signs the papers and it's all finalised before gloating,' suggested Ellie. 'Who's going to write the story? When is Sally starting back at the *Chronicle*?'

'She said she was ready to start work anytime, so I've asked her to come in this morning. We need to figure out the story for Wednesday's paper but I haven't told her anything yet about what transpired last night,' said Patrick. 'Ben will have told her about it, of course, assuming he's been informed himself. I want to give her all the details we know in person rather than load her up with that news over the phone.'

'Good idea,' said Ellie, accepting the cup of tea Patrick handed her. 'Thanks, Poppy. Well, at least we know that if Seamus renews the lease, the caravan park will most likely be safe for the next fifty years,' she added.

'That's right. I'm going to call Meredith and update her,' Patrick said. 'Want to meet us for lunch?'

'Thanks, Poppy, but I think I'll relax at home this morning. Mike said he'll be here in time for a late lunch, so I'll go into town then.'

'Ah, yes. It will be good to see him again,' said Patrick.

'Now don't you go telling him the same old war stories,' Ellie said, laughing.

'Oh no, I have heaps of others I haven't told you both.'

'Save them for your book, Poppy.' She stood up and gave him a hug.

\*

When Ellie walked into the office at around noon, she heard Sally and Jon laughing. Patrick was perched on the corner of Maggie's desk talking to her, and Sam was eyeing Maggie, watching every crumb of her biscuit disappear.

'Wow,' Maggie said as she glanced up at Ellie. 'Is that a new dress?'

'Yes, I bought it here in Storm Harbour,' said Ellie. 'It's that soft lightweight wool.' She held out the delicate embroidered skirt.

'Look at you!' said Sally.

'Where's the party?' asked Patrick.

'Oh, for goodness' sake . . . I just made a bit of an effort for a change,' said Ellie.

'Wouldn't be because you're meeting Mike for lunch, would it?' asked Patrick.

Jon smiled. 'You look gorgeous, Ellie.'

'Thanks, guys. So what's going on? Is this a coffee break or a conference meeting?'

'Both,' said Patrick, biting into a muffin. 'What're you up to?'

'Mike's picking me up here. I thought I'd check in first and find out if the development article is in the works. I can imagine the headline: "*The story at last: no development, council confirms no changes at the river*",' she said.

'Sally and Jon are collaborating on it now,' Patrick said.

'Yes, this has been a bit of a wake-up call, so we're also mulling over a feature: "*What does Storm Harbour want for its future growth?*"' said Sally.

'Good point. Council should be considering a twenty-year plan at least,' said Ellie. 'It could be a really controversial and thought-provoking article. You should talk to Dave from the community bank, he has some really interesting ideas. Poppy already knows about them.'

'First things first,' said Patrick. 'We cover the caravan park story and reaffirm there won't be any development. There's no need to involve the sideshow antics of certain O'Neill family members, because they have nothing to do with the town. We can't publish any of the murkier details, anyway, since a lot of it is hearsay,' he said. 'We'll write that the new lease arrangements will be finalised early this week, and the caravan park will be open for business for the next fifty years.' He picked up a folder of papers. 'These are the proposed plans for the caravan park site that Ronan and Susan's developer mates were going to try to push through if they acquired the land. I think it would have been horrific. Here, Poss, have a look.'

'Where did you get this?' asked Ellie, taking the folder from Patrick.

'Seamus gave it to me this morning. He told me that Susan is packing her bags and Ronan has begged forgiveness from Seamus, and hopefully from Cynthia as well,' said Patrick.

Ellie opened the folder and spread the plans out on the desk, then pored over them for a few moments. 'These are hideous. They would be so out of place in Storm Harbour.' She held up the architect's drawing of steel and glass apartments. 'Did Seamus share anything else with you?' she asked.

Patrick shook his head. 'Nothing we can publish,' he said. 'Ronan declared to Seamus that it was all Susan's idea.

She had opened the first reminder letter to Seamus about the lease renewal being due and saw an opportunity. She quietly went to Ronan with an idea, he says. Mind you, we saw Susan deny that so we can't be sure what the real story is. Besides, it doesn't really matter whose idea it was. They were clearly both invested in it.'

'Yes. They must have had some sort of relationship to join forces in a plan to go behind his father's back,' Sally said.

'It looks that way,' Patrick agreed. 'I think Ronan is ambitious and greedy. He didn't want to wait for his inheritance, which of course he'd have to share with his siblings. I think the two of them wanted to make a buck and they didn't care who they hurt in the process or how they went about it.'

'So let me get this straight,' said Jon. 'Susan hid the first reminder letter from Seamus, and Seamus was away and unreachable when the other letters came through. So when our council source wondered why Seamus had never answered his reminders, it was because Seamus never saw them.'

'Correct,' said Patrick. 'Ronan and Susan were so cocky about pulling it off that they went to the expense of working in partnership with a developer to start drawing up plans. From what I can gather, they planned to sell off the land at an exorbitant price, once they'd bought it from council for peanuts.'

'So that's why that architect and the surveyor guy Jon and I met were snooping around, waiting in anticipation. They thought the deal was in the bag!' said Ellie.

'There's more,' said Patrick. 'Meredith rang me this morning before I had a chance to call her, and it seems dear old Councillor Lowe is suddenly suffering some health issues and is going to resign. Meredith is surprised but delighted he's quitting.'

'I bet,' said Ellie.

'The main thing is, Seamus is meeting with his lawyer today and plans to sign the lease first thing Monday morning. When he's with the lawyer, he's going to revoke the power of attorney he gave Ronan before he went away on his cruise.'

'Do you think Seamus might take shorter holidays from now on?' Maggie said dryly.

Patrick shrugged and smiled. 'Nothing anyone can do about hurricanes! But Susan and Ronan definitely capitalised on Seamus being away. It was always easy for them to keep things from Kathryn, with Susan as gatekeeper. By the way, Seamus has made it absolutely clear that Kathryn is not to know anything about the swindle her grandson was trying to pull off.'

'And luckily, we know Kathryn never reads the paper,' said Ellie.

'What does Ben think about all this, Sally?' Ellie asked.

'I haven't had the chance to talk to him about it apart from one quick phone call as I was driving home last night. He was angry about something but there wasn't time to talk. I didn't want to stay over at Craigmore and Ben said he needed to keep his grandmother company on her party night. So I drove home as soon as the storm died down,' Sally explained. 'I didn't know any of the details till I came in this morning.'

'I wonder how Ben'll take it,' Maggie said, standing up to return her mug to the kitchenette.

'Why don't you ask me?' said a voice from behind them, and they turned to see Ben in the doorway. 'I suppose you're all sitting around discussing my family.' He turned to Sally, a pained expression on his face. 'You reported on the development ages ago, Sally. Did you know any of this then? Did your source ever mention that my family was involved?'

Sally jumped up, her face creased with worry. 'Ben, I didn't know anything more than what I said on the radio. I promise you, I had no idea Ronan was involved.'

'Oh yeah?' he said, but the sting had gone out of his voice.

Ellie broke in. 'Ben, Sally's right. None of us had any facts. All we had were a lot of rumours and suspicions, that is, until a whistleblower contacted me about the lease. I promised him I wouldn't reveal his identity so he wouldn't lose his job. It's a basic tenet of journalism to protect our sources. Otherwise people won't speak up.'

'I'm really sorry, Ben. If I had known about your family's involvement with the development I would have told you,' said Sally.

Ben looked at her, then finally exhaled and said, 'I just didn't like the feeling of there being secrets between us, Sal.'

'Oh, Ben.' Sally hugged him. 'There won't be.'

'So, have you two got any plans for the day?' asked Ellie, trying to shift the mood in the room.

Ben nodded. 'Sure have. My father asked me to go over to see Cassie and Steve and give them the good news that there is nothing to the development rumours. They've got the next fifty years here if they want it.'

'They'll be so relieved. As will everyone at the caravan park,' said Ellie.

Ben dropped his arm around Sally's shoulders and looked at them all. 'I haven't told you my big news. We had a family meeting this morning, but without Grandy as Dad doesn't want her to know what Ronan tried to do to our family. Anyway, Dad has decided to send Ronan back to the cattle property in Queensland. He'll be close to Cynthia and her family so maybe they can work things out between them.'

Ben gave Sally a big smile. 'And he has asked me to move to Craigmore permanently and help him run things there. I told him I couldn't give him an answer until I'd talked to you, Sal, and you'd had time to think about it, because I'd like you to move there with me.'

Sally leaned against him and gave Ben a kiss. Then she turned to Patrick.

'Patrick, after Jon and I have written this piece we're working on today, do you mind if I take a few days off before I start back here?' Sally asked.

'Of course, my dear.' Patrick smiled. 'You and Ben take all the time you need to work out what you want to do next. Sounds like it's a time of change for both of you, in the best possible way.'

Ben gave Sally a quick kiss. 'I can't stay. I'm on my way to see Cassie and Steve and put them out of their misery.'

*

Mike leaned back and grinned. 'Man, that was good. Fresh crayfish on a homemade bread roll. It's great to be here again!'

'When I rang to book, I asked them to keep a cray for you,' Ellie said, smiling.

'Thank you. It was almost as good as the news about the caravan park. That Susan must be a piece of work. To go after Patrick's dog, troll the mayor and you, blindside Kathryn O'Neill, and try to push through an inappropriate development.'

'She is,' Ellie said, laughing. 'But she didn't do it alone. She and Ronan O'Neill are as bad as each other. I'm just glad we were able to stop them in time. So, speaking of developments, tell me what your plans are.'

Mike leaned forward enthusiastically. 'Not development: reinvention. Resuscitation. A heritage architect guy who worked with me on my app has restored a lot of old places. When I told him about the buildings along the river here he came down to Storm Harbour to see for himself. He was so keen he suggested we team up. So we are applying for government grants as well as approaching the council and state government for heritage funding to restore them.'

'Wow, that's big. But some councils are known for not having much imagination,' said Ellie.

'Ah, but Storm Harbour has an enlightened leader. Meredith is definitely forward thinking. I'll pay her an official visit when the time's right.'

'That's true. She's always thinking about the future and what's best for the town,' Ellie said.

'If you've finished, let's walk to the river and look at the buildings.' Mike smiled.

They paid and went outside into the sun.

'There doesn't seem to be a lot of storm damage,' said Ellie when they reached the riverfront walkway.

They strolled through the little park by the lighthouse causeway to the row of old closed buildings that had once been the School of Arts, a warehouse, a clubhouse for the Sea Scouts and Rangers, and a storage shed used by the early seamen for their small boats, nets and fishing equipment.

'Apparently these buildings have had various incarnations over the years,' said Mike. 'There have been attempts to do things with them on a small scale but they've just been forgotten. Growing towns want the newer stuff till they wake up to the value of reworking heritage buildings.'

'So what would you do with them? They look so run-down. Aren't they past their use-by date?' asked Ellie.

'According to my architect partner the interiors are in better condition than the façades, and structurally the buildings are sound,' said Mike.

They stopped as they came to the School of Arts with its fading Federation façade.

'Let's start here. The caretaker told me where he'd leave a set of keys for me.'

'Wait. What's that? I hear music!' exclaimed Ellie.

'Oh, he said someone uses one of the rooms for music classes on the weekends. Let's see,' Mike said.

The moment they pushed the wooden double doors open and went into the old building, Ellie felt a rush of nostalgia. She grabbed Mike's hand. 'You can smell the history!'

'What, dead mice and chewed red velvet curtains?' Mike winked at her.

'No! Of course not.' She giggled.

They could hear voices, and then as they went into a small auditorium the sounds of an amateur chamber music group floated across to them.

Ellie gasped. On the dusty stage area, beneath a few dim lights, sat a small circle of musicians. Roly, playing his cello, was surrounded by kids in their early teens playing violins, a viola and a cello. It was a classical piece but before they finished, Roly stopped and rapped his bow on the floor for attention.

'Let's repeat that last phrase, minus the flaw. Begin, one and –' Two of the musicians noticed Ellie and Mike and stopped playing.

'Please don't stop,' called out Mike. 'That sounded great.'

'Roly! What on earth is this?' said Ellie.

Roly spotted them and pulled an exaggerated face. 'Oh, wretched girl. This was to be a surprise!'

'Are you running a chamber music class?'

'Yes, Mr Bolton has been teaching us. We love it,' exclaimed one of the girls.

'These fine young people love music and I am happy to share what expertise I have. We are the Chronicle Ensemble, and our plan is to perform at Patrick's eightieth birthday! As a surprise,' added Roly a bit huffily.

'But that's next year!' Ellie was trying to stifle a laugh.

'Quite. So you are sworn to secrecy. We want to be perfect, *mais non*, troupe?'

'*Oui, oui,*' the teenagers called in unison, laughing.

'So they practise their French as well? *Très bon*,' said Mike. 'Well, don't let us disturb you. And our lips are sealed.'

An hour or so later, Mike and Ellie had completed the inspection of the interior of all the buildings and emerged back into the sunlight.

'It's staggering,' said Ellie. 'On the outside they look as if they're just abandoned buildings ready for demolition. Though now I see how the interiors could be restored. There're so many beautiful fittings and fixtures. The window panes, the architraves and doorways, so much that could be re-used.' She turned to Mike. 'Just what would you do with these places?'

'I'm not sure yet. But I'm certain we can give them a new life, repurpose them while keeping their magic and history.' He smiled broadly, and his enthusiasm was infectious. 'Actually, the possibilities are almost endless. They could be anything from a restaurant to a ballet school, specialty shops, an artists' enclave, a foodie co-op, craft places to learn and sell goods, an IT central hub, an animal hospital . . .'

Ellie nodded. 'I see what you mean, only your imagination is the limit!'

'Exactly. What does this town need? No – not need, but what will make this town inspiring, a drawcard for locals and visitors? That's what we should work towards. It's exciting,' said Mike.

'Totally,' breathed Ellie. 'I'm blown away. But how would you pay for the full box and dice?'

'Down the track the project will need seed funding and the backing of locals to support and market it,' said Mike. 'Then we'll look for investors, government funds, council help and so on.'

'You'd need a pile of money, though,' said Ellie. 'But if people can see the vision . . .' She paused as an idea came to her. 'Actually, I might know someone who could get the ball rolling,' she said.

Mike raised his eyebrows. 'Someone local? Not the O'Neills?' he said in surprise.

'Nope. It's my mate Tommy.'

'What! How on earth . . .?'

Ellie smiled. 'Tommy's been something of a hermit, getting over the tragic death of his wife. But he does a lot of good work quietly behind the scenes for the people of this town. He has no family other than his friends in Storm Harbour. He wants to give back where he can. Tommy has the bit between his teeth now, so I'll ask him.'

Mike shook his head. 'For a small town there's a deep sense of family and community here. That's why I admire your grandfather and his newspaper. And it's transformed you, too, Ell. You radiate strength and self-confidence now. The shadows have gone.'

Ellie gave a little smile and shrugged. 'Guess this place agrees with me.'

'It's more than that. This town has brought out the best in you. I see now that you've inherited your grandfather's passion, persistence and bravery, Ellie,' he said softly.

Ellie reached for his hand and held it tightly, overcome by his words and the dawning realisation that she knew she would fight, tooth and nail, for all that Patrick and his country newspaper stood for – the right to call out cheats and liars, praise and promote the modest and those who did not ask for recognition for living life by simple rules: loving family, respecting others, helping in their community.

'While I'll always be involved with IT in one form or another, I have decided this is my community and home now,' she told Mike. 'I will always be part of the *Chronicle* and Storm Harbour. "To thine own self be true", Poppy always told me, and now I know what he means.'

'Yes. Like Roly. What a guy. You never really know about people, do you?' said Mike as he reached over and touched her lips with his fingers.

Ellie leaned towards him, then suddenly stood back. She looked up at him. 'Mike, I have to tell you something. Like you said, you never really know about people. Kathryn said it to me, and in a way, so did Meredith; that the worst thing you can do is to keep a secret.'

He looked surprised at the tone of her voice.

'Secrets? You have a secret?'

'Yes. I do. And I'd like to tell you.'

'Of course, if you're sure. Let's sit down.' They moved to a seat by the water's edge.

Ellie sat on the wooden bench, her hands clasped between her knees. Mike sat beside her, staring at the river.

Haltingly, Ellie began to speak, returning to the painful memory of a young woman, still in her teens, swayed by the attention of a handsome and influential young man in town.

She related how flattered she'd been by his attention at a dance, the unfamiliar drinks, how sick she'd felt, how she'd trusted him to help her and, instead, he'd tried to force himself on her. She described how she had fought him off and fled, leaving her terrified and traumatised, wounded in heart and soul.

'I felt I could never trust a man again. I was physically safe, but badly scarred from the experience. I survived that night, but I never realised the damage it caused me. I blamed myself, and unknowingly that blame sabotaged any relationship I've ever had with a man since. He held that power over me. It's a painful secret I've kept buried, but it's time to let it go now.' Ellie paused to draw a breath.

Mike sat still, not moving, not looking at her, not touching her, and asked her, 'Do you want to tell me who it was?'

Ellie sucked in a breath. 'Ronan O'Neill.'

And she waited for Mike's reaction.

He was silent and still a moment before saying, 'It must be hard for you to see him and his family and be involved with them. A constant reminder of your nightmare.'

Ellie looked at him. 'You know, I finally confronted him last night, at Kathryn's birthday party. He had no idea who I was or any memory of what he'd done. I suddenly saw him for the weak and pathetic person

407

he is, and I knew he had no hold over me anymore. I felt free. So now I want you to know that this is what happened. I blamed myself. I've never really trusted anyone since. Never trusted myself to feel worthy, or to truly love someone. I see now that I've never been totally honest in any relationship, always holding back.'

Mike shifted, but Ellie stilled him, resting her hand on his arm, determined to get the words out.

'You have been so patient and kind and such a good friend, Mike. I thank you for that.' Ellie turned and looked at him. 'But now I realise I want us to be more than that. I don't know if it's too late, but I want you to know that something has changed in me since confronting Ronan. I'll understand if you don't want more than just keeping our friendship. I want you to be my best friend still, but I also want to show you that I love you with all my heart. I ache at how I've let something hold me back, stop me from living my life as I want. Kathryn told me not to keep a secret from the person I love. Now I understand what she meant.' Ellie took a deep breath. 'So, there you are. I don't mind what happens, I just needed you to know.'

Mike slowly lifted her hand and kissed her palm, curling her fingers closed over his kiss.

'I always felt you were wounded in some way. But you never made it easy for me to ask. I thought by being your friend I could stay close to you.' He put a finger under her chin and tilted her head. 'But now I want to be more than your friend.' He lowered his mouth to hers. 'I love you, Ellie, always have. Now it's your turn to love me back. If you want. No more secrets.' He kissed her slowly, gently. Until some dam burst in Ellie and she pulled his head to hers, clasping him, kissing him amid a torrent of tears, passion, laughter and love.

Ellie and Mike walked through town, arms linked, and turned into the *Chronicle* office.

The front bell jingled and Patrick, followed by Sam, came into the reception area. Patrick looked up and saw Ellie and Mike, hand in hand, Ellie's face aglow, Mike with a huge grin.

'Aha. Are congratulations in order?' he asked, a smile breaking out on his face.

Suddenly Sam loped over to Ellie, plunging at her side, and rubbing his head against her, trailing his leash.

Ellie stroked his velvet ears. 'It's okay, Sam. I'm not going anywhere.'

Mike looked into Sam's deep brown eyes and reached to pat the old dog's head. 'Sorry, mate. Me either.'

Di Morrissey
**The Last Paradise**

Grace has the perfect life: a job she loves, a beautiful daughter and a rich, successful husband. But one night, when their world falls apart in a shocking disaster, Grace suddenly sees what she couldn't admit – her marriage and her husband are a fraud.

With the life she knew in tatters, she takes an assignment promoting the launch of a unique luxury hotel, hidden in a stunning, untouched oasis in the heart of tourist-crazed Bali.

Here, in this last paradise, Grace gathers the strength to take charge of her world. And, inspired by a woman's story from long ago, she discovers a path to a future she'd never dared to imagine . . .

'Enchanting, life-affirming' *Brisbane News*

'This story is a wonderfully uplifting celebration of women . . . finding strength within themselves and in friendship with each other.' *Newcastle Herald*

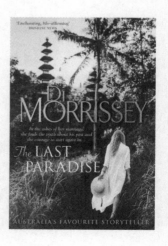

Read the opening pages of Di Morrissey's captivating
*The Last Paradise* . . .

# Prologue

GRACE STOOD AT THE window staring into the late summer garden of neat lawns and beds of heavy headed roses about to rain petals. The roses would need pruning soon.

She almost smiled. Since when did she care, or even know anything about pruning roses?

Since she'd married a successful businessman, moved into an elegant house with a sprawling garden, and become mummy to adorable Daisy, that's when.

Their home in Dural was the last house in the street, next to an empty field that had become an informal local park. The area had once been the end of the line, on the rural fringes of Sydney. It was where homes were estates, and locals kept horses; the remnants of pastoral wealth still on display.

What was it her mother had said when she'd first seen this house? 'You've done well, Gracie. I'm happy for you.'

But sometimes Grace missed the buzz of the city. Her favourite café on the corner, a quick meal with friends and colleagues, recognising familiar faces and eccentric locals from the urban neighbourhood. Entertaining in her small Paddington apartment.

Now she lived in a quiet street of nice neighbours, where groomed dogs with expensive accessories were walked on fancy leashes. Voices were never raised and children were rarely heard, unless they were splashing in a pool. On the weekend you might catch the *thwack* of tennis ball meeting racquet, and occasional laughter and the clink of glasses from a patio in the late afternoon.

Grace poured herself a glass of mineral water and debated whether she should call her mother to see how Daisy was, but resisted the urge. After all, Daisy was only away overnight. If Grace called too often her mother thought she was checking up on her.

She heard the car in the driveway, then the sound of the door opening and closing as Lawrence came in and went straight to his office.

'Hey, Lawrence, you're not working, are you?' She poked her head around the door. 'Don't forget we're going to dinner tonight at the Robinsons'.'

He didn't look up straight away, and it struck her that his hair was thinning on top. She knew he had the hairdresser put a colour rinse through it regularly to hide his greying temples, although she wondered why he bothered now he was only a few years away from fifty. He was also looking a bit pudgy these days, though, being tall, he carried it well. He just never did any kind of exercise other than walking to his car and the occasional game of tennis, she thought.

'Hi,' he said, glancing up and smiling at her. 'Is Daisy with your mother?'

'Yes. I thought it was better than getting a babysitter.' Daisy adored her grandmother, who lived alone in her home on a clifftop overlooking the beach. Grace knew her mother and Daisy would go down to the surf first thing in the morning for a swim. 'You promised to take me out for a fancy breakfast tomorrow, remember?' Grace leaned against the door frame and crossed her arms.

'Of course. I'm looking forward to it.' He pushed his laptop aside but continued sifting through the papers on his desk, putting them in the briefcase she'd given him.

'We should leave soon. Unless you want a sundowner before we go? They're only a few blocks away.'

'Thanks, but I'll wait till we get there. Did you get the champagne for them?'

'It's in the fridge. I couldn't find the one you wanted, but the one I bought is very good apparently.'

'Are you sure?'

'The guy in the bottle shop went on and on about it. It's from 2012. Pierre someone and Sons. Do you really think the Robinsons will know a superior from a mediocre?'

'Yes, actually, I do. Give me ten minutes or so to finish off here and get ready, and then we can go.'

He seemed a little distracted so she straightened up, quietly closed the door and went out onto the patio to watch the sunset. Typical Lawrence, wanting to spend money on an expensive bottle of champagne the Robinsons might not even care about. Grace was sure they would be just as happy to share cheap bubbles with friends. Socialising was all about friendship as far as Grace was concerned, while for Lawrence, it was about making an impression. Or as her best friend Melanie had once said, 'Lawrence always has to big-note himself. He just can't help it.'

Melanie made no bones about the fact she didn't like Lawrence. And the feeling was mutual. Grace knew that most of her friends avoided Lawrence, but Mel was the only one who'd told her bluntly that she should never have married him. And, more and more lately, Grace was wondering the same thing.

They'd been married seven years, after a whirlwind courtship. She'd met him at a cocktail party for movers and shakers in the business world after she'd done an advertising campaign for a big, newly merged financial institution. He was English, with an Australian-born mother who'd lived in England most of her life. Lawrence had come to Australia to go to university and stayed. When Grace met him, he'd recently come out of a long relationship, and he'd told her he wanted to settle down and start a family.

Grace had been on the cusp of travelling, looking for a job overseas, but Lawrence had swept her off her feet, taking her on luxurious holidays and surprising her with expensive gifts. He'd proposed after six months, with a very large Bvlgari diamond ring. He had been working on a major contract at the time and, if it came through, he'd suggested that they could live in Italy for a year or so. 'Then you can choose to work or not. Or just take assignments if you want to, not because you have to,' he'd said.

She was thirty at the time and suddenly she'd been able to see her life pattern: being a mum and working when she wanted. Come her forties she'd have kids in school and could concentrate on a career in visual advertising, finish her film and video production course, maybe start her own company. Well, it had all seemed very appealing.

There was a lot to be said for a doting, older, well-to-do husband, she'd thought.

Her mother, Tina, had agreed, if not too enthusiastically. She confessed she would have been happier if Grace had chosen someone like the boys she'd gone out with when she was growing up on the Northern Beaches.

'They might look like surf bums,' Tina had said to her once, 'but some of those lads have done very well for themselves. Marty Davidson, who won all those Bells Beach championships, has his own law firm now. He still surfs here every weekend.'

'Mum, you're such an old surfer chick.' Grace had laughed. 'You've never got over your wild hippy times in Bali.' Tina had spent some time in Bali in the seventies, well before it was the tourist mecca it had since become. She spoke about it often as one of the best times of her life.

Tina had given her a quick smile. 'Yep, Kuta back then was something else!'

So Grace had married Lawrence and looked forward to the sparkling future she pictured for them. However, the big contract Lawrence had anticipated didn't pan out, and Italy was off the cards. Perhaps it had always been a pipe dream, Grace thought. Anyway, by then, Lawrence had been very keen for them to have a baby.

Out on the patio, Grace checked her watch. Just as she was thinking about pouring herself a glass of wine, Lawrence called out to her. 'You ready?'

'I'll grab my bag.' She shut the French doors and turned the key. 'Is everything locked up?'

'Yes. I've checked. You look nice.'

She smiled. Lawrence had a habit of suddenly looking at her as if he hadn't noticed her for a while, despite them sharing a house. A home. A life. 'Thanks, darling.' She'd been told often enough that she was pretty, with her naturally sun-streaked blonde hair, tanned skin and svelte figure. And when she was with Daisy, a tiny replica with bouncy blonde curls and a sunny nature, people often remarked that they should be the ones in the TV and magazine ads that Grace created.

Impulsively she gave Lawrence a hug, although he didn't hug her back. She'd got used to him not being as affectionate as she was, but sometimes, especially lately, she felt he was pushing her away. She pressed herself against his solid body. How long had it been since they'd made love?

If she were honest, her relationship with her husband was wearing her down. Lawrence could be difficult – no, actually nasty. Spiteful. But then, was that the trade-off for having a darling daughter, a comfortable lifestyle, a nice home in a good area? Could she be happy with a husband who lavished gifts on her instead of affection and fun? The thought suddenly made her feel cheap and avaricious.

In the past, she'd always fallen for the sweet guys who had nothing. She liked to think that she was generous and thoughtful towards other people. But as she stepped back from the embrace and saw the emotionless look on her husband's face she wondered, had she traded genuine unconditional love for security? Was it too late to do something about it?

Lawrence turned away. 'I'll get the champagne.'

As he slipped the bottle into the leather wine cooler, she noticed he'd changed his shirt, and was wearing the peachy-pink Lanvin she'd bought him. He patted his coat pocket. 'Right, I've got the keys.'

'It's only a couple of blocks. Let's walk, it's such a nice evening. Do us good,' she suggested.

'Me, you mean.' She had been gently nagging him

to exercise. 'I'd prefer to drive. My sprained ankle from tennis still hasn't healed.'

'Oh, too bad. You are such a killer on the court,' she teased. 'You really do play to win,' she added, echoing something he'd once said to her.

'I do, darling, and why not?' he said lightly. 'Okay, let's go.'

Grace pulled the front door closed, leaving the light on outside. The air was fragrant with roses as she got into the passenger seat of Lawrence's Mercedes. Her feet bumped against his briefcase, which sat in the footwell.

'Why are we taking your car?' They usually used Grace's when they went out locally.

'I left it out the front so I thought it was easiest. Is that okay?' he asked, raising an eyebrow.

'Yes, sure, that's fine. You're the designated driver.' Grace smiled at him.

Turning out of their street, Lawrence drove past a bush block where a stand of gum trees almost obscured the view of the big homes that had been built in the 1970s and eighties.

'What's that on the road? Lawrence, stop! It's a koala!'

As he pulled over, the young koala waddled towards the trees.

'Oh, he's adorable. Let me take a photo for Daisy.'

'They're around all the time,' Lawrence said, a hint of annoyance in his voice.

But Grace jumped from the car and lifted her phone to snap a photo, saying quietly, 'Where're your mumma and papa, little fellow?'

'Hurry up, Grace. We're running late.'

'It's okay. How cute is this little guy? I hope people drive carefully round here at night.'

'No one goes out at night here. This is the 'burbs. Country style,' Lawrence said as Grace scrambled back in and the car glided forward.

'You've always been a city boy,' said Grace. 'Do you miss it?'

'And you're a water baby. Do you miss the beach?' he countered.

'Well, Mum's there so I still have a connection to it. But it's such a trek into the city from the Northern Beaches.'

'You can say that again. Okay, so who else is coming tonight?'

'Just the Robinsons and some of their neighbours. You said you wanted to get to know George Ashton.'

'The bank guy? Yes. Just don't leave me stranded with Holly Ambrose and that husband of hers. I don't give a shit about soccer and swimming and all the sports stuff they talk about.'

'Okay.' She didn't bother to argue with him. Lawrence was intolerant of subjects he had no interest in and people who he perceived to bring no value to his world. But she liked Holly, and her husband Roger did so much for the sports teams at Daisy's school.

Lawrence pulled up and parked in front of a white, ranch-style house with a basketball hoop on the garage, a trampoline to one side, and two small bicycles lying on the front lawn.

'There's Holly now,' Grace said, waving to her as she got out of the car.

*

The evening felt long. Grace had hoped they might get home early but for once Lawrence seemed in no hurry to leave. He rarely drank, but was nursing a glass of red, probing George Ashton for his views about bank rates and where certain investments were headed. George must have turned out to be a useful contact for him, Grace thought.

Finally, the other guests started to stand up. Grace carried some glasses into the kitchen and found Holly there, stacking the dishwasher. Holly glanced up and smiled. 'Been lovely to see you guys. You must come over. Bring Daisy to use the pool any time. Roger can teach her to dive properly.'

'Thanks, Holly, we'd love that. Daisy can swim pretty well now, but a few tips would be great.' It was a shame, Grace thought, that Lawrence would never want to take Daisy round to the Ambroses' place, but she made a mental note to do so herself. She and Lawrence didn't have a pool and it had been such a hot summer.

Heading out of the kitchen, Grace called to Lawrence that they should be leaving. She picked up her bag and walked with Holly to the front door, where the Robinsons were saying goodbye to their other guests.

Suddenly, they heard the thunderous boom of an explosion. The night sky lit up with a bright orange glow. They all stared in horror as a crackling red fireball erupted into the air a few streets away. Then they all spoke at once.

'What the hell was that?'

'Where is it?'

'It's not that gas storage place, is it?'

'No, wrong direction . . .'

Grace's shriek was ear-splitting. 'It's near our place! Lawrence!'

Lawrence swore as he hurried to the door where they all stood, stunned, looking into the distance.

'Where is it?' cried Grace. 'Oh, God no. I think the fire's in our street!' She screamed again and broke into a run.

'It can't be! Grace, get in the car, come back here!' shouted Lawrence.

Grace was propelled by fear, horror and disbelief. Her mind seemed frozen as she sprinted towards their home.

Lawrence jumped in the car and caught up to her.

'Jump in, Grace, for God's sake,' he called.

She was driven by some wild terror. For a moment or two her husband drove beside her, begging her to stop and get in. But she was running as if her life depended on it.

Lawrence gunned the car and sped ahead.

By the time she reached her street, the full horror had begun to dawn on her. Their house was alight, a wall of leaping orange flames and smoke. She could hear glass breaking and timber crashing.

'Oh, my God, no, no, no . . .' she panted as she saw Lawrence's silhouette and the dark shapes of other figures as they came up and clustered around him.

The flames were higher and hotter now, and she picked up the strong, searing smell of smoke.

She had fallen into some unreal, terrible nightmare. Everything moved in slow motion. She felt hands on her arms, holding her back, and heard voices bouncing around her, as if she were in an echo chamber. Her own wailing voice sounded far away, drowned out by the noises that would continue to haunt her in the nights to come. The cracking and groaning as their home, their beautiful house, disintegrated.

It was impossible to take in that everything she owned and treasured from her past and present was being swallowed in this licking orange inferno of heavy smoke and searing heat.

Sirens wailed. People held her. She couldn't see Lawrence.

'Where's my husband?' she screamed.

A man in orange overalls and a helmet put his hands on her shoulders. 'Is anyone else inside?'

'Where's Lawrence? Stop him . . .'

'He's here, it's all right, Grace,' came the shaking voice of a neighbour, who was holding her back.

More sirens, more people hosing down nearby houses. The smell, oh the smell.

Then Lawrence was beside her, pulling her to him, trying to turn her face away from the sight of their world imploding.

'Don't look,' he shouted at her.

**The Storm Harbour Chronicle**

15 Dec. 1923 | REPORTING COMMUNITY NEWS AND VI...

**The Storm Harbour Chronicle**

24 May 2019 | REPORTING COMMUNITY NEWS AND VI...

SHIRE SHOW WINN...

**The Storm**

11 Feb. 1901 | REPORTING C...

DROUGH...

**The Storm Harbour**

22 Aug. 1982 | REPORTING COMMUNITY NE...

WEATHER WARN...

**The S...**

8 March 2000 | R...

MIS...